ACCLAIM FOR CHA

The Kissi

'A perfect escapist cocktail

Mail on Sunday

Love Song

'A perfect example of the new, darker romantic fiction . . . a true 24-carat love story'

Sunday Times

'A poetic and poignant love story'

Sunday Post

The Love Knot

'The author perfectly evokes the atmosphere of a bygone era . . . An entertaining Victorian romance'

Woman's Own

'Hearts are broken, scandals abound. It's totally addictive, the sort of book you rush to finish – then wish you hadn't'

Woman's Realm

The Nightingale Sings

'A novel rich in dramatic surprises, with a large cast of vivid characters whose antics will have you frantically turning the pages'

Daily Mail

To Hear a Nightingale

'A story to make you laugh and cry'

Woman

'A delightful novel . . . Pulsating with vitality and deeply felt emotions. I found myself with tears in my eyes on one page and laughing out loud on another'

Sunday Express

The Business
'A compulsive, intriguing and perceptive read'
Sunday Express

'Compulsively readable'
Options

In Sunshine or in Shadow
'Superbly written . . . A romantic novel that is romantic in the true sense of the word'
Daily Mail

Stardust
'Charlotte Bingham has produced a long, absorbing read, perfect for holidays, which I found hard to lay aside as the plot twisted and turned with intriguing results'
Sunday Express

'Irresistible . . . A treat that's not to be missed'
Prima

Nanny
'It's deckchair season once again, and Charlotte Bingham's spellbinding saga is required reading'
Cosmopolitan

'Excellent stuff'
Company

Grand Affair
'Extremely popular'
Daily Mail

'A stirring tale of a woman struggling to overcome her past'
Ideal Home and Lifestyle

Debutantes
'A big, wallowy, delicious read'
The Times

'Compulsively readable'
Daily Express

The Blue Note

'Will satisfy all of Bingham's fans'

Sunday Mirror

'Another offering of powerful romance and emotional entanglement from an author on whom I am most keen'

Sarah Broadhurst, *The Bookseller*

Change of Heart

'Charlotte Bingham's devotees will recognise her supreme skill as a storyteller . . . A heartwarming romance which is full of emotion'

Independent on Sunday

'A fairy tale, which is all the more delightful as it is not something one expects from a modern novel . . . It's heady stuff'

Daily Mail

The Season

'Her imagination is thoroughly original'

Daily Mail

Summertime

'Destined to become one of the season's bestsellers, this is great summer escapism'

Choice

Distant Music

'Bingham's characters are warm, empathetic, and endearingly cosy. Their unfolding story is as comforting and nourishing as a hot milky drink on a stormy night. Her legions of fans will not be disappointed'

Daily Express

The Chestnut Tree

'As compelling as ever'

Woman and Home

Also by Charlotte Bingham:

CORONET AMONG THE WEEDS
LUCINDA
CORONET AMONG THE GRASS
BELGRAVIA
COUNTRY LIFE
AT HOME
BY INVITATION
TO HEAR A NIGHTINGALE
THE BUSINESS
IN SUNSHINE OR IN SHADOW
STARDUST
NANNY
CHANGE OF HEART
DEBUTANTES
THE NIGHTINGALE SINGS
GRAND AFFAIR
LOVE SONG
THE KISSING GARDEN
THE LOVE KNOT
THE BLUE NOTE
THE SEASON
SUMMERTIME
DISTANT MUSIC
THE CHESTNUT TREE

Novels with Terence Brady:
VICTORIA
VICTORIA AND COMPANY
ROSE'S STORY
YES HONESTLY

Television Drama Series with Terence Brady:
TAKE THREE GIRLS
UPSTAIRS DOWNSTAIRS
THOMAS AND SARAH
NANNY
FOREVER GREEN

Television Comedy Series with Terence Brady:
NO HONESTLY
YES HONESTLY
PIG IN THE MIDDLE
OH MADELINE! (USA)
FATHER MATTHEW'S DAUGHTER

Television Plays with Terence Brady:
MAKING THE PLAY
SUCH A SMALL WORD
ONE OF THE FAMILY

Films with Terence Brady:
LOVE WITH A PERFECT STRANGER
MAGIC MOMENTS

Stage Plays with Terence Brady:
I WISH I WISH
THE SHELL SEEKERS
(adaptation from the novel by Rosamunde Pilcher)

THE WIND OFF THE SEA

Charlotte Bingham

BANTAM BOOKS

LONDON • NEW YORK • TORONTO • SYDNEY • AUCKLAND

THE WIND OFF THE SEA
A BANTAM BOOK: 0 553 81398 6

Simultaneously published in Great Britain by Doubleday,
a division of Transworld Publishers

PRINTING HISTORY
Doubleday edition published 2003
Bantam edition published 2003

1 3 5 7 9 10 8 6 4 2

Set in 11/13pt Palatino by
Phoenix Typesetting, Burley-in-Wharfedale, West Yorkshire.

Bantam Books are published by Transworld Publishers,
61–63 Uxbridge Road, London W5 5SA,
a division of The Random House Group Ltd,
in Australia by Random House, Australia (Pty) Ltd,
20 Alfred Street, Milsons Point, Sydney, NSW 2061, Australia,
in New Zealand by Random House New Zealand Ltd,
18 Poland Road, Glenfield, Auckland 10, New Zealand
and in South Africa by Random House (Pty) Ltd,
Endulini, 5a Jubilee Road, Parktown 2193, South Africa.

Printed and bound in Germany by
Elsnerdruck, Berlin

THE WIND OFF THE SEA

Prologue

When they all looked back on that time, it was as though he had come into their lives like the wind off the sea. It was as if, without realising it, he had determined to draw their thoughts away from the dreary toil of their days, from the heartache caused by relationships for ever stilled, from the destruction that still sat around in awful witness to the past conflict.

As the winter wind moaned around their houses and cottages, and they sighed at their memories, staring into smouldering fires and looking back to happier times, he seemed somehow to have strolled into their lives, bringing with him not just the promise of spring, but the certainty of summer warmth.

With his arrival they started looking up to that far distant line known as the horizon, looking towards a future which, although it might be stormy, would be far from grey. Naturally – and there can be no guilt attached to them because we are all the same – no-one thought of the effect they might be having on him, as people don't when someone fascinates them.

Nor did anyone fall to wondering why he was there, what ghost he might have come to lay, or what mystery might be strong enough to have drawn him back to the beautiful old harbourside village that faced the English Channel.

WINTER 1947

Chapter One

The frost had lain heavy on the latch when Mr Todd had made to leave the cottage with his grandson Tam, making it unusually difficult to open the planked wooden door with hands already half frozen. The weather had turned so cold that water had frozen inside the window panes, while outside Tam and his grandfather could see icicles hanging from the guttering as thick as a man's fingers. When the door had finally been prised open the first thing the little boy saw was a big black bird dead on its back on the hard white ground, its clawed feet thrust skywards as if in one last protest. His grandfather picked the poor little corpse up, and chucked it away without ceremony into a nearby ditch.

'The rats can have him. No good comes of seeing dead crows,' he muttered, half burying his face in his thick grey muffler as the east wind bit into his skin. 'Dead crow in the morning always comes with a warning.'

The little boy by his side said nothing. He knew that his grandfather was right: even the rats needed feeding in a winter as cold and hard as this one. The bitterness of the weather made him feel as though life was on the verge of stopping, that it would just get colder and colder until nothing could survive, until everything and everybody was dead, frozen stiff beneath one huge sheet of ice.

'Don't know what we's bothering to come out for, Tam,' his granddad muttered on. 'Ground's that frozen we'd need a pickaxe to get anything out of it. A pickaxe, or a ruddy pneumatic drill.'

The wind sharpened as they reached the end of the lane and turned into the road leading to the allotments. Mr Todd hunched his shoulders tightly together and buried his chin further in his muffler while Tam gasped out loud as the ice-cold blast seemed to hit the back of his throat.

'Think it'll snow now, Grandpa?' he cried bravely, as tears of cold trickled down his cheeks. 'Must snow soon, surely, Grandpa?'

'Too cold for snow, Tam. Far too cold for snow.'

'How can it be too cold to snow, Grandpa?'

''Cos the clouds freeze up, that's a why, boy. And the snow can't fall out, that's a why.'

The two of them continued on their way in silence, as silent as the frozen countryside around them.

'Can't remember when I last seen the estuary froze over, and that's true,' Mr Todd said, gazing out to sea and suddenly flapping his arms round his body in a hopeless attempt to gain some warmth. 'They say sea's froze too, to a quarter a mile out.'

His grandson frowned, staring in the direction of the sea, wondering whether he dare ask to be taken to see the boats glued into the ice, the snow carpeting the boatyard. But his grandfather always liked to do the suggesting; he knew that, as so he should. His grandmother had told him often enough.

You best leave any ideas you have well alone, she'd say, ruffling his hair, which Tam hated. *Your granddad's sort of man who'll run in the opposite direction you tell him, just for the sake of it. So you just leave any suggesting things to him.*

Hardly daring to breathe in or out now, so painful did it seem to have become, Tam wished with all his heart that he was back at home with his granny, huddled over the few lumps of coke and half-dry driftwood that afforded them the only warmth available in this most bitter of winters, rather than trying to curry favour with his granddad by agreeing to accompany him to the allotments to see if there was any food that they could dig up out of the unyielding ground.

'Don't know why we bothered fighting damn war,' he heard his grandfather mutter as they reached their destination.'You can bet Jerry isn't half freezin' to death on a diet of tinned snoek – nastiest tasting fish ever put on a plate is snoek – or trying to dig a frozen turnip out of the ice. Makes a man wonder what it was all about, it does really.'

'What what was all about, Grandpa? An' who's Jerry?'

'Never you mind, young Tam,' Mr Todd told him, with a sudden deep sigh. 'That's all a dead and buried now. 'At's all a dead and a buried now, and that's for sure.'

As if to amplify his point, he undid the spade he had strapped to his back and started to try to prise some turnips out of ground that had seemingly turned to stone. As he did so, it began to snow. Five minutes later the two of them could barely see each other, let alone the vegetable patch, so thick was the blizzard. Finally Tam heard his grandfather throwing down his spade.

''Tis bloody hopeless,' he swore. 'Completely bloody hopeless.'

Mrs Todd glanced at the clock and, seeing it was five minutes after the time her husband had said he would be back, immediately began worrying; it was that same worrying that had driven Mr Todd half to distraction during their long marriage. But it was something she couldn't help – *born with a frown*, as her own mother had frequently told her. *Never seen such an anxious child*. Little wonder, however, that the poor woman did worry. Born into the kind of poverty that her marriage did nothing to alleviate, she hardly had two pennies to rub together for the first few years with her new husband. Perhaps lack of money had brought on her miscarriages, for they followed each other so regularly that it seemed she would never have a living child. Finally, Rusty, her first live child, was born, followed by the two boys. Now there were only Rusty and Mickey left to her – Tom, her elder son, having been killed on a rescue mission to Dunkirk.

With a deep sigh, Mrs Todd pulled another thick knit cardigan on over her first one and knelt down at the grate to attend to the vaguely smouldering fire. She worried that her husband and young Tam would be frozen stiff by the time they returned from what she knew must be going to prove to be a fruitless quest. She stared furiously at the few remaining miserable lumps of coke that were refusing to ignite and the lumps of driftwood that were too green even to hold a spark. She had to warm the house somehow, if only for poor little Tam. She just had to warm the house.

Desperate for warmth, and even more desperate to have some sort of welcoming fire going when her husband and grandson returned, Mrs Todd started to scour the house for something dry she could burn. She was so cold that for a moment she even found herself contemplating breaking up one of the kitchen chairs and throwing it into the grate. The truth was that had they been hers to burn, and not her husband's property, she knew she could not have resisted the temptation. Instead she pulled her wardrobe away from the wall and prised up two of the short loose planks on which it stood in one corner of their bedroom. It wasn't the first time she had been reduced to this desperate measure, and if the freezing weather continued she imagined that it wouldn't be the last.

Minutes later, the fire having leaped thankfully

and cheerfully into life, she heard the outside latch rise and fall at long last.

'Hang that soaking wet coat on the clothes horse, Grandpa,' she called out to her husband as he ushered a half-frozen grandson into the room. 'And for goodness' sake sit you both down by the fire while I brew you some hot sweet tea.'

'Hot maybe, sweet'll be the day.' Mr Todd winked at Tam who was too cold even to respond.

As tea was being prepared Mr Todd rolled himself a cigarette that was nearly all paper and precious little tobacco while Tam went to fetch their precious mound of Swan Vestas, all of which had been cut neatly down the middle, such was the shortage of matches. The little boy reached forward eagerly to light his grandfather's cigarette.

'Now go and put a light on, lad,' Mr Todd suggested, once his pipe was lit. 'I know it's not time yet, but five minutes one way or another won't break the law, will it? No, well, I don't rightly reckon it will.'

Tam, a serious and dutiful expression on his young face, stood on the chair by the door, and pushed the light switch down. Just as solemnly he watched the low wattage bulb flicker into life, because he was not so old that it did not seem to be some sort of miracle how the turning of a switch could make a piece of glass light up.

'Word is, on the wireless that is, it's going to snow for a week or more,' Mrs Todd said, as she put down her wooden tray, loaded with a teapot carefully covered with a cosy, and cups, their faces turned to their saucers, not to mention a precious jug of hot water, and a tiny jug of milk, on the table under the window. 'I can't remember a winter like it, I can't really.'

'How's our Rusty?' Mr Todd wondered, as his wife handed him a plate holding a slice of brown bread scraped lightly with margarine and a cup of steaming tea.

'She's lying in bed with a face as long as a wet week,' Mrs Todd sniffed. 'Peter's gone to the garage, although I should imagine this weather'll bring him home soon enough. No-one's got any petrol coupons they want to waste in this weather, and there'll be no mending neither, I shouldn't have thought, so much good it'll do him, but gets him out and away from Rusty, so that's something.'

Mrs Todd sighed and shook her head slowly from side to side, which was enough to tell her husband what she was feeling. The Todds had been married long enough for Mr Todd to understand that the slow shaking of his wife's head meant that their daughter was no better.

'Mickey still in the churchyard?'

'Can't think why,' Mrs Todd replied, sitting down to her own tea on the other side of the fireplace. 'Ground's like rock. Vicar says there's that many funerals being delayed, but they can't do a thing about it. Suppose they're stockpiling them, back at the undertakers, poor souls. But it doesn't bear thinking about. They were saying in the village, people are being found all the time, all over the country, dead in doorways, frozen stiff – tramps mostly, mind. But not just tramps, waifs and strays too – and not only waifs and strays neither. Ex-servicemen too, standing about in this weather with trays of matches for sale, and after what they've done for their country. Makes you think.'

'What can you say?' Mr Todd sighed. 'Risk your life for King and Country and come home to die from neglect in a doorway.'

'It simply isn't right. It just doesn't make sense.'

'When did war ever make sense? That's what I'd like to know. You tell me when a war ever made sense. I tell you, it never did.'

Tam stared from one old face to another as they sighed and grumbled, wishing with all his heart that he could read the time. He knew his father came back at six o'clock every evening. He just didn't know when six o'clock would come; soon he hoped, silently, swinging his legs slowly under him, as his grandmother switched on the wireless, and his grandfather held out his cup for more tea. He'd just like it to be really soon.

As she lay in bed in the dark, Rusty could hear her parents' voices floating up from down below. She had only just woken up from a sleep from which part of her wished that she had never woken, yet she knew exactly what time it was, without even having to look at the clock, because there was yellow in the white of the falling blizzard from the glow of the one dim bulb that lit teatime by the fire side downstairs. Despite the twilight falling beyond the window, however, she made no move to switch on the light by her bedside, perhaps because the coming darkness outside the window matched her feelings so precisely.

In her imagination she could feel the warmth of her newborn baby lying in her arms, imagine the softness of the face held close to hers, see herself carefully folding the shawls around it to keep it snug. But although Peter had taken the precaution of heaping her bed with extra blankets and coats before leaving to go to his garage, she knew the room to be colder than it had ever been, for her baby was dead, and Mickey was down at the churchyard with it, and she imagined there would never be a day for the rest of her life when she didn't think of it, wondering over and over why it had been taken from her.

Even at this time of day there was still ice on the inside of her window panes. The short dark bitter days of cold, the endless nights when her mood seemed to be echoed by the winds that constantly moaned around the cottage, the shortages of every needful thing – everything conspired to make her wonder why she now faced not new life, but yet more death. Too miserable to cry and too cold to feel anything except misery she tried turning her thoughts to spring and summer; towards flowers and a warm sea running up the harbour full of brightly painted boats. But since all she could see were black leafless trees outlined against darkening skies, even the idea of warm spring weather and blue skies seemed like a hopeless fantasy, something that, like her dream of motherhood to come, would never now happen.

You'll have another one.

To other people the baby was just a baby, whereas to her a baby was a person. You couldn't replace people, so why did the cruel unthinking world believe you could replace a baby?

You'll have another one.

If she heard that said one more time Rusty thought she might kill herself. Even the vicar, as he parted from her at the baby's funeral service, pressing her hand and turning to go, had said the same.

You'll have another child, Mrs Sykes, I feel sure of it.

Rusty had nearly shouted at him – so very nearly. She was so upset that she wanted to take hold of him and tell him – tell him that a lost baby wasn't like a broken plate. You couldn't just apply to the shop for another one with the same pattern. But she hadn't. She had just looked at the ground and nodded silently, before moving away from the vicar as quickly as politeness would allow.

Now propped up on her cold pillows in the growing darkness Rusty stared numbly at the ceiling, which seemed to be growing less like part of the room and more like the dark lowering sky outside, a firmament that was reaching down, it appeared, with every intention of eventually smothering her. Hot tears trickled down her half-frozen cheeks as she rocked herself to and fro, one of her pillows cradled in her arms while darkness fell around her, enclosing the world outside her window. She heard the sounds of her husband returning, but rather than talk to him she feigned sleep when he quietly pushed open the bedroom door to check on her, a mock sleep that soon became a real one as she drifted off, only to wake again shortly afterwards when her son was brought up to bed by his grandmother. With a deep sigh she turned on to her other side, thankful that yet another long meaningless day was nearly at its end.

Pulling her bedclothes up high, almost over her head, she buried herself as deeply as she could, and found herself hoping against hope that perhaps there would be no tomorrow, or at least if there were she might not wake up to it. Much as she hated the dark, for once in her life she found herself hoping that this particular night would have no end, and day would never break; that no faint light would creep through the thin curtains, and for her there would never be another winter's morning – no voices would murmur, no doors would open and shut, and there would be no sounds of people going about their business. That there would be no more life, in fact; no more seemingly endless bitter days or long drawn out freezing nights, no more pain, no more utter misery, no more anguish. At this moment in her young life, all Rusty wanted was for it to come to an end. Now.

* * *

Judy Tate was due to go and meet Meggie at Cucklington House, but a change in the weather had delayed her departure. To pass the time, she sat in the window of Owl Cottage watching the skies for a break in the snow with Hamish, her black Scottish terrier, sitting beside her on the window seat, seemingly as intrigued by the blizzard outside the diamond-shaped lead panes as his mistress.

'I don't think it's ever going to stop, old boy, do you?' Judy asked him, stubbing out the end of her cigarette. 'Having been frozen stiff I now think we're all going to be buried alive under a blanket of snow.'

Hamish leaped to his feet and started to bark at a cat streaking across the snow in front of the sitting room window. Judy was brushing some ash off her tartan skirt, reluctantly giving in to the idea of having to cancel her lunch date, when she saw the sun coming out, lighting up the snow which had stopped as suddenly as it had begun, and at once changed her mind, eager to get out of the cottage that, because of the bitter weather, had of late become something of a prison.

Five minutes later the sun was shining so brightly off the deep, crisp snow that when she opened the front door to step out she had to shade her eyes to look over the winter landscape. The beauty that greeted her raised her spirits immediately, but once outside she found it was still as bitterly cold as ever, a cold that burned into her lungs when she breathed it in, forcing her to wrap a thick red wool scarf around the lower part of her face. Holding Hamish's lead tightly in one gloved hand, she made her way slowly and carefully, passing only a few other brave souls trying to go about their business, or keep appointments somewhere in Bexham. The trek took her twice as long as usual so it was with some relief that she finally arrived at Cucklington House, where in answer to her tug on the old iron bell rope to the side of the wood-panelled, black-painted front door Meggie Gore-Stewart arrived to greet her, wearing an old fur coat, a matching hat and sheepskin gloves.

'No Richards?' Judy wondered, looking around the hall and suddenly noticing some missing paintings. Judy knew better than to pass comment. She was aware that Meggie's financial circumstances had become somewhat straitened since the war, what with overdue taxes and debts she had been obliged to pay off following the sudden death of both her parents, killed in a car accident in America the previous summer. The tragedy had left the already chaotic Gore-Stewart family affairs in a bigger mess than ever, forcing Meggie to try to raise the necessary funds from everything she had been previously bequeathed by her adored and adoring grandmother. Judging from the increasingly bare walls of Cucklington House, and the lack of any silver on the sideboard, the going was not likely to get any easier.

Meggie pulled a comically over-tragic face as Judy rephrased her question about the missing butler, wondering if he too had been hocked?

'Richards is upstairs in his sty,' she sighed, narrowing her eyes and taking hold of Judy by one arm. 'Determined to keep warm with the help of a bottle of nose paint. Come on – come through to the kitchen at once. I've found some sardines in the larder and some biscuits for the cheese in an old tin – and best news of all, the biscuits have no weevils. Imagine? Besides, it's almost warm in there.'

Following her friend's example and keeping on her overcoat, Judy trod carefully down the dark flagstones into the large kitchen. The room was dominated by an old cream-coloured range to which they both immediately gravitated, as towards an open fire, putting their still gloved hands on its comfortingly warm exterior.

'I've got some brandy – or would you rather a gin?'

'Anything. Anything as long as it's alcohol.'

Meggie poured them both large brandies, and then, still in gloves, hats and coats, with even Hamish carefully pushing his backside against the stove to warm himself, they raised their glasses to each other in a toast.

'To hell with rationing and the Labour government and God save all here.'

Meggie sat down on one side of the old table, while Judy pulled up another chair to sit opposite her.

'So Richards has taken to his bed, has he? What a bother. I suppose that means you have to do everything, and in this place that's not funny. I remember even your grandmother said it was too big for her, and she had plenty of people to help her.'

'And wasn't Madame Gran a lucky devil, to say the least of it. Even so, Richards can stay there and rot for all I care, even if the dust gets thicker and the cobwebs heavier. When all's said there's no-one to see them but him and me – and he can't see much through his eternal hangovers anyway.'

'Have you thought of kicking him out of bed?'

'No, but I have contemplated murdering him. Only the thought of ending up swinging on the end of a rope is stopping me. I don't think being driven mad by your grandmother's lunatic old butler is enough to risk being topped. Funny really, him taking to his bed now that the war is finally over – I mean, it just doesn't seem to be in character. He was so utterly resolute when the bombs were dropping, a rock upon whom we all leaned, day and blooming night, really he was.'

'Perhaps he's missing all the excitement?' Judy wondered. 'Lots of people are missing the war. That could be the trouble. Or he could be just plumb tuckered out?'

'I know just how he feels,' Meggie sighed, lighting up a cigarette. As she offered Judy one, she saw the look of surprise in her friend's eyes. 'Don't say you don't miss it, Judy? Since I've come back from America, I don't know why, but I seem to miss it more and more. It's as if, having been wholly alive, I am now half asleep.'

'I suppose that now you come to mention it, I suppose I do – a bit,' Judy said after a moment, surprising herself with her reply. 'I hadn't really thought about it before. War seemed so awful, and I just thought, well – peace is going to be—'

'Course you do,' Meggie interrupted as she topped up both their glasses. 'God, after all that danger and excitement, everyone pulling together – life is so *dull*. Don't you find it dull, and grey, Judy? Walter must, surely?'

'In a way I'm just glad to be still alive, Megs. I think I could take any amount of so-called austerity in return for us all still being here. Particularly Walter. Seriously – don't you feel the same?'

'About Walter?'

'*Seriously*.' Judy laughed. 'I know it's all a bit grim right now, but isn't that the rough with the smooth thing?'

'I suppose.' Meggie sighed. 'It's just not quite how one saw it all. Not quite what one was brought up to expect. Still, long as you've got a bit of whoopee water in the drink cupboard, and a few friends to chew the old cud with, I suppose one must not grum. Only bugbear I have personally speaking is fighting the old ennui, as the song has it.' She tapped the ash off her cigarette into the ashtray in the middle of the kitchen table in front of them. 'Although must say – after the States, life here has an altogether greyer hue. Not a morning goes by but I don't wake up and find myself missing real coffee that tastes of coffee, and fresh bread rolls and curls of cold butter . . . how I wish I hadn't said that.'

'How I wish you hadn't.'

Judy sighed gloomily, the idea of real coffee and equally real rolls and butter filling her with inexpressible longing. She turned her thoughts away from such unimaginable luxuries, and sipped at her drink instead. At least that was real. Rather than think about the change that had obviously come over them all, she turned her mind to the present, to the shift in Meggie's circumstances, to this new strange life her friend was being forced to lead, all alone in a large echoing house, trying to find the wherewithall to survive. To say that she was curious would be understating it.

Having finally warmed up due to the heat from the stove as well as the brandy Meggie slipped her fur coat off her shoulders and draped it over her knees. As Judy followed suit, she laughed.

'My God, we both look like Madame Gran when she was being driven about Bexham in the old Rolls.'

They both laughed again, then fell to silence.

'Are you all right, Megs?' Judy enquired, reading a sudden dark expression on Meggie's face.

'Yes. Of course. Why shouldn't I be?'

'Nothing. You just suddenly – you suddenly looked a little sad, that's all. Is it still your parents?'

'Is what still my parents?' Meggie asked tetchily. 'You know I didn't get on with them.' She averted her eyes and lit another cigarette from the one she was just finishing.

'You've never really talked about it. The accident, I mean.' Judy shrugged. 'I just wondered whether you wanted to talk about it.'

'Nothing really to talk about, darling. Besides its being a bit of a bore. Having to scratch round to pay their dues. I mean they really were quite hopeless. Not just with me – with money. With their affairs. I don't think it's quite fair, actually. Leaving such a terrible mess behind one. For someone else to clear up. I don't consider that to be quite the thing. So there you are – that's it. That's how all right I am. I'm fine, darling. Just a mite miffed.'

'Are you having to – are you having any difficulty?' Judy corrected herself. 'Getting the necessary, I mean.'

'You're wondering about the missing paintings?' Meggie flashed a sudden smile, much to Judy's relief. 'It's all right, I haven't flogged them – yet – although dare say I'll have to surrender them sooner or later. At the moment they're only up in London being cleaned – just in case. Anyway, this is boring. I hate talking about money, et cetera. Much more interesting – how's it feel to have a husband again?'

Judy went to say something, and then stopped.

'It feels strange,' she said, finally and reluctantly. 'I don't know why, and I never thought to say it, but having Walter back after six years, after thinking he was dead – it's a bit odd actually.'

Meggie nodded, as if she hadn't paid much attention to this admission.

'Does Walter talk about his war much, or is he

how they were when they came back from the last war? A lot of them wouldn't talk about it, you know. Not a word. According to my grandmother. It was as if four years in the Flanders mud had never happened. Is Walter a bit like that?'

Judy hesitated, not wanting to be disloyal to the only man she had ever loved, and at the same time longing to talk about the state of her marriage.

'A bit,' she admitted, finally. 'You'd think that after all those years in Norway fighting with the Resistance he'd have a bit to say on the subject, but all he ever really says is *later, Judy, later. All in good time*. It's a bit hurtful actually. At first I thought perhaps he had a mistress over there that he couldn't tell me about – or something or other. But then I saw this look he has in his eyes and I know it couldn't be that.'

'Why?'

'Because he looks so lost. He looks as if he still doesn't quite know where he is. Maybe it's because he had to kill people, that kind of thing.'

'Hardly surprising, darling. There was a war on.'

'But then you don't talk at all about France and being in the Resistance,' Judy continued. 'Not even to me, so I suppose it's hardly surprising if Walter doesn't either.'

'We're probably all afraid of being war bores, darling. Better by far to put it behind us, yes? It is actually all over now, you know. Better to leave be and not become a bore about it.'

'You could never be accused of that.' Judy laughed, pointing accusingly at Meggie. 'You even turned down a medal without telling me! I only found out by chance!'

'A medal's a medal, for all that – that's all it is,' Meggie replied, getting up out of her chair. 'Now then – I don't know about you, but I'm famished. As always. Let's eat.'

Far from the expected sardine on stale bread with a bit of old cheese, much to Judy's surprise and delight Meggie had performed a small culinary miracle, and from such basic ingredients as she had found made a delicious meal of sardines and anchovies – a lucky discovery apparently – served in a delicious dressing miraculously concocted out of some old white wine dregs, long ago turned to vinegar, and the last of an ancient bottle of olive oil, stuffed into two large baked potatoes, followed by slices of farmhouse cheddar served on hot toast.

'Don't tell me you've learned to bake.' Judy stared at the loaf on the side. 'You'll be wearing a pinny next.'

'Wouldn't be caught dead. As a matter of fact I learned to bake bread when I was a child – Grandmother's cook taught me, under Madame Gran's insistence. Only three things a girl needs to know how to do to make her way in the world, she used to say. You've got to be able to make love, bread and Three No Trumps doubled and vulnerable.'

Further fortified by a bottle of claret Meggie had luckily brought up earlier from the cellar but which had only thawed out sufficiently to be drinkable after being stood on the stove for a full twenty minutes, the two young women reminisced about their times together at the start of the war, remembering those dark days now almost fondly, for all the world as if they were the good times that would never roll again.

'Things can only get better, I suppose, Meggie,' Judy mused as they moved back again to sit close to the stove. 'Things always seem worse in the winter, particularly a winter as hard as this one.'

'I don't know about you, but I was brought up to believe that the spoils of war were what came with peace. Prosperity. Optimism. Triumph. Not shortages, queues and misery. I mean, *regardez nous*, would you? You'd think we'd lost rather than won the war, wouldn't you?'

'Perhaps we did. What an awful thought.' Judy stared ahead of her at something she couldn't quite name. 'In fact, in more than one way we just might have lost, you know, and no perhaps about it. In fact, in one way, I think that we actually did lose.'

'And what way is that, do tell.'

'I think maybe we've lost our innocence.'

Ellen flicked her duster idly along the top of the desk, much more interested in what her employer's daughter was doing than in the little bit of housework that was required that morning.

'You're smoking yourself to a standstill, since you and Master Max have come back from your London visit, Miss Mattie,' she said, looking at the thin blue spiral of smoke that was rising from the sofa, and giving an extra flick of her duster as if to underline her point. 'That's the third cigarette you've had since I started doin' in here this morning, and I think that's too much, really I do, Miss Mattie.'

Mattie didn't even bother to look up from her copy of *The Tatler*, flicking her ash inaccurately into the fireplace as she stared at a particularly foolish-looking set of young people enjoying a joke on the stairs at a dance in some particularly gloomy-looking country house.

'You'll find furniture gets much cleaner, Ellen, if you move the articles on top of it while you're dusting, rather than threatening them with your duster,' she countered, throwing Ellen a look, which was promptly greeted with a sniff and a shrug. 'Or counting how many cigarettes I might or might not have had for that matter,' she finally decided, as she closed her magazine. 'Anyway, I'm only doing my duty. In case you may have forgotten, smoking is a government directive. Everyone in London's smoking like chimneys. The Prime Minister, Mr Attlee—'

'I know who the Prime Minister is well enough, thank you, Miss Mattie,' Ellen interrupted. 'Having helped to have him voted in.'

'Mr Attlee wants us all to smoke as much as we can. Be patriotic, smoke your way through the day, that's the maxim.' Mattie picked up a fresh magazine. 'By lighting up a ciggie every twenty minutes I happen to be doing my duty for God and the King.'

'I can't see the point of it, really I can't, can't see

the point of smoking, Miss Mattie.'

'I suppose the point behind their thinking, Ellen, is that the more we smoke the less we will feel the hunger pangs, that's the point. They want us to smoke to make up for the fact that there's no tea, no butter, no bread, no eggs, no nothing really.'

Momentarily distracted from the magazine, Mattie breathed out a beautifully shaped smoke ring and watched it drifting across the sitting room before it disappeared against the Japanese-style pre-war wallpaper.

'Well, I wouldn't know about that,' Ellen muttered. 'Not being a smoker meself. And isn't that young Max just waking up and calling for you?' Once more she stooped, pretending to dust a chair leg, at the same time cocking her head to the ceiling above. 'He's a healthy pair of lungs on him, and that's certain.'

'Even if I haven't,' you mean?' Mattie returned, throwing her now finished cigarette on the fire. 'Coming, Max!' she called. 'Mummy's coming!'

'We'll go out to the village green and make a snowman,' she promised Max a little later, as he jumped down the stairs in such a state of excitement over the snow that he could barely stand still long enough for his mother to dress him in a thick home-knitted hat, gloves and socks. Having put on her own overcoat, the much darned lining of which was a tribute to the needlewoman in her, Mattie stepped outside into the front garden and straight on to the green.

After the loss of her mother in a wartime fire, she and her father had moved from Magnolias to the Place, a light and roomy house directly overlooking Bexham village green. To their mutual surprise they found they had both settled into the new house without any sense of regret for their previous home, perhaps because, among many other advantages, the new house was considerably nearer to the Three Tuns where Lionel Eastcott liked to go for a regular drink at certain equally regular times of the day.

Out on the green Mattie and Max found that they hardly noticed the cold, so engrossed did they become in building their enormous snowman. They weren't alone, because the green was already dotted with groups of other children similarly employed, under the vigilant eyes of their mothers.

'Now that really is a snowman. That is going to be the best snowman of them all, Max,' Mattie said. 'If there was a prize for best snowman, undoubtedly you would be the winner, sweetie pie.'

Having carefully inserted the two old black coat buttons for the eyes that she'd brought out especially for the task, Mattie stood back to admire their handiwork. As she did so she noticed a figure walking nearby, a young woman carrying a large pink-blanketed bundle in her arms. As soon as she realised who the woman was, Mattie caught her breath. The last thing she'd heard about Rusty Sykes had not been good – and yet here she was out walking with a baby cradled in her arms.

For a moment Mattie stood motionless, not knowing what to do, hoping against hope that Rusty might not have seen her, or that if she had she might be just as anxious as Mattie to avoid contact. As she stood watching Rusty seemed about to pass on by, so Mattie thought her wish had been granted, until Max suddenly pointed.

'We forgot the carrot for snowman's nose, Mummy!' he called back to her, already on the move. 'We'd better go back home and get it!'

'No! No. In a minute, Max!' Mattie called hastily, running after the fleet little boy. 'Let's just finish off his chin first!'

By the time she had caught Max up and had him safely back in hand, she found herself directly in Rusty's path. Rusty stopped when she saw Mattie, looking at her with uncertainty, before bowing her head and looking away at the ground beyond them both.

'Hello, Rusty,' Mattie said sparely. 'I thought it was you.'

'I didn't see you,' Rusty muttered. 'I didn't see you at all.'

'We've been building a snowman, Max and I,' Mattie said, not knowing what else to say. 'Snow's perfect for it, isn't it, Max?'

'Want to come and see our snowman?' Max asked Rusty hopefully, before standing up on tiptoe. 'Can I see your baby please?'

'It's all right, Max,' Mattie said, trying tactfully to pull her son away. 'Why don't we go and get that carrot you were talking about?'

'I want to see the baby, Mummy. Please can I see the baby?'

'Max—'

'Is it a little boy or a little girl baby?'

Max was pulling hard at his mother's hand, straining to get a sight of the baby wrapped in the pink shawl.

'It's a little girl,' Rusty said suddenly. 'You probably wouldn't like that. Not everyone likes little girl babies, unfortunately.' She turned her face to Mattie and stared at her almost accusingly.

'Not me, Rusty,' Mattie replied, trying to smile. 'That's what I'm hoping for next – a little girl to make the pigeon pair.'

'Well if you don't get one, don't worry, Mattie. *You can always have another one*.'

'Can I *see* your baby, please?' Max persisted, jumping up and down on the spot. *'Please?'*

'My mother didn't want a little girl, so it didn't matter in the end,' Rusty said, looking down at the bundle in her arms. 'I did. I wanted a girl. Just like you, Mattie. But my mother said it didn't matter because no-one can take the place of Tam. *You can always have another one*, she said. These things happen. Lose one and you can always have another. Provided it isn't a little boy.'

Rusty leaned forward and tucked the pink blanket round the bundle in her arms.

'Truth to tell,' she continued. 'I don't think

Mother can even remember what she had *me* christened. I think she still imagines she had me baptised Rusty to go with my hair, rather than Katherine with a K.'

'Please can I see your baby?' Max, like most children his age, was refusing to concede defeat. 'Please?'

'Later, Max,' Mattie suggested, tightening her grip on his arm to prevent any more jumping.

'It's all right,' Rusty assured her. 'If he wants to have a look, that's perfectly all right. Here you are – say hello to Jeannie.'

She stooped down over the little boy, turning the bundle in her arms to him so that he could see it better, holding it at the height of his own face. Max looked, then looked again, staring at the bundle then up at his mother.

'It's a doll,' he said to her. 'It's a doll, Mummy.'

'I know, dear,' Mattie whispered back to him. 'A little girl doll.'

'A pretty little girl doll,' Rusty said, standing back up and rocking the doll in her arms. 'My pretty little Jeannie Katherine with a K.'

'It's a doll, Mummy,' Max hissed urgently up at his mother again. 'This lady's carrying round her dolly.'

'My pretty little Jeannie Katherine,' Rusty repeated, cooingly. 'Time to take little Jeannie home.'

'I want to go home too, Mummy Please can we go home please?' Max pleaded.

'What about your snowman? We haven't

finished our snowman. We've got to get a carrot for his nose, remember?'

'I want to go home now, Mummy. Now.'

Max tugged free from the hand that was holding him and began to run in the direction of his house, straight towards a gang of local lads who were busy making an arsenal of snowballs.

'Max?' Mattie called after him anxiously. 'Max, wait for me! Max? Sorry, Rusty – but I can't have him rushing off like this. Sorry.'

'Little boys, Mattie,' Rusty smiled, rocking the doll in her arms. 'Little girls are so much easier.'

But Mattie was now out of earshot, running as best as she could through the snow after Max who was skipping along, unaware of the danger that lay ahead. The lads had seen him coming, but had pretended not to notice him, laughing and throwing snowballs at each other over the top of his head as he ran between them. Mattie knew exactly what they were up to, because she knew this gang. She'd run across them before with Max. They'd been trouble then. With one last shout to her son to wait for her, she tried to make up lost ground, but the snow was deep and inevitably she fell flat on her face in a drift. By the time she was back on her feet it was too late. One of the bigger boys had taken careful aim with a huge snowball and thrown it straight at Max. The force of it sent him flying onto his back, and he was howling in angry fright long before Mattie could reach him.

'Little bastard! That'll teach you to look where

you're going, won't it! Cry baby bastard!'

The boys ran off laughing, leaving Mattie to comfort Max while behind her she heard Rusty yelling out furiously after them as she hurried to Mattie's side. Max was still howling when she arrived although happily his pride appeared to be the only thing that was really hurt.

'See what I mean about boys?' Rusty said, looking after the gang that was disappearing into a new flurry of falling snow. 'Little roughnecks.'

'Don't worry, Rusty,' Mattie sighed. 'We're quite used to it.'

'You never get used to it, not to that taunt. Tam comes home practically every day saying he's been insulted like that at school, even though his dad and I are married now. You know who's worst of all? The other mothers. Nice, isn't it? Think they'd be a bit sympathetic, but not a bit of it. Can't wait to point a finger, they can't – even them who've got a little bastard of their own in tow – they're even worse sometimes. As if by calling out loudest of all no-one'll guess their secret.'

'And it's hardly the child's fault, is it, Rusty?' Mattie said, dusting the snow off Max's coat. 'It's not as if they've been party to it. Come on, Maxie – let's dry those eyes of yours and go and get that carrot we forgot for Mr Snowman's nose.'

'Don't want to,' Max grizzled. 'I want to go home.'

'It would be a shame not to finish Mr Snowman off, dear.'

'I don't want to.' Max gave another worried

glance up at Rusty, who was too busy looking at the bundle in her arms to notice. 'I want to go home.'

'I must go home as well,' Rusty said, swaddling her doll even more tightly. 'Getting too cold for Jeannie to be out – and anyway's it's time for her feed.'

Her eyes drifted back towards the place from where she had come, her mind seesawing with difficulty between the past and the present before settling for its present nightmare state.

The two women said their goodbyes before making their separate ways home. Mattie had only a matter of a few yards to go until she and Max reached the front door of the Place, but the short journey seemed to take for ever, time hanging the way it always does when you are anxious to close the book on an unhappy chapter, such as this short episode with the bully boys and poor half-demented Rusty and her wrapped up china doll. At last they reached the gate and then the door, which Mattie shut thankfully behind her, putting a barricade between herself and her son and the harsh reality of Rusty's mistery.

Ellen was in the kitchen when Mattie entered in search of something hot to eat and drink for herself and Max, whom she had left with his grandfather by the fireside to get himself warm. Mattie went to fill the kettle, only to find it taken out of her hands by the housekeeper.

'That cold out there is it?' Ellen enquired. 'You look half frozen to death.'

'And half startled, too, Ellen. I just bumped into poor Rusty Sykes.'

'Poor Rusty Sykes, yes, I know.' Ellen sighed. 'Still, at least she's up and about now. Which is something.'

'She's up and about, Ellen, carrying round a china doll in her arms.'

The housekeeper stared at her frowning as if she could not possibly have heard aright.

'A china doll, you say? What sort of china doll would that be, Miss Mattie?'

'What do you think, Ellen?' Mattie replied in exasperation. 'A china doll. A child's china doll. All dressed in pink and wrapped up in a pink shawl. She's carrying it round like a *baby*.'

'Like her baby?'

'Like her baby, if you prefer. Frightened the life out of poor Max.'

'Poor Rusty. She's carrying round a china doll for a baby, now? Oh, the poor child. The poor unhappy thing. I had no idea she'd taken it that hard.'

'How long since she lost the baby, Ellen? It's not long, is it?'

'I don't know exactly, Miss Mattie. All I knows is when you were up in London they had the funeral for her – while you were away up in London. So it must be near two week now, I suppose. Course they couldn't bury the poor little mite, could they – spite of having the funeral service for her. They couldn't bury the poor little mite on account of the frozen ground. Couldn't even dig deep enough for a grave that size. Maybe that's what gone and turned poor Rusty's mind a bit.'

'It frightened the life out of Max. I have to say it spooked me a bit, too.'

'Mind you, some is saying it were Rusty's own fault losing her baby. You know what a tomboy Rusty's always been. What an independent-minded lass. Mrs Minton what lives opposite said she never stopped for a moment during her time. Hardly sat down to draw breath. Always busy about the place, running here there and everywhere – doing what she shouldn't, at any rate. So she brought it on herself, that's what a lot of folks is saying. Might even be down to eating green potatoes. That's what my mother always warned us against. Eating green potatoes when you're not expectin's bad enough, goodness knows, but if you is—'

Ellen stopped for a moment to shake her head disparagingly before continuing.

'It's not just Mrs Minton who's saying she done too much. So does her mother – Rusty's mother not Mrs Minton's that is – she's sure as eggs is eggs that the girl went and brought it on herself, doing too much of what she'd been told not to do. Doesn't feel sorry for her at all, not at all, her mother doesn't. That's according to Mrs Minton, mind. Don't take my word on it. But that's what Mrs Minton is saying, and what some other folks think and all.'

For a moment Mattie thought of defending Rusty whom she had always liked and whom she now felt desperately sorry for, convinced it couldn't be her fault, only just pure circumstance, but thought better of arguing with Ellen, since in common with most of the village Ellen always did suspect that people brought bad things on themselves, even Hitler and the war.

Even so, as she settled herself into her bed later that night, tucked up warm and cosily with two hot water bottles wrapped in sweaters against her back and feet, and her own child safely tucked up in bed in the next-door room, she found she could not get rid of the strange image of the china-faced doll, and Rusty carefully pulling the pink blanket round its head to keep out the cold. It was the saddest of sights, and it worried her no end to think that a friend's mind might have been turned by a tragedy which was none of her fault; that it might have affected her so badly that she had become quite unable to cope with her loss. Try as she would she could not get the memory of the events of that afternoon out of her mind. It was a long, long time before Mattie finally drifted off to sleep and into a series of fitful and unhappy dreams which, when she woke from them, made her feel as though she had spent the night on the opposite side of the looking glass.

Early the following day Meggie caught sight of Judy passing her house, with Hamish trotting by her side as best he could, given the depth of the snow. As she watched, an unaccustomed wave of jealousy hit her. Judy was probably on her way back to her cottage to get ready for her husband's return from London, while all Meggie had to look forward to was being entertained by yet another of Richards's dreadful hungover litanies of how his life was never going to be the same again with Madame Gran gone and the blessed war over.

Unable to bear any further thought of Judy's domestic bliss, Meggie found an old apron in the kitchen to protect her still stylish pre-war black and white coat and skirt and set about trying to light herself some sort of fire from the last of the wood Richards had managed to chop and bring into the drawing room before succumbing once again to his ever ready friend – the bottle.

As she searched on the top of the fireplace for the box of Swan Vestas she thought she had put there she found herself stopping and staring at the photograph of herself and Davey aboard the *Light Heart*, a snapshot taken one weekend before the war when all had still seemed safe and they had sailed down the coast as far as Lyme Regis to spend the night together making love on deck underneath a blanket of stars.

She frowned at the image of herself with both her arms tightly wrapped around one of Davey's, imagining for a few seconds that he wasn't really dead, that one of these days he would, like Judy's husband, Walter Tate, turn up as if from nowhere, swinging through the front door of Cucklington House, suntanned and full of life, not to mention merry as a cricket from the hospitality at the Three Tuns. He would swing her round as he had used to do, sweeping her off her feet, and Madame Gran and Richards would be there, and they too would be waiting for him to wrap them round his little finger with his charm and his gaiety.

Holding the little silver-framed photograph in one hand and forgetting all about the fire, Meggie sank down into the old chintz-covered armchair behind her as she continued to stare at her lost and much missed love.

'Of course you're dead,' she told the photo. 'You were drowned at sea, yet another dead hero, lost and gone for ever with no tombstone to speak of your passing, or mark your life.'

Her grandmother had told her to wait until the war was over before marrying Davey. If they hurried into it Meggie might find she had made a mistake. Or Davey might discover the very same, she had warned. Once the war was over they might be different people, and she had advised Meggie to think of the consequences if they were married.

But so what? Meggie now thought. *Really, so what?*

So what if they had married and had made one huge colossal mistake – at least they'd have had some time together, be it only a few weeks, days or even hours. Instead, what remained of Davey lay somewhere on the bottom of the English Channel, while Meggie, who had so loved him from childhood onwards, sat alone, by an unlit fire, in a land impoverished by victory.

If she had married Davey she would not have gone to France. She would have stayed at home in

Bexham, married and safe, or safely married, and very likely a mother to Davey's children by now. If she had married Davey she would never have allowed Judy's father-in-law, Hugh, to encourage her to join SOE; she would never have been dropped into occupied France. She would never, through a combination of loneliness and necessity, have found herself first having an affair and even falling a little in love with Heinrich Von Hantzen, the German officer who had saved her from the Gestapo at terrible risk to himself.

As the thought came to her Meggie glanced up at the chimneypiece, as if to assure herself there was no photograph of herself and her German lover there, so there could be no possible evidence of their affair. Now Heinrich too was dead, killed in action during the D-Day campaign as she had learned in a letter from his sister after the war had finished.

My God, now she came to think of it, what *would* they have made of such an alliance here in Bexham? What would they make of it now?

Realising it was not a thought that she had really faced up to before, in typical Meggie fashion Meggie suddenly found the whole notion quite hilarious. They would probably have shaved her head and paraded her in the streets with a bill-board around her neck, and possibly they would still do the same if they should discover the truth. Certainly no-one would ever ask her to their houses again; she would be shunned by all, the lowest of the low. She would be that simply awful

Meggie Gore-Stewart who all the time she was meant to be doing heroic things for her country was in fact sleeping with the enemy. Never mind that Heinrich was not a Nazi, never mind that he was a highly civilised, articulate and kind human being – the fact that Meggie had consorted with a German would banish her to Coventry for the rest of her life, at least as far as the folks of Bexham were concerned.

A strange noise woke her out of her reverie, and looking round she saw the dreadfully bedraggled but all too familiar post-binge figure of Richards in his well worn tartan dressing gown and equally well worn grey winceyette pyjamas, with a pair of faded black slippers on his slowly shuffling feet. He was staggering into the dimly lit and freezing drawing room looking like something that not even a cat would bother to bring in.

'It is I, Miss Megs,' he announced shakily. 'All but arisen from the grave.'

'Looking at you as you are now, I'm not sure I agree about the *all but*, Richards, really I'm not,' Meggie replied tartly, at once getting up and replacing the photograph she was still nursing, before Richards shuffled up the drawing room towards her. 'Why don't you wander off and find yourself something to eat, and try to sober up for what remains of the day.'

'I do not require anything to eat, thank you, Miss Meggie. All I require is a pen and a fresh sheet of paper – and for good reason. I wish to sign the Pledge.'

'I could repaper this room with the number of pieces of paper you've signed to that effect, Richards.'

'This time I mean it, Miss Megs. I have visited Lethe's portals and it was not an experience I would recommend even to my worst enemy, not even to Herr Adolph Hitler should he still be alive and in rude health somewhere.'

Meggie smiled to herself as she watched Richards weave to the walnut bureau and search for pen and paper while gently but not altogether inaudibly moaning to himself yet more incantations about having visited Hades, but now having seen the Light.

'When you've quite finished making your Pledge, Richards,' she said, collecting her cigarettes and lighter and going to the door, 'I'll be in the kitchen, making you something a little more realistic.'

However she couldn't help feeling sorry for her wrecked butler, so much so that she decided to raid her emergency stores on his behalf. Her underground larder was a place she had somehow managed to keep undisclosed to anyone, most of all Richards. It was here that she kept a small supply of luxury provisions collected before her return from the States, and thereafter obtained via the black market, either from smugglers who ran the provender in from France, or simply from the fairly constant stream of spivs who passed through the village, stopping to make themselves known either at the Three Tuns, or at the grocery store. The few tins of veal, pâté and ham, the Belgian coffee and bars of Swiss chocolate, were all kept in top-secret storage under a thick stone slab in the floor of the cold room. Much as she longed to share Richards's meal of ham on hot toast washed down with a huge mug of fresh black coffee, Meggie abstained from the luxury, allowing herself only one cup of coffee, albeit with brandy added, to go with yet another appetite-stunting cigarette. Meanwhile in front of her Richards was visibly, minute by minute, pulling himself together.

'I don't know about you, Miss Meggie,' he said, once he'd wiped his plate clean with the last crust of bread. 'But you can keep this post-war life for a game of soldiers.'

'And I think I probably agree with yous, bedad and to be sure,' Meggie agreed in a cod Irish accent. 'So what'll we do? What'll we do? What'll we do? To be sure, to be sure, to be sure?'

'I have heard it rumoured upon the grapevine—' Richards eyed her now with slightly less reddened and bleary eyes. 'I have heard that the Three Tuns might be up for sale.'

'I dare say. With your weakness, I would say you would be just the man to buy it, Richards. Talk about the perfect job.'

'You may mock, and I cannot complain at your mockery – but I have been reliably informed that there is no better path to sobriety than to watch others getting regularly shipwrecked. If that doesn't stop me from drinking then we must all sure as rationed eggs give up the ghost entirely.'

'Does this mean I shall be losing you, Richards?'

'One could hardly say you will be losing me, since no-one could say that I have been exactly present in recent times, Miss Megs.'

'How could I manage without you?' Meggie asked in all seriousness. 'You and I are joined at the hip, like it or lump it, old thing.'

'You will manage a whole lot better without me, dear.' Richards suddenly sighed, losing all his former decorum. 'The way I am at the moment, I'm just one great big waste of valuable space and time, and please do not try to convince *moi* otherwise.'

Meggie smiled, although she did her best to hide her amusement, just the way she always did whenever Richards lapsed into what he called his *theatrical*.

Buying the Three Tuns might not sound the most likely of salvations, but in an odd way she realised Richards might have a point – as he so often did. Immediately after the war there had been some talk of Richards's taking over a small restaurant on the other side of the harbour, but for one reason and another his plans had come to nothing. Now, buying a pub might indeed be a kill or cure for her grandmother's old butler; and besides, Meggie rather relished the thought of the more than theatrical Richards behind the somewhat stuffy bar of their local hostelry. If that didn't stir up the natives, she didn't know what would, and for that reason alone it surely had to be a good idea.

* * *

It froze hard again that night, so hard that rumours abounded that out at sea the waves themselves were freezing, their white tops stilled into shapes resembling whipped white of egg as shipping all but ceased.

Rusty, still clothed, lay silently in her bed once more. Downstairs her mother was listening to Children's Hour on the radio with Tam. For a second or two Rusty thought she could hear Uncle Mac's soothing voice floating up through the floorboards, but it did nothing to settle her. She closed her eyes and wished she could pray, but she couldn't. It was as if she had fallen into a well of unhappiness and was slowly beginning to drown, no longer strong enough to tread the waters surrounding her. She had thought her walk with Jeannie might do her some good, blow away at least some of her black thoughts, and for a while it had indeed seemed to work. When she had been with Mattie and Max everything had been fine, momentarily. Even the incident with the snowballs and the name-calling had been galvanising rather than depressing. It was only when she had returned home again that the black clouds had descended once more.

Why would her mother not allow her baby up here with her? Why did she insist that Rusty left Jeannie in the pram downstairs instead of letting Rusty have her upstairs in her bedroom so that she could cuddle her?

It might have been different – in fact everything

might have been different – if she'd had her own home, the way things were when Tam was born. Just her and the baby, that had been bliss, no-one nagging and carping, no-one to tell her what to do at all times of the day and night, just her and her baby. But then the war had ended, and the people who owned the house she had rented had needed to have it back, and what with money being so short Peter had suggested the best thing – in fact the only thing open to them – was to live with her parents, just until they got back on their feet, just for a few weeks. But the weeks had turned to months, and now they had been under the same roof for over two years with the result that they had no privacy and thus really no proper marriage. Worst of all, Mother had taken little Tam over, and since to her way of thinking nothing was good enough for her grandson, nothing being good enough was very bad for little Tam.

Nor would Father hear a word said against the little boy. Everything Tam did was right and everything his parents did – particularly his mother – was wrong. Small wonder then that Peter was out all the time, seemingly caring less about his wife or what happened to her, not until the baby arrived that was. After that he was out even more. It was as if with the baby lost for ever Rusty had caught a highly infectious disease, something like tuberculosis. Peter seemed unable to come near her, apparently afraid that if he came too close he might catch her grief. So, kind man that he was, or that he used to be, he offered Rusty no shoulder for her to cry on and absolutely no moral support. As early as he could make it every morning he disappeared off to the garage where he remained working until long after his son's bedtime and in turn that of his young wife.

Rusty had to face the fact that at the moment Peter seemed more sorry for himself than he was for her. On top of everything he never once attempted to say anything to Mother in Rusty's defence. He never contradicted her about the cause of their baby's death, never said *the baby didn't die because Rusty helped you hang the curtains* or *we didn't lose her because Rusty ran everywhere in the early months* or because she might have eaten a green potato. Never once did he say *the baby – our baby – she died, Mother-in-law, because the little thing had the cord round her neck, and that was all there was to it.*

Never the once.

Never once did he leap to her defence. Instead all Peter could do was rush out of the house to try to mend the motorcars that people brought to him, and spend his day fiddling about in his garage, day after day, day after day.

'Summer'll soon be here, Rusty,' was about all he could think of saying to her when he found Rusty yet again lying in a darkened room, trying to come to terms with her loss. 'Soon as summer comes you'll be feeling better, you mark my words.'

But as she lay in her bedroom long after Peter had left for work it seemed that summer would never in fact come. All that happened was the weather worsened and with it so did Rusty's state of mind. She would spend morning after morning lying in a ball under her covers, crying her eyes out while trying not to be heard by her mother as she went about her housework. She could just about handle the food shortages and the terrible grim and freezing weather, the lack of money and heating, the deprivations that seemed universal and wholesale, but what she couldn't deal with was the lack of any love and compassion. She didn't want anyone feeling sorry for her – she just wanted some love and some tenderness. Instead of which all she got was blame and half-hidden accusations of wilful carelessness. She even began to consider the possibility that it might be her own fault, that whatever lay at her door did so because she had brought it there. Until they moved in with her parents she thought she had really loved Peter, but after two years under the same roof as her mother and father, Rusty had come to fear that she had only married Peter after the war out of pity rather than for love – and because of Tam, because she thought he should have a proper name like other boys, that she should give him a proper father, and that if she did that her child would be safe from taunts and insults. And when Peter had come home such a hero, albeit a hero minus a leg, out had come the village band to greet him, bright had shone the medals on his chest, and Rusty loved a hero as much as anyone, and so they had married.

It had been so good at first, Peter proving to be as gentle and sweet as he had always been when they had all been growing up in Bexham. Neither had his wartime experiences, let alone the loss of his leg, seemed to have made him bitter. They were happy together, even when they'd moved back into the tiny house that had been her home – until they realised that with the loss of privacy came a loss of intimacy, not only physical but mental. Now this new loss, the major one, the tragic one. Rusty suspected that what she'd fallen in love with was the uniform, the heroism, rather than the man inside the uniform, because the man she now shared her life with showed no love for her, no compassion, not even a little tenderness.

It's not that I don't love So-and-So, it's just that I'm not in love with him. That was what Rusty used to hear girls in the wartime factory where she worked saying time and time again. She thought that was how it must be now with Peter. She did like Peter, even though he was so hopeless at dealing with her grief. She still liked him in spite of his inability to help her. In fact – she sat up as the thought occurred to her – in fact she liked Peter so much that the one thing she knew now was that she couldn't possibly go on living with him. It just wouldn't be fair.

She became quite determined, now that she knew what was in her mind. Whatever happened, one way or the other, Rusty was now convinced that she had to go. Somehow she had to get out of this suffocating little cottage, get away from Mother and Father, and from a marriage which was little more than a friendship. She had to run away from home. She had to run away and leave it all behind her.

But where was she to go? And when? It was all very well making these life-changing decisions as she lay in her bed upstairs while her husband worked all the hours God gave him to put food on the table, to clothe them somehow, and help her parents keep some sort of roof over their heads, but when it came down to practicalities a feeling of utter hopelessness came over Rusty, the same feeling that she used to have when she was little and realised that being a child was like being a prisoner. You were helpless, always waiting around for someone else to feed you or clothe you, quite unable to do anything for yourself. And that was just how she was beginning to feel again now.

She was a prisoner once again, but this time she was incarcerated not by the helplessness of childhood but by her marriage vows.

She climbed out of bed as quietly as she could and carefully opened the door. The voices she could hear talking below were all coming from the kitchen, which would mean if she was very quiet – and very careful – she could get up and down the stairs without being heard.

'Sshhh!' Mrs Todd said suddenly, knitting needles held still in mid-air. 'Thought I heard something.'

They all listened, Mr Todd, his wife and their son-in-law Peter, but the house was completely silent.

'Probably just them floorboards again,' Mr Todd said, resuming his reading of the single sheet of print that nowadays represented the local newspaper. 'Creak as if they've a life of their own so they do.'

'Could be Rusty.'

'Don't think so, Mother-in-law. She was fast asleep when I looked in. Out to the world.'

'State of mind she's in she could walk in her sleep,' Mrs Todd said, picking up the stitch she had dropped. 'Time she pulled herself together. Which is why I did what I did.'

'What was that, Mother-in-law? What did you have to do?'

'Nothing that need concern you, Peter,' Mrs Todd replied, with a sharp look. 'Least not unless you want that wife of yours locked away.'

She gave one last glance towards the closed door but the house had once more fallen completely silent, the only noise to be heard being the moan of the winter wind outside, the rattle of the windows.

On the other side of the door, still as a mouse, Rusty stood on the bottom stair, her eyes on the pram by the door, the little pram with the pink blanket still pulled up into place. All she had to do was wait, take a deep breath, tiptoe over to the pram, take Jeannie and tiptoe back upstairs. That's all she had to do to be safe, and since she had got down here without anyone noticing, she surely could get back upstairs. As soon as she could, she would wrap Jeannie up in her warmest clothes, then in the thick wool blanket, dress herself as warmly as possible, take the little money she had saved away in her purse under the mattress, climb out of her bedroom window on to the roof of the outhouse, drop down into the snow and be off. Where, she didn't yet know, nor did she care. All she knew was that once she had Jeannie in her arms and was out of the house, she was safe. She had enough money to pay for several days' food and lodgings somewhere – anywhere, as long as it was miles from Bexham – then once she was settled in her mind again, once everything was back to normal, she would get a job. She didn't mind what she did, just so long as they didn't mind her bringing Jeannie, and Jeannie'd be no trouble anyway. Jeannie was a good little girl. Jeannie would just lie there and sleep without making a sound until her mother had finished her work, and could take her home again. So now all she had to do was tiptoe over to the pram, pull the blanket back, lift Jeannie up and take her away with her.

When she saw the pram was empty Rusty screamed. She couldn't help it. She screamed as loudly as she could, she screamed at the top of her voice. Someone had stolen her baby.

Chapter Two

'If we'd had a winter like this during the war, Jerry could have marched across the bloomin' Channel, and no mistake,' Gwen announced as she began to clear away her mistress's breakfast things. 'And look at you leaving those perfectly good crusts. You shouldn't leave good bread like that, Mrs Tate. The way things are, you shouldn't be leaving good bread. Not a crumb.'

'OK – so you take it, Gwen. Why don't you? See what you can get for it on the black market.' Judy's mother-in-law laughed, pushing her chair back from the table and getting up. 'And while you're at it, see if you can beg, steal or pay through the nose for some more fresh eggs, will you? I would die for some freshly scrambled eggs.'

'At two and six a dozen? It's enough to make anyone drop dead, Mrs Tate. Don't know how they dare as to ask that sort of money, I really don't. Not only that – who's to say they're fresh? I'd like to know where they find chickens laying in this dreadful weather. You ask me them's foreign eggs they're selling on the quay. You won't find those to be British fresh farm.'

'I don't care if they come from Timbuktu, Gwen,' replied Loretta Tate – Loopy to her friends – pulling her second cardigan around her tightly against the wind that was whistling through the gaps in the window frames. 'I just have this simply awful desire for just one plate of soft scrambled eggs and bacon, or some thick French toast dripping with butter. Oh, for crying out loud, what did I have to go and say that for? Now I shall go completely out of my mind.'

'You'd need to send to your folks in America if you want bacon, Mrs Tate,' Gwen muttered, flicking the crumbs off the table and straight onto the floor with her mistress's discarded napkin. 'You've as much chance of getting your hands on rashers of bacon here as I have of marrying Errol Flynn.'

'My, I quite forgot to tell you,' Loopy called, pulling a face of mock innocence behind her maid's back. 'Mr Flynn called again last night, Gwen.'

To the sound of further grumbles and protestations Loopy ambled out of her dining room and into the small sitting room where she had already taken the precaution of lighting a wood fire. She was due to have lunch with her daughter-in-law, but since more heavy snow had been promised she thought perhaps it might be wiser to telephone to Judy, and cancel the engagement now.

'The roads haven't been cleared, darling,' she told Judy on the telephone. 'Not even half. I'm perfectly prepared to walk, but even that's mighty hazardous – and if it snows as they say it's going to . . .' She stopped, disappointed suddenly at the idea of not going out to lunch, and perhaps Judy sensed this because she changed tack at once.

'Tell you what, Loopy. If it doesn't snow any more, and given that it's too much to walk all the way over here, why don't we meet at the Three Tuns? I know we won't get much of a lunch, but at least we'll be able to see each other.'

'OK, darling. If it doesn't snow any more, that's a date. I can't bear all this enforced isolation. It's like living in Alaska.'

To pass the time, Loopy sat by the fire putting the fine detail to her latest painting. Unsurprisingly really, considering they were enduring the coldest winter weather on record, it was a snowscape, but she was rather pleased with the way she had managed to capture the over-bright light as well as the blues and yellows in the snowdrifts.

When she had finished she removed the canvas from her work easel and propped it on the top of her little desk, wondering if anyone would comment on it, or whether it would go unremarked the way most of her paintings did, ignored by her family as if they found them embarrassing, which, for all she knew, they quite probably did. That would appear to be the case since, except for Gwen of all people, everyone else in the household seemed to pretend that Loopy didn't paint, that what she was doing was merely keeping herself busy, as if her increasingly good artwork was nothing more interesting than someone's darning or yet another shapeless knitted garment, a hobby which they could happily ignore, which was in fact what indeed they did. Sometimes Loopy thought that if she filled the drawing room with every single canvas she had painted, her family would still come into the room at drinks time and fail to pass a single comment. The fact that Gwen noticed her work became a source of strength and inspiration for Loopy. If Gwen was prepared to comment, actually to talk about her painting, it meant that it existed, even though the maid's remarks were invariably accompanied by what Loopy mentally called *Gwenisms*.

'I don't know nothing about art, not a single stitch,' she once said seriously, as she stood regarding a self-portrait Loopy had just finished. 'But what I do know is I know what I *don't* like.'

'Naturally,' Loopy had replied, as if conversations like this were the norm. 'So do you not like this?'

'The colour's nice. I like the way you paint colour. That red rug, for an instance. I can sort of feel its texture, and that's clever. Then there's the sea beyond, out of the window there. I love all that light you got on the sea. I really do like that.'

'I'm glad you like that, because that's my favourite bit – and it was a perfect swine to get right.'

'I can imagine, Mrs T. I don't know how you get light like that on water. That I really do like.'

'So if you like it, that's good, Gwennie.'

'I can't see as to why, Mrs T. I can't see what jot of a difference whether I likes it or not will make.'

'On the contrary, Gwen. If you like it, then that means there's a strong possibility that someone else might, too. Although possibly no-one that *we* know.'

'I like this one, Mrs T.,' she said on this particular morning, the day Loopy finished the snowscape. 'Really wintry that is. Makes you want to stoke up the fire. Course, it'll be even nicer when the trees come out, won't it?'

Happily this particular morning seemed determined to stay cloudless and sunny, although still bitterly cold, with the result that at midday Loopy wrapped herself up in her long fur coat and matching hat, and set off to make her way to the quay that ran by the side of the estuary, and the historic old inn that stood at the head of it.

As soon as she swung through the double doors into the main bar, Loopy could see Judy ahead of her, already there waiting, two gin and tonics at the ready, a most welcome sight. The saloon bar was surprisingly full, the number of people gathered helping to add warmth to a room heated by only the smallest of coke fires.

'Cheers.' Loopy raised her glass. 'To the day when we can drink unwatered gin.' She raised her eyes to heaven. 'And may it please come real soon.'

'I heard they're selling this place,' Judy said. 'Walter heard it on the grapevine when he was down last weekend.'

'I'm not surprised, honey. It must be the very devil to try to make money at times like these. Someone said to me it should be called the Three Millstones, not the Three Tuns.'

'It's always full, Loopy. Granted it is the only pub in Bexham, but they always seem to do good business.'

'So why sell it if it's so completely perfect?'

'Walter said – although apparently it's not meant to go any further – that poor Valerie isn't too well.'

'That *is* sad. I'm fond of Valerie, a lot fonder than I am of that over-cheerful husband of hers. Too busy playing Mine Host to general applause and leaving her to do all the work. So how's my favourite daughter-in-law been, despite the weather, the weather – and the *weather*.'

Judy and Loopy chatted for the next ten minutes or so, both of them careful to keep the conversation commonplace, despite their genuine affection for each other. In fact it was their mutual respect which prevented Loopy from confiding in her daughter-in-law that she thought she could sense a vague feeling of discontent in her husband Hugh when he came home from London at the weekend, and Judy from discussing with her mother-in-law the fact that, despite every possible effort, she did not seem to be able to conceive. Instead they talked about the weather and the general shortage of most of life's necessities, before being interrupted by a loud exchange aimed, it seemed to Loopy, in their particular direction. The conversation, if it could be called such, was between two red-faced local gentlemen seated at the bar, and it was about the fact that all the real troubles in the country were being caused by the demands of the womenfolk.

'Who if you want my opinion have had it all to themselves for far too long during the war. It's them what's demanding to get everything their own way, that's what's the matter with this country – it's the women.'

'Excuse me?' Loopy called suddenly, from her seat.

'Loopy . . .'

But Loopy merely flapped one hand at Judy, looking, for her, purposefully determined, her mouth set in disapproval. 'Excuse me, sir?'

One of the men at the bar looked round in mock astonishment.

'You addressing me, madam?'

'I am sir, certainly, because I am most interested in how you have become such an authority not only on this poor country's problems, but on its women, if you please.'

The man in the tweed cap looked round at his colleague as if he was being addressed by a lunatic before turning back and staring at Loopy, while breathing deeply in and out.

'Madam,' he said, carefully doing up the top button of his tweed sports coat. 'You may not find this palatable, you being a member yourself of the fair sex, but I have to tell you none the less that the general consensus of opinion is that a certain number of you ladies nowadays, now that the war is over, are finding it very difficult to remember that your place is in the *home*. That home is where you belong, where you should return and where you should stay.'

'You've gathered this, I imagine, from pieces in the newspapers, from opinions expressed mainly by – let me guess – by members of the unfair sex. By men.'

'That is quite beside the point, madam.'

'I don't see why. Men seem to write opinions for other men to talk about in their local hostelry, while all that is supplied for us ladies to read is recipes or how to make an evening dress out of an old sofa cover. Let me tell you something, sir. We women do not have *a place* any more than you men do. Why should we? If we didn't have *a place* when the war was on, which we most certainly did not when you remember what a lot of us women did during the war, then why should we be expected to have a place now, may I ask? You men were only too happy to have us women working in your factories, driving your buses, nursing your injured – doing all the things in fact that up to that time only men had been allowed to do.'

'Naturally. Because we were at war. But we're at peace now.'

'Of course. And because of that we women are expected to drop everything, put our pinnies and aprons back on again, and spend the rest of our lives tied to hearth and home and stove looking after you lot.'

'That is what the sacred articles of *marriarge* are all about.'

'And for those of us who aren't *marriard*?' Loopy wondered, echoing his mocking pronunciation. 'What are they meant to do?'

'Things might be different across the Atlantic, madam – and what isn't, pray? But here single unmarried women stay at home and look after their parents. That is what single unmarried women do, what they are for. That is what is expected of them: to do their duty by their parents.'

'Oh, come along, sir. Really. The same thing goes in some places across the other side of the Atlantic, you know. American men are just like you – they expect young women to sacrifice their lives and become unpaid drudges in family households, and believe you me it's no more attractive over there than it is over here. So, no, no, we're not so very different as you imagine,' Loopy retorted. 'On both sides of the water I'd say you guys are in for a bit of a shock one of these days. You just wait and see.'

Most of the men listening had laughed at her, but now more and more people joined in the public debate, and having got them all well and truly stirred up Loopy gave a slow smile and sat back to light the cigarette she had just pushed into her long, ebony holder.

'Nothing like a well lobbed hand grenade to liven things up,' she murmured to Judy, inhaling smoke. 'I like that. The nerve of them. Keep women in their place indeed.'

'You don't think that's right, Loopy?' Judy said hesitantly. 'You don't think a woman's place is in the home?'

'Not necessarily. Should she choose it – well, that's fine, and if it brings her fulfilment, absolutely right, but if she'd rather be out there climbing Mount Everest or flying around the world in a Tiger Moth – why in hell not? Are you quite happy to be tied to the stove by your apron strings, Judy? I doubt it – not after all you did in the war, surely?'

'You surprise me, Loopy. But then you usually do. I know you value your free will and all that, but I always thought you stood rather strictly by what our friend at the bar referred to as the articles of *marriarge*.'

'You bet I do – at least by the sanctity of marriage. That's how I see it and I won't hear a word against it. But I wouldn't sacrifice my life for it – for love maybe, but not for *marriarge*.'

Feeling vaguely embarrassed by the conversation because it happened to concern the doubts in her own mind, Judy diverted her mother-in-law away from further argument by ordering lunch from George, their over-convivial host who, with an exaggerated wink of his rheumy eye, promised them a good slice of chicken each in their Spam sandwiches, provided, of course, that they didn't tell everyone.

Over another watered down gin and tonic Judy and Loopy seemed to forget all about their earlier discussion and gossiped instead about what had, or was rumoured to have, happened in Bexham since they last met. Then the skies suddenly clouded over and the threat of yet another blizzard sent them hurrying off home in opposite directions.

As Judy passed the end of the lane that led up to the church she saw a pair of car headlights coming slowly towards her in the snow which was now falling thick and fast. A moment later the car began to slide across the road as in spite of the chains on the tyres the driver lost control on the compacted and frozen surface. Suddenly aware of the danger she was in, Judy jumped sideways into the lane, falling into a deep drift as she did so, then rolling over just in time to avoid being crushed by the car that had come to a standstill only a couple of feet from where she lay.

'My God!' she heard through the snow as the driver wrenched his door open and tumbled out into the snowdrift. 'My God – are you OK wherever you are?'

It was, oddly enough, another American voice, and it was accented so much like Loopy's Southern tones that Judy thought hazily that the owner might even prove to be some sort of relative of her mother-in-law.

'Yes, I'm fine!' she called back. 'I'm over here – in front of the car!'

The driver was by her side in a moment, half stumbling and half falling through the snow.

'Dear God, I thought I might have killed you,' he said, falling to his knees where Judy was now slowly sitting up. 'I am so – so sorry.'

Judy looked up and, finding herself staring into a pair of intense dark eyes, she started to laugh.

'Don't be silly, I'm fine, really, I'm *fine*. It was just an accident, no more and no less,' she assured him.

'No, I really am so very, very sorry.'

Taking the arm held out to her, Judy looked round for Hamish and bent to retrieve his lead.

'Don't be silly, worse things happen at sea, and all the time.' She started brushing the snow off her coat. 'I'm Judy Tate, by the way, and you are?'

'A great deal better now that I see you're unhurt. I'm Waldo Astley.'

Waldo took Judy's gloved hand and shook it. It was only as she found herself staring into a pair of large, dark eyes that Judy started to realise that the drama that had just taken place was as nothing compared to the one that might be just about to happen if she continued to hold the hand that was shaking hers.

'What a wonderfully absurd name,' Meggie exclaimed, lighting a cigarette expertly with one hand, at the same time cradling the telephone receiver between her face and her shoulder. 'Does he look as absurd as his name?'

'No.' Judy cleared her throat. 'No, absurd is not the word I personally would use about Mr Waldo Astley. He dresses beautifully, by the way. Cashmere camel coat, hat at just the right angle – pure Long Island, I would imagine.'

'What else did you discover? Anything interesting?'

'You don't think the fact that he nearly killed me is remotely interesting?'

'Of course he didn't nearly kill you, Judy. He merely gave you a bit of a nudge with his car.'

'It was an American car. A rather large Buick motor car.'

'All American cars are large, Judy darling.' Meggie sighed and blew a smoke ring into the air, watching it without much interest. 'So, tall dark stranger nearly knocks local woman over but doesn't – talk about no news is no news, Mrs Tate. I want a bit more colour than that.'

Judy thought for a moment. 'Well, as a matter of fact, I thought he was a bit odd. Gave me goose bumps.'

'There are goose bumps and there are goose bumps, Mrs Tate. And before you tell which sort he gave you, remember you are a married woman.'

Lionel Eastcott was the next to meet Waldo Astley, and he furthered his acquaintance with him at a location where only a few months before he would certainly not have wished to find himself, that is in the house of a woman with whom he had once imagined himself passionately in love.

Gloria Morrison, née Bishop, lived in a pretty faux-Jacobean house that stood in an acre of garden on the corner of the road that turned to the left in front of her grounds to lead around the top end of the now completely frozen estuary. Built in Edwardian times, the house had thick walls of what had once been dark red brick, and small latticed windows that did not take best advantage of the lovely view beyond the low wall surrounding the property. Nevertheless, compared to more modern houses it was definitely handsome, and when spring finally arrived and turned to summer visitors would be reminded of the beautiful garden the previous owner had laid out, the house covered with a fine wisteria on its south side and the grounds laid to lawns and borders of sweet-scented shrubs. All in all it could be said to be an enviable property, and it would have attracted much more interest when it had come on the market had times been different, but the last owner had died suddenly in the autumn, and his executors had been forced to sell in a winter that had turned into one of the worst in living memory.

Their misfortune was Gloria Bishop's good luck, for when on a flying visit to West Sussex she passed through Bexham for old times' sake and saw the For Sale sign outside a house she had always coveted she immediately decided to buy. To her great delight her offer of three hundred and fifty pounds below an already much reduced price was snapped up at once, and six weeks later she found herself comfortably installed at the Starlings.

Of course, given the position of her newly purchased house, Gloria had soon spotted her old flame Lionel Eastcott playing with what she realised must be his grandson on the village green. Watching him from the privacy of her motor car, Gloria noted that Lionel, unsurprisingly, had aged considerably. Not that this did anything to prevent her from planning to surprise him with an invitation.

Remembering as she did that Lionel had once been a fanatical bridge player Gloria started to make plans for a bridge weekend.

A few days before Judy's stirring encounter with the beautifully dressed American, Lionel Eastcott stared into the dining room. His daughter, Mathilda, had laid out what seemed to both of them to be a sumptuous tea for grandson Max and two small friends who lived across from them on the other side of the village green. Somehow, in all honesty Lionel did not like to think how Mathilda had begged, borrowed or stolen the ingredients for the birthday tea, determined that her little boy should be able to celebrate his big day in style with a few of his friends.

'Mr Eastcott – the telephone! It's a Mrs Morrison, I think she said her name was. Yes, it was a Mrs Morrison all right, I would say. Yes.'

Lionel had noticed that Ellen always looked quite worried when the telephone in the new hall rang, principally, he supposed, because it hardly ever did ring, so unsociable had he become. Besides, few people in the village actually possessed a telephone, so it was still very much a novelty in Bexham, with women like Ellen always imagining that, like the arrival of a wartime telegram, its ringing must herald bad news. Novelty or not, Lionel found himself hesitating before he went to pick up the receiver, feeling both shy and awkward. He hadn't spoken to Gloria since her daughter had been killed the night his grandson Max was born as the bombs were dropping all around the estuary, and many of the outlying timber-framed farmhouses went up in smoke long before anyone could get to them. It had been in one of those that Gloria's only daughter Virginia had died, a terrible coincidence, his old flame Gloria losing her only daughter just as little Max had put in his first appearance in this world. Virginia had gone to the farm to fetch a midwife for Lionel's daughter, and perhaps it was the awful embarrassment he still felt about this that made him hesitate, as if in some way it was his fault that Virginia had volunteered to go for the midwife, which of course it hadn't been.

He was about to instruct Ellen to tell Mrs Morrison that he was out when he thought better of it, realising that it was going to be a bit difficult to be permanently out to a woman who had moved in so close to his new house. Besides, he had written to her about Virginia, and she had written back. They had communicated, and now that Gloria had moved back to the area it would prove more than a little difficult to avoid her in the village, Bexham being such a small community.

'Very well, I'll take the call,' Lionel told Ellen, realising that his daily maid was staring at him in a really rather over-interested way as he went into the hall to pick up the black Bakelite telephone.

'Come for a bridge evening on Friday night,

Lionel, oh do!' said the voice on the other end. 'Gossipy – nothing serious.'

She was still Gloria, still deep-voiced, and doubtless still smoking too much too. If he could not remember precisely how much she had despised him when they were young, Lionel might even have been tempted to tell himself that she was still *his Gloria*. But the war years had brought him up with a start, and although he had remained head over heels in love with Gloria long after she had married her first husband, Lionel could not deceive himself as to Gloria's true feelings for him, either then or now.

The truth was that Gloria had broken Lionel's heart, and, strictly on the rebound, he had married Mathilda's mother Maude, to whom, effectively, he now realised in his great, grand maturity, Gloria had handed him over, lock, stock and barrel.

So it was that having set his eyes on what he thought was a beautiful rose, Lionel had, emotionally speaking, been thrown a daisy. Probably because of this, he had never managed to make Maude at all happy, not even when they were young. He realised now that poor Maude had only really found true happiness and fulfilment in the war, finally to die a heroine. Unfortunately the manner of her tragic death, even some years on, still acted as a dreadful reproach to her husband.

Why had he never even suspected poor Maude of possessing the qualities that she had displayed so conspicuously once she joined the WVS? Why had he never recognised her courage? Most of all why had he constantly mocked her the way he had? As the years passed, it was his stupid and eternal facetiousness more than anything that came back to haunt him.

Even so, for some reason, possibly loneliness, the idea of spending at least a little bit of time with people of his own age, who did not make him feel not just old but quite past it, suddenly seemed more than attractive. He heard himself telling Gloria that he would come over for an evening of chatty bridge, for old times' sake, but that he couldn't be late.

'It's because of Max, my grandson. I like to get up and have breakfast with him at an early hour.'

Gloria gave what sounded to Lionel like an over-familiar laugh. It was a laugh that floated down the years, the before-the-war years. The laugh that had rung out around the tennis courts, and in the fields where all the young in Bexham had loved to walk, gathering primroses, listening to the skylarks overhead, watching for hares boxing in the bright sunlight, and pursuing other occupations which now seemed heartbreaking in their innocence.

'Still the golden charmer, eh, Lionel? Half past six drinks, dinner seven thirty, bridge eight thirty. Don't be late, now, there's a good fellow.'

Gloria's ability to dominate him, her dangerous brand of charm, and her devil-may-care attitude came back to Lionel in a rush. He found himself staring at the telephone receiver, which he had just replaced. He should have refused. He should have said he was otherwise occupied. If he had been thinking on his feet he would have realised that he really did not want anything more to do with Gloria. Gloria was a doodlebug of a woman. You never knew when her engines would suddenly cut out, not until that sudden silence, and once they had, you never knew where she was going to hit you.

Indeed, Gloria quiet was still a dreadfully frightening thought. As he turned to go back to the new sitting room with its pale green walls and old chintz curtains, Lionel made up his mind that on Saturday night he would arrive at Gloria's house on time, and leave early. It was the only solution. He must not get embroiled with her again. It would be quite fatal.

'That's nice for you then, Mr Eastcott.' Ellen peered round the corner at him.

'What is, Ellen?'

'You going to bridge with Mrs Morrison. I hear she's been a bit of a lonely old thing since she came back to live in the village.'

Lionel carried on into the sitting room. As if it was not enough that Ellen listened in to all his telephone calls, now she was giving out a verdict on his social life. And to hear her calling the once divine Gloria a lonely old thing was a bit of a shock, to say the least.

'I expect you have finished the house now, Ellen, So why don't you take the rest of the day off?'

Ellen shook her head. 'Gracious no, Mr Eastcott. I've hardly started. Besides, there's no-one at home for me now, not since my Harry was killed. So what is there for me to go home *for*, Mr Eastcott? That's what I keep asking myself, what is there to go home for?'

Lionel sank back into his favourite old leather armchair. It seemed that Gloria Morrison was not the only lonely old thing living in post-war Bexham.

Despite having made new friends in London, Waldo Astley, armed with only his precious guides, had made it a point to motor down to Bexham in his Buick quite alone. It was an arduous journey made worse by the ghastliness of the small hotels at which he was forced by the weather to stop all too frequently. It seemed to him that it was for this reason that, when he had eventually reached his destination, either from fatigue or misjudgement he had come so near to knocking down Judy Tate at the entrance to Church Lane.

He was still mentally running through the horror of the incident and longing for a large drink when he signed into the Three Tuns, and gratefully surrendered his luggage to an aged retainer. Useless to tell himself to stop thinking what would have happened had he run the girl and her little dog over. It was not until after his second drink that he finally managed to put that thought out of his mind, and, finding his eyes wandering to the other occupants of the bar, realised he was being watched intently by a white-haired and white-moustached tweed-suited gentleman. He smiled at him, because after a couple of drinks Waldo usually felt it was perfectly all right to smile at strangers, particularly strangers who were staring at a fellow. Besides, this particular stranger seemed to possess one of those faces that encouraged friendliness.

'You're a stranger in Bexham, sir?'

'If you don't mind me saying so, that sounds like a line from a Western.'

Lionel Eastcott smiled. 'Yes, quite so. And I must say, I do agree. I actually only ask because in this weather it is unusual to say the least to see an unfamiliar face in here. In fact I doubt if we've seen a stranger in our midst for weeks, so of course we take note. We have to. We're that short of excitements.'

An exchange of introductions followed, as also another round of refreshment, and it wasn't long before Lionel and Waldo were well enough acquainted to be exchanging the sort of intimacies induced by taking drink in convivial establishments. Thus it was no surprise that within half an hour of their introduction Lionel discovered that Waldo Astley was as keen a bridge player as he was himself.

'Can't say I'm surprised, Mr Astley. You look every inch the bridge player. Intelligent face, high domed forehead, conservative cut to your clothes – the sort of opponent one would think twice about playing against. Which is why I hope maybe that if we play sometime we'll be partners rather than opponents. Except – as it happens . . .'

'Go on – surprise me,' Waldo said with a grin. 'There's a game coming up.'

'As it happens I'm desperate for someone to make up a four tonight in the house of an old friend who has moved into the village. Colonel Wetherby – a regular – sadly he's down with flu – gone to his chest, poor fellow, running a high temperature and confined to barracks – otherwise he'd be there. Nothing else would keep him from the bridge table, other than his own demise – hence the panic. I'm particularly anxious to make up the numbers as I have no wish to disappoint the lady in question, having once, in my youth, had pretensions to her hand.'

'This sounds so interesting it would take someone a lot less curious than myself to refuse.'

'Good.' Lionel beamed at Waldo before leaning forward and confiding, 'Besides which, the food here is terrible. You'll do a lot better for grub *chez* Mrs Morrison.'

Some few minutes later, Waldo having washed and brushed up, the two set off in good spirits, making towards Gloria Morrison's house with the kind of optimism that always precedes a game of cards, a bottle of wine or two, and a good and very welcome dinner.

As soon as Gloria saw Lionel's new companion standing in her hall, the light illuminating his head of thick dark hair and his handsome face, she knew that the evening was going to be considerably more interesting than if Colonel Wetherby had been taking up his usual position at her bridge table. As she always did, in spite of food rationing, Gloria had managed to lay on an excellent supper, courtesy of a one-eyed gentleman who had called at her door not only with pâtés and wines from France but with some well hung steaks and fresh vegetables too, all of which more than made up for the previous week's diet of whale meat in onion sauce and the sort of offal that she had truly never imagined finding herself eating, ever.

So what with the table neatly laid with fresh cards, and the excitement that a handsome stranger's entering a house necessarily brings, Gloria was so pleased with Lionel's find that she could almost have become engaged to the poor man on the spot – almost, but, happily for Lionel, not quite.

Lionel quite thought he had the cut of the American's jib during the first couple of rubbers, having noted the young man's style of bidding and card play which appealed as being, to say the least, reckless. He seemed to revel in gambling on card placements without ever thinking the hand through, and playing finesse after finesse even when it was unnecessary. Naturally he was only too happy when Gloria, who had elected to make Waldo her playing partner for the evening, suggested upping the stakes from a penny to sixpence a hundred. Lionel was no gambler, most especially not at the card table, yet judging from the level of play he had been witnessing he could only be encouraged into thinking that he was as near to a sure thing as was perfectly possible. This indeed was what the next rubber effectively proved. Waldo and Gloria played ever more recklessly only to lose ingloriously, and go down a further two thousand points.

'Look here,' Waldo laughed as Gloria passed him the score pad. 'Look here, this really will not do at all. We are down fifteen shillings here, Mrs Morrison, and I for one simply cannot afford such losses! So what do we all say to making it a shilling a hundred? Give us poor dopes a chance to repair a little of this terrible damage to our finances?'

After consulting with Mrs Highsmith, his partner, who in his experience was one of the better women bridge players in the village, Lionel gave their joint consent and dealt the first hand of the new rubber. From that moment everything went downhill, as without even changing their style of play Waldo and Gloria went swiftly from fifteen shillings in arrears to a profit of four pounds two shillings and sixpence.

'Well, you know what they do say?' Waldo gave an easy, slow smile, as his opponents paid up. 'Lucky at cards, et cetera.'

'I do hope not,' Gloria cut in with what she hoped was a sufficiently coquettish look. 'I for one have had quite enough of being unlucky in love.'

'We did have a run of exceedingly good fortune, Mrs Morrison,' Waldo reminded his playing partner. 'All our finesses suddenly got lucky, and as for your remarkably perceptive double on that last bid of Five Diamonds . . .'

'Pure chance.'

'Absolute nonsense. The call of a very fine player, if I may say.'

So the evening drew to a close, Lionel and Mrs Highsmith doing their best to take their leave in as light-hearted a manner as possible while Waldo continued his elegant flirtation with their by now enthralled hostess.

'I say, where on earth did you find your innocent seeming card shark, Mr Eastcott? He must have come off an ocean liner, surely?' Mrs Highsmith wondered, as Lionel took her by the arm to help her down the frozen path to the gate.

'I found him, as you put it, Mrs Highsmith, in the Three Tuns, earlier in the evening. We were quite desperate, as you may imagine. The colonel had only just gone down with a high temperature at teatime. Not like him to miss an opportunity for friendly bridge, not to mention a good dinner.'

'Yes, but do you think Mr Astley played entirely straight, Mr Eastcott?'

'I certainly didn't see any cards falling out of his sleeve. Unless of course he did it all by mirrors.'

'I'm being perfectly serious, Mr Eastcott. I simply can't afford to lose that sort of money playing bridge. I am a widow, you know.'

'Then I'm very much afraid you shouldn't play with the grown-ups, Mrs Highsmith,' Lionel retorted, suddenly fed up with her carping. 'No, you shouldn't play with the grown-ups if you don't want to lose, unless of course what you really mean is that you don't *like* losing money.'

Mrs Highsmith laughed, and at the same time squeezed Lionel's arm. 'That's exactly what I mean, you dear man. I do hope it wasn't my bad play.'

'I think not, Mrs Highsmith. I think what happened was – as our American friends are fond of saying – like it or not, we were well and truly *hustled*.'

With the temperature having fallen to well below freezing early in the evening no trains ran that night out of London because of heavily frozen points. None the less, Hugh and Walter Tate, who were both equally determined not to be denied the company of their wives that weekend, agreed to take a chance on the road conditions and drive down in Walter's MG TC. Wrapped up to resemble nothing more nor less than Arctic explorers, and with extra Thermos flasks of hot coffee laced with brandy on board, they set off more full of hope than expectation, but only managed to make it halfway to Bexham. In fact a journey that normally took them little more than an hour and a half ended up by taking them nearly six.

Half frozen into imbecility they stopped off at Horsham and spent the rest of the night thawing out in the bedroom of a pub whose own temperature wasn't that much above freezing point. The next morning they woke to bright sunshine and the start of a good thaw, conditions which while not making for carefree motoring did at least enable the benighted travellers to get to Bexham in time for lunch.

Arriving home at last Hugh found Loopy still well wrapped up in her furs painting in the room upstairs that she had temporarily turned into her studio, the conservatory having proved far too cold in this coldest of cold winters.

'I couldn't resist it,' she said, after welcoming him home. 'It's even freezing up here despite being so near the airing cupboard and all that heat that rises from the kitchen, but do look at this *light*. I mean look at that light over the sea, Hugh, doesn't it take your breath away!'

Hugh did indeed give it a cursory look, which was more than he afforded the canvas upon which his beloved wife was working, his mind directing itself with considerably more enthusiasm towards pouring himself an extra large gin and tonic.

'How was London?' Loopy called after him, as he headed back downstairs.

'Very cold!' Hugh called back. 'Now don't stay up there all day! I am absolutely starving!'

But by the time Loopy came back to reality, tearing herself away from her intense painting session, she found Gwen had already served Hugh his lunch, quite alone, and having finished he had disappeared, in all probability to go for a walk.

Hurrying to the dining room window, she saw her husband making his way as quickly as he could through the banks of snow that had blown up into frozen billows along the edge of the estuary.

Grabbing her fur hat and gloves from the hall stand Loopy hurried after him as fast as she could, but she stumbled through the deep snow and fell hopelessly behind, and before long Hugh was gone from her sight.

Following what she hoped were his footprints, which were fast disappearing under a fresh fall of snow, she finally reached the rise that led up to the headland. Looking up into the snowstorm she could just make out two figures, seemingly in conversation, and one of them she recognised quite definitely as being her husband.

'Hugh?' she called. 'Hugh honey, wait, will you?'

The snow thickened, swirling round her in the wind that was now getting up fast as the tide began its turn. For a moment she lost the figures entirely; then the knoll came into view again as the snow drifted in the other direction.

But now there was only one man standing there, all alone. Hugh.

'But I swear I saw two people,' Loopy insisted as they made their way back home through the snow.

'Me and my shadow, darling.'

'Maybe I'm getting double vision in my old age.'

'I could do with a double gin at mine.'

'Hugh – it isn't even teatime!'

'Doesn't stop a chap thinking ahead. In this weather all one can think of is the inner man. Makes petty bleak thinking, too, as a general rule.'

'You sure you weren't talking to someone, Hugh?'

'Only the Spirit of Times Past.'

'I definitely saw someone.'

'Then you were definitely seeing things.'

Hugh smiled round at her as if to reassure her. But Loopy knew that particular smile of old. It was the smile Hugh always employed when he was determined to get away with something.

Chapter Three

Judy put the tea tray down in front of Walter, who had fallen fast asleep in front of the fire and was now waking up pretending that he had only been daydreaming.

'Tea. And honey sandwiches.'

Walter rubbed his eyes and stared at the luxury on the plate Judy had placed on his knee.

'Who have you been flirting with?'

'Who do you think? Mr Bee the Bee-Keeper.'

'Old Mr Adams gave you some honey?'

'Old Mr Adams *sold* me some honey.'

'It's delicious, worth every penny,' Walter told her, carefully eating a dripping honey sandwich.

'In that case I can tell you how much I had to pay to Mr Bee the Bee-Keeper—'

'No, no – it will only give me indigestion.'

There was a small silence while Judy watched Walter eat all the sandwiches, one by one. Then, having sipped at her cup of tea, she said, 'What I didn't tell you, Walter, was—' Judy was about to begin to embark on an account of her near miss with the car in the snow when she thought better of it. It was as if Mr Waldo Astley was her particular secret, and if she told Walter about him he would somehow vanish. Whatever the reason, she found herself changing tack in mid-stream. 'What I didn't tell you was Meggie's back from America,' she finished seamlessly.

'You told me that on the telephone.' Walter looked instantly bored, as he always did at the idea of having to listen to something twice.

'Did I? I don't think I did.'

'Then I must have dreamed it.' Walter took another sip of his tea.

'I haven't told you about our lunch,' Judy continued, disregarding her near faux-pas. 'Meggie told me all about her trip. It's absolutely fascinating really – what America is actually like in comparison to us – to poor old us.'

'Less of the *poor old us*. Gracious heavens, we won, didn't we? That's what counts – the fact we won. Whatever the cost now.' Walter frowned, and turning pointedly away from his wife he picked up one of his law books.

'That really wasn't what Meggie and I were talking about actually, Walter. It was more to do with what you can get over there, what the general standard of living is like.'

'Meggie was staying on Long Island, wasn't she?'

'And Newport.'

'Quite.' Walter yawned and turned the page of his book. 'Wealthy parts of America. I dare say there were other parts where Meggie didn't venture, where their standard of living wasn't quite so hot.'

'Yes. But that was really what I was going on to say. Meggie said she got the impression that over there you really feel that there hasn't been a war, except in the films.'

'As in Errol Flynn saving Burma single-handed.'

'You should hear her talk about real coffee and butter and rolls,' Judy continued, enviously. 'And about Hershey bars and ice creams made with real cream.'

Walter looked round at Judy, the longing in her voice getting to him in a way that nothing she had said previously had done.

'I am trying to study, Judy – in case you haven't noticed.'

'Sorry,' Judy replied and fell to silence. She would have liked to put the radio on, but knowing that too would disturb Walter, instead she lay back in her chair and stared round their little cottage sitting room. After listening to Meggie's tales of America, it seemed to her that her own life was suddenly rather dull, even duller and certainly drabber than it had been before. In fact with a start she realised that what Meggie had said to her was right – she *was* missing the war. During the war she had known excitement and comradeship, she had witnessed heroism and self-sacrifice. But now the only thing to get excited about was the possibility of getting a new pair of nylons and the only sacrifice to be made the amount of black market butter one spread on one's toast.

Time passed, its only companion the sound of the still green wood burning miserably in the little fireplace. Nowadays Judy somewhat dreaded Walter coming home, because due to the size of the tiny cottage, and Walter's need to spread out his law books on top of every conceivable available flat space, there seemed hardly the room for one person let alone two. Open books were everywhere, there was a pile of clothes that needed washing and ironing before Walter's return to London first thing Monday morning, there were endless meals to be made and washed up and there were Walter's other needs and desires to be taken care of. As always, after Saturday lunch while she was working her way through the mound of washing, besides worrying how much the weekend would cost them, Judy also found herself wondering if this time her husband had at last made her pregnant.

Not very romantic, she thought to herself as she began ironing. *Not quite the way I imagined it somehow.*

A moment later Walter put his head round the door and announced he was going for a walk.

'If you hang on ten minutes we could go together,' Judy replied, carefully folding the sleeves of Walter's best white shirt.

'It's OK,' Walter replied, whistling to Hamish to come to him. 'I have a lot of stuff to learn by heart, so it's better I go off by myself. Won't be long.'

With Hamish safely on his tartan leather lead, Walter disappeared.

Judy's heart sank. Walter was now always taking himself off alone at weekends with only Hamish for company, to learn things by heart – things that Judy knew he could learn a whole lot quicker with her testing him as they always used to do when Walter first started studying for the Bar. But not any more. Every Saturday afternoon whatever the weather the front door would bang closed and Walter and Hamish would disappear out of her life for two – sometimes three – hours. And just as she always did, Judy watched him go from the small latticed window of the room she was in, head bent down, woollen muffler wrapped around his throat. She knew people would greet him as he passed them by and that he wouldn't see them, so intent was he on staring at the ground with his head full of torts or whatever it was he was learning by heart at that moment, but no-one would mind he hadn't acknowledged them because they were just so glad to see Walter Tate back. The only trouble was, Judy sighed as she dropped the curtain back down into place, that the Walter Tate walking on by with his eyes on the ground, the Walter Tate who had suddenly re-appeared in their midst out of the blue, was not the same Walter Tate who had left Bexham when the war broke out, head held high, his blue eyes fixed firmly ahead.

Even though the weather was still as bitter as ever, with the snow thick frozen on the ground, there was a good congregation for Matins in the village's beautiful old Saxon church, albeit a well wrapped up one since the heating system had yet again packed up under the strain of more heavy use than it had seen in years. It was so cold inside the church that when everyone sang or prayed aloud it seemed as though the church was full of smokers, so long did their breath hang white and heavy on the air.

However, the cold could not conceal the enthusiastic female interest in the stranger in the congregation's midst. Waldo Astley had sat himself quietly down in a small pew in a side aisle, attracting attention before he had even bent his knee to pray, and he had been well and truly marked out long before the notes of the first hymn had faded and gone.

Meggie, who had joined Judy and Walter in their pew, was one of the first to notice the American's presence, nudging Judy gently before slowly rolling her eyes in the stranger's direction.

'Tall, dark, beautifully tailored and a total stranger,' she whispered. 'Is that the swine who so nearly snatched you from the bosom of your family?'

'Later.' Judy rolled her eyes towards Walter and then back to Meggie again.

'He looks the hit and run type, and that's without a motor car,' Meggie went on, mischief in her eyes, her mouth pulled down mock-solemn.

Mr Lowering, one of the churchwardens, half turned round from his seat in front of Meggie and knitted his thick, bushy eyebrows at her in disapproval. Meggie smiled brightly and mockingly back, then hugged her furs enthusiastically around her in an effort to retain as much body heat as she could for the rest of the service.

In spite of the fact that it had begun to snow yet again, most of the unattached young women who had been kneeling in worship, as well as several of the older and very much attached ones, hung about as long as they dared, pretending their delay was caused by a pressing need to congratulate the Reverend Anderson on what was definitely one of his more tedious and long-winded sermons while waiting to see if the stranger in their midst was in fact known to anyone in the congregation. It seemed not, since Waldo wandered out of the old church all by himself, producing a silver cigarette case and a cigarette he proceeded to light with a Zippo lighter, much impressing the three teenage daughters of George the publican who like so many of their peers found anything even vaguely transatlantic utterly enthralling.

'Guess who's caused a flutter in the female dovecote, then?' Meggie whispered to Judy, before deliberately sidling up behind the vicar to try to hear the conversation he was having with the American.

'I found your sermon interesting, to say the least,' Waldo was telling Mr Anderson, who was busily stamping his shoes on the ground in an effort to stop his chilblains from paining him. 'Particularly your choice of text.'

'Thank you, how very kind. Really most kind,

most kind.' The vicar's lips were purple with cold, and on attempting a smile his upper lip seemed to have frozen to his lower lip.

'It put me in mind of Sterne's *Tristram Shandy*? The excellence of this text is that it will suit any sermon. And of this sermon that it will suit any text?'

'One may prefer fresh eggs, sir, though laid from a fowl of the meanest understanding. But why fresh sermons?'

'Very good,' Waldo nodded. 'George Eliot if I'm not mistaken. Although I must confess I would prefer no sermon whatsoever. I sometimes imagine Hell to be having to sit reading all the sermons ever preached here on earth – although the better part of my nature hopes that even Hell hasn't come to that.'

Waldo's deep bass voice, a surprisingly rolling and mature sound from a young man, seemed to echo round the churchyard. Certainly it carried over to the rest of the congregation, who paused momentarily before hurrying on.

'You are staying here in Bexham?' the vicar enquired, as politely as he could. 'Or perhaps just passing through?'

'I had just come down for the weekend, Reverend. But you know I have taken such a liking to your parish that I am seriously considering renting somewhere here. Maybe even buying a house. Oh – an excellent choice of hymns, by the by. Good day to you.'

Waldo touched the stylish black hat he was

wearing half tilted over his brilliant dark eyes and strolled out of the snow-covered churchyard.

'Well,' Hugh said over lunch as the subject came up for discussion once again. 'I suppose we're only all still talking about it because it's something someone should have said ages ago. I quite envied the fellow as it happens.'

'So, you *should* have said something years ago, Hugh darling,' Loopy chided him. 'It's not like you not to say *something*.'

'Problem is I always fall asleep during the poor chap's sermons, so I have no proper ammunition.'

'*By our pastor perplexed – how shall we determine?*' Walter rhymed. '*Watch and pray says the text – go to sleep, says the sermon.*'

'Anon?' his father queried.

'Who else but good old anon?' Walter laughed, raising his wine glass. 'To good old anon – who says all the things we all wish we had said, sometimes even some of the things that we have said, and plenty of the things that ought to be said.'

'Does anyone know anything about our mysterious visitor?' Loopy wondered. 'Surely someone has heard something on the grapevine.'

'I think I was nearly run over by him,' Judy suddenly admitted. 'But only nearly,' she continued, noticing Walter and Loopy of a sudden staring at her. 'It was nothing. It was when I was walking back home after lunch with you on Friday, Loopy – a rather large car suddenly slithered right across the road. The next thing I knew it was coming straight for me.'

'And Mr United States was the driver, was he?' Walter asked, immediately bristling at the idea that someone had put Judy in danger.

The expression in Walter's eyes immediately induced Judy to quickly shake her head. 'Heavens no! It wasn't his fault. I slipped, and the next thing I knew this car was slewing towards me.'

'And that fellow was driving, was he?'

'I think so, I told you, I don't know. I had to run after Hamish,' Judy lied, wondering why she'd mentioned the incident at all.

'I expect it was that fellow, and he was driving too fast. People coming from London always drive too fast. I bet he didn't think twice about the speed he was doing.'

'It was just a very slow skid, nothing important, really,' she added quickly, afraid that Walter might make a fuss.

'Oh, come, come, Judy!' Hugh teased. 'The sudden death of a house fly or the trapping of a mouse is a matter of enormous importance to the citizens of Bexham! Had you said something about it earlier, by now the story would have it that the handsome American was drunk in charge of a tank which he had commandeered during the war and it was only you throwing yourself under its tracks that saved Bexham from being razed to the ground by a maniac ex-GI.'

'What had he done to go mad, do you reckon,

Father?' Walter wondered, joining in the fantasy and happily forgetting the incident. 'Or, even better, what had driven him mad?'

'Us winning the war, undoubtedly. He's really a Nazi sympathiser who has been living undercover in Bexham, plotting an invasion that was to begin right here in Bexham Harbour.'

'But they forgot all about him,' Loopy joined in. 'Hitler changed his plans but forgot to tell Mr United States, and he spent the rest of the war cooped up in Curley Sidelow's Farm, eating faggots and lights.'

'After that exchange with the vicar he'll be lucky to be asked anywhere for faggots, or lights, for that matter. Hardly the thing, was it, criticising the sermon.'

The subject changed after that, the interest turning to other events that had taken place in the village, while Judy began to clear away the dishes. As she carried them through to the kitchen – Gwen having taken the day off to visit an ailing relative about whose illness Loopy actually had severe doubts – Judy once again found herself thinking about Waldo Astley. From the fleeting moment that she had met him he hadn't seemed to be the church type, and yet there he'd been in the next door pew, looking round at everyone – and through Judy as if they had never met, which of course they had, if only by way of an accident. Tall, handsome, with a magnetic presence and style which made the rest of the male population of Bexham look drab and ordinary, what was he doing in a small Sussex seaside village? Why had he seen fit to visit Bexham of all places?

'A dollar for them—'

Loopy's voice behind her made Judy turn quickly, knocking a precious glass fruit bowl to the floor, where it shattered.

'Oh God—' Judy exclaimed, and her eyes flew to Loopy's face, knowing that the men would have been sure to overhear.

'What's happened now?' Walter stood in the door, frowning. 'Oh, not Mother's precious fruit bowl. Did you do that?' He looked from the broken glass everywhere to Judy and back again.

'No, I did, Walter,' Loopy drawled, smiling. 'And the fruit bowl is mine to drop as it happens, so go back to your brandy, and leave me to clear up.'

Both women waited for Walter to leave, which he seemed to do almost reluctantly, as if he suspected some sort of feminine cover-up yet dared not say anything.

'I'm so sorry, Loopy,' Judy whispered, once he'd gone. 'So, so sorry!' She covered her mouth with one hand, tears hovering in her eyes.

'Couldn't matter less, sweetie. Really!' Loopy grabbed a dustpan and brush. 'It's people not things that matter, the war taught us that, if nothing else. Let's get cracking – although that's not quite the right phrase, is it?' She laughed. 'What I mean is let's clear it up, and then have ourselves a coffee and a cigarette, and forget all about the damn thing.'

'I'm terribly sorry.' Judy got down on her hands and knees and began carefully to pick up the larger broken pieces.

'What were you thinking about when you dropped it?'

'Nothing really.' Judy looked briefly at her mother-in-law. It was a strange fact that she found it easier to talk to Loopy than she did to her own mother or father.

'Ah yes, nothing – I often think of nothing, and for some reason straight away after I have thought of nothing – a painting results.'

Loopy finished her brushing up, and sat back preparing to talk, but Judy got quickly to her feet, turning away and tipping the broken glass she had collected into the pail below the sink. She kept her head averted, not wanting Loopy to see the mixture of emotions on her face. Behind her, Loopy stood, her own head on one side, and went on as if Judy had replied to her, which of course she hadn't.

'I'm sorry,' she said. 'I really mustn't be so facetious. Hugh's forever telling me it's my most dreadful habit – it's just that I sense you're not quite yourself.'

'I'm quite happy,' Judy said quietly, staring out of the window over the sink at the wintry landscape beyond, knowing that the very opposite was true.

'Good. Well, as long as nothing's the matter.'

Judy turned round of a sudden. 'Except, you know, the fact that I can't seem to have a baby. I don't know why but – you know. It's just – it's just not happening, Loopy. And the less it happens, the less it seems likely to happen, and I think it's getting Walter down.'

Loopy said nothing but taking the filled kettle she put it on the gas hob, lighting it with her cigarette lighter before pulling out two chairs at the kitchen table.

'OK – so let's have a cup of what passes as coffee nowadays, and a smoke.' She patted a chair for Judy as she sat herself down. 'First things first. Do you *want* to have babies?'

As Judy looked surprised, Loopy poured the coffee and added some dried milk, before lighting another cigarette.

'Don't look shocked. Women don't always want to have babies, just because they marry. I know I didn't long to have them first off. It's not such a natural state after all. I believe when horses have their first foal they're completely amazed, no idea where it's come from. However, when I did, I was really pleased, even with John, even with the first, which is always the most difficult one to adjust to. Being a mother doesn't arrive with a rush, it comes along bit by bit, rather like being in love. Not many people realise that they've been smitten by love, until they start to hear singing when there's no-one there, and all sorts of other sensations.'

'Oh yes, I want babies, of course I do.' Judy could hardly keep the surprise out of her voice. 'Of course I want to have babies.'

Loopy smiled wryly and tapped the end of her

cigarette on the edge of her saucer, dislodging a long length of ash.

'Well, I don't know that there's any of course about it; until you actually have a child, children are just a notion really. You like playing with other people's children, you enjoy cooing into other people's prams, but when you have one yourself it goes from being a pretty indulgence to being a major reality, believe me. Like you, I had a sort of sense of duty. My mother-in-law – oh, and my mother – were forever telling me that my responsibility – once I was married, I mean – that my responsibility was to give my husband a whole clutch of children, and of course by that they really meant *sons*. And you know what? For a long time I thought *really? Why?* I know this isn't exactly *orthodox*, in fact it's kind of heretical, particularly in England at the moment. So that is why I asked you – do you really *want* a baby?'

'Well, of course.' Of a sudden Judy sounded a lot less sure, because she knew Hugh and Loopy had already suspected that she and Walter might not actually want children.

Of a sudden, out of the blue, Judy remembered the moment in her mother's conservatory when she and Walter had just made love for the first time. War had broken out, at least that was how she remembered it, and they thought they might never have another chance.

'It's none of my business really,' Loopy was saying. 'I am sorry – I shouldn't have asked. It's just the latent grandmother in me popping out. I'm afraid I just can't wait to have a clutch of smalls round the place, taking them sailing and swimming, and all that, and then promptly and happily handing them back to you at the end of a long and tiring day.'

'It's only natural.' Judy's face grew sad. 'Only natural for us all to want another generation.'

Seeing Judy's vulnerable expression, how she looked away into the middle distance, and hearing the tiny sigh she gave that was hardly a sigh at all, Loopy quickly advised her to go easy on herself, adding that she was sure if Judy did so, it would happen.

'Believe me, honey – just take it easy, and it'll be. It'll happen. And as far as I'm concerned, we haven't spoken.'

Loopy gave Judy her most enchanting smile, and they finished their coffee, stubbed out their cigarettes and walked back to the dining room where Walter and his father were drinking smuggled brandy and smoking contraband cigars that Hugh had bought from a contact in the Three Tuns. Loopy surveyed the scene before her, and smiled.

'Well, well, it seems that the shortages have turned us all into law breakers.'

Refusing her father-in-law's offer of a brandy, Judy wandered over to the sitting room window, gazing out at the overcast day, and thinking over her talk with Loopy. As she listened in a desultory way to the general conversation, she saw a man stop at the gate that led into the lane and stand looking directly into the house, hands sunk deep in the pockets of his long black overcoat, a large black hat pulled down over his eyes. She knew at once who it must be, and putting a hand to her mouth she found herself catching her breath, trying not to laugh at his impudence as he doffed his large hat, his head to one side, smiling at her, before turning and continuing on his way.

For a good half-minute more Judy continued to stare out of the window to where the man had stood, then she turned and carefully sitting down put one of her hands over Walter's, as if to remind herself of how married to him she was.

'And what have you two been talking about? Hair styles and beauty tips as usual, I suppose?' Hugh asked Loopy.

'That's right, just hair and beauty, and fashion, and all that. Nothing else interests us women actually, Hugh.'

Loopy caught her daughter-in-law's eye with one of her most falsely innocent looks, widening her own dramatically in order to make Judy smile.

As the family round her continued to talk, Judy could not stop her eyes straying once more to the window. How had Waldo Astley found the Tates' house? And more than that, why had he risked doing something so outrageous? After all, it might not have been Judy who had gone to the window. It might have been Loopy, or even Walter. Was he mad, or was he something worse – enchanting?

Chapter Four

Much to her delight Gloria now found herself at the hub of a flurry of social activity, for at her invitation, and following an uncomfortable night at the old inn, Waldo Astley had moved out of the Three Tuns and into her best guest room. Waldo's quite obvious lack of interest in her as a woman while initially faintly irritating soon became entirely acceptable, particularly when Gloria discovered that his presence in her house gave her an ever-growing social importance, which she did all too soon.

As in all small communities, much of the real life of Bexham was hidden from view, certainly from the view of the casual visitor who saw only what appeared to be a small and idyllic West Sussex fishing village. What no visitor could know was that it took at least half a decade before any of Old Bexham would ever accept any of New Bexham. The only people who invited anyone new were other new people, or the less desirable old residents who all had what Loopy always called a 'known fault', being either permanently drunk or agonisingly boring. However, thanks to the immediate impact that Waldo had on the village, Gloria found that doors that would otherwise have remained permanently shut were now being flung open to her. Social success was beckoning at an almost alarming rate. To start the ball rolling, Waldo and herself received an invitation for cocktails at Cucklington House.

'This Miss Meggie Gore-Stewart,' Waldo wondered after the invitation had been hand-delivered by Richards. 'Tell me what you know about her. Besides the fact that I gather she's blonde and beautiful, if a trifle snooty.'

'I can only tell you what I know from Lionel, which is only what I have gathered at the bridge table—'

'A propos of which, Mrs Morrison, a jump bid of Two No Trumps over an opener in a minor suit is a shut out bid – not an invitation to go three down doubled and vulnerable. If you get my drift.'

'I thought we had agreed to play Strong No Trump, Mr Astley?' Gloria looked suitably innocent, which of course when it came to bridge she was certainly not.

'My dear Mrs Morrison, as you well know, that is not Strong No Trump. That is Enfeebled Thinking. And it will cost you dear – if you insist on playing so damnably, very dear indeed. Anyway, to get back to Miss Meggie Gore-Stewart, if you don't mind. Someone told me she played the heroine during the oh-so-recent fracas commonly known as World War Two. Dropped behind enemy lines, it seems she covered herself in glory. Is this so?'

'Something like that,' Gloria half agreed, her interest straying as it always did when another woman was mentioned. 'Although you know how it is, Mr Astley – once wars are over, it's amazing the tales of bravery one suddenly hears.'

'Do you have any specifically, that relate to yourself?' Waldo asked, his eyebrows raised and knotting in expressive wonder. 'Or did we stay at home by the fireside knitting socks and gloves for Our Boys Over There?'

'My late husband was a war hero, I *think*.' Gloria pulled a slightly comical face, which made Waldo laugh. 'Anyway, he did die in the war. although some people say he was so incompetent his own men had to shoot him. You know – it was he or they, at least that is what *they* say. Although of course I don't believe them, because I wasn't there. I never do believe anything unless I see it with my very own eyes.'

'I doubt there were many fatalities who died a coward's death, do you know that? To my way of thinking anyone who joins up voluntarily deserves a chest full of medals. However, to get back to the subject in question, I caught a glimpse of a young woman who might have been Miss Gore-Stewart after that lamentable church service on Sunday. Isn't she tall and blonde with a somewhat disdainful stare? Is she resident here? Or does she just have estates here?'

'I don't know that much about her nowadays,

alas, Mr Astley. Just that her grandmother left her Cucklington House, but as to whether or not she is going to live there permanently, I couldn't tell you. She has only just returned from America, that I do know. I also know she is unmarried, and living alone at the house.'

'I spied the house the other day on my rambles. It is a rather fine piece of Queen Anne architecture, quite different from the rest of Elizabethan Bexham.'

'It was kept only as a holiday house by the late Mrs Gore-Stewart, at least to begin with, but when her little granddaughter's health was not good she brought her down here for long summers to build up her strength.'

'We must find out what might be her intentions for the house. We wouldn't want a place like that to fall into the hands of some dreadful *parvenu*, like myself, now would we?'

Gloria wondered for a brief moment quite what her house guest's exact definition of some dreadful *parvenu* might be, before happily concluding that since he had seen fit to make fun of himself, he could not possibly mean that Gloria was one too.

'And by the by,' Waldo added. 'Don't you think it's time we got all American and called each other by our first names? Rather than keep abiding by this somewhat antiquated British formality? I'd certainly be more comfortable.'

'Of course.' Gloria smiled in return. 'I think I should be considerably more comfortable, too.'

After which Waldo seated himself happily at her boudoir grand piano and proceeded to play a selection of Rodgers and Hart, while she settled herself down by the fire to read *Fowler on Bridge,* paying particular attention to the chapter on *The Proper Bidding and Responses in No Trump Contracts.*

There was plenty to drink at Cucklington House that Friday, thanks to the fact that Richards was now on the wagon. Determined as he was on becoming the next owner of the Three Tuns and having already tendered an offer that he had been officially informed by the agent was actually being seriously considered, Richards took advantage of the present incumbent's book of contacts and arranged delivery of several cases of under-the-counter contraband liquor to the back door of Cucklington House during the dead hours of the night.

Meggie was too delighted with both Richards's enterprise and his sobriety to quibble with the exorbitant price she had to pay for the smuggled booze, not to mention food. Richards had contacts on the coast that were open to none but himself. He took a special pride in keeping their whereabouts from everyone, murmuring only *laces for my lady, brandy for the parson* at regular intervals as if to remind everyone, himself included, that smuggling had always gone on, and that being so it was almost a duty to the past to keep up the national pastime.

'I shall just have to cut back on my dress allowance,' Meggie told Judy who, on arriving half an hour early as requested had been taken to see the amount of drink that was set out in the kitchen preparatory to the cocktail party.

'What dress allowance, Meggie?'

Since Meggie was wearing a pre-war cocktail two piece composed of a white crêpe jacket embroidered with gold beads worn over a black crêpe skirt, and Judy was wearing an equally venerable black cocktail dress of ridged satin with ruffles at the throat and rhinestone decorations instead of front buttons – reluctantly loaned to her by her mother – neither of them could be said to be looking exactly up to the minute. Unsurprisingly Christian Dior had not yet made his mark on Bexham, where the New Look in any case would have been considered not just shocking, but wasteful, disrespectful, and what's more – unpatriotic.

'Let's just put it this way – I *was* thinking of giving myself a small dress allowance, but I have now been forced to put that to one side. Anyway – it's all in a good cause. The Let's Cheer Up Bexham Cause – never seen so many glum faces. And now that the thaw has started and spring isn't that far away, it's high time for a bit of fun, *don't-cher-know*.'

'Do you honestly think Richards is going to be up to it?' Judy whispered as she and Meggie made their way back to the drawing room, leaving Richards resplendent in his white tie and tails to mix the drinks.

'It's a kind of do or die stroke, I suppose.' Meggie sighed lightly. 'Either he does or he dies. I think he gave himself such a fright he has to reform; he was reduced to a mumbling jelly, if indeed jellies do mumble. He knows how close he sailed to the wind, *and* its three sheets. And if he doesn't make it, we can be assured of quite a swan song.'

Judy lit both their cigarettes, and gave Meggie a mock serious look as she handed her one.

'What's the poison you're going to be giving them then, old thing?'

'Something called Rob Roys.' Meggie nodded towards the table where the glasses were set out, a gleam in her eye. 'That is one of the really great advantages of having a drinking butler. They know how to hit the spot. Apparently, made correctly, Rob Roys taste quite innocent, and induce people to behave quite dreadfully. So, heigh-ho the cocktail hour, and let's see who ends up in the estuary!'

It was only when the Reverend Anderson started telling Judy risqué stories that he had learned as an army chaplain that the full strength of Richards's concoction became apparent. Judy, not willing to risk even one cocktail, could only feel sorry for the loquacious cleric, hoping, for his sake, that when he woke up the following morning he would not – as can happen – remember a thing.

Fortunately Loopy too was unwilling to risk drinking anything but lime juice. Being the only ones therefore in the room who were destined to stay temperate, they were able to observe the growing mayhem caused by the Rob Roys from the sidelines, as guest after guest succumbed to the potency of Richards's particular mix.

'No need to pile any more logs on the fire, Judy

darling.' Loopy laughed, holding up her glass in front of her face to stop anyone seeing her giggling. 'We can warm ourselves by the gentlemen's complexions. My heavens, do look at dear Hughie! He's so lit up, if we put a bit of tinsel on him he could stand in for a Christmas tree!'

'Am I standing behind the only two guests who elected not just to be sensible, but to remain as much?' a voice drawled immediately behind them both. 'Or perhaps you ladies had prior warning?'

Waldo had taken them by stealth, easing his way so quietly into their company that they had no idea how long he had been standing behind them. Realising this, Loopy caught her breath, trying desperately to remember whether or not either of them had been indiscreet, while Judy, without quite understanding why, immediately decided that she had never before seen or met Waldo Astley in any way socially.

'I have to confess Meggie did mark my card about the Rob Roys,' Judy replied. 'This is my mother-in-law Mrs Tate.'

'Waldo Astley. How do you do?'

'I gather you all but ran my daughter-in-law over, Mr Astley.'

'Unfortunately, yes. Even more unfortunately she refused all succour and walked off with her dog, leaving me not only in her debt for ever, but with a lasting admiration for true British grit.'

Loopy laughed, and Judy too smiled, but when she tried to continue the conversation she found herself for once hopelessly tongue-tied in front of

Waldo, and ended up feeling only deeply grateful for the company of her spirited mother-in-law.

'So, Mr Astley,' Loopy was saying. 'And what brings you to England? And most particularly to these parts? Were you stationed here during the war?'

'Alas, no, Mrs Tate. No – no I wasn't stationed here, nor indeed anywhere in fact during the late, great military debate. Having volunteered the day after the Japanese paid us a surprise visit, I discovered to my fury that I was found unfit for military service.'

'How galling.'

'Yes, it was. But I got my revenge on the military medical boards. Joined up with the American war film unit. Moral – if you're not allowed to shoot, you can at least shoot those who are shooting, and it's just as satisfyingly dangerous, believe me.' He gave them both an enchantingly warm smile.

'I'm sure.'

'And you, Mrs Tate. Did you have a good war?'

'No, terrible, like everyone in Bexham, but please don't imagine that we spent our time knitting socks for soldiers because we did our bit, believe me.'

'Naturally. Why would I believe any different?'

'Take my daughter-in-law – Judy here – she fought fires, helped with ambulance work; there was nothing to which she didn't turn a hand.'

Loopy's sudden and somewhat gauche attempt to include Judy in the conversation only caused her daughter-in-law to change her mind about remaining abstemious, and she quickly exchanged her empty lime juice glass for a cocktail from the tray of freshly made drinks that Richards was calmly distributing; managing as he did so to look about as innocent as Nell Gwyn and her tray of oranges.

'So, you had an active role in battle proceedings, Mrs Tate Junior?' Waldo asked, with an exaggeratedly straight face.

'No – no, I wasn't in the armed services, or anything.'

'She was in the WVS. Women's Voluntary Service, a service without which I truly think Britain would have been defeated.'

'I was in the WVS,' Judy agreed, a little too late. 'Yes. The Women's Voluntary Service . . .' she went on, sparely, unable to look at Waldo, feeling on tenterhooks lest he mention the fact that he had stood outside the Tates' house mischievously raising his hat to her. She didn't want Loopy suspecting her of flirting with him she loved Loopy too much for that.

'Was there a Men's Voluntary Service? If so, I think I would have joined it at once.' Waldo looked from Loopy to Judy and back again.

'Will you excuse me?' Judy said, of a sudden, with a small glance at Loopy, unable to bear her own inner tension any more. 'I really should circulate.'

Thoroughly discomforted by the magnetic Mr Astley, Judy made for the door, and fighting her way through the noisy scrum of people who were now crowding the drawing room she escaped to the hall. Walter was meant to be arriving soon. He was coming down on a later train. She wished that he was there, if only to remind her that she had a husband, that she was a married woman.

'I do hope I haven't upset your daughter-in-law.' Waldo nodded after the departing Judy. 'She seems more than a little tense, and now – shall we say – she is past tense.'

'That's just Judy,' Loopy replied, shrugging her shoulders and accepting a light for her fresh cigarette from Waldo's gold Zippo. 'Or rather that is just Judy at the moment. She's a little bit on *edge*. Can't settle to anything, and little wonder after what she has been through. She has not had an easy time of it. Tell me, Mr Astley – I shouldn't have to ask a fellow American, I know, but where exactly are you from?'

'Why, Mrs Tate, should you have to ask?' Waldo drawled, and Loopy smiled at the exaggerated Southern accent that he had of a sudden assumed. 'I was born in West Virginia, but I have homes in New York and San Francisco; and we still have property in the South.'

'A man of substance. I'm impressed.'

'A man of straw, my dear Mrs Tate. A Jack of a lot of trades and a master of not many. And how do you spend your time?'

'I have a husband, and a family, Mr Astley. That sort of thing takes up a lot of a person's time.'

'Something tells me there's more to you than just

a diligent wife and mother. Your children are obviously grown up – and your husband works?'

'My husband works. At least when I last looked at him he was still working. In London.'

Waldo smiled, and as he did so Loopy could not help realising that she had become fascinated by his looks, in a perfectly painterly way, of course. The dark eyes, the nose with its slightly ski shape, so unusual in a man, the curved lips, and sculpted chin. He was not beautiful so much as arresting. 'What does Mr Tate work at then, Mrs Tate?'

'Government work,' Loopy replied. 'But if I say another word I shall be dragged off and imprisoned in the Tower of London.'

'If you were, you would only adorn that ancient institution with your elegance and your art.'

'My art?' Loopy said in very real surprise. 'What art?'

'You paint, don't you?'

'What makes you say that?' Loopy blew out a long stream of smoke, and for a second she watched it, rather than looking at Mr Astley.

'Instinct, masculine intuition, if there is such a thing,' he replied, then lifted one of Loopy's elegant hands. 'As well as a distinct trace of cerulean blue on your left hand.'

'Not just instinctive but a detective, too!' Loopy laughed. 'You should work for my husband. He needs to recruit people with sharp eyes, and ears.'

'What do you paint? No, sorry – I'll rephrase that. How do you paint? I'll rephrase that too, before you say *badly*. In what *style* do you paint?'

'I don't really know, Mr Astley. Perhaps being such a man of the world you could tell me?'

'I'd need to see your paintings to do that.'

'I'd need to invite you for you to do that.'

'So? When may I see them?'

'Don't count on it, Mr Astley.'

'You'd rather not invite me?'

'I've never invited anyone to see my paintings. Only my family—' She stopped, realising it wasn't true. She had long ago given up even talking about her painting with her family.

'And what do your family say?'

'Not a lot.' Loopy smiled and looked for somewhere to get rid of her cigarette. Waldo searched and found her an ashtray. 'I'm hogging you, Mr Astley. You must circulate, most especially since I take it you're a bachelor?' Loopy turned to go, but Waldo stopped her.

'Yes, I am a bachelor, but don't worry – I like being hogged, Mrs Tate.'

'I really think I should introduce you to some more Bexhamites.'

'Sounds like some sort of particularly fierce Biblical tribe.'

'You are sailing closer to the wind than you think, Mr Astley. I'm afraid some of the things the Bexhamites do are positively Biblical. Now come along, I'm going to make sure you talk to your hostess. Have you made her acquaintance yet?'

Waldo looked round to where he could see the ever elegant and seemingly always poised Meggie talking easily to a group of men.

'No,' Waldo said thoughtfully. 'No, I haven't made Miss Gore-Stewart's acquaintance yet. Mrs Morrison brought me here, so I fear I am a bit of an intruder.'

'Come along then, and I'll introduce you.'

With a light hold of his arm Loopy steered Waldo skilfully through the throng until they were part of Meggie's court.

'I hope you're enjoying yourself, Mr Astley,' Meggie said as they shook hands. 'That you're meeting enough people.'

'I never really enjoy myself at cocktail parties, Miss Gore-Stewart,' Waldo replied with a smile. 'A roomful of people standing and shouting at each other while getting progressively drunk is not my idea of Nirvana.'

'You could always have stayed at home, Mr Astley.'

'I could, Miss Gore-Stewart, except by staying at home one never gets out and meets anybody. That is very much the point, I find. I mean, look at me tonight. I have already met Mrs Tate and her charming daughter-in-law, Judy, and now I am enjoying the pleasure of meeting you.'

Meggie smiled at him vaguely, as always entirely resistant to his, or any other man's, charm. She turned to the man on her left.

'I don't think you've had the pleasure of meeting Laurence Nicholson, who is a collector of fine art. And Jeremy Wilson-Bennett, one of our most noted local scribes. Mr Waldo Astley.'

As the three shook hands or nodded an acknowledgement, Meggie gave another polite smile and eased herself away from the group.

'If you'll excuse me,' she said, and left them to it, safe in the knowledge that she had landed her guest with two of the most professional local bores. Laurence Nicholson never listened to a word anyone else had to say, and Jeremy Wilson-Bennett was the author of some particularly long biographies of local personalities, which he published privately but spoke about publicly and at length.

'Was that altogether fair?' Loopy wondered, following Meggie across the room having observed what she had done.

'Perfectly fair. Mr Astley's far too charming for his own good,' Meggie replied. 'And cocky with it.'

'No-one, surely, no-one in the whole world deserves to be landed with those two collapsing tents, Meggie darling. But no-one.'

'It'll test his social skills, Loopy.' Meggie stopped, looking around. 'I don't see Judy – she surely hasn't gone home? Hardly – because there's Walter just arrived.'

'She hasn't gone home, of course not. She excused herself a few moments ago – probably went to powder her nose.'

Loopy was watching Walter who was standing apart from everyone else, talking intently to a diminutive and attractive-looking brunette whom Loopy couldn't quite place. Seeing her look, Meggie supplied the necessary information.

'Fiona Carrington's first public appearance since

she lost her husband in France. Day before they entered Paris.'

'Poor kid. What terrible luck.'

'Worse than terrible. They'd only got married two months before, on his last leave.'

'She looks very young. Can't be more than twenty.'

'About that, I should think. Why don't you go and interrupt them?' Meggie asked, half hooding her large eyes with her hand as if she was at sea. 'I meant talk to them, rather, while I go in search of your errant daughter-in-law.'

Loopy needed no second invitation to introduce herself to Fiona Carrington who seemed almost pathetically grateful, while Meggie went upstairs in search of Judy. Seeing one of the guest bedroom doors wide open, she found her friend sitting in the freezing spare room absentmindedly brushing her hair in front of a dressing mirror.

'What on earth are you trying to do, Judy?' she asked mock crossly. 'Catch frostbite?'

'I'm fine,' Judy said, quickly turning round. 'In fact this lovely cool room is just what I needed. It's terribly hot down there.'

'Can't say I noticed.'

'It is actually. I nearly fainted.'

'Too many of Richards's specials, probably,' Meggie said, sitting down at the dressing table and checking her appearance. 'Or else there is a little visitor on the way. Feeling faint can be a true sign of—'

'I had literally half a glass of Rob Roy, Meggie,

truly, that's all. I couldn't have managed any more.'

'Very wise. Richards's made them far too strong, bless him. Still, it's made the party go with a swing and it's going to be quite fascinating to see who leaves with whom – and indeed if they notice. Come on – we don't want to miss anything.'

Meggie extended a hand to pull Judy up from the dressing table stool, but Judy hesitated.

'Something wrong, darling? Somebody done or said something to upset you?'

'Not really. No, no, of course not.' Judy stood up and bent down in front of the looking glass on the dressing table to check her own looks, pushing her hair back, once more, with both hands.

'Not really generally means yes.'

'Not in this case, Meggie. Nobody did or said anything to upset me.'

'Fine – then try this. Did *someone* upset you?' Meggie started to walk out of the room, at the same time holding out her hand to Judy to follow her.

'No*body* upset me either,' Judy finally replied. 'I just got very hot.'

'And not a little bothered. It's OK – I understand. Now, we must go down and rescue the elegant Mr Astley. I left him being bored to death with Laurence Nicholson and Bexham's very own vanity author Jeremy Wilson-Bennett. He'd need to be a social Houdini to escape from their conversational clutches.'

But on their return, far from finding Waldo stiff with boredom, Meggie and Judy saw him with a seemingly deeply interested expression surrounded by an animated group of people.

'I'd say our Mr Astley is already really quite popular, wouldn't you?'

'So long as he doesn't prove to be a show-off.' Without giving him another look, Meggie took herself off to talk to some of her other guests.

'John,' she said mock sternly to Walter's older brother who was standing with a nearly finished drink in his hand gazing without any interest whatsoever at a very dark eighteenth-century landscape that was badly in need of cleaning. 'John Tate, I did not invite you here to stare at the paintings, particularly highly insignificant ones such as this one. I want you to come and meet a friend of mine who's driven all the way from Arundel to meet the eligible young men of Bexham.' She put her hand in John's to lead him back into the fray, and at once felt his resistance.

'Sorry, Meggie. I'm much too drunk.' John sighed. 'Don't know what your man put in this concoction but it has rendered me near speechless and without the use of my legs. Hence my trying to make out this gloomy depiction by some obscure dauber.'

'I want you to meet Angela Gower,' Meggie insisted. 'She's pretty, grand, and rich. Just what the doc ordered in fact.'

'I will meet her when I can see one of everything, rather than three. In fact, all things considered, I think I shall wobble off home.'

Meggie glanced at her friend, who was hovering

in the background waiting to be introduced, but it was too late – John aimed a kiss at Meggie, and missed, before stumbling out of the nearest door, colliding with two equally tipsy guests and one very upright door post. Meggie watched him go with a sigh, knowing how much he had been in love with Judy during the war when Walter had gone missing, how desperate he had been to marry her, and how Judy had hardly seemed to notice him, longing only for Walter's return, which somehow had made it much worse for John.

The problem was not finding John a suitable partner but somehow convincing him to put what had happened behind him, in the past where it belonged. He could still hardly bear to look at Judy, let alone talk to her for any length of time without being reduced to a helpless silence. It sometimes seemed to everyone that Walter had married the only girl that John imagined he could love.

'I really don't know what we can do for him,' Loopy confided to Meggie as they both watched his uneven progress out of the drawing room. 'I keep introducing him to pretty, bright girls, and he keeps showing absolutely no interest whatsoever in them. If John wasn't quite so resolutely the son of his father I might begin to suspect he'd turned into a wildflower.'

'I don't think so, Loopy,' Meggie returned, at the same time shaking her head at Richards who had just appeared with yet another jugful of danger. 'He might just decide to become a monk, but a wildflower? No, I don't think so.'

'He's going to have to find himself *some*body.'

'The right somebody though, not the wrong one.'

As John stumbled out of Cucklington House he passed a young woman seated on a bench pushed up against the house. Seeing what a bad state he was in she found herself wondering fleetingly whether she should go to help him, but then she saw Hugh Tate's car stop alongside where John was hanging on to a lamppost as if his life depended on it. A moment later John had been swallowed up into the dark comforts of the family car, which proceeded home at a slow if not quite steady pace. Getting to her feet she too made her way towards the road, intent on walking off the Rob Roys in her own good time.

Gloria too was leaving the party, although resolutely not alone.

'Come on, Mr Astley,' she cried to Waldo, dangling the Buick's car keys at him from one small, white hand on which a large diamond sat as a toad on a stone. 'Time to go home and play Patience, whoever she is.'

'Is this wise, Mrs Morrison?'

Waldo's large, round dark eyes swept from his party hostess to his permanent hostess, and he nodded significantly from Meggie to Gloria as if to encourage Meggie to say something.

'Nothing that is fun is wise.'

Waldo shrugged his shoulders, placing his hat carefully on his head.

'Do you enjoy taking your life in your hands, Mr Astley?'

'Doesn't everyone?'

'Mrs Morrison? I do think that perhaps you should let Mr Astley do the steering bit—'

'And so I shall, Miss Gore-Stewart, always providing he can find his keys.'

With a roguish look at Richards, who was standing surveying the break-up of the merry party with some evident satisfaction, Gloria swept laughingly out into the drive only to be restrained by Meggie from climbing into the wrong car.

'That's mine, Mrs Morrison. I think you'll find that Mr Astley's Buick is over there.'

'I can honestly say, thanks to your mix, a good time was had by all, Richards,' Meggie said once they were back in the hall. 'And if it wasn't, then they must be teetotal or members of the Salvation Army, and that is the plain unvarnished truth.'

Richards sighed with sudden nostalgia, his eyes full of quiet contentment.

'Nice to hear the old place ringing with social chat and laughter once again. Just like in Madame Gran's day. Just like the old days, before the war.'

Waldo was forced to let Gloria take the wheel, since not only was she in possession of his car keys, but, as he said to Gloria as soon as he had walked out into the drive of Cucklington House, it made very little difference who drove, since they were both five sheets to the wind.

'What is more my driving record in Bexham is not all that it should be,' he continued. 'However. *However*.' He stood back, seeing Gloria weaving towards the Buick. 'However, seeing the state you're in, Mrs Morrison, maybe we should walk after all.'

'Nonsense. I'm as sober as a bishop at a confirmation.'

Waldo sighed, followed her into the car, and having spent some time helping her find the ignition sat back and lit two cigarettes for them, handing Gloria hers as she drove slowly but surely into the hedge outside the gates of Cucklington House.

'The very place to stop and have a quiet smoke,' he said, pulling slowly on his own cigarette, his hat lowered onto his nose.

'The trouble with hedges in Sussex is that they are such party poopers, Waldo darling. If you have noticed, they are party poop-poop-poop-poopers, always placing themselves just where you don't very well want them, and where they know they're going to be at their most annoying.'

Gloria reversed, narrowly missing a gatepost, after which they shot forward.

'My oh my,' Waldo exclaimed. 'This *is* an interesting new route, but it might help if you watched the road and not me, you know, on account of the estuary. Only because I haven't packed my bathing trunks, Gloria honey . . . another time perhaps.'

After this short episode Gloria settled down to driving too fast, imagining herself to be Veronica Lake, peering sexily out from under a peek-a-boo curl of hair, chatting gaily as she bounced the

Buick along the Sussex lanes, with Waldo beside her smoking nonchalantly, for all the world as if she was the greatest and safest driver in the land.

'Watching the road isn't really your forte, is it honey?' he asked at one point as Gloria took another lit cigarette from him, and thanked him while she continued to drive with her face turned fully towards him.

Gloria certainly wasn't watching the road as she finally swung the large car into the lane behind her house to park it. Instead she was too busy teasing Waldo about the effect he was having on the womenfolk of Bexham.

'You're stirring up all the hens in the coop, Waldo darling, as I knew you would.'

There was a sudden bump as, still laughing at her own observation, Gloria tried first to back and then to straighten the Buick and in doing so hit something horribly hard, which caused the car to lurch and both its passengers to reach for the hand brake.

'My God, Waldo – I'm sure I've hit someone. I do, I think I've hit someone.'

Unsurprisingly Waldo was out of the car in a matter of seconds, while Gloria remained sitting at the wheel, her cigarette burning a brown hole in her evening glove.

'Oh, my God,' she shouted through the open car window. 'Oh, my God, what have I done.'

Waldo came round to her side of the car.

'I'm sorry to tell you, Gloria my sweet, you

appear to have run over a very large stone mushroom. It is now mortally injured.'

'You mean a saddlesone?' Gloria's voice came out in what she knew to be a strangled whisper. 'I mean you mean a *staddlestone*?'

'If that's what large stone mushrooms are called in Bexham, yes. Its head has just rolled down to the gate, and its body is even now settling itself into the hedge. Shall I call the police or will you?'

Gloria threw her cigarette past Waldo, and leaning forward she put her head on the steering wheel. As always when she had sinned against herself and humanity in her own eyes she vowed to God that from now on she would always be good, forever and ever, amen.

'Come on, Gloria. Time to go in and make heavy work of that cold collation your housekeeper left us, bless her.'

'Coming, Waldo darling.' Gloria stood outside the car. 'Oh dear, I fear I might have scratched your Buick's backside.'

'Oh, dear. Well, I dare say that's better than someone else's. Now where do you think you might have put the front door keys?'

Gloria smiled. 'Don't be so American. We don't use front door keys in Bexham, never have and never will. If you can't trust the village, who can you trust, is what we always said when we were growing up here.'

'Well, that's novel at any rate.' Waldo turned the handle of the front door, his face now lit by the dim porch lamp. He stood back to let Gloria pass, and hardly had she done so when he reached out and flattened her against the hall wall, at the same time raising a finger to his lips to quieten her as he saw a door opening at the back of the hall.

'What?' Considering her state Gloria's whisper was commendably quiet. 'What?'

'There's somebody in the house.'

'Where?'

Waldo dived towards the end door. 'Here!' He brought the figure down with a flying tackle, pushing it to the floor as Gloria put the light on.

'My God!' Gloria cried. 'And what *is* that?'

Waldo stood up and looked down. 'That,' he said feelingly, 'is a girl, I do believe, unless you grow them different here in Bexham. And I appear to have just knocked the poor kid out.'

By the time Waldo had examined his victim's head, and Gloria had helped clean the superficial cut with warm water and antiseptic, they both concluded that the only real damage had been the stunning blow the girl had received when falling.

'Do you think she ought to go to the doctor, darling? Do you think she's seriously damaged?' Gloria wondered, putting a hand gingerly to where a bandage now covered the brow of the slowly awakening girl. 'Or do you think she's going to be all right?'

'Maybe it's a question of let's wait and see. If she gets a headache, shall we say, or starts getting double vision, then a visit to *el médico* will have to be considered. As it is since she is now coming to perhaps it's time we introduced ourselves.'

The girl sat slowly up, looking understandably dazed.

'Hello there. I'm Waldo Astley,' he said affably. 'And this is Mrs Morrison – who lives here. And you are? Not a potential maid come to apply for a job here, I hope? Because if so I dare say you might be thinking better of it if Mrs Morrison regularly entertains guests who knock people out.'

The young woman frowned, looking at the doorway through which Gloria had just disappeared.

'Mrs Morrison?' she repeated, then frowned deeply as if the name puzzled her. 'Mrs *Morrison*.'

'That's right, Mrs Gloria Morrison – in whose house I am a guest at the moment. And you still haven't told me who you are. Can you remember who you are? Perhaps you don't know who you are?'

The girl looked round at him and Waldo was aware of the dark shadows under her eyes and her over-pallid complexion.

'My name's Sykes,' she said quietly, her eyes back on the doorway. 'Rusty Sykes.'

'OK, Rusty Sykes – and so what were you doing out this late? Were you on your way home or what? Is there someone we should call?'

'There most certainly is, Waldo darling,' Gloria announced, having just come back into the kitchen. 'The police.'

'The police? What for, Gloria?' Waldo stared at Gloria, remembering her parlous state of a few minutes before, her terror at the idea that she might have run someone down. 'I hardly think we need to bother the police because this poor young woman here slipped over and banged her head.'

'We need to call the police, Waldo, because someone has been in here while we were out and helped themselves to some of my silver, not to mention some money that I left out on my writing desk.'

Rusty was on her feet at once. But Gloria was standing right behind her and the moment Rusty rose Gloria put both her hands firmly on her shoulders and pushed her back into the chair, while Waldo stared down at her with a sympathetic look on his face.

'Try her pockets, Waldo,' Gloria suggested. 'As well as that handbag of hers.'

'Do you want to turn out your pockets, Rusty? Or shall we have to do it for you?'

Rusty eyed Waldo, but since Gloria still had her hands firmly on her shoulders she sank both hands in her coat pockets and produced several small articles of silver – snuffboxes, a cigarette case and lighter. Finally she gave her pockets another rummage and took out a ten-shilling note and three half-crowns that she placed on the table alongside the other loot.

'The brazen cheek of it. You keep an eye on the little thief, Waldo darling, while I go and telephone the police.'

'Gloria honey – if you don't mind – since I am a fully registered and paid up liberal, let's first hear what this young lady has to say, shall we?'

'I don't see why.'

'I think you do, Gloria – after all, only a moment or two back there you thought you'd killed someone. And let's face it, driving the way you were driving, with what you had on board . . . ?' Waldo looked at Gloria, hooding his big dark eyes the way he normally did only when he thought she was about to make a cracking ass of herself at the bridge table. 'Good. So, now then, Miss Sykes.'

'Mrs Sykes.'

'I beg your pardon. *Mrs* Sykes. Now I may be wrong here, but you don't look like a hardened criminal to me. In fact you look like someone who could do with a long soak in a hot bath and a square meal. Is that perhaps why you broke in here – because you're hungry? Because you're far from home – and longing for a nice hot shower? Which you won't get here, I'm sorry to tell you. Here what you get is a tub only – a truly dreadful English custom to my mind. Sitting in dirty water.'

Rusty shook her head. 'I live in Bexham. I was born and bred in Bexham, and so were my father and mother and both my brothers, and my grandfather.'

'Take it easy, slow down – take it easy.' Waldo smiled and held up a hand. 'All I was trying to do was to lighten the atmosphere. In other words, get you to relax. After all, we're never going to understand why you're here with a pocketful of silver and a bump on your head unless we find out a little about you, and – well, when people like you commit this sort of crime they generally have good reason. I say generally because of course some people are just greedy and lazy, but most people have some sort of reason why they steal – or commit murder or whatever – and theft as a pretty general rule is usually based on need.'

'I don't understand what you're talking about.' Rusty put a hand back to her head and frowned at him as if in pain.

'You just need money? Or do you need money for something? That's what I mean.'

Rusty frowned. 'I don't know. I don't remember actually.'

Gloria rolled her eyes to heaven, impatience written all over her. 'Guess what – she doesn't remember.'

'So let's start again, shall we? You know your name, Rusty Sykes – so that is at least something. Now, if you can remember your own name, can you remember where you live? You have just said that you live in Bexham, so that much you do know – but whereabouts precisely?'

Rusty glanced fearfully from one face to the other. 'I don't know. I can't remember.'

'I think you can.' Waldo told her gently but firmly, seeing the fear in her eyes. 'I think you do remember, Rusty. I also think you don't want to tell us, in case we tell your family you were caught here stealing Mrs Morrison's silver. Because that might be just a trifle embarrassing, mightn't it?'

'There's a Sykes who's a *garagiste*,' Gloria recalled. 'Runs that shabby little garage at the top of North Hill. Nice young man though. Poor soul lost a leg in the war. Peter Sykes – that's right. War hero. Remember his father from before the war.'

They both knew at once they were on the right track since Rusty immediately dropped her eyes at the mention of Peter Sykes.

'I suggest we telephone him. Just to see if his wife is home, or if she's still out somewhere. Or if he's looking for her.'

'No,' Rusty insisted very quietly. 'Please don't.'

'Any particular reason why we should not?' Waldo enquired.

'Every reason,' Rusty replied. 'I've run away.'

'In that case we *won't* ring anyone—'

'If I may say so,' Gloria sighed, 'a crime is a crime is a crime.'

'And all sorts of crimes that aren't crimes are crimes. Such as driving when you're five sheets to the wind. This is a spur of the moment crime, Gloria – there was never any danger that someone might get hurt. Or killed. Or even run over. And no-one runs away without good reason. Now I suggest we allow this young lady the comfort of a good long hot soak – since half of her seems frozen, and the other half, petrified – while we talk this thing through.'

Forced to agree, Gloria took Rusty upstairs holding her firmly by one arm and locked her in the bathroom to have a long hot bath while she and Waldo decided her fate over several cups of strong coffee.

'As a woman you should be able to understand

her predicament far better than I,' Waldo reasoned. 'You would have to be not quite in your right mind to leave house and home during weather such as this unless you had a pretty darned good reason.'

None the less, Gloria was still reluctant to let her burglar off scot-free. She had little sympathy for anyone who stole from other people simply because they were too idle to earn for themselves the things they stole. As far as she was concerned, if the girl at present locked upstairs in her bathroom preferred to steal rather than work for a living then Gloria was damned if she could see why she should go against her better judgement and offer the girl forgiveness and understanding.

'The little so-and-so just walked off the street and helped herself to things that don't belong to her. So why on earth should that deserve any tolerance, understanding and patience, I have to ask myself.'

'Try the long view, Gloria. There's no real harm done, in as much as we got here and stopped her before she could get away with anything. So instead of retribution, maybe some good may come out of it. It happens sometimes, believe me.'

'Very well, Waldo,' Gloria agreed, with extreme reluctance since the last thing she was feeling was clement. 'If you insist we shall let her go. But you mark my words – the moment I let her out of that bathroom and send her on her way, you can bet your last farthing she'll go straight to someone else's house and do the very same thing all over again.'

'Maybe, but I don't think so. I don't think the young lady is a professional thief. I think something has happened to her – something disturbing perhaps, certainly unsettling – and because of whatever it is, I don't think she's quite herself. Don't ask me why – it could be the look in her eyes, or the way she talks. There's something not quite right with her, and maybe that's why she's behaving out of character. And hell – maybe it's better to risk being too tolerant rather than being too harsh and condemning someone out of hand for the wrong reasons. I really do believe that this young lady did what she did out of sheer desperation.'

'Oh, Waldo darling.' Gloria sighed, and laughed. 'You are such a ragged trousered philanthropist, aren't you? With such a tender heart but still such a fool. You just wait and see – young Mrs Sykes will soon prove how wrong you are.'

Even so, Gloria took herself upstairs to let her burglar out of the bathroom on whose door she was now busily knocking. Waldo, meanwhile, pulled a curtain to one side to stand and stare out into the darkness of the winter's night to consider what he might be able to do for the sad and pretty young woman found burgling Gloria Morrison's house.

Chapter Five

Waldo walked Rusty home, having decided that one post-cocktail party incident behind the wheel was enough for one evening. At least he walked her wherever it was she was going, since at first neither of them seemed to have any definite idea of their final destination.

'You don't want to go home?' Waldo asked her again, having made the initial enquiry as to which direction they should take. 'But I thought—'

'Assumed, you mean,' Rusty muttered. 'Though why – search me. After all that stuff in there about something awful happening and all that.' She nodded her head backwards in the direction of Gloria Morrison's house, sinking her hands deep in her coat pockets and trudging down the lane that led only to the estuary.

'That where you intend spending the night?' Waldo wondered as he fell into step beside her.

'What's it to you?'

'A matter of some concern, that's all. I don't particularly like the idea of you sleeping rough.'

'Who said anything about me sleeping rough?'

'This only leads down to the estuary – at high tide. Which is what it is now. At low tide – OK. You might be able to take a short cut to the quays and huddle in a hut somewhere for the night, but for the next couple of hours you're not going any farther than the water's edge.'

'So what?' Rusty muttered. 'What's it matter to you?'

'I don't like the thought of you stuck there at high tide. Anything wrong with that?'

Rusty just shrugged by way of an answer.

'Why don't you go home?' Waldo persisted. 'If I don't say anything – and I'll make good and sure Mrs Morrison doesn't say anything—'

'That's not the point,' Rusty interrupted, coming to a stop at the top of the shingled beach. Only a matter of a few yards below, large dark waves were breaking noisily on the shore. 'The point is I can't go home.'

'Why ever not?'

'Because – because I can't. Because I've run away.'

'You haven't run very far, Rusty,' Waldo observed with a smile, before turning up the collar of his coat to shelter a match for the cigar he began to light. 'I mean if I was running away from home I'd have run a hell of a sight further before breaking in somewhere to try to bolster my exit funds.'

He glanced over the end of his cigar at the small, diffident figure who was standing idly kicking stones.

'Forgive me for my curiosity,' Waldo continued.

'But when a young lady is married she might leave home, or leave her husband – but she doesn't really run away, surely, does she? Not unless – not unless something awful has befallen her.'

Rusty said nothing. She just shrugged again and continued to kick at the pebbles.

'Has something upset you, Rusty? Married folks have arguments, we all know that – and sometimes the arguments get a little heated—'

'It's nothing like that. I haven't had no argument – and Peter – Peter would never get angry or anything. He'd certainly never raise a hand to me. Or anyone come to that.'

'Yet you're running away from home. So you say.'

'Yes.'

'Or maybe you're just running away full stop. From something that has happened to you.'

'Maybe I am.'

'OK.'

Waldo said nothing more. He just stood on the edge of the beach smoking his cigar and watching distant lights bounce off the dark waters of the estuary. Rusty said nothing for a while either. She simply continued slowly kicking pebbles, with her hands sunk deep in her pockets and her shoulders hunched.

'If you really want to know,' she said out of the blue, 'I lost my baby.'

'You poor kid,' Waldo said. 'That's a terrible thing to happen to anyone. You poor kid.'

Rusty stopped kicking the stones and took a

sideways glance at the tall man beside her who was standing still looking out to sea as he spoke. She frowned, wondering when the inevitable question was going to be asked, when he would wonder how she lost it, and why. But the tall dark American said nothing more for the moment. He just shook his head sadly once and continued to smoke his cigar.

'I've got another child, a little boy. Tam,' Rusty volunteered after another long silence. 'He's a lovely little boy, and the – the baby I lost, it was a little girl.'

'I see.'

'My mother would have preferred it if it had been a boy, but then it wasn't, was it.'

'I can never understand why so many women only want sons. If every baby born was a boy the world would very soon run out of women – but then maybe that's how some women would prefer it.'

There followed another long pause, broken only by the crashing of the waves and the pulling back of the shingle.

'Who's looking after Tam then?' Waldo wondered, tapping the ash off the end of his cigar with one little finger. 'That was the name, right? Tam?'

Waldo had deliberately repeated the name with an added resonance, in the hope of agitating Rusty into a fuller explanation. Instead, all he got was silence.

'Your mother, I guess,' he continued. 'And she must be a good pair of hands – or sure as anything you wouldn't have been happy to leave your little boy with her. Had you any idea of where you might be headed?'

'Mother's taken Tam over,' Rusty replied angrily, ignoring the second part of Waldo's question. 'Even if I'd wanted to bring him with me she wouldn't have let me. Like the way she took Jeannie.'

'Jeannie?'

'Doesn't matter.'

'But I thought you only had one—'

'I said it doesn't matter!'

Rusty was looking at him fiercely now, breathing in and out deeply before turning on her heel and walking back up the path away from the sea. Waldo let her go ahead of him before ambling along after her.

'I lost my sense!' she called out loudly. 'I just lost a bit of sense! That's all that happened! Hardly surprising neither! I lost a bit of sense!'

This time it was Waldo who chose not to reply at once, gambling on the fact that now she had somehow been touched on the quick, she might drop her guard and consequently be a little more forthcoming. He'd already concluded that the loss of a baby might make anyone unstable, be it only for a short space of time.

'Not surprising at all.' Waldo deliberately kept his voice low, so that Rusty might not hear exactly what he said. He saw the ruse had worked as Rusty stopped and turned back to him.

'What did you say? I didn't quite catch that.'

'Nothing important.'

'If you think it's easy – if you think I'm just feeling sorry for myself—'

'I didn't say anything along those lines, I assure you.'

'If you think leaving your little boy behind, and your husband – if you think losing a baby and leaving your little boy behind and thinking you don't love your husband no more – if you think that's *easy*—'

'On the contrary,' Waldo assured her, having now caught up with her. 'I imagine what you're going through must be perfect hell. That's why I want to help you.'

'You want to *help* me?' Rusty stared at him with a deep, suspicious frown. 'Why do you want to help me? How?'

'I'm not altogether sure. In any way I can, I suppose. I don't have anywhere of my own to live, otherwise I could offer you accommodation until—'

'I wouldn't take it.' Rusty shook her head at him fiercely. 'I wouldn't take nothing from any stranger.'

'You were quite prepared to take something from Mrs Morrison.'

'I'd lost a bit of sense!' Rusty yelled at him. 'Don't you understand! Don't you understand I'm not exactly in my right sense!'

'Then why don't we take you home?' Waldo suggested.

'Home? Home's the very last place I'm going, I can tell you!'

'Tam'll be missing you.'

'Tam'll be fast asleep!'

'He'll miss you when he wakes up and finds you're not there.'

Rusty looked at him silently for a moment, considering this. 'He's got his gran.'

'Little boys prefer their mother. Believe me. I was a little boy once.'

'I'm not going home,' Rusty said finally, but not with quite as much certainty as before.

'OK. I know – the vicarage. I'm sure the good vicar will be able to help.'

'I don't need no help from no vicar neither.'

'OK. Just a thought.'

'Yes.'

They walked on up the lane, going nowhere in particular.

'OK,' Waldo concluded when they reached the T junction at the top. 'Right then. Long as you're all right – and don't need any more help from anyone, let alone me – this is where I say goodnight. And I hope you find somewhere warm and dry to rest your head. *Cheerio*, Rusty.' He doffed his big black hat, smiled, and turned to his right to retrace his steps back to Gloria. In his head he gave her twenty but she was running up behind him before he had even counted to ten.

'Wait! No – please, please wait! Please?'

Waldo waited, but without turning.

Rusty came all the way round him so they could be face to face.

'I can't go home,' she said quietly. 'They'd murder me.'

'I don't think so.'

'You don't know my parents.'

'And they don't know me.'

Rusty frowned up at him, unable to make sense out of this person who'd come into her life. 'I don't understand.'

'Do you trust me?'

'I don't even know you.'

'Easier, then. To trust me.'

'Forgive the intrusion,' Waldo said as he took off his hat to stand in the cramped living room of the Todds' house. 'I know it's awful late but I simply had to stop by and tell you personally how grateful I am to this young lady here. To your daughter, Mr Todd. Mrs Todd.' He nodded to both of Rusty's parents before turning to smile at Peter. 'And I guess you must be Peter.'

'We've been worried sick,' Mrs Todd said, wiping her perfectly clean hands down on her apron. 'We been worried sick wondering what become of her.'

'I really should let Rusty here explain,' Waldo said before Rusty could say a word. 'But I guess her modesty would prevail and you wouldn't hear the half of it. So if I may?' He cleared his throat. 'As of course you are all aware,' Waldo went on refusing the offer by Peter of a flimsy-looking chair. 'As you are all perfectly aware, young Rusty here has been suffering from an emotional upset. This is none of my business of course, but I mention it because Rusty mentioned it to me and because it explains her sudden disappearance this evening. But your loss was someone else's gain, the way these things often turn out to be. My gain in fact. Because if it hadn't been for young Rusty here, I would be a much poorer man and so too would my good friend Mrs Morrison, with whom you may well be acquainted.'

'We know who Mrs Morrison is,' Mr Todd nodded, taking his old pipe out of his coat pocket, only to have it immediately confiscated by his wife. 'Lives in that fancy house up on the corner of the quays.'

'I happen to be staying with Mrs Morrison—'

'We know that and all,' Mr Todd added.

'And the both of us were attending the party that was held this evening at Miss Gore-Stewart's.'

'That right.'

'It certainly is. Anyway, to continue—'

'Please do,' Mr Todd remarked, trying unsuccessfully to wrest his pipe back from Mrs Todd.

'On our return to Mrs Morrison's house,' Waldo continued, 'we were confronted by the sight of a youth wearing some sort of woollen helmet over his face—'

'A balaclava,' Peter offered helpfully. 'They're known as balaclavas.'

'Thank you, Peter. Yes, we were confronted by

this youth in a balaclava wool helmet running hell for leather out of Mrs Morrison's house with his pockets bulging with what I imagine we would all call loot.'

All eyes were on Waldo, and none more intently than Rusty's.

'He was gone down the lane before I could give proper chase,' Waldo said. 'But just as I was about to try to go after him, out of the lane just beyond the house appears this other figure, smaller than our fugitive but I dare say equally determined, except happily her determination unlike the fugitive's was for the good. Rusty in other words. Your very brave and resolute daughter, Mr Todd, who went after that villainous youth like a terrier after a rabbit. And you know what? She caught him. She threw herself at his legs, wrapped her arms round them and brought him crashing to the ground – whereupon she jumped on him, pinned his arms to the ground and sat on his chest.'

'That's my Rusty,' Peter said proudly. 'Brave as a young lion.'

'That's Rusty all right,' her father sighed. 'She's thrown her big brother across this room more times than I like to remember, a tomboy to the last.'

'By the time I'd got to the thief he was still quite helpless, in spite of his struggles. We frogmarched him back to Mrs Morrison's, emptied his full to brimming pockets, and – ah—' Waldo hesitated as he realised he had arrived at a part of his story that he hadn't prepared. If he said he had handed the youth over to the police, what with Bexham being such a small community his lie would soon become apparent. Even if he made out that he had handed him over to the police from the nearest big town, he guessed the Todds would be scouring every local newspaper report for news of their errant daughter's heroism. Happily, it was Rusty's turn to leap in and come to the rescue.

'It wasn't your fault about the window,' Rusty put in.

'You don't reckon?' Waldo said, with as much sangfroid as he could muster.

'Mrs Morrison and the gentleman here locked the lad in the downstairs toilet while they called the police – and he got out through the window. Somehow.'

'The one thing we didn't think of was the window.' Waldo nodded, hoping the Todds never visited Gloria Morrison's and needed to use the facilities, when they would soon discover that in order to escape through the rest room window you would need to be either a child no older than two or three or a circus midget.

'And the blighter was out of there in a flash,' Rusty added. 'Although he'd need to have been some sort of contortionist.'

'But you got a good look at him,' Peter said. 'Good enough to recognise him again if you saw him.'

'The other thing we failed to do, Peter,' Waldo sighed, 'was to remove his bacalava.'

'Balaclava.'

'His balaclava. Anyway – the good thing is Mrs

Morrison and I recovered all our chattels – and the main thing was your daughter's act of amazing heroism.'

'Amazing's the word for it,' Mrs Todd said. 'Seeing the state she's been in.'

'I think we'd all be surprised what a long walk on a bitterly cold night can do for the head,' Waldo said gravely. 'Followed by some quite unexpected adventure—' He smiled at the assembled company and made as if to take his leave. 'Whatever,' he said. 'The point is Rusty here did a brave and unselfish thing for two people she didn't know. And although it's no business of mine, other than to congratulate you both for having such a remarkable daughter – and you, sir, for having such a remarkable young wife, and to thank Rusty here for her heroism, I feel sure that whatever upset Rusty might have caused you by her sudden disappearance this evening, and whatever might have happened to have caused that disappearance, you can all of you put it behind you now and be very proud of this fine young lady here – who really has made this evening quite a night.'

No-one said a thing, not even Rusty, tempted as she was to throw her arms around this stranger's neck and smother his face with grateful kisses, which would not have been at all like her. All that happened was that Peter put his arm around Rusty's shoulders and hugged her to him, shyly kissing the top of her head, while Mrs Todd reluctantly handed her husband back his faithful pipe.

A minute later Waldo was striding back home to

Gloria's house, whistling 'The Battle Hymn of the Republic'.

'Tell you what we have to do and do it pretty quick,' Peter said to Rusty later, after he had brought her up a mug of hot cocoa to sip in the comfort of their bed. 'First thing we have to do is find us somewhere to live. By ourselves. We can't go on living like this. It isn't right or fair, not on anyone.'

'First we got to have something to live *on*,' Rusty said, with a half-smile, sipping her cocoa.

'We could try my wages,' Peter replied with a grin, sitting down slowly and carefully on the bed.

'Mind my cocoa!' Rusty warned, as the bed rocked despite his care.

'I know I'm not bringing home enough, but perhaps if I had to—' Peter stopped and looked at her.

'Up to you,' Rusty replied. 'Whatever you want, I'll go along with. Particularly if it means getting out of here.'

'I got some ideas, Rusty. And as soon as we get some capital—'

'Pete?' Rusty interrupted. 'Sorry.'

'You don't have to apologise for nothing, Rusty. I'm the one who should be apologising for neglecting you.'

'It's going to get better now, Peter. I can feel it. Just as they say – things have to get worse to get better.'

'I think you're right, Rusty. I can feel it, too. And

let's face it, they can't get much worse so they've got to get better.'

Peter grinned at her and so infectious was the smile that Rusty laughed. They both laughed and it was the first time for as long as both of them could remember.

Waldo knew this was only a beginning, but Waldo was a patient man so he bided his time. His favourite uncle's business motto had been contained in three words – *Don't Be Previous.* Although for a long time, as a young boy growing up, Waldo had always felt impressed by the axiom, he had absolutely no idea as to what it meant, until he finally plucked up the courage to ask.

'It means, my boy, don't be hasty and don't rush at things,' his Uncle Harry had told him, taking off his glasses and staring at Waldo. 'It means always take time because time is all it takes. The longer people have to wait for your decision the more important it will seem. The very same goes for any offer you might be thinking of making. The longer you take to make it, the more of a bargain will it be considered, and the better for you the reward. Nobody ever won anything by being previous. But they sure have lost things, kid. Believe me.'

So when Waldo finally drove his Buick up North Hill to refill its large petrol tank with as much fuel as he could obtain on the coupons he'd been given, he was able to congratulate himself for being well this side of previous. In point of fact he had allowed more than a fortnight to pass since the night he had caught Rusty Sykes stealing from Gloria.

'You get quite a view from up here,' Waldo remarked as he counted out the petrol coupons he had obtained, heaven and Mrs Morrison only knew how. 'Particularly now the weather's improving so dramatically. Bexham really is what we Americans love to call *quaint*.'

'Quaint,' Peter Sykes smiled. 'I've heard it called a lot of things, sir, but never quaint.'

'No, really? Oh, it's a word I sometimes think we Americans have become infected with,' Waldo replied. 'Soon as we set foot on these shores. I don't mean it to sound insulting – I suppose it's simply because we don't have a word good enough to describe what appeals to us as a small but somewhat mystical country. Maybe I should just stick to beautiful, after all? Because that's really what your little port here is, it's beautiful.'

'You staying long in Bexham? Or just passing through?'

'I was thinking of just passing through, but Bexham seems to have caught a hold of me. So much so I was actually thinking of renting a property here for the summer.'

'Well, now, sir. That does sound a good plan, if I may say so. Bexham is a lovely place in the summer, particularly if you sail.'

'Yes, I sail. As a matter of fact I was thinking of hiring somewhere along the estuary – be grateful for any local knowledge. I imagine you must hear quite a lot of tittle-tattle from your regulars. So if you do hear of any houses for hire – I'm staying with Mrs Morrison as you know.'

'Indeed I do, sir. And if I hear tell of any houses for rent—'

'Or even for sale—'

'I shall let you know at once, sir.'

'Most kind. Very kind. If you'd be good enough to check the oil and water while you're at it, Mr Sykes?'

Peter nodded and eyed the dial on the pump as it spun towards its allotted six gallons.

'Lovely car, sir, but she must drink a fair bit,' Peter said, as he hooked the nozzle of the petrol hose back into the Shell pump. 'If you don't mind me saying so.'

'No more than the average Sherman tank.' Waldo sighed. 'For some crazy reason my father brought this car over with him before the war, some time in the nineteen thirties, and left it here. Couldn't be bothered to ship it back. I have been toying with the idea of finding myself something a little less thirsty and a little more suitable for the winding English roads. Do you deal in cars at all? Do you have any second hand stock?'

'We used to deal quite a lot before the war, sir, my father and I that is. But as you can imagine the market is more or less non-existent now, particularly in these parts.'

Peter replaced the petrol hose as Waldo opened up the Buick's big bonnet.

'I could look around for something if you wish, sir. If you tell me your requirements.'

'Something for the summer days, I think, Mr Sykes. Something *sportif* – a ragtop I'd say. A car to, as they say, ruffle one's hair.'

'I'll see what I can find for you, sir. And you're very low on oil.'

'Mmm, so I am.' Waldo smiled hugely. 'So I am. Just as well I came to see you, Mr Sykes. Just as well. How's that heroic young wife of yours, by the by?'

'She's very well, sir, thank you for asking. In fact she's altogether well in herself now.'

'That's good. Maybe that famous deed of daring helped her turn. Who knows?'

'Who knows, indeed, sir. Who knows indeed.'

Loopy was taken quite by surprise the coming weekend. She had been shopping in Churchester with Judy and they had returned earlier than expected, empty-handed. Judy had dropped Loopy off at the end of her driveway and refused tea since she suddenly found herself anxious to get back to Walter. Loopy smiled to herself as she wandered up the drive to her own house. It wasn't so very long ago that she would have been behaving in exactly the same fashion, waiting to hear the shutting of the car door outside and Hugh's tread on the gravel, the opening of the front door, and his call into the house as he tossed his hat onto the stand. Although she still looked forward to seeing him home, she nevertheless now often found herself only too relieved to be alone for a few days a week, happy to be painting rather than waiting for the sound of his step. It wasn't that she no longer loved him – in fact she often thought that possibly she loved him even more than she had ever done – it was just that inside her head she had grown older, perhaps even older than her actual years, thanks she imagined to the war.

When Walter had been declared missing presumed killed part of her had gone missing with him; and although she was past that terrible crisis, redeemed by her middle son's miraculous return, she was aware that the experience had changed her. For some reason she could not precisely name, it seemed to have changed her more than it had her husband, who as always appeared to have taken everything in his stride, so much so that it sometimes seemed to Loopy that Hugh no longer loved her the way he had loved her before her wartime crisis when he had stayed in London so much, pleading security matters. Of course she was aware that love changed – not that it altered when it alteration found, but that as one grew older so its very nature shifted. But whereas she hoped her love for Hugh had matured and strengthened, she suspected Hugh's might have gone in the very opposite direction. She worried that he had become bored with her, that she no longer amused him, that nowadays when he sat down at the piano he played and sung more to himself than to her.

Even so, she still entered the house with a light step at the prospect of seeing him. There was still enough of that old feeling of anticipation, enough of the hope that she could bring a smile to his face, or perhaps make him laugh out loud when she recounted Judy's and her farcical shopping adventures earlier. As she opened the drawing room door Loopy thought that maybe she might be able to charm her man so well that he might once again be persuaded to play 'Night and Day' before he mixed the cocktails as he had always used to do.

'Oh. Oh, I'm so sorry, honey – I didn't realise you had a visitor.'

It wasn't the fact that Hugh had somebody with him that surprised her. It was the look of what seemed to her to be a strange complicity between them. The way they both started when she came in, the way Hugh's visitor got quickly to her feet while stowing something away in her pocket as if she didn't want anyone to see what it was, the look of irritated surprise on Hugh's face, as if he was really rattled, then finally his diplomatically urbane smile.

'Loopy, darling. I didn't hear you come in. I wasn't expecting you back so early.'

'We had a kind of frustrating afternoon so Judy and I decided to cut our losses. Meggie – how nice to see you.'

She kissed Meggie on the cheek. Her behaviour was impeccable. So impeccable in fact that Meggie could never have suspected for a moment how Loopy felt on discovering her so unexpectedly at Shelborne.

Moments later Loopy turned to see Gwen ushering Waldo Astley into the house.

'Hugh seems to have decided to hold a house

party here without telling me,' she joked to Meggie. 'May I introduce Mr Waldo Astley, Miss Gore-Stewart.'

'We've met already, Loopy darling—' Meggie laughed.

'Of course. You two met at Meggie's cocktail party, didn't you?' Loopy smiled, feeling foolish.

It was Hugh who was smiling at Loopy now, repeatedly tapping an untipped cigarette on the back of his silver case before lighting it.

'Mr Astley and I bumped into each other in the Three Tuns at lunchtime, so here we all are, hands across the sea, and all that. Will you ask Gwen to bring us in some tea, darling?'

'Yes, of course.'

Given the nature of Hugh's government work Loopy always knew better than to ask too much, yet she couldn't help wondering what it was that Meggie had been showing Hugh when she came in.

'Come on, Hugh.' Meggie was teasing him now. 'I'd say the sun was sufficiently over the yard arm for something a little more serious than tea, wouldn't you?'

Loopy turned at that. It was difficult not to feel irritated by Meggie's easy manner with her husband. She tried to reassure herself that it came purely and simply from their wartime relationship, when Meggie had worked as an agent for Hugh, but she suspected it might also come from something a little less official, namely that Meggie was an extremely attractive and beautiful young woman, and that Hugh was an extremely susceptible middle-aged man.

'You're right, Meggie. Sun's dropped well and truly down below the yard arm, so out with the nose paint,' Hugh agreed, drawing on his cigarette. 'Whisky? Mr Astley? The real McCoy I assure you, not watered down cough mixture. Meggie?'

'Only the very quickest of quickies for me, Hugh, because I have to dash.'

Taking the shot of whisky and soda Hugh handed to her, Meggie raised her glass in salute then drank it down in two.

'Excuse the rush, but I suddenly – remembered an appointment,' she said, picking up her gloves and bag. 'Goodbye, Mr Astley. Hugh darling.' Meggie nodded at Waldo, blew a kiss at Hugh, and quickly kissed Loopy once again. 'I'll leave the men to you, Loopy darling. I must go and see to more important matters.' She sighed and looking at Loopy with the air of a conspirator she whispered, 'Namely – destitution!'

Meggie quickly left the room and the house, and shortly afterwards Loopy slipped out after her. By the time she had dressed herself for the evening and returned downstairs the two men were finishing what must be their second large whiskies, since they were chatting and laughing as easily as old friends.

As soon as Loopy came back into the room, both men were on their feet and a moment later Hugh was at the cocktail shaker, ready to mix Loopy's favourite Sidecar. As she collected her glass gratefully from her husband she noticed Waldo had detached himself and wandered into the conservatory to look at some of the paintings stacked up against the wall.

'This is rather fine,' he called, stopping and peering at a small contemporary beach scene. 'In fact, it's very fine.'

'That's just one of Loopy's daubs.' Hugh turned to Loopy and they both laughed, because it was a family joke – Loopy's daubs.

'That's why it's in the conservatory. It's not allowed in here. Eighteenth-century watercolours only, please observe. My paintings are far too bright for my husband's taste.'

'Is this really by you, Mrs Tate?' Waldo turned to Loopy.

'It is only – as my husband has just warned you, Mr Astley – one of my daubs, that's all.'

'Actually this is a very fine painting, if I may say so.'

Hugh turned to Loopy. 'I think he just wants another drink, darling.'

'Did you train at all, Mrs Tate? I often think those who don't go to some sort of school are the most expressive. They haven't had that vital sensitivity stamped out of them by the leaden boots of some half-talented teacher.'

'Mrs Tate is entirely self-taught, aren't you, darling? Self-trained entirely. Strictly a Monday to Friday painter, because on Friday she starts thinking about her old man coming back from London, which is only proper.'

'May I see some of your other work?'

'I wouldn't want to embarrass you, Mr Astley, really not.' Loopy shook her head. 'My husband's right. I'm a Monday-to-Friday painter – I don't have to do it. I don't have to do it to earn a living.'

'I would still like to see more.'

Loopy glanced at Hugh who simply widened his eyes in mock amazement.

'If you will allow me the privilege.'

Loopy hesitated. She wanted very much to take Mr Astley upstairs into the room she was using as her studio and show him her work, because she was simply burning to show someone who would not just dismiss her work as daubs, as her family had always done. But she was all too aware that to do so would be to incur Hugh's jealousy. She looked from one man to the other hoping that Hugh would concede, that he would suddenly smile at her, wink and tell her to go on upstairs and show the man what he wanted to see. But she could see that Hugh's expression had grown dark at the very idea, while Waldo Astley's remained entirely impassive.

'It's getting rather late,' Hugh said suddenly. 'Don't you have to get back to Mrs Morrison, Mr Astley? She eats early, doesn't she, before the inevitable bridge game?'

'Not for quite a while yet, Mr Tate,' Waldo replied with a slow smile. 'Not for quite a while.'

'Well, I'm terribly hungry,' Hugh complained. 'Perhaps you ought to ask Gwen to get a move on with dinner, Loopy.'

'I have already spoken to Gwen, Hugh. Dinner won't be ready for half an hour yet.'

'Plenty of time, then, for you to allow me to see your work, Mrs Tate.'

Loopy looked again at Hugh, but since he had turned his back and poured himself a third whisky she could not see the expression on his face, or even guess at his feelings, whatever they might be.

'Very well.' Loopy suddenly announced her decision, loudly enough and with enough determination to cause her husband to spill the whisky he was pouring from the decanter. 'Why not? Maybe I shall find out whether or not I'm a dauber, a part-time painter, perhaps even an undiscovered *genius*.'

Giving her attractively husky laugh, Loopy held the door open for Waldo Astley to precede her out of the room and up the stairs and so to the moment that would change the second half of her life for ever.

As Waldo was standing looking at each canvas held up in turn by his elegant hostess of that moment, high up on the hill above Bexham harbour Rusty was emerging from the back of her husband's garage block covered in grime and dust.

'We could easily move in here, Peter,' she said to her husband, who was locking up the premises. 'There's three rooms over the old stores which would make up into two bedrooms and a bathroom, then if we moved the stores—'

'It would cost too much, Rusty,' Peter interrupted. 'When I said find us somewhere, I wasn't thinking of converting any property.'

'We could do it ourselves. I can turn my hand to a few things – I didn't learn exactly nothing in Dad's boatyard. And you're good with your hands – you're a mechanic, and a good electrician.'

'Don't get carried away, love.' Peter stopped her. 'Just look at the building, will you? It's a shed. It's nothing more than a large wooden shed. It isn't suitable for human habitation.'

'We could *make* it suitable. Long as it's got a roof and walls. And floors.'

'You're forgetting the building restrictions. To do what you're saying we could do we'd need permissions – and they're not giving those out to the likes of you and me, not to convert half-rotten old timber buildings into some sort of house or flat.'

Rusty was about to protest further, but realised there was no point. Peter was right on both counts. The place wasn't fit or even meant for human habitation, and to make it so would mean a great deal of construction work for which they would most certainly not get the necessary permission. Only recently there had been a case where a well known resident of Bexham had been taken to court and fined a hundred pounds for redecorating and painting his quite substantial house without licence, while someone else who had applied perfectly properly was only allowed to spend fifty pounds on repairing incendiary bomb damage to his property.

In view of these cases, Rusty realised that there could be precious little chance of the likes of them getting permission to renovate a place that wasn't even their residence, even if they did have the money. At this realisation the immense feeling of despair that she had been managing to keep at bay ever since suffering what her mother now described as her *funny little brainstorm* began to surface once again, so much so that Rusty found herself running out of the garage towards the little wood opposite, while Peter slowly limped after her and took her by the shoulders.

'Don't cry, Rusty,' he said gently. 'I know things are bad, but we've just got to be patient.'

'It's easy to say that, Peter. But this isn't what it was meant to be going to be like.'

'What isn't?'

Rusty gestured hopelessly. 'This, all this. Everything was going to be better, everything was going to be for something, not less than nothing. Things weren't meant to be like this, not for anyone, least of all those of us who lived through it.'

'I know. We all thought that somehow everything was going to be all right, just like that, overnight. That having won we were going to wake up to some brave, new and wonderful world. But that's not going to happen now, is it? Not unless we make it happen. Not unless we try to rebuild it with our own hands. Blood, sweat, toil and tears, all over again, but we can do it, we can rebuild our little world.'

'How? How can we rebuild anything?' Rusty cried. 'They probably wouldn't give us the blooming permission until we're nearly a hundred!'

Peter wiped the tears from her face with a grimy handkerchief. 'We've just got to stick at it, Rusty. Long as we have each other and long as you believe in me, we'll get there.'

'I don't know as to how. But I hope you're right, Peter; but don't ask me as to how.'

The man who was going to supply the answer to that particular question had just finished his examination of the collection of paintings that had been put before him. He still held one, a small oil measuring no more than one foot wide by ten inches high. It was of two young women sitting on a sunlit sandy beach under coloured umbrellas. By any standards it was an outstanding piece of work in the way that the artist had captured the haze and the heat of the day, as well as the delicate use of colours that were never for one moment too hot for the scene that was depicted, but by the standards of a so-called amateur painter, and a rank unschooled one at that, it was a work of considerable talent.

'I am really at a loss for words, which as a matter of fact, Mrs Tate, is not my usual state of play.'

'You're not actually making sense, Mr Astley,' Loopy remarked from her position at the window where she had been standing nervously smoking a cigarette while her guest spent what seemed to her to be an inordinately long time staring at her paintings.

'What I meant to say, but must have omitted to do so, is that you possess a quite exceptional talent.'

Loopy stared at him, her heart seeming to be suddenly in her mouth, unable to think of anything to say, which was probably why she stubbed out her cigarette only half smoked and with unusual ferocity.

'Very well,' Waldo continued. 'You might well say, and I wouldn't blame you, what does he know? And I might well answer – really very little, which would be the very truth. I'm no art critic, and I haven't studied art at any level other than a domestic one. But I can also answer that, possibly above everything else, I love fine painting. I have always loved painting, ever since I was young. I even wanted to be a painter. But guess what – I found I couldn't paint. I couldn't draw a box let alone paint it. I have absolutely no talent whatsoever, and as soon as I found this out – well before the war as it happened – I determined to discover as much as I could *about* painting. See as much as I could, learn to know what I liked – and I have to say I really like your work, Mrs Tate. Really. I like it quite inordinately. Nor am I judging it as the work of some unschooled amateur – I can assure you that your talent is up there along with that of many contemporary painters. These seascapes particularly are exceptional. I don't know how you developed this style—'

'Neither do I.'

'It's a kind of cross between pointillism and post-expressionism, but no matter how you came by it this is your style and it is both quite original and utterly beguiling.'

'Are you sure you're not just being kind, Mr Astley? I won't mind if you are because I have to tell you – and this really is to go no further – you're the first person, apart from my maid, who has actually noticed my work.'

'Is that so? I can't believe that.'

'I can.' Loopy laughed, and lit a fresh cigarette, even though she didn't really want one, but she felt so excited that if she didn't do something she thought she herself might go up in smoke, not just the cigarette.

'And I'm not just being kind. If I were being kind I would say quite different things, in different words. I would say these paintings are *fun* – and *colourful* – and I would say that I imagined you got a lot of pleasure out of your *hobby*. And I would more or less leave it at that – and most certainly I would not have taken the best part of half an hour to come to these conclusions. But since I have, and I can hear your husband calling us from downstairs as well as the gong being sounded for dinner, I suggest we abandon the topic of your genius for the moment and pick it up again at a time convenient to you.'

'What are you going to tell my husband, Mr Astley? Because he's never thought too much of my paintings. I don't want him to make fun of you.

You've been too kind for that, really you have.' Loopy carefully closed the door behind them, as if closing it on their secret.

There was a pause as they both stood looking at each other, Waldo realising at once where her problem might lie, and Loopy knowing instinctively that she could trust him.

'What would you like me to tell him, Mrs Tate?'

'Maybe that you liked my works. That you didn't think they were a waste of time, but nothing more. Don't *eulogise* about them, whatever you do. Too much praise might be embarrassing for both of us.'

'Very well. Then that is all I shall say.' Waldo nodded, understanding completely.

'Thank you, Mr Astley.'

'It is entirely my pleasure, Mrs Tate. I assure you.'

By now, to the relief of both himself and Meggie, Richards was well and truly installed as the new landlord of the Three Tuns. If there had been a good time to question his determination to maintain his sobriety Meggie knew that this had to be it, Richards let loose in his own public house. Yet as he explained to Meggie after his first week in residence – paraphrasing Shakespeare as he so often did – the more he saw people putting liquids in their mouths to take away their brains, the less he felt inclined to follow suit.

'In fact, Miss Meggie, to be absolutely frank, when I see how utterly daft people become when they're under the influence, I wonder not only how Madame Gran and you put up with me, but how in all honesty one put up with oneself.'

Although she said nothing to him Meggie was slightly concerned as to how the check cap, blazer and cravat brigade would react to someone of Richards's character and demeanour running what they considered to be their local hostelry. She wasn't worried about the fishermen and the boatmen. They would drink in the Three Tuns as long as the beer was good and as long as it was competitively priced. If the beer got cloudy and the prices got fancy, then first they would complain and then if their complaints were not attended to they would vote with their feet and take their trade elsewhere, even if in this case it meant having to travel another mile and a half to the Crown and Anchor, further along the estuary.

The check cap and blazer brigade, however, were of a totally different complexion, particularly since many of its members came from the ranks of the local Yacht Club. Meggie was concerned lest some of their number might find it funny to subject Mine Host to a barrage of what Richards always liked to call *unsolicited comments*. She knew such a type of person always found confirmed bachelors like Richards fair game, and took cruel enjoyment in trying to discomfort them.

Happily she had reckoned without Richards's lifetime ability to deal with mockery.

'Excuse me, miss?' one of the Blazers enquired on the retired butler's first day as landlord. 'A pint when you've a moment, please, my sweet.'

'Certainly, sir,' Richards had replied with great aplomb. 'With a straw?'

'No. Straight from the tap, please, miss.'

'Very well, madam. Coming straight up.' After which Richards had placed a pint of water in front of the Blazer with a smile.

'No, no – I meant a pint of ale – dearie.'

'Whoops – my mistake, but you know how it is.' Richards had sighed, taking the drink away. 'I didn't think we were quite adult enough to try alcohol yet.'

Having witnessed that early exchange and others similar, Meggie soon found her worries diminishing. In fact the more she observed with what panache Richards was able to handle contentious moments the more she realised her concerns had been quite groundless. Just as Richards had coped superbly with the vagaries of being a manservant before his drink problem overcame him, so too did he seem to quickly master the art of being a landlord. Besides, the years he had spent as a butler stood him in excellent stead, since not only did he have an encyclopaedic knowledge of drink, but he had also long since mastered the art of tact. He knew when to continue a conversation and when not to prolong it, when to pass comment and when to stay silent, and when to give advice and when not to, always bearing in mind the most important point of all: that, just as in the drawing room or dining room, those in his bar who asked for counsel must only be given the counsel they wished to hear.

As a result it was soon very obvious that Richards's tenure of the Three Tuns was proving to be more successful than any of the village could have hoped, and of course his stock went up even further when the regulars learned of his record in the Great War. Naturally Richards never volunteered this information himself, leaving it to others to find out, which of course they soon did, the old inn being the centre of so much of the life of the village. So it was that after only a short space of time, Meggie found that she could stop worrying about the abrupt change in both their lives and turn her thoughts to other things.

The only advice Richards himself found he needed was about catering for large numbers at a time, since not only were supplies of most foodstuffs still rationed, but there were often acute shortages of the foods that were meant to be more freely available. Although he was not at all happy with having to deal with the only alternative suppliers, it soon became abundantly clear, as always, that if you could not beat them then you had to join them, particularly if you wanted your business to stay solvent. Fortunately he soon discovered that the local police were more than prepared to turn blind eyes to the ever ready stock of victuals at the Three Tuns, since they themselves were only too pleased to be able to frequent a local where they were assured of an unwatered down drink, and the sandwiches and pies had a decent and appetising filling.

One of Richards's more original innovations was to section part of the saloon bar off into a *Ladies Only* snug, since not only was it still frowned upon by many for women to frequent public houses, but, as with clubmen in London, a high percentage of his male custom did not enjoy doing their drinking in the presence of women. His sympathy did not just extend to the women of the village, however. Realising that many of Bexham's young men had few sociable places to meet members of the opposite sex, Richards soon redecorated one of the many small bars, renaming it the cocktail lounge, he made sure it was warmly lit and comfortably furnished. Meggie wondered about the wisdom of such a conversion when the supply of spirits was still noticeably short, only to be told by the new landlord that his youthful clientele met in the cocktail lounge not to drink cocktails but to be smart.

'I should imagine that most of the young men who frequent the lounge think a Sidecar is something in which to drive their lady friends to the Three Tuns,' Richards replied, delicately slicing a hardboiled egg. 'Although the other day we did have the dearest of older couples in – down from the north on holiday. They were most taken with the cocktail lounge – so much so that when the gentleman came up to the bar he ordered a pint of brown and mild for himself, and for the wife – *a bottle of cocktail*. Too dear for words it was really.'

As always, regulars to the Three Tuns had their

favourite seat, stool or position at or in their chosen bar, and Hugh and Loopy were no exception. They always called in for a drink Saturday midday after they had finished their shopping and this particular Saturday they made no exception, taking their place in their usual window seat from which they could watch the comings and goings on the quays. When Hugh went up to the bar to order a second round, Loopy saw the now familiar figure of Waldo ambling along the street that led up to the quays, a cigar stuck in one corner of his mouth and his big black slouch hat tipped at a rakish angle almost over one eye. As if feeling her stare, Waldo looked up at the bow window of the pub high above him, saw Loopy and stopped, doffing his hat with an extravagant flourish and bowing equally excessively. Loopy put a hand to her mouth and laughed then waved back in greeting with the other, amused not only by Waldo's theatricality but most of all by the reactions of the fishermen who had witnessed the flourish.

'Who are you laughing at?' Hugh wondered, putting down their drinks and glancing out of the window. 'Oh. The Yank. I might have known it.'

'I imagined you liked the Yank, as you call him,' Loopy replied. 'Do you still think of me as a Yank, I wonder?'

'Of course not,' Hugh replied grumpily, taking out his packet of cigarettes and shaking the last one out. 'Don't think I ever thought of you as anything other than you, really. Cheers.'

He lifted his glass and drank, then lit his

cigarette, just as the door swung open behind him and Waldo ambled in.

'Greetings, local people,' he said generally, taking off his hat and his long black overcoat preparatory to making himself comfortable somewhere. 'A little bit warmer today, I think. Spring can't be long now.'

'Will you join us, Mr Astley?' Loopy asked, indicating an empty chair, accompanied by an indicative frown from her husband.

'Most kind, Mrs Tate, most kind,' Waldo replied, looking round the crowded bar. 'But I am otherwise engaged for the moment. Perhaps later.'

'Delighted,' Hugh said, drawing on his cigarette, safe in the knowledge that by the time Waldo might have prised himself free he and Loopy would be well on their way home.

'I have to look into what is somewhat quaintly known as the public bar,' Waldo mused, folding his coat over one arm. 'As if the other bars in here were for private use only. A business contact you understand. Until later, perhaps.'

Having excused himself, Waldo went in search of his quarry, whom he found just as he hoped he might finishing a pint of light and bitter in the public bar.

'Good day to you, Mr Sykes,' he said, joining Peter at the bar. 'Please – let me buy you a beer. I see your glass is empty. While you tell me if you have any news for me yet regarding any suitable sports car that might be for sale. I trust you have heard of something?'

While their drinks were being poured, Peter told Waldo about the few cars of which he had indeed so far heard. Unfortunately nothing seemed really suitable, judging from the disappointment he saw on his new client's face. But that was just a snare and a delusion, a trick of the trade. Peter hadn't learned his business at his father's knee for nothing. Peter Sykes was keeping the best until last.

'It isn't definite,' he said slowly, loading his words with as much doubt as possible. 'It is only hearsay. But there is word of a Jaguar SS 100 that might be coming up for sale. Belonged to an RAF chap, Battle of Britain pilot, so I gather. Survived the Big One, only to get killed in the last week of the war flying his kite on some exercise or other. Doesn't bear thinking about, does it? Getting through the war, and then your number coming up coming in to land after some pointless exercise. Anyway – about this motor. It's been laid up since 1940 – never driven during the war at all – which again is odd, seeing how the fighter lads liked to show off to the girls, know what I mean? Anyway, this chap laid his pride and joy up instead of joyriding, and now it might be up for sale. Might be of interest. Like new, so they tell me, sir. A Series 3 it is, three and a half litre, or if you want to be precise three thousand, four hundred and eighty-five cc.'

Waldo nodded appreciatively, but said nothing.

'Which is a fair old lump of engine, sir,' Peter continued. 'The Series 3 was built in 1939. This example has only done just over fifteen hundred miles and when it was out of action it was properly laid up – wheels off, bricks under the axles, engine and sump drained, whole body covered with several layers of dust sheets. So it really should be like new. She's barely run in yet. In a way you'd be buying a better than new car.'

'Then no doubt you'll want a better than new price for it, Mr Sykes,' Waldo smiled, lighting up a fresh cigar, much to the interest of the locals in the public bar. 'You have a figure in mind?'

Peter hesitated. Having bought the car well below the market value, at a figure of two hundred and eighty pounds, and having obtained an agreement to delay final payment for a week, he was hoping to double his money at least. Yet, being disinclined to take the American for a fool, he was a long way yet from counting his chickens.

'You know what they cost new, sir?' he wondered aloud instead. 'New they cost one thousand two hundred pounds.'

'In that case go no further. If that is what the car costs new, then that is what I shall pay. Plus your buyer's commission, of course.'

Peter Sykes stared at Waldo, whose expression was deceptively innocent.

'Is that not enough? You look surprised, Mr Sykes. What sort of figure did you have in mind then?'

'The car is eight years old, Mr Astley,' Peter stuttered. 'When I said it was better than new—'

'It was just a *façon de parler*? Your sales pitch? A little bit of an exaggeration?'

'Well, no sir, no, not exactly. What I meant by better than new was that what with the engine being just about run in now, and the fact that if there had been any teething troubles they're all over and done with – and the fact that it has been so well stored, as I said – what I meant was that I don't imagine you would find a better one anywhere. They only built the Series 3 for a year, sir, so they're as rare as rocking horse droppings – if you'll pardon the vernacular.'

Waldo smiled broadly and drew on his cigar.

'Go on.'

'I think you'd have to pay a London dealer well over seven hundred for her, sir,' he said, plucking a figure out of the air. 'But that's not the figure I have in mind.'

'You have a better than new figure, Mr Sykes!' Waldo laughed. 'And why not? Something good, rare and beautiful is worth good money. Tell me what you were thinking.'

For some reason Peter felt himself outrun, and yet he didn't know why. The American's benign affability and apparent willingness to pay whatever was asked plus commission had unnerved Peter, unused as he was to this sort of negotiation. He wished devoutly his father was still alive to handle the deal for him, because he knew his old man would have got every available penny out of the Yank plus a few more, but Peter wasn't made like that. All he wanted was to get a fair price for the car plus say a twenty per cent commission. If he could get that, then he and Rusty would be able to afford to rent the little flat above the greengrocery in the main street; have a proper home of their own.

Yet he still hesitated, feeling that to try to achieve his aims by what amounted to cheating someone as affable and generous as Mr Waldo Astley would be iniquitous. He sincerely believed he would not be able to live comfortably with his conscience after that.

'The thing is, Mr Astley, sir. The thing is the car would cost you a lot of money anywhere else, particularly one with this history and such a low mileage, but I'm prepared to let you have it for five hundred and sixty pounds, plus commission.'

Waldo frowned. 'I can't accept that, I'm afraid, Mr Sykes.'

'I understand, sir—'

'I can't accept that for the simple reason that you can't be making enough money on that deal. That is sheer economic lunacy, besides being appalling business.'

'You asked me to find you a car, sir—'

'The deal didn't include cutting your own throat. Look, what I propose to do – if the car is as good as you say I propose to pay you what you and the car deserve. I shall pay you one thousand pounds and that will include your commission. As long as the car is as described. If it isn't, then woe betide you. Now, have we a deal, young man?'

Peter looked at his client with renewed anxiety, only to find with relief that Waldo Astley was still smiling and was now holding out a hand to be shaken on the deal.

'Mr Astley sir—'

'If you're not going to take it, Peter, then I shall leave it. That is my final offer, so take it or leave it.'

'But, but it isn't right, Mr Astley. It isn't right at all.'

'So, tell me what's so wrong about it, will you?'

'You're paying me too much.'

'Isn't that my business?' Waldo laughed good-humouredly.

'I know – yes, I'm sure you're right, sir – but the point is—'

'The point is, my dear fellow, you have told me what you want for the car and I have told you what I am prepared to pay for the car. Is that not how car dealers do business with their customers? Is not that the way you do business? You name your price, I name mine, and we agree a sum. So all we are waiting for here is for you to agree the sum.'

'I'm not sure I can, really I'm not.'

'Then you will never do well in life. If you refuse this, you will always do badly.'

'I don't see why,' Peter replied stubbornly.

'Because that is the way of the world. This is your last chance, friend. My offer stays valid for one more minute – after that I won't even pay you a penny for the car. But if you accept my offer, I promise you I shall make it doubly worth your while.'

'But you haven't even seen the car, sir. It isn't as if you know the model either. You'll be buying something blind – something you'll be paying miles over the odds for – something whose value you can never hope to recover.'

'Thirty seconds,' Waldo merely replied, looking at his watch.

'I think I must be dreaming.'

Waldo continued counting. 'Twenty-five, four, three, two—'

'Yes, all right, I agree!' Peter suddenly yelled, startling those drinking near their corner table. At which Waldo put his head back and, removing his cigar from his mouth, roared with laughter.

'My dear fellow! For one awful minute I thought you weren't going to make it!'

'You wanted me to agree?'

'Of course I wanted you to agree! What kind of game did you think I was playing? Now – when we have finished our drinks you can take me and show me the car, which I imagine you already have locked up in that garage of yours – and provided it is as good as you describe I shall pay you cash, there and then.'

'It's actually better than I say it is, Mr Astley.'

'I'm very glad to hear it.'

'You have no idea, sir, what this money will mean to us. To Mrs Sykes and me.'

'Of course I don't,' Waldo replied with a smile. 'I have absolutely no idea at all.'

'That was a stupid thing to say, sir. Sorry.'

'You will be able to do everything you had been hoping to do except maybe a few years sooner.

And when you throw another five hundred into the kitty—'

'Another five hundred, Mr Astley? But why?'

'Because we're going to join forces.' Waldo smiled, but this time the smile was for himself, as he remembered Rusty the night he and Gloria had caught her in Gloria's house, and the state she was in both then and particularly afterwards.

'Astley and Sykes. I like the sound of that, Peter,' Waldo said. 'How about you? Astley and Sykes. Who knows – it might even become a hallmark of quality.'

The look on Peter Sykes's face was one that Waldo wished that he could have captured on a camera. But, then again, like so much in life, perhaps it would be even better left as a glorious memory.

Chapter Six

By now a spring that had brought floods to the country to compound the misery of a terrible winter had turned just as dramatically to a baking hot summer, bringing with it yet another change of mood for the bewildered population. Naturally, just as first the heat waves were welcomed by a people still recovering from the vicissitudes of the coldest weather any of them could remember, by the time the end of April had arrived, people were in two minds as to which had been worse, the bitter cold or the universal damp.

Then all of a sudden, just as everyone thought their misery could grow no deeper, out came the sun, and along came clear blue skies and blessed warmth. The warmth was what everyone wanted, sun enough to dry the ground out and to be able to throw open windows and air houses full of condensation, mould and dampness. Everywhere people spring-cleaned, washing and hanging out their nets and their curtains, beating their carpets over the washing lines with sturdy bamboo paddles, turning articles of furniture out onto front or back lawns to dry out in the rays of the long forgotten sun as if they were grazing animals being put out to grass. As the population spring-cleaned postmen began to whistle again, as did dustmen and delivery boys, while incoming swallows swooped and soared in their perpetual quest for food, and larks hovered high above fields full of burgeoning crops. Now a mood of sudden optimism was everywhere, for at long, long last it seemed that perhaps the bad times were over and the sudden change of weather presaged the start of the new age of which everyone had been dreaming.

Then the warmth turned into a sweltering heat wave, bringing with it soaring temperatures unrelieved by any cooling winds. Cities and towns became unbearably hot and every weekend there was a mass exodus in coaches and trains to the beaches, where a stupefied population sat in deck chairs on the burning sands trying to find relief from the scorching sun. Without their realising it, their escape to the seaside brought with it if anything worse conditions, the relentless sun beating off the water and on to the sweltering figures stretched out on sand and pebbles. Naturally it did not help that most of those who sat in serried ranks along every available foot of beach remained partially dressed, the men in their trousers and shirts with only a foot or so of trouser leg rolled up, the women in cotton dresses with large cheap hats flopping over their reddening faces and stockings rolled down over their sunburned knees, while children in knitted woollen bathing trunks hopped in and out of a tepid sea, avoiding swarms of vicious little crabs that floated inwards in search of sustenance, or bruised their feet on the inevitable shingle that seemed to constitute any decent stretch of beach.

Added to which there was no ice, and few households could boast a refrigerator, so there were no cold drinks to assuage the raging thirsts that a scorching sun reflecting off a shining sea engenders. There were no cold drinks on sticks and ice cream was at a premium, if you were lucky enough to be able to find any. Halfway through what was turning out to be the hottest summer on record, with people roasting at work and scorching at play, most of the population found themselves wishing the skies would cloud over and the April rains would return once more. Life now seemed, once again, to be a series of tortures, with no relief in sight.

The heat in London was certainly proving too much for John Tate, whose appointed annual holiday came round just in time to provide him with a welcome escape.

'One more day and I thought I would expire,' John told a barefoot Loopy as she fetched him from the station in the old family car, which was still like an oven, even though his mother had all the windows open.

'You're one of the lucky ones, sweetie. Imagine what it's like for people who can't get away.

Your father says you can fry eggs on the London pavements.'

John settled himself into the seat beside his mother. All the way home in the stifling train he seemed to have been able to smell the sea and see the beloved view from his bedroom window. He could almost feel the cold stone of the conservatory floor, followed by the cool of the grass, the shingle of the beach, and finally the pleasure of the sea bathing his dripping body, so much was he longing to get to Shelborne, throw off his work clothes and head for heaven.

After he had enjoyed his first swim and returned home to bath and change, John sat for a while at his bedroom window in his silk dressing gown, enjoying the slight breeze that had got up and was blowing in off the sea as the tide reached full. It was a perfect evening and Bexham was looking its best, the mouth of the estuary beginning to fill with sailing boats waiting to run in home to their moorings on the tidal water, and small commercial traffic also arriving with the turn of the tide, which would still be full enough for them to sail into the busy little harbour by the time they reached it. Lovers strolled along the path that ran parallel to the estuary, or sat with their arms around each other on benches and seats placed on mounds to provide the best view of the surrounding landscape.

Seeing the couples dallying, John felt vaguely restless, wishing that he too was part of a couple, one of a pair of lovers walking in the evening sunlight and holding hands by the sea, strolling happily into a future where they would live together in perfect harmony. So attractive was the prospect before him that for a moment he considered changing his job – giving up London to return to his roots, to buy a little cottage in or near Bexham where the two of them – once he found a suitable partner – could start their married life while he made his way up the ladder of some local firm. He was good at what he did, a good businessman, particularly when it came to understanding money, and given the lack of any serious opposition to his talents in the neighbourhood he knew that it wouldn't be long before he had risen to the top of the tree. The only trouble with this daydream was the fact that as yet he had not met anyone he could possibly consider taking as a wife. Truth to tell he had never enjoyed a full relationship with a member of the opposite sex and had only once ever fallen in love, and that was with Judy, his brother's wife, the wife of a man they both thought was dead. Walter's return had proved that particular belief to be wrong, but by that time John had already scotched the notion that Judy felt anything for him except friendship.

So John had been as thrilled as the rest of his family at his brother's return; yet as time went by he found himself becoming first jealous of his brother, then resentful. He deliberately distanced himself from both Walter and Judy, emotionally and physically, coming home as little as he could, and, when he did, avoiding their company whenever possible. Eventually he came to the realisation that he had a duty to shake himself free of his heart-break, and after making an immense effort to be more friendly and sociable he really believed and hoped he had now closed the gap.

So this sunny summer evening as he sat enjoying his favourite view, he found to his satisfaction that he felt truly content, so much so that he actually found himself smiling as he saw Judy arm in arm with Walter as they walked out of the house and into the garden, pre-dinner drinks in hand. For a while he watched them unnoticed, observing how they seemed easy in each other's company, walking side by side, with Walter doing most of the talking and Judy the listening, the sea breeze blowing her dark hair, her old but carefully preserved silk evening skirt blowing back towards the house, showing off tanned legs, high heels, and a slim figure. Walter was some lucky fellow, but he need not be the only one, because the way John felt he too could be some lucky fellow one day. Finally he leaned over the balcony and called down to his brother and sister-in-law. They turned and called back to him to hurry up and get dressed and come down and join them, which after another wave John went inside to do, singing happily as he went, for some unknown reason now utterly convinced that the bad, black days were over and the bluebird of happiness was just about to land in his heart.

The next day dawned even hotter than the one it had succeeded. In fact by ten o'clock it was so hot that all Mattie Eastcott wanted to do was flop out in the deep cool of the house with some iced tea and a good book. But Max was on holiday from kindergarten, and each day, regardless of the heat, he demanded to be taken to his favourite beach round the corner from the mouth of the estuary. Before the war Lionel had sensibly bought a beach hut on the edge of a nearby perfect golden strand, and now, instead of offering shelter from prevailing winds and rain, as was more usual in England, it was affording the Eastcotts welcome shade and respite from scorching sunshine.

Every day Lionel would arrive with a lunch for the three of them that he had carefully prepared himself and put into his treasured dark blue leather picnic case, perfectly packed with boxes and bottles, cups, saucers, plates and cutlery, and of course food. Tomato or egg sandwiches in greaseproof paper, an undressed salad of lettuce, radish and beetroot all picked from the garden, and a big Thermos of nearly cold homemade lemonade. By lunchtime even Max was feeling the heat and was glad to sit inside the beach hut to nibble at his sandwiches and bat at the ever persistent wasps with the fly-swat his grandfather never forgot to bring with him, or watch gleefully as they drowned in a bottle full of watered down honey.

Later, when the sun had moved off its zenith, Mattie would take Max down to the sea for his second long paddle. Another game with his beach ball followed before they paddled off the heat in the sea once again and returned to the beach hut for tea, brewed on a Primus stove and accompanied by slices of Mattie's homemade fruit cake.

Every day followed the same ritual, Mattie carefully covering her little boy's head from the scorching heat of the sun and his body with Nivea Cream. Unsurprisingly within a week of constant exposure to sun and sea they were both as brown as berries. Mattie in particular was privately delighted with the colour of her now fashionable tan, which set off her eyes and hair better than ever. Day by day she and Max grew darker and darker, until Lionel started to refer to them as his little Red Indians and would make whooping sounds when he joined them on the beach for lunch.

'Daddy, do stop, you're shocking the people in the next-door hut,' Mattie would mutter, but her father refused to take any notice. As far as he was concerned he had bought a beach hut and if he wanted to yodel, sing, or make Red Indian noises such as he had heard on cowboy films, that was his business.

Mattie started to lay out the picnic, not bothering to cover herself with her towelling beach top, because even that seemed too heavy for the stifling heat.

'You would honestly think that there would be some sort of breeze coming off the sea, wouldn't you? But no, the air is as still as a graveyard.'

She shook up a bottle of ginger beer for Max, and sat him well into the shade of the beach hut. Strolling past their hut, stopping every now and then to admire the sea view, walked couple after couple, some with children, some without. Normally Mattie never noticed, but today for some reason as she sat back down on her father's travel rug it seemed to her that every person who passed was one of a couple. For a second she contemplated the idea of what it must be like, to be part of a pair, to be part of someone else. It seemed unimaginable. To have someone else to whom she could talk at the end of the day, laughing over what had happened on the beach, regaling him with tales of her father's yodelling in his beach hut and embarrassing her and all those around him, of how Max's attempts at swimming in his water wings were coming on, about how many shrimps they'd caught, about everything and anything really – just to have someone to talk to would be unimaginable.

That was what being one of a pair meant. It meant you could share everything in a way you couldn't share your thoughts with an old man or a young boy. You could love them, but you couldn't share your thoughts with them, because they were at a different stage from you. It was as if they were all waiting at a bus stop, and Lionel was posted way ahead of her, and Max way behind, so when the bus came along Lionel would catch it long before her, and Max long after.

'These hardboiled eggs are a bit overdone, Daddy.'

'Not for my taste they're not. Don't like them anything except nice and floury inside and nice and hard on the outside.'

Mattie sighed and raised her eyes to heaven. They didn't even share a taste in hardboiled eggs.

John had got up late, breakfasted late, and was downstairs late. As he walked into the conservatory where Loopy was busy painting he was so late up he actually felt guilty, the way he did when he was late for church, or for some important date, instead of just being on holiday, when after all a chap had every right to do what he liked.

'Gwen's done you up a picnic lunch, it's by the door!' Loopy called back without turning round to where John was still standing by the door. Her smock was covered in oils and her hair caught up in a scarf and tied on the top of her head, as if she were working in a factory. 'Sandwiches, hardboiled eggs, and a bottle of cider.'

'Then God bless, Gwen.'

'God bless Gwen, I'll say. How she puts up with us all, I don't know.'

Picking up the picnic basket John laughed and strolled off down to the beach without giving Loopy's new painting a second glance. He was dying for a dip. He couldn't wait to feel the cold water closing over him. Once again the day was already boiling, and he had seen all too little of it. Behind his back Loopy shook her head a little sadly and mixed herself a new pot of turpentine and linseed oil.

John strolled along the beach to the family beach hut, dark glasses on, towel rolled up under his arm, swimming shorts under his yachting trousers, unable to think what a lucky chap he was to be on a beach while the rest of the world was toiling in London. He had just undone the hut door and hung up his towel when he heard quite a commotion coming from nearby.

'Is anything the matter?' he said, arriving at the scene of the disturbance. 'Can I help?'

'It's all right, it's nothing,' the pretty young woman called, finally glancing up at his precipitous arrival. 'It's just my son. First of all it was his beach ball – and now he's been stung by a wasp.'

'It hurts!' the child was yelling, holding the side of his arm. 'It really, really hurts!'

'I have some blue bags,' John told her, about to disappear back to his hut. 'I always carry blue bags this time of year, for this very reason!'

Once the blue bag had been allowed to do its magic, Max's yelling ceased and was replaced by a look of such tragedy that as he held the application to his arm John found it hard not to smile. In order to divert the little boy's attention from both his pain and his loss of dignity he at once began to examine the deflated beach ball for a puncture, a hole that he soon found by way of submerging the ball bit by bit in sea water collected in a bucket. Ten minutes later the puncture was repaired thanks to a large sticking plaster from John's emergency kit.

'Do you always travel to the beach this well equipped?' Mattie smiled, knocking the big coloured bouncing ball back to Max.

'Afraid so. Blue bags for stings, and sticking plasters for the repair of ailing beach balls. I'm a bit of an old woman like that. Actually, I only carry blue bags because if I get stung I swell up rather like your beach ball over there – and I happened to have a box of plasters on me because I cut my foot yesterday, and I thought I might need a fresh one. And I don't know why I'm telling you this really, because it really is really rather boring.'

There was a short silence.

'I don't know whether you remember me,' Mattie finally said, to break the ensuing silence. 'I'm – I'm Mattie Eastcott.'

'Of course I remember you. Actually I was wondering if you remembered *me*. Last time I saw you – good Lord – last time I saw you properly, that is, it must have been before the war, I imagine. Some party or other, wasn't it?'

'I think it was Caroline Nesbitt's dance. You and your brother were there, you and Walter, and I danced with you both.'

'Yes, you did. But I seem to remember that you danced with Walter more.'

Mattie found herself just about to say, as a tease, *well who wouldn't?* but she stopped herself in time, before – as her mother was so fond of saying – the devil got her tongue. Instead she fell silent and just smiled, at which John smiled back and looked shyly away at little Max.

'Max is my son,' Mattie said at once, determined for some reason that this was something John should know as soon as possible. 'I had a baby during the war. But if you're a Bexhamite, you probably know that already.'

'As a matter of fact I didn't,' John replied, trying to keep the disappointment out of his voice. 'I didn't know you were married.'

'I'm not.'

John looked back at her sharply. 'I see. What – killed in the war was he? Your husband?'

'No. I'm not married now – and I wasn't married then, when I had Max. I've never been married.'

'I see. That's war for you, isn't it? Really? Good-looking little fellow, isn't he?'

John ruffled Max's hair.

'His father was very handsome,' Mattie replied, feeling her cheeks colouring. 'His name's Max – Max's that is. Not his father.'

'I like the name Max. It has a kind of heroic twang to it. Like an air ace – or a dashing sportsman. Max Eastcott scores a hundred at Lords. Max Eastcott wins Wimbledon. Max Eastcott wins the Open. I can just see it, can't you? The child is bound for the Hall of Fame, no doubt of it.'

Mattie smiled, throwing the ball back to Max who caught it and put it down, now more interested in the sandcastle he was busy building.

'Down for your summer holiday? You don't live in Bexham any more, do you, John?'

'No – not full time. I still come home for weekends. Sometimes.'

'Home, to Mum's cooking.'

'That's right. I'm down here on holiday now. Couldn't get out of London fast enough. Hot enough to fry eggs on the pavement, as the saying goes.'

'I can imagine,' Mattie replied. 'I couldn't stand this sort of heat in a city.'

'It's utterly appalling. It's suffocating. In fact it's so hot they're growing coconuts in Hyde Park.'

Mattie just stared back at him, refusing to laugh. John widened his own eyes at her in return, wondering why he found her so easy to tease. Then he remembered, because he remembered her. Those times in Bexham before the war felt so far off nowadays, halcyon days, full of laughter and eternal sunshine, days so distant that it now seemed to John that they might well have been from another century. Yet as he looked at Mathilda Eastcott standing before him it was as if the last time he had seen her had been only the day before, so fresh had her memory become. Today she was a picture with her brown hair cut fashionably short, her tanned body clothed in a bright blue all in one bathing suit over which she had thrown a pale yellow cotton shirt for protection and also perhaps, a little modesty; a vision from yesterday that had become a picture for today.

She had to be resolute as well, John realised, strong-minded and determined enough to bring up her illegitimate child in the small, inquisitive society that was Bexham. No helpless woman then, but a character strong enough to withstand the barbs and arrows that would inevitably be aimed her way.

'Mattie—' he began, suddenly nervous after a short silence. 'Mattie, I was wondering if—'

'Whom are you talking to out there?' a voice

suddenly boomed from the darkness of the beach hut as Lionel Eastcott awoke from his post-prandial snooze. 'Mattie? Who the devil you talking to out there, eh?'

Lionel appeared at the entrance to his beach hut, shading his eyes against the sun as he tried to make out the identity of the tall figure standing talking to his daughter.

'Good afternoon, sir,' John called back. 'John Tate. How are you?'

Lionel frowned as his brain clicked into operation trying to remember which exactly of the three Tate sons he actually was. Then, as he shook the hand being offered him, he remembered John was the eldest of them.

'Hello,' he said. 'Home for a holiday I imagine. Certainly got the weather.'

They exchanged pleasantries about the heat wave and the general situation while all the time Lionel watched John watching Mattie, and wondered uneasily at this sudden meeting outside the beach hut. Finally, John made to take his leave, only for Mattie to prevent him by suggesting that it might be a better idea for him to stay and have some tea with them. Lionel, inwardly reluctant, nevertheless agreed politely and disappeared back into the hut to light the Primus and prepare for the daily beach hut tea ceremony, while John stood outside the hut talking to Mattie and throwing a beach ball at Max.

'Odd how cooling tea is in hot weather,' John remarked as they sat in the shade of the hut finally drinking Lionel's precious brew, which had seemed to take hours to prepare.

'Law of opposites, I suppose,' Lionel announced, staring ahead of him as if talking to himself rather than John. 'To cool down drink hot tea; the law of opposites,' he repeated.

'Rather like the proper state of affairs between a man and a woman,' John heard himself saying, but he looked at Mr Eastcott, despite his not looking at him. 'My father's a great believer in the union of opposites – and at certain times it has seemed to me that there's none so opposite as my mother and father.'

'By opposite do you mean mettlesome, I wonder?' Lionel asked, slowly stirring his tea.

'Not at all, sir, far from it. It's just that women's characters are so completely different. What's more they really seem to enjoy begging to differ, which makes for what we all call a happy marriage, I suppose. Besides, women must have a greater say in things, don't you think, sir? It's only fair.'

Lionel paused for careful thought, wondering whether this was what had been amiss at times in his own marriage to Maude. As a general rule she had always held distinctly different points of view from his yet he himself hadn't enjoyed the experience at all. On the contrary, he hated being bested by a woman, particularly his wife. In return Maude had resorted to sighing deeply, clicking her tongue loudly and staring at him with narrowed eyes. All in all they had certainly not enjoyed begging to differ, and reflecting on this now Lionel realised, for perhaps the thousandth time, how wrong he'd been. Undoubtedly they would have enjoyed their life together a great deal more had he taken more time to listen to what his wife had to say. Not that it had all been dreary, far from it. Their times on the beach with Mattie had always been fun, which was probably why he still liked to keep the beach hut on, the memories keeping him more than warm, keeping him kicking on, still wanting to be up and about in the morning. That and little Max, the light of his life, the next generation coming leaping along with all the same uncertainties, all the same weaknesses, all the same joys to come.

'No doubt you're right,' he said, returning from his reverie. 'And if the suffragettes have their way, we'll see women doing everything men do. Probably even have a woman Prime Minister one day – though God forbid such a thing ever happens in my lifetime.'

'The union of opposites isn't a particularly contemporary idea, sir,' John offered, after a small pause. 'The Greeks were great believers in that sort of thing.'

'You don't say?' Lionel stared at him briefly before continuing. 'But then the Greeks were very peculiar people, young man, with some very peculiar ideas. Little wonder their civilisation tumbled – little wonder at all. They've always appealed to me as being nothing but a crowd of pansies.'

'I'd rather them than the Romans. I think Churchill might too – seeing how much the Greeks preferred jaw-jaw to war-war.'

'Nothing comes of trying to talk to people who want to make war. Best get in there early, and get it over with. That's why we're in the mess we're in now, because we failed to grasp the nettle ten years ago. In hesitation and rhetoric lies only the threat of defeat, with the threat of defeat finally we have recourse to war, and if you leave it too late you're ill prepared – and what was the result in this case? Much greater losses than we'd have sustained if we'd been ready and willing earlier. Your Greeks would have been no match for the Hun, while your Romans would have been. They'd have been in there first. Beauty is all very well but it's a luxury. What matters is a country being in a state of readiness.'

'Perhaps. But then again with the benefit of their great wisdom perhaps the Greeks might have foreseen a situation such as we faced long before it became dangerous and lanced the boil early. They had a pretty fine set of soldiers, too, you know. They weren't all pansies.'

Lionel frowned at John over his teacup and sniffed, making a sound more eloquent than words, a sound that said *I don't know what to say to that*, a tactic Mattie suddenly remembered that he had often employed against her poor mother. In return John just smiled. Realising that Mattie had been left out of the conversation for some time, he turned to her, intending to include her.

'Good cuppa, at just the right moment.' Lionel started to collect up his precious picnic things. 'Well, it's been very nice seeing you, young man.

Perhaps we'll see you down here on the beach some other day.'

'Every chance of that, sir,' John replied happily. 'Seeing I have the beach hut next door but one.'

Lionel smiled weakly as he realised that if the hot spell continued as indefinitely as was forecast, then there was indeed every chance of seeing John Tate on the beach not on *an*other day but on many days to come.

'Jolly good.'

Lionel clipped his picnic case tightly shut, picked up his panama and prepared to leave.

'Time to go home, Mattie. Collect up Max's things, if you would.'

'Why don't you go on ahead, Daddy? There's a wind getting up and it's a bit cooler now the tide's coming in. Max and I will come back later.'

Max piped up. 'Can we go shrimping, Mummy?'

'Why not. Good idea – we'll go to your favourite pool.'

'You know I don't like you two playing on the rocks when the tide's coming in,' Lionel grumbled. 'There have been far too many accidents.'

'I'll help keep a good eye on him, sir, if that's all right?'

Lionel saw the question was directed less at him than at Mattie. Sticking his empty pipe upside down in his mouth and giving a grunt of farewell, Lionel departed, reminding Mattie not only to lock up the beach hut, something she'd never yet forgotten to do, but also to be home in good time since he was playing bridge at Mrs Morrison's that evening.

Left alone, Mattie, John and Max fished happily for shrimps for the next hour, until finally the incoming tide defeated them and they retired back to the safety of the beach hut.

'Mind if I have a quick dip? Before I see you both home?' John enquired. 'I haven't really had my swim, and I'm a bit broiled.'

'I should think you are. In fact you've caught the sun terribly on your shoulders. After you've swum I'll rub some cream on – a girl in the village brought lots back from France. Well, smuggled it back actually.'

'That's terribly kind of you. Thanks.'

'Come on, Max – one last splash to cool off.'

While Mattie and Max splashed about in the breaking waves, John swam out to sea, so far that when Mattie looked for him of a sudden she found she couldn't see him. Filled with fear she shielded her eyes against the still brilliant sunshine that was dancing off the water. It was then that she saw him, probably two hundred yards out from the shore, treading water and waving at her. Now he was waving both hands at her, then all of a sudden he disappeared under the water. Mattie put both hands to her mouth and was about to look round for an able-bodied man whom she could call on for help when she saw John reappear, swimming strongly through the sparkling seas. On his way back to the shore he kept disappearing and reappearing in the sea like a seal or a dolphin, vanishing on one side of a wave only to surface on the other. Finally he rolled on his back and lazily backstroked his way in, riding the crest of the incoming waves, until he flopped down on the sand at Mattie's feet.

'That was great.'

'Not for us it wasn't.' Mattie retorted as she towelled off Max's little feet. 'I cannot imagine why you thought that might be funny. Swimming out to sea as far as that, and without saying a word.'

'Bit difficult when you're a couple of hundred yards from the shore.'

'You could have said you were going to swim out for miles, couldn't you? You could have said *don't worry, I'm a strong swimmer and I'm going to swim quite a long way out*. That's all.'

'Yes. Yes of course.' John got to his feet, doing his best to keep a straight face. 'It was very thoughtless. Please forgive me.'

Mattie glanced at him, more to see if he was being serious than anything, and when she saw how very serious his face was she gave him a small smile of pardon.

'You're forgiven. You're obviously a very strong swimmer.'

'Father insisted we all learned from the age of dot. Living by the sea, and all that. Spending as much time on and in the water as we all did as kids. My brothers and I were known as the Shelborne seals.'

'Next time you feel like swimming to France, just let me know first.'

'Of course.'

'Now let's get on home, shall we? Before you do something else to worry the life out of me.'

'Whatever you say, Miss Eastcott.' John gave a naval salute, in reply to which Mattie gave a reluctant smile.

If he had been by himself, he would have probably skipped home, probably even done a cartwheel, so ecstatic did he suddenly feel that Mattie had actually worried when he had swum so far out to sea. As it was he walked home slowly behind her and Max, carrying everything that he could, and thinking that if he had known what a wonder-filled day it was going to turn out to be he would have got up a whole lot earlier.

John and Mattie's meeting on the beach had a bad effect on Lionel. As he dressed preparatory to going to have dinner and play bridge at Gloria Bishop's house, he had plenty of time to reflect on a subject he had kept confined to the back of his mind, namely the possibility that one day his daughter would once again fall in love.

Next time round the new man in Mattie's life might well do the so-called decent thing and marry her, with the result that it would be Lionel who would be the abandoned one, abandoned not to live alone, but to live with just Ellen for company, and the thought of spending the rest of his life left to Ellen's tender mercies sent a very real shiver down his spine. Ellen was tolerable as long as she was a background figure, and the very presence of Mattie in his household ensured she remained so, since Mattie was extremely good at what she liked to call *managing Ellen*. Ellen needed managing, too, since she seemed to find it all but impossible to say anything kind or charming about anything or anyone as well as being excessively pessimistic. With Mattie around to keep her under control, Ellen's idiosyncrasies were almost tolerable, and as a result Lionel was able to live in comparative peace. Now, with John Tate hovering on the horizon, Lionel had to face the idea that with Mattie married, gone would be his best line of defence against the extremes of Ellen. The idea of having to tackle Ellen every morning was more than he could take. Such a prospect was truly daunting to an ageing widower.

Lionel suddenly groaned out loud, more at the thought of what the future could hold for him than over the fact that he had made a mess of his bow tie. As he began the meticulous process of retying it, he stopped and took a good look at himself in the mirror, an activity he had once enjoyed but now dreaded as he saw the obvious manifestations of his increasing age. *Yes,* he thought after a good moment of introspection, *I am still a reasonably good-looking man. I haven't run to fat, I still have most of my hair, and I haven't entirely lost my looks – but*. He took another look, lifting his chin to try to hide not only the beginning of double chins but also the dreaded turkey neck, as well as to alleviate the now quite pronounced jowls that were developing at the bottom of cheeks that had always been slightly pendulous. *But who is there whose fancy I might take? Gloria is obviously not interested in me, more's the pity because nowadays we might well have suited each other – but she is so taken with this American she's got staying that she doesn't spare me a second glance unless I make a wrong cue bid at the bridge table. Besides her, I cannot think of a single soul here in Bexham or its environs who might have even the slightest interest in me.*

He paused to make a final adjustment to his bow tie, cocking his head to one side and sighing deeply, knowing that since he hardly ever set foot outside Bexham there was precious little chance of his meeting anyone else who might be suitable for a man of his standing.

I'm afraid it looks like Ellen, he told his reflection gloomily. *I'm afraid it very much looks as though I am to be stuck with the dreaded Ellen as occasional company, until I am finally gathered to my maker. Dear Lord above us – perish the thought, and let this Waldo Astley leave Bexham before too long so that Gloria will notice me.*

With a last look at his now fully dressed and dapper self in his dressing glass, Lionel gave another sigh, packed his silver cigarette case into his inside pocket, checked the wad of notes in his front money pocket, and headed downstairs. He met Mattie on the stairs, happily with only his grandson in tow.

'The very man we were coming to see, all pink

and perfect, bathed and ready for bed,' Mattie told him. 'Come for our goodnight kiss.'

'Goodnight, Nipper,' Lionel said, picking up the little boy and smiling at him. 'Sorry we don't have time for a bedtime story tonight.'

'It's all right, Daddy,' Mattie reassured him. 'John's promised to read to him.'

'John?'

'John Tate? Remember? This afternoon?'

'John Tate?' Lionel repeated, trying to feign ignorance. 'What's he doing back here?'

'I asked him in for a drink. If that's all right.'

Lionel was about to tell her that it most certainly was not all right, what with him going out for the evening and Mattie being left all alone in the house, when he suddenly realised the absurdity of the situation. He couldn't possibly play the strong father, not with a daughter who not only was well and long over the age of consent, but had a five-year-old son whom he was standing holding in his arms. With a weak smile he gave Max a kiss on his cheek and handed him back to his mother.

'There's some gin in the dining room cabinet, and some whisky,' he told her. 'He'll probably prefer whisky.'

'Thanks.' Mattie smiled suddenly. 'Have a lovely evening, Daddy. And don't let Gloria hog the auction. It only makes you overbid. Remember what Mummy used to say – it's only a game, not a gunfight.'

'Try telling Gloria that – her and her pearl-handled pistols,' Lionel said gloomily, making his way downstairs, knowing all the same that Mattie was right.

Ever since Gloria had teamed up with Waldo Astley it seemed to Lionel that he had never suffered such a run of defeats at the bridge table, and it was precisely because he was letting the two of them get to him that he was overbidding, something which would normally be entirely against his nature. With that very much in mind he left the house, determined that this would be the evening when he would resume his former conservative style of play. No damn Yankee was consistently going to get the better of Lionel Eastcott at the bridge table, no sir. Tonight he would show them how to play bridge by the British book.

Unfortunately Waldo Astley was there before him, with, it would seem, his own plan well and truly already mapped out.

By the time John had finished reading *The Tale of the Flopsy Bunnies* he realised that Max was fast asleep, obviously knocked out by his exertions on the beach, not to mention the wonderful sea air. Carefully brushing a lock of hair from the child's eyes, he pulled his sheet tighter round him, and tiptoed downstairs to where Mattie had bottles and glasses ready for their drinks.

'Every time I return to Bexham, I seem to see it as if for the first time,' he confessed, after his first generous whisky. 'Everything anyone could ever want is in Bexham, wouldn't you say?'

'Bottoms up!' Mattie replied, raising her refilled

glass because she did not want to be drawn on the subject of Bexham.

'Cheerio.' There was a pause, before John continued. 'Isn't it strange that we've both lived in this village since we were small and yet we hardly know each other.'

'Exceptionally strange, but probably just as well. I was a beastly little girl, and I know from everything that was said about the Tate boys that you, on the other hand, were quite perfect.' Mattie pulled a mock straight face and John laughed.

Mattie stared at him for a second. After another day on the beach his town pallor was already being supplanted by a healthy colour. He looked boyish, and handsome, but most of all reassuringly kind.

The hurt that Mattie had known getting over Max's father's wartime exit from her life was, she thought, enough to have left its mark on her for ever. Handsome, older, American and married, following his call to duty, Max's father had left Mattie behind in London. Mattie who probably really was no more than his London fling, his pretty little driver, who had not unsurprisingly fallen in love with the handsome American general in the back seat. He might sometimes have given her a thought when he returned to the States, but, she reckoned, no more than a thought and he certainly never knew about Max.

Mattie Eastcott – pretty little driver I used to have in England during the war – I remember her. That's all she would be now, a recollection, a memory. Not the very real part of his life she had been during the terrible bombardment of London when together they had dodged the bombs and made passionate love in Michael's little apartment in Marble Arch. When they were together, it seemed as though that is how they would stay: as one, lying there in bed listening to the bombs whistling down from the skies above to explode in a neighbouring part of the city. They never talked about their future because they knew they had none, yet such was the intensity of their affair – a love affair that had sent them both to heaven in the middle of a terrible war that even though no mention was made of the impossibility of its enduring beyond the moment, while they were together both of them truly believed that they could never be apart. That was the nature of that sort of love, its very insecurities locking it into some mad non-existent security.

And then suddenly Michael had gone, forced to leave her as suddenly as he had come into her life, ordered back to the States to help lead the invasion of Europe, leaving Mattie alone and, as she'd already known, pregnant. For a long time Mattie thought she might never recover from either shock – that of Michael's sudden departure – although she had always known such a thing was inevitable – or from the reality of her pregnancy. She had wanted the baby, had never considered anything other than having the baby, but in her moments of solitude she had wondered how she would now cope with the aftermath of her passionate affair, or with the reality of bringing up a child alone. But now, as she sat talking to the sweet-natured and thoughtful John Tate, for the first time since the war had ended Mattie found herself thanking God that she hadn't married Michael, that he had gone home without any knowledge of the physical state in which he was leaving her, that he knew nothing about Max. Now John Tate had come into her life Michael had all of a sudden become the past, a figure quickly becoming dim and distant, a memory to be buried for ever in the mists of time, just as half of their London had been buried in the thick choking dust of the bombed-out buildings.

She felt so different now, sitting there with John. It seemed as they talked and laughed that they had always known each other, and yet the questions they asked were the questions strangers ask. In other words it was a classic case of two casual acquaintances, who had grown up in the same place at the same time, suddenly falling in love and finding themselves to be almost perfect strangers. They talked into the night, until long after the moon had taken the place of the summer sun, when just as suddenly as they had begun their long conversation, they fell to silence, not because they had nothing more to say to each other but because their emotions had finally overtaken their words.

'It's getting late. I think perhaps it's time I went home,' John said, after they had spent what seemed like an immeasurable amount of time staring into each other's eyes. They were still sitting well apart from each other, Mattie on the edge of the stone balustrade that fronted the terrace and John in a wooden armchair that was part of the garden furniture, yet such was the feeling of intimacy that hung in the summer night air that they might just as well have been lying in bed together.

'I really think I ought to go home,' John repeated, but still he made no move.

'You don't have to go,' Mattie said, trying to sound matter of fact but not succeeding at all. 'At least not on my account.'

'I think I ought to,' John insisted. 'I don't think really I should still be here when your father gets back. Might not quite be the done thing. Not as early on as this.'

'Early on?' Mattie laughed. 'I thought you said it was getting late.'

'I meant as early on in – in our – well. In our – I mean it is the first time we've been – I was about to say been out.' John grinned. 'But of course we haven't actually. We've rather stayed in I'd say, haven't we? Anyway – I think it might be better if I went now, before your father came back – came back and said – you know – *I say – what, you still here, John Tate? Isn't it high time you made some sort of tracks?*'

John's more than passable imitation of Mattie's father made her laugh, much to John's relief.

'I shouldn't worry,' Mattie assured him. 'When Daddy's out playing bridge at Mrs Morrison's he loses all trace of time. Him and his bridge. Honestly.'

'The first resort of the lonely, and last of the loveless,' John said, getting to his feet. 'Hope I don't become a hardened bridge player.'

'It's not the real reason you're going,' Mattie said quietly as she too stood up to move in front of John and look into his eyes. 'Is it?'

'Of course not,' John admitted after a moment. 'But it won't do any harm to make a good impression.'

'Very crafty.' Mattie laughed. 'A sort of Trojan horse really. It won't fool Daddy, don't you worry. Daddy is not that easily gulled.'

John grinned and was just about to lean forward to kiss Mattie when he thought better of it and wished her good night instead.

'You really are going then?'

'Yes. But it's been a wonderful evening.'

'I was forgetting what good boys you Tates were.'

'Absolutely, Mattie,' John agreed with a straight face. 'But I wouldn't count on it for too long, Miss Eastcott.'

John was long gone by the time Lionel arrived home in the best of spirits, having enjoyed a surprising triumph at the card table. He was loth to think his success was in any way due to Waldo Astley, yet as he now sat on the edge of his bed slowly undressing and reviewing the events of an evening that was turning out to be wholly remarkable, he had to admit that his good fortune had started the moment Waldo had taken charge.

'Mr Eastcott.' Waldo had greeted him on arrival, taking him aside at once. 'I have a little strategy, in which I am sure you might take an interest. I noted your card skills from day one, if I may say so, and am a little envious of your generally scrupulously correct bidding.'

'Generally being the operative word here, Mr Astley,' Lionel returned. 'Of late I've become somewhat quixotic. It's not like me to be sorry rather than safe.'

'No, I wouldn't consider you a safe player by any means, Mr Eastcott. It's just that you have been increasingly handicapped by the partners you have been allotted, and quite deliberately so.' Waldo glanced with an indicative smile in the direction of their hostess. 'Which brings me to my strategy, Mr Eastcott. Namely that tonight I shall be your partner. I think we shall make an excellent team. Now before you protest—' Waldo held up one beautifully manicured hand. 'The die is already cast. I have already had the matter agreed by Mrs Morrison, but for entirely different reasons from the ones I have given you. I'm afraid I made out that it was your partners who were suffering, rather than you.'

Waldo stopped and looked at Lionel, smiling a sideways smile at him as if challenging him to protest. To his surprise, Lionel did not feel affronted, so, having agreed their playing conventions, after a brief buffet supper they sat down to play.

This time there was no upping or downing of stakes since all rubbers now played in Gloria's increasingly select bridge school were set at the daunting level of one shilling a hundred, meaning that rash bidding and careless lay were felt very hard in the pocket.

But from the moment Waldo teamed up with Lionel the wind was in their sails. It was a marriage made in Contract Bridge heaven. Lionel's classical conservatism and intelligence allied to Waldo's brio and bravura made them a formidable team, so that by the end of a long evening of cards they got up to leave the table thirty pounds the richer. Lionel finally got his way about how to split the winnings, managing to persuade Waldo to take half despite Waldo's initial and very genuine reluctance to take any part of the winnings whatsoever.

'My dear fellow,' Waldo had said. 'It was purely your skill that saw us through tonight, and my pleasure has been to play as your partner. That is reward enough. But wasn't I right about us? Didn't I say we would make a splendid team?'

So Lionel had left Gloria's house well pleased, an emotion not shared by Gloria who he was convinced had actually slammed the door behind him. Or perhaps the slam had been directed at Waldo, since he had found himself being joined very shortly after his own departure by his partner at cards.

'Might I offer you a lift, Mr Eastcott?' Waldo had said genially, puffing away at his cigar, which was fast becoming a trademark. 'Do you have far to go, sir?'

'Very kind of you, but no, I don't have far to go. As you must surely realise by now, Mr Astley, there isn't a great deal of Bexham.'

'Perhaps not, my good fellow. But there is certainly quite a lot to it. Do you get up to town much? There's quite a game arranged for the beginning of October, and I would be delighted if you would consent to play as my partner again. I assure you we shall be well within our depth.'

Lionel had looked at his companion with a certain amount of interest tinged with a certain amount of trepidation. He had never in his life before played bridge for the sort of money he was now playing for, and which he could certainly not afford to lose. Yet he sensed that the offer Waldo Astley was making might well entail stakes considerably higher than one shilling a hundred.

'I know what you're thinking, Mr Eastcott, but don't you worry about it, sir.' Waldo had smiled. 'I shall underwrite the entire enterprise. You won't have to risk a penny of your own cash.'

'You must know so many players who are better than I – richer too.'

'I am asking you for your great card skills and those alone, my dear fellow. Don't look so worried – there are no catches, no bear traps.' Waldo grinned hugely, puffing on his cigar. 'Life is for the living, sir – and if you come along with me, we shall live it to the full.'

'Might I let you know?' Lionel had wondered. 'I'm getting a little long in the tooth to go rushing into things headlong.'

'Take just as long as you like, Mr Eastcott. Provided I have a "yes" by the end of the month. Goodnight to you, sir.'

Doffing his large-brimmed summer hat, Waldo had disappeared into the darkness.

So yes, Lionel considered, leaning back and slipping off his thin silk black socks. Yes, all in all, it had been a most interesting evening, as well as a most rewarding one – spoiled only by his growing concern over his daughter's relationship with young John Tate.

Mattie had still been up when Lionel had returned. He found her in the drawing room listening happily to her Bing Crosby records on the gramophone, sitting by the open French windows with her feet up on a footstool in front of her gazing happily up at the stars. Lionel didn't even have to ask how her evening went or how she was feeling. He simply poured himself a nightcap, wished her a gruff good night and took himself off to bed.

His daughter's happy frame of mind managed to take more than a little gilt off the night's gingerbread, jolting Lionel back to reality. On his way home he had been contentedly imagining himself sitting at the smartest of London card tables making a lot of money in partnership with his new colleague, only to open his front door and find himself being reminded of his current nagging fear, that of the possibility of losing the daughter he had counted on to take care of him in his old age in return for the way he had taken care of her in what he thought of as her time of extremis.

It wasn't a lot to ask for, he told himself as he continued to prepare himself for bed. He certainly wouldn't stop her from having any relationships with the opposite sex, but not anything serious and certainly not with anyone like young John Tate. The Tate boy would just take her for a ride, and even if he didn't, as soon as his parents found out they would have a blue fit. Their eldest boy having a liaison with a young woman with an illegitimate child? It would be quite out of the question, and Lionel doubted very much that young John Tate wasn't already aware of the inevitable opposition. So what would he do? He would just muck about with Mattie's affections. He would flatter her, make it look as though he was serious, have his wicked way with her and then vanish over the hills in a cloud of dust. In fact he probably had it all mapped out to fit nicely in with his seaside holiday.

Over my dead body, Lionel growled to himself as he turned his bed down. *Let him just try – because it will be over my dead body.*

Chapter Seven

'Don't you *sometimes* wonder what he's up to?' Meggie demanded of Judy, lighting up another cigarette before continuing to pace the drawing room of Cucklington House. 'He arrives here out of the blue, gets himself installed as the house guest of that perfectly dreadful Morrison woman, and imposes himself on the rest of us.' There was a short pause as Meggie stood drawing on her cigarette. 'I dare say he seduced the stupid woman, flattered her, made love to her, and is now in the process of scalping her at the bridge table.'

'Oh, really, Meggie,' Judy protested. 'Mrs Morrison may be a merry widow, but she's surely not the idiot you make her out to be. Anyway, from what I heard Mr Astley is the perfect gentleman, whatever you say.'

'That is such a contradiction in terms, Judy. An American? A perfect gentleman? Mr Astley is what most of his fellow countrymen are, Judy, believe me. He's a businessman, or an out and out adventurer. Look at what he's up to in the village! Buying up Peter Sykes's garage? Why? Why buy up some run-down, hole in the wall garage in a village that is practically falling down, never mind closing down? You can't tell me that's either a bargain or a good investment. Yet along comes Mr Waldo Astley and what happens? He buys the tumble-down garage and not only that – he starts to invest in it! Someone told me they're planning to build a showroom up there now. A *showroom*, Judy. In Peter Sykes's old garage? That's little more substantial than the privy that stands behind it? And that's not all – Mr Astley it seems has also taken a fancy to the Wiltons' house on the opposite side of the estuary. You know the house I mean. Markers – that lovely old house right on the edge of the water . . .' Meggie pointed across the estuary.

'I love Markers, I always have,' Judy said. 'We used to go to lovely parties there, before the war. Even my mother likes Markers. And you know what a house snob she is. She can't generally abide Edwardian houses, but she's managed to make Markers an exception.'

'It seems Mr Astley has decided that this is the house where he would like to live,' Meggie continued inexorably, as if Judy hadn't even spoken. 'So what does he do? He knocks on the door and proceeds to make the poor bewildered Wiltons an offer for their home that they could not possibly refuse without appearing to be utterly unreasonable. Never mind that they have nowhere to go – he just *buys* them out.'

'The Wiltons are hardly poor, Meggie, and of course they have somewhere to go,' Judy protested. 'They have three other houses – one in London, one in Scotland and another waterside house down in Cornwall. They were probably delighted to get rid of Markers. They've hardly been in Bexham since the war, and as they readily admit – according to my mother-in-law – they far prefer Cornwall.'

Meggie stared at her, rather crossly.

'Loopy told me,' Judy assured her. 'She knows them through the Yacht Club. In fact according to Loopy the Wiltons couldn't believe their luck when Mr Astley made the offer on the house. No-one wants to buy old houses at this moment, as you well know. They were actually delighted by the offer.'

'Even so,' Meggie said, lobbing her cigarette out of a window, the wind blown considerably out of her sails. 'It seems more than a little bit what you might call *patronising*.'

'Oh, for goodness' sake, Meggie!' Judy laughed. 'You'll be going on about the War Debt soon.'

But in spite of her laughter, Judy felt a little cross with Meggie. She very rarely got on a high horse and took unreasonable exception, yet to Judy that seemed to be exactly what she was doing now. That she was taking particular exception to Waldo Astley annoyed Judy even more because what no-one was ready to admit was that Mr Waldo Astley was bringing more than a little excitement to Bexham, and not just at the card tables.

'Why have you taken against Mr Astley?' she asked. 'Was it something at the party? Was he rude to you? I can't imagine him being rude to anyone, actually – and he certainly didn't get as drunk as everyone else, most of whom disgraced themselves.'

'I don't know what he was doing at my party, if you really want to know, Judy. I can't think why I invited him.'

'I know why – seeing what a shortage of young men there is in the village.'

'I'm not in the habit of asking people to my house whom I don't know. Particularly ne'er do wells such as Mr Waldo Astley. And what sort of name is that, for crying out loud? Waldo, for heaven's sake. I don't know where Americans come up with these names, I really don't.'

'Of course you could be taking such an exception to our Mr Astley for quite a different reason, couldn't you?' Judy suggested provocatively.

'Do tell,' Meggie said icily. 'I cannot wait to hear.'

'Because you've developed a bit of a pash.'

'A bit of a pash? A bit of a *pash*?' Meggie threw her head back and laughed.

'You're showing all the classic signs of falling,' Judy replied.

'And how would you know?' Meggie asked lightly and she lit a fresh cigarette. 'You're hardly an expert – and no, I most certainly do not have *a bit of a pash* on Mr Waldo Astley. In fact I'd say if anyone's developed a bit of a pash on our confidence trickster, I could well be looking at her.'

'Me?' Judy protested with a squeak, colouring

bright pink at the same time. 'How ridiculous! Me? Don't be absurd!'

'You've gone a jolly interesting colour.' Meggie grinned, triumphant.

'No I haven't,' Judy argued. 'All I think about Mr Astley is that I can't see what actual *wrong* he has done, at least not yet. Maybe he will prove to be a complete horror and take everyone for the most awful ride, but as things stand now I can't see how Bexham's become a worse place because of Mr Astley's generosity, misplaced or not.'

'Really?' Meggie stubbed out her cigarette. 'Let's just wait and see, shall we? Meantime I'll bet you my best new nightdress, not to mention my last pair of silk stockings, that Mr Astley's motives are not exactly altruistic. That whom he is out for is in fact Number One. You just wait and see.'

'I shall,' Judy said. 'And you're on.'

'On what, darling?'

'The bet, silly. I accept your wager.'

Judy smiled and extended one hand to cement the bet.

'The roof will last the summer all right,' Peter Sykes assured Waldo as they inspected Markers, Waldo's newly acquired Bexham home, together, while Rusty and Tam played happily in the garden. 'In fact, I don't think it's near as bad as everyone's making out. The trusses are perfectly sound – really the tiles more than anything. Where they got dislodged in the winter gales, and all the snow got in.'

'That could account for the main bedroom ceiling collapsing, I suppose,' Waldo agreed. 'Not to mention all those large damp patches.'

'Frankly, a few days spent refixing the tiles on the north side would sort out most of the troubles,' Peter went on. 'Probably have to do all the battens again because a lot of them have rotted – but that's no great problem, is it, Mr Astley?'

'Then let us go to it.' Waldo smiled, tipping his hat back from his face, and putting his hands in his pockets. 'If we muster a bit of extra labour I don't think we have the need for any permissions, do you? We're not going to be using any new materials.'

'We can repair from old, Mr Astley – that should do the trick all right.'

'Good. Now follow me, Peter – I want you to see something else. And call your wife and your little boy in too – this is something I think they too should see. It is, as they say, of interest.'

Waldo led the way through a pass door in the east wall of the house into a self-contained wing that contained two bedrooms and a bathroom upstairs, and a living room, kitchen-diner and cloakroom downstairs. The windows of the main bedroom and the living room below had a southern aspect looking out over the grounds at the back so there was abundant light.

'Room for a couple, dare I say – or even a young family.' Waldo turned round and looked at Peter and Rusty.

'Very nice too, Mr Astley,' Peter agreed. 'Make

a perfectly good home for a live-in couple.'

'Yes, perfectly good. I would agree, Peter. Plenty of room to swing an army of cats, I'd say.'

Rusty eyed what seemed to her to be unbelievably spacious accommodation, and tried to imagine what it would be like to live in such a place.

'Besides which, the Wiltons have been gracious enough to allow me to buy all the furnishings in here. They're not bad furnishings either, as furnishings go. That is to say, they're well made, and not soaking with mildew after all that rain in spring.' Waldo sat himself down on the sofa and bounced up and down as he tried it out. 'Yes, not bad at all,' he pronounced. 'Properly sprung, I'm happy to tell you. And note the electric wall fires in all the rooms. No more freezing in winter, eh?'

'Not for those that can afford such luxury,' Rusty agreed shyly, feeling slightly awkward as she always did in Mr Astley's company, since she had never quite got over his kindness the night he had found her in Mrs Morrison's house. 'Electricity doesn't come cheap, you know, Mr Astley.'

'I intend to throw the heating in as part and parcel.'

'Someone's going to be lucky then.'

Peter gave Rusty a brief look, raising his eyebrows as he did so.

Rusty frowned, wondering where all this was leading, yet finding herself oddly excited because she thought that Mr Astley could not possibly be cruel enough to lead a couple such as her and her husband up such a pretty garden path. There might well be more than an outside chance that this proposed enterprise would involve them.

'No,' Waldo continued. 'I wouldn't make anyone pay for their heating on top, not at today's prices.'

'Like I said, Mr Astley,' Peter replied, interrupting hastily. 'Excellent accommodation. Someone would fall lucky to have this.'

'And what is your wife's view?'

'I agree with my husband, Mr Astley. It's really lovely actually. Whoever lives here is going to be – well – very lucky.'

She bit her lip as if to stop herself saying too much, if she hadn't done so already. Since Peter had got his windfall from the sale of the Jaguar to Mr Astley, Rusty had begun imagining that her dream about the flat for rent above the greengrocer's shop in the High Street might now become a reality, but however well they did it up it would never measure up to accommodation like this. This was so much more spacious and light, being more like a small house in itself rather than a somewhat cramped set of rooms stuck above the smell and noise of a busy greengrocery. Of course, compared to how they were living now at her parents', any place of their own would be a blessing, but a place like this would be more than just a blessing, it would be heaven.

Even the ultra-conservative Peter, a man who worried night and morning about money and security, had finally allowed that with the huge profit he had made from the sale of the Jaguar to Mr Astley they could now seriously consider a move to an apartment such as they had found in the High Street. However, thanks to the expressions of foreboding and repeated forecasts of economic doom and gloom that had emanated from Mr Todd following the announcement of the Sykeses' proposed evacuation, Peter was now having second thoughts, believing his father-in-law's assertion that economic recovery was far from certain, and that if this was indeed so, rather than find themselves over their heads in debt, the best move to make was no move.

'If the government fail in steadying the ship,' Mr Todd had taken to warning the young marrieds, 'which in my opinion they have every chance of doing given the present economic climate, we could all find ourselves even worse off than we were before. So much the best thing to do with this windfall of yours is to save it for the famous rainy day, which as far as I'm concerned could be any day now.'

Mindful of her father's prognostications, Rusty decided that much the best thing was not to say another word, just in case of quite what she wasn't at all sure, but just in case. In order to make absolutely sure she wasn't going to be responsible for anything that might somehow jeopardise her little family's future, she took her little boy's hand and began to lead him towards the doors that opened on to the garden, only to find her way blocked by Waldo.

'Rusty? Is something the matter? You've said so little about this place, I am beginning to wonder whether you really like it one bit.'

'Sorry, Mr Astley.' Rusty looked mortified. The last thing she wanted to do was upset Mr Astley because ever since the night she had been discovered in Mrs Morrison's house she had always had it at the back of her mind that if Mr Astley should suddenly take against her, or if she did something stupid and upset him, he would tell on her, tell the whole of Bexham, and what small and relatively unimportant life she had would be well and truly ruined.

She felt a tug on her sleeve, and coming back to earth saw from Peter's frown that she had been quite carried away by her worries.

'As far as I can gather you said this would be an agreeable place to live, Rusty,' Waldo was saying, in a tone that suggested he was repeating himself. 'But what you did not say was whether or not *you* might find it agreeable.'

Now Rusty was completely at sea, able only to imagine that during her reverie she had missed some vital part of the conversation. Unable to respond sensibly, she found herself staring from one man to the other, from Peter to Mr Astley and then back to Peter.

'I don't think she heard a word you said, Mr Astley.' Peter smiled. 'Or else she didn't quite catch your drift.'

'Then we shall have to start over, Peter.' Waldo took an exaggeratedly deep breath, half closing his eyes while he prepared to begin again.

'Mr Astley is suggesting that we live here, Rusty,' Peter chimed in. 'That we have this quite splendid accommodation in return for working for him.'

The information he was about to repeat having been relayed for him, Waldo closed his eyes entirely and sighed.

While Rusty frowned.

'I don't understand, Peter,' she said. 'How could we live here – I mean how could we possibly work for him? For Mr Astley here? What about the garage?'

'The garage will not be affected, Rusty,' Waldo assured her. 'You could both live here, and Peter can still work at the garage – in fact I shall insist that he does, such is my investment in the place – the only condition being that you agree to be my housekeeper. Because I am most definitely going to need a cook-housekeeper. You're looking at a fellow who boils eggs in a kettle, and has absolutely no idea how to make toast let alone a pot roast.'

Rusty smiled shyly. Encouraged, Waldo continued.

'The idea, Rusty, would be for you to look after me and my house, while your husband looks after my business interest in his garage. You can both live here rent free, since you will be working for me, and I can keep a weather eye on your husband in case he decides to take the day off and spend it in bed rather than go and plough our joint furrow.

So what do you say? Seems a very sensible arrangement to me.'

Rusty wanted to agree, more than anything else in the world. But she knew it couldn't be. She knew it had to be a daydream or a cruel joke, because no-one had thought it through properly. No-one had considered the one thing – or more properly the one person – who could prevent this dream from becoming a reality. So she said nothing, hoping that as long as she remained silent on the subject the others might agree to it before they discovered the snag.

'It's Tam, isn't it?' Waldo asked out of the blue. 'You're worried about your little boy. You're wondering how could you manage with Tam running about all over the place – and not only that, you're worried about how I would cope. Well, don't. I don't see any difficulty with your boy, Rusty. If you were at home rather than here doing your housework, what would you do? You'd have Tam running about the place while you set about your duties, and anyway he'll be starting school soon. When he does, you'll have more time to yourself, and in the meantime he's old enough to play by himself in the garden here, which we shall make quite childproof. Lord above, when I was his age I spent most of my time playing by myself, being an only child just like young Tam. It's good training. Teaches you to be resourceful and independent.'

'Mr Astley's right, Rusty,' Peter put in quickly to prevent Rusty saying anything more. 'Besides being extremely generous. There's really nothing to stop us agreeing to this proposal.'

At the mention of Tam's being an only child Rusty had immediately retreated back inside her head. There was no reason now why Tam should have to go on being an only child. If the three of them moved into this wonderful accommodation there'd be plenty of space for a new baby. And what a wonderful place to bring up a child – large, light rooms that overlooked the estuary from the front and the wonderful big garden that ran out to the rear. Perhaps now she would be able to make up for the loss of her baby, for the death of little Jeannie, and if not bury at least assuage the hurt she still felt so keenly. No-one had understood – nor, it seemed to her, tried to understand – what the loss of a baby meant to its mother, to the person who had been carrying the tiny life around within her for nine long months. Having gone through two pregnancies Rusty now believed there was something mystical in that state, that being pregnant must be part of a mystery that had to do with the rhythms of the universe, the movement of the stars and the moon – that this all too common human condition lifted a woman into a state of spiritual consciousness that made others either envious or wilfully uninterested, so that perhaps it came as a strange relief when they found you had lost your baby, such were the primal and numinous sentiments having a baby encouraged. Once some people knew your mysterious odyssey had ended not in joy, but in tragedy, they felt this strange relief, and consequently were all too ready to come up with idiotic reasons why the baby had died.

Listening to the radio too much was one. According to one mean-minded old woman in the village this was the reason Rusty had lost Jeannie, because she'd been listening to too much *radio*. Radio waves killed babies, didn't she know that? Just as eating green potatoes might – or at the very least could – leave you with a deformed child, which again would be entirely your fault. But now if they lived in a place of their own, away from the know-alls, the wiseacres and the prophets of doom, Rusty might be able to have a beautiful brother or sister for Tam, and Peter and she could bring up a family in peace, health and happiness, which was a heart-stopping thought.

'Yes,' she announced suddenly, to the two men's surprise. 'I think you're right, Peter. I think we should accept Mr Astley's very kind offer.'

'You will?' Waldo's face lit up with a mix of genuine relief and pleasure. 'You really will?'

'I think so. Yes. I can't see any reason why not to.'

She wanted to ask him why. Very badly she wanted to ask why he was singling them out to help, why her and Peter and no-one else in the village. There were other deserving cases he could have considered, some perhaps even more deserving than their own, yet he had picked them, and Rusty was curious to know why. Yet she dared not ask just in case she might learn something that would quite spoil the pleasure and excitement of the moment, or, even worse, something that might jeopardise their whole future, that might be so dreadful that they would not be able to take up his offer after all and would be forced to go back, cap in hand to her mother and father, to live with them once more in abject misery. So of course she didn't ask the question. She simply affirmed her decision, thanked Mr Astley as best she could and stood aside while the two men talked through the fine details. And it was just as well she did. For by doing so, by remaining silent, she was able to see why Mr Astley was being so benevolent. It wasn't that he felt sorry for them, although she was sure that might well have been the reason for his Christian behaviour the night she was caught in Mrs Morrison's. No, it wasn't pity at all. This time Mr Astley's charity was motivated by something entirely different. Rusty saw it as she stood by watching the two men talk business, making plans and foreseeing their joint future. Mr Astley was doing what he was doing not because they were some deserving cause, but because, unlike her own father, Mr Waldo Astley believed in Peter.

With this realisation came an enormous surge of relief. Rusty didn't need any more pity. Rusty reckoned she had endured from certain people recently enough pity to keep her humble for the rest of her life. But now that Mr Waldo Astley believed in Peter enough not only to invest money in his enterprise and make him a business partner, but also to take on his once errant young wife as his housekeeper, she knew that she could rebuild her life, that she could pull her shoulders back to where they had been during the war, stand straight again and walk as tall as she should. She could look people in the eye again, rather than pass them by with her eyes on her feet, trying not to notice how they shook their heads sadly at her, at *that poor Rusty Sykes who lost her baby and used to wander round half demented clutching a dolly, poor soul.*

Once everything had been agreed in principle, Waldo drove off in his beautiful, newly acquired Jaguar, a car that seemed to Rusty to have been tailor made for him, so well did it go with his flamboyant personality and extraordinary good looks. Rusty watched him drive away down the causeway that led back to the estuary road, the hood of the car down, the wind blowing through his thick dark hair, his famous hat chucked onto the back seat, with the sunlight dancing off the brightly polished chrome, and felt a sudden pang. His dash and his style, and above all his huge appetite for life itself, reminded her of the late Davey Kinnersley, Meggie Gore-Stewart's great love, a passion Rusty had secretly shared. Rusty was reminded of how Mr Kinnersley would arrive back in Bexham aboard his yacht the Light Heart, standing at the helm with the wind off the sea blowing through his shock of fair hair, and how Rusty and her brothers would be there lined up on the quays to watch him, enthralled by his seemingly carefree manner, his style, and his dash. Rusty would have given anything she had to be seated in the passenger seat of the beautiful white sports car with Waldo Astley driving. To be driven away by him into the unknown would be like going to heaven. It would be like taking the open road leading only to unimaginable happiness and bliss.

Instead he had left her another taste of paradise, the right to live in the lovely wing of Markers, to be a resident in one of Bexham's most elegant of houses.

'Do you ever wonder why he's doing all this?' Peter asked Rusty as they wandered back, towards the centre of the village. 'Do you ever wonder why us?'

'Course I do, Peter,' Rusty replied. 'All the time. It worried me at first – but now I know why, I'm not the least bothered by it no more.' She picked up Tam and swung him onto her hip, walking along more jauntily than Peter had seen her move for weeks and months.

Peter hesitated then hurried on after her, as best he could with his gammy leg. 'Wait!' he called. 'Hey – wait for me, Rusty!'

She waited, smiling happily to herself while Tam played around her feet, chasing a big coloured butterfly that was fluttering over the wild flowers along the verge.

'What did you mean – now you know?' Peter demanded, once he had caught up. 'Now it doesn't bother you any more. Why *did* he pick us?'

'He didn't, Pete,' Rusty answered simply. 'He didn't pick us, love. He picked you.'

* * *

Waldo's next port of call was Shelborne. He had telephoned Loopy earlier that morning to ask if he might pay her a visit because he had some important news for her, and after the briefest of hesitations Loopy had agreed to see him at lunchtime over a glass of sherry.

'That's one of the few drinks which I don't enjoy, if you wouldn't mind,' Waldo said as he was offered a glass from a cut crystal decanter. 'Once when I was at Harvard we were very bored, as students perpetually seem to be, even though they have everything at their feet, and I overindulged in dry sherry. I thought it was a nothing drink – the kind of drink you gave to your maiden aunts at Thanksgiving and Christmas. Next thing I knew was waking up in hospital. I actually don't want a drink, to tell you the absolute truth. This is actually a business call, not a social one.'

As Loopy smiled and poured herself a tonic water, as much to mark time as anything else, Waldo stroked her little dog's head and noted with admiration how trim and lithe Loopy Tate's figure still was.

'Sure I can't tempt you to something?' she called from the other end of the room.

'I can be tempted to most things, Mrs Tate, believe me – but not sherry wine.'

'Yet so far no-one's tempted you into marriage.'

Loopy turned back to him and looked at him with a slight smile intended to hide her deliberate provocation. She was interested to note that for once Mr Waldo Astley was at a loss for words – but only temporarily.

'If I were to be married, Mrs Tate, I would not want to be tempted into it. I'd really want to be married for love.'

'How delightfully old-fashioned.'

'Being a Southerner – like yourself, Mrs Tate – I declare some of the oldest fashions still to be the best.'

'Then forgive my modern impertinence – and this is a lot to do with living in this country, particularly in these parts and at this time in our history – but given that there is generally a great shortage of eligible young men, I simply must know if you have ever been even close to what my husband calls the state of unholy deadlock.'

Waldo laughed and shook his head. 'I rather agree with whoever it was,' he replied. 'Voltaire, I think. That marriage is the only adventure open to the cowardly.'

'Thank you.'

'Present company excepted.'

'Would you count your parents as cowards too, Mr Astley?'

'Do you think you might call me by my first name? And I you by yours? After all, we are fellow Americans.'

'But of course, Waldo. So, to get back to what we were saying—'

'My parents were a classic case of two people marrying only to wake up the next morning and find they'd married someone else.'

'If I get your drift,' Loopy said, taking the easy chair opposite Waldo and indicating with an elegant hand that he should also sit down, 'if I catch your drift, you're saying your parents – what, didn't know each other that well before they married?'

'I have to wonder why you're so curious not only about my marital or non-marital status but also about my family, Loopy,' Waldo said with a smile, taking his cigar case from his inside pocket as he saw Loopy lighting herself a cigarette.

'I'm a naturally curious person,' Loopy replied, exhaling a long line of blue smoke. 'Particularly about people who interest me.'

'I'd far rather talk about your paintings than my parents, if it's all the same to you, Loopy,' Waldo replied as he cut the end of his cigar with a small silver implement. 'And I've changed my mind about a drink, if that's all right? No, don't move – I'll help myself if I may. Is that whisky in the other decanter?'

'I have a terrible feeling they're both sherry wine. One dry one sweet.'

'Then I'll have a pink gin, if it's all the same to you. I've developed a bit of a taste for this most English of drinks.'

Shaking a couple of drops of Angostura Bitters into a glass, Waldo swilled them round then tipped the remains into the fireplace before adding a generous amount of gin with a dash of water. As he prepared his drink Loopy smoked her cigarette, wondering privately why he seemed so unwilling to elaborate about his background. But she knew better than to ask further. She had been far too well brought up not to recognise the fine line between polite curiosity and impolite nosiness.

'I have some rather exciting news for you,' Waldo announced, as he sat back down once again. 'I find it so, at least, and I sincerely hope you do as well. Do you know of Richard Oliver, the art dealer?' Loopy nodded and frowned. 'Richard's a good friend of mine. His gallery did some business on behalf of my father some years ago in New York – or rather his late father who was running the Oliver Gallery then did, and his son and I became friends. Whenever Richard was in New York, he and I played a lot of cards together, drank a lot of whisky and listened to a lot of jazz. But to cut to the chase, I showed him the four small pictures you kindly allowed me to borrow and he demands to see more. I mean *demands*. He was suggesting he might come down here, to see the body of your work – but I sense that might prove difficult.'

'I don't see why,' Loopy protested. 'They're my paintings and surely I can show them to whomsoever I choose.'

'I seem to remember you had a certain amount of difficulty showing them to me.'

'This is different. This is business.'

'Excellent. I'm glad to hear such determination,' Waldo replied. 'Now of course you know what this could mean? If Richard gives you an exhibition, your whole life could change – and that might not be quite as convenient as it sounds.'

Waldo smiled at Loopy but she just nodded, anxious for him to proceed.

'You might become not just successful, but famous. And because of that, you might want to think about it some. It opens up all kinds of maybes. So you might want to think about it, because once you've opened Pandora's box, afterwards is way too late.'

'I shan't become famous, don't worry. If my work is any good I might become moderately well known, but I shall eschew fame. It really would not suit me. But as for something changing my life, why not?' Loopy smiled and shrugged. 'Look – I've lived my whole adult life at the disposal of other people – to me the most important people in the world, namely my family – waiting on them, worrying over them, thinking only of them, but that part of my life is over now. So I really have no intention of remaining at their beck and call for what's left. It wouldn't be good for them, and it would be even worse for me. And even if the absurd did happen and I became monumentally famous, it's a little late for me to have my head turned. I'm getting too old for that.'

'OK! That's settled then,' Waldo said cheerily, draining his glass and standing up. 'No more talk of you getting spoiled by the trappings of fame – we shall stick strictly to business. Richard is genuinely very excited by your work, just on the evidence of those four small pictures. He feels you have an original talent, and after all that is what art is all about – producing something unique and original. But I have to say here, I can't understand why none of them hang in the house. I do find that odd.'

'Let's just say Hugh finds my colours too bright for his taste.'

'Don't you think that's something that husbands do? And fathers as well? I sometimes think it's because they feel it distracts from them. Why do so many male birds have brighter feathers than female birds? So that the males can strut and show off, and no-one will even notice the poor old drab female behind them. The male sex are born show-offs, Loopy, believe me. Nature has given us a love for centre stage and we don't like relinquishing it.'

'Does the same thing go for you, Waldo? Do you like to strut?'

'You are looking at the prime example, my dear Mrs Tate, believe me.'

'Good. Then I insist you stay to luncheon and expound your theory some more, so that I shall be able the better to handle my husband on his return. Come on, Beanie,' she called to her little dog. 'We shall eat al fresco.'

They sat out on the terrace eating a sardine salad dressed with a strange mayonnaise Gwen had invented during the war and to which she had become oddly addicted, but since both Loopy and Waldo were far more interested in their conversation the state of the salad dressing was by the by.

What was not by the by was that it seemed that Loopy really was going to be invited to have an exhibition at a famous London West End gallery.

But however much Waldo kept insisting it was true, the more he did so the more impossible the notion seemed, particularly since if the show was in any way successful it very well might establish Loopy as a professional artist. As she listened to Waldo expound, Loopy couldn't help imagining the reaction of her family and friends, and wondering what on earth they would make of it. Not even her children had ever bothered to comment on their mother's 'daubs'. As far as they were concerned Loopy's paintings were just the reason she was often late for dinner, or was forever catching them up when they went out for a walk on the Downs. Not one of them had ever considered her paintings might possibly have some merit.

'So what's the next step, Waldo?' Loopy enquired as he prepared to take his leave of her. 'Will young Mr Oliver really come to visit?'

'I really think he will,' Waldo replied. 'Unlike a lot of gallery owners, Dick likes to come to artists' studios himself. Doesn't send a subordinate; he comes in person. That way he gets a much better feel for their work. He'll go anywhere in search of fine art, sometimes to the most outlandish places. He really is very dedicated.'

Picking up the large straw panama hat that he now always wore during the heat of the day in place of his slouch hat, Waldo smiled in farewell and made for the door.

'I wonder why,' Loopy said quietly, as she opened the front door for her guest.

'I just told you, Loopy. Because Dick really is one dedicated fellow.'

'I meant why me? I meant I was wondering why you have spent all this time and bother on me. Is this something you do? Find artists for your friend Richard? Or is there some other reason you're taking all this trouble?'

Waldo looked at her carefully, then at his hat, on whose perfectly clean brim he seemed suddenly to find some small traces of lint which he carefully picked off. Finally he put his hat in his other hand, preparatory to donning it, and cocked his head to one side as he looked back at the beautiful woman standing before him.

'No, Mrs Tate,' he said slowly. 'No, this is not something I do. This isn't something I do at all. In fact this is something I have never done before. So why you? Why not you? Why not ask yourself that? Why *not* you?'

With an enigmatic look, Waldo gave a smile and a small bow before donning his hat and departing, leaving Loopy with an almost irresistible urge to pull an infuriated face behind his back. Instead she went back inside, changed her dress – for reasons she knew not – dotted some scent on the inside of each wrist and in the centre of her neck and suddenly smiled happily at her image in her dressing glass.

'I am going to be famous,' she told herself. 'I am going to become a painter of some renown.'

She had already decided to take a walk down by the estuary and was about to put Beanie on his lead when she thought better of it, remembering how the little dog had suffered in the heat the last time she took him out in the afternoon. So with another pat to his fond little head she left him in the cool of the kitchen and took herself out the back door.

She had meant to take her sketchpad with her, but the heat had become so oppressive that she decided if she sat somewhere to draw she would simply frazzle in temperatures that must by now be well in the nineties. So armed only and very sensibly with her parasol she was wandering along the path beside the water in the direction of the quays, meaning to stop and sit for a while on the jetty when she got there before returning home via the lane that ran past the church and back round the top of the village, when suddenly she saw her husband's car.

At least at first sight she thought she saw the big black Humber, before realising she could not possibly have done so because Hugh was still in London and not returning as always until Friday evening. So cupping a hand over her eyes to protect them from the sun into which she was looking, she stared across the estuary again to make sure she was right and that she was in fact not seeing things.

There was a car and the car was large and black, of that there was no mistake. It was driving west, on the road on the far side of the estuary, heading for the abandoned boatyard on the promontory that lay beyond Markers, Waldo's new house. From such a distance it was impossible for Loopy to clearly identify the vehicle, yet something told her it was their car, not just because it was the only one of its sort in the neighbourhood, because such a car might easily belong to some incoming stranger or visitor, but because of the way it was being driven. Why she could identify their car for such an absurd reason Loopy had absolutely no idea, yet she was convinced enough to hurry to the quay and to pay one of the boatmen to ferry her across the stretch of water which was now at high tide.

As to what she was going to do once she got to the other side Loopy had no real idea, other than to have it confirmed or denied that the big black Humber was their car or not. If it was, she might ask Hugh what in hell he was doing home – and then again, remembering her husband's line of business, she might *not*. But if she possibly could she would find out what exactly Hugh might be up to here, in his own backyard, in the middle of the week.

In line with her instructions, Jed the boatman dropped her well east of the derelict boatyard so that she could not be seen disembarking. Loopy instructed him not to wait for her, so Jed turned the motor dinghy about, to return to the quays. Ahead of her, Loopy could see the big black car parked with its back to her next to the boat shed, to one side of the jetty that ran out from the front of the yard beside the slipway. Unfortunately whoever the driver was had parked the car behind the upturned hull of an old boat so that the number plate was obscured from Loopy's view. In order to get close enough to identify the vehicle Loopy would have to get to the back wall of the boat shed, from where she would be able to get the clearest of views. Unfortunately to do so she would have to run the risk of being spotted by the driver in his rear view mirror, should he chance to look into it. But, as Loopy realised, that was a chance she would have to take, and if the driver was her husband she would have to somehow convince him either then, or later, that she was out for a stroll, even though she was the wrong side of the estuary, and with the tide still running high a good three miles from their front door.

It was a fifty-fifty shot and Loopy took it, gambling that there was more than one person in the car. To her way of thinking there had to be, because it seemed unreasonable to believe that if a solo driver wanted to feast his eyes on a beautiful view, some broken old boats and rusting up machinery would hardly be his choice.

So as quickly and as quietly and as circuitously as she could Loopy made her way to the cover of the boat shed, from where she could observe the car and its occupants.

She was right – there was more than one person in the car. There were two. On the passenger side, Loopy could clearly see a woman's elbow resting on the sill of the wound down front window while the fingers of one red-nailed hand drummed a slow tattoo idly on the roof. Beyond the woman, who had her head turned away from her, she could also see the driver, an outline she recognised at once as belonging to her husband Hugh, whose own elbow was also resting on the sill of his open window as he talked to his companion.

Despite being well hidden from the car, Loopy pulled back further into the shadows. What exactly she was going to do now she wasn't at all sure, except perhaps just look and listen, which was what she did.

It was a very quiet spot, the nearest building being Markers which stood a good half-mile down the lane. Apart from the mournful hoot of a distant ship somewhere out in the Channel, the only noise was from the run of the tide, but it was a windless day and the sea was running calm. So from her hiding place Loopy could hear what was being said almost too well.

'But I need you,' Hugh was saying.

'Of course you don't,' came the reply. 'I don't think you really need me so much as I happen to be readily available. And, most important of all, I'm still single – but you needn't start trying that line on me because it won't wash. I'm not that wet behind the ears any more. Not like before, not like I used to be. I really have no desire to play the heroine any more. Germany was enough.'

She had known from the very first words the woman had uttered who she was – but even if she hadn't that last phrase would have revealed her identity. Meggie Gore-Stewart.

Then she heard her husband laugh, laughing his delighted flirtatious laugh, the laugh that still entranced his wife.

'Your problem,' Hugh said, his voice carrying to Loopy all too clearly, 'your problem is that like so many members of your sex since the war, you've lost any idea of your worth – of your value. You'd rather people saw you as a social butterfly now than as the person you really are. But I know you better than that. I know the real you. And however much you protest, you'll come round to saying yes in the end.'

'Do you know what you have, Hugh Tate? A nerve. You really do have a nerve thinking that all you have to do is smile and lift your little finger and I'll come running back to you. As if I was like a wireless set you just turn on and find it's still playing exactly the same programme as it was the last time you listened to it. Not me, Hugh. I'm playing something quite different now, and I'm very much afraid you are just not part of my programme any more. Got it? I sincerely hope so.'

'You don't mean that.'

'Yes I do – and stop looking as if it's the end of the world. Because it ain't.'

'You really have no idea how much I need you. Really, Meggie.'

'Then you're just going to have to go on needing. Now can we go home, please? I have things to do.'

Hugh went to say something but he was cut short by his passenger's suffering a sudden coughing fit.

'You all right?' Loopy heard him asking anxiously.

'Course I'm not bloody well all right!' came the

angry reply. 'I'm half choking to death – can't you hear!'

'That really is a dreadful cough,' Hugh said, as the fit eased.

'It was that damned winter,' Meggie spluttered. 'I got the worst cold, and I've never been able to get rid of the cough since.'

'Nothing to do with cigarettes, of course.'

'If it was, that's got nothing to do with you,' Meggie replied shortly. 'Now take me home or I'll get out and swim, I really will.'

Loopy waited until the car was completely out of sight before taking another breath, let alone moving. While she waited, she wondered what on earth was the true import of the conversation she had just overheard. Knowing Hugh and his security work it could be anything – but then knowing men it could equally well be something else altogether.

Meggie and Hugh? It seemed the most unlikely of liaisons. As a rule Hugh, while admiring Meggie's courage, had only ever joked about her. It was always 'Meggie-Long-Legs' or 'Meggie-Won't-Settle'. Loopy had always stood up for Meggie whom she very much liked as well as admired, particularly after her heroic actions during the war. Yet Loopy also knew that according to Judy, Meggie could be notoriously unreliable or even, dare she think it, unstable, given to sudden fancies which Judy described as Meggie's *whims*.

So there might be good reason to suppose that

her very own husband had been the subject of one of Miss Gore-Stewart's *whims*.

Once the car and its occupants were well out of her range, Loopy began her long walk home. She made no attempt to take any short cuts this time round. She had far too much to think about.

Chapter Eight

The fact that Lionel Eastcott was apparently stepping right out of character by accepting Waldo's invitation to join him in London for a schedule of high stake and standard bridge games was of far less interest to Bexham society than the question of *quite was what going on*. There was an air of curious disquiet abroad, as if the little seaside port was a pond whose normally tranquil surface had been disturbed by a succession of stones being skimmed across it as their American visitor – who it seemed must now be recognised as having semi-residential status – continued his game of ducks and drakes with their normally placid existences. So although Lionel's possible temptation was certainly of interest to those who frequented the local bridge tables, it was small beer compared to the rumours and whispers about much more important matters, most particularly the precise nature of the business Mr Waldo Astley was undertaking in Bexham.

There were all sorts of rumours flying about, the first and most obvious being that Waldo had been Gloria Morrison's lover but had left her bed for that of another, someone who could possibly be Loopy Tate who was going around behaving really rather strangely. Then there was a very positive notion that Meggie Gore-Stewart was having a torrid affair with a married man, the no-surprise being that the most likely candidate had to be Judy Tate's husband Walter who had also been seen acting in uncharacteristic fashion (this to include going out regularly on weekend walks all by himself). The ostensible reason for the affair was that Meggie and Walter had always been in love – at least Meggie Gore-Stewart had always been in love with Walter Tate and everyone knew what a man-eater Miss Gore-Stewart was. Then there was the tale that Peter Sykes was trading in cars that his father had stolen during the war and had kept hidden away ever since, the enterprise now given a cloak of respectability by the investment of Waldo Astley who was also deeply involved, an added refinement being that some of the cars were American and contained guns being run for the hoodlums back in Mr Astley's home country. Then some let it be known that the father of Mathilda Eastcott's illegitimate child was not some GI Johnny as first supposed but actually John Tate, and that Miss Eastcott was finally blackmailing him into marrying her, while her father apparently had lost so much at the card tables that Waldo Astley had paid off his gambling debts in return for some sort of Faustian deal that involved cheating at high-stake card games.

For the few good people in Bexham who

preferred the truth to these Chinese whispers, it was as obvious as ever that the knowledge gleaned under the chestnut tree on the village green was about as accurate as the Reverend David Anderson's spin bowling during the village cricket match.

But not so the gossipmongers. And such is the power of gossip that the rumour spreaders were able quite to change the atmosphere of Bexham, an alteration that they all too willingly ascribed to the arrival of Mr Waldo Astley in their midst. Happily the incomer appeared to be totally oblivious of the sensation he was creating, continuing to conduct himself in a way that was, on the surface at any rate, totally without reproach. He greeted everyone with a smile, a touch of his hat or a wave of his hand as he wandered blithely through the streets on his way to or from the Three Tuns, or drove around the lanes and the immediate vicinity in his new Jaguar. His constant good humour might have given the lie to at least some of the rumours, yet the fact remained: everyone refused to take him at his face value.

For a short while it seemed even Loopy might have begun to doubt his integrity, particularly after witnessing what she now suspected to be collusion between her husband and her new found friend, although she was unable to ascribe such a liaison to any reasonable motive.

'I have to ask you something,' she said to Waldo one Friday morning when he had telephoned her about her forthcoming art exhibition. 'You don't have to answer if you don't want to – but I believe I saw my husband leaving your house last Saturday, early evening.'

'You saw this from where, Loopy?' Waldo enquired politely. 'Were you out sailing perhaps?'

'No, no I wasn't,' Loopy said quickly, now well and truly annoyed with herself for saying something without thinking it properly through. She knew what Waldo was going to say next, and sure enough he did.

'The only way you could have seen what you say you saw would be from your house, right? Through field glasses?'

'I was watching some birds on the water. Some egrets I think they were.'

'And you happened to put your glasses up just as Hugh was leaving my house. That's OK – I don't have anything to hide.'

'My husband might have. He never mentioned it.'

'Chaps' stuff, as your husband would say. Men's palaver.'

Seeing the door from the drawing room beginning to open and knowing that Gwen was about to emerge and listen in to her side of the conversation, Loopy walked into the porch still holding the telephone and firmly shut the door between.

'Your husband called because he said he needed to talk to me,' she heard Waldo continuing. 'Actually not quite true. He needed *someone* to talk to, would be a whole lot more accurate, and he was passing my house, he saw me out on the stoop as it were – and he stopped by.'

'You hardly know each other.'

'Confucius say – better the ear of a stranger.'

'Can I ask what it was about?'

'If I may make so bold, you should ask your husband. I'm bound by convention not to tell you any more. I really think this is something you must discuss with Hugh.'

Waldo excused himself with his usual perfect manners, at the same time explaining that the reason he had called was to tell her he had to hurry off up to London to see Richard Oliver on her behalf and as soon as their meeting had been concluded he would telephone her again.

Puzzled by their enigmatic exchange mid-conversation, Loopy lit a cigarette and returned to the conservatory, which was once again serving as her fine-weather studio. She had made no mention to Hugh of his mysterious midweek appearance at the deserted boatyard, simply because she saw no way to bring the matter up naturally. Her husband had arrived home as usual at his appointed time on Friday evening as if there were nothing untoward. He behaved as he always did nowadays when he got home – pouring himself a couple of large drinks, the first of which he drank far too quickly, before bolting his dinner and then taking himself off to the Yacht Club to meet friends and enjoy a few more drinks. But Loopy knew in her heart that even if the opportunity had arisen to ask Hugh what had been the purpose of his apparently mysterious meeting she would not have taken it for fear of finding out an unpalatable truth. And now, as darkness fell outside, and the landscape she had been painting slowly disappeared into the night, she found herself hoping against hope that Hugh's meetings might indeed be just part of his work. After all, Meggie had worked for SOE during the war, and Loopy thought it was perfectly possible that Hugh might have been trying to re-recruit her, which would make sense of the conversation she had overheard. But Meggie was also an extremely attractive young woman, perhaps made even more attractive by her courageous underground exploits, and, as Loopy knew too well, younger, prettier, and particularly singular women always posed a threat to any marriage, however stable it had previously been.

Having washed and dried her paintbrushes she covered her canvas and took herself inside for a drink. As she sat sipping her whisky and smoking a chain of Du Maurier cigarettes, she tried to put all suspicion out of her head, but finally found it impossible. The trouble was that anyone engaged in undercover work for the government was more or less untouchable. Other than your superiors, no-one had the right to know what you were doing and when and why, so as Loopy very soon concluded security work was surely the greatest cover for having an affair ever invented.

She finished her drink, stubbed out her cigarette and went out onto the terrace for a breath of the fresh night air. She stood gazing up at a star-filled sky and came to her conclusion, namely that she would believe that Hugh was innocent until proved otherwise. She must and would believe that whatever he was doing was for the best reasons, and above all she would always believe that he loved her as much as she loved him. To do otherwise would not only be unfair, it might well destroy their happiness.

Hugh was late driving down from London that evening, and by the time he got in it was midnight and Loopy was fast asleep in bed. He went straight to his dressing room rather than disturb Loopy, who must have guessed that he would, because on his pillow he found a handwritten note. It simply said *I love you – as always – Night and Day*.

He sat slowly on the edge of his bed with the note in his hand, staring at it.

I love you – as always – Night and Day.

Then screwing the scrap of paper slowly up he lay back on the bed and stared at the ceiling, worrying yet again that the figure he thought he had caught a fleeting glimpse of ten days ago, half hidden in the shadows behind the old boat shed, might possibly have been his wife.

Waldo was hardly able to contain his delight when he arrived at Shelborne the following Wednesday with news from London. It seemed that although Richard Oliver had been called away on business to New York and thus could not make his planned personal visit to see Loopy's work he was nevertheless perfectly happy to take Waldo's word for the quality of the rest of her portfolio and so to let him go ahead and make all the arrangements for the exhibition in his absence. Moreover there was a week that had suddenly become free in October so Waldo had taken the liberty of pencilling Loopy's exhibition in for that date.

Such unexpected news at once threw Loopy into a state of panic and she began to hurry round her conservatory studio going through the paintings Waldo and she had selected for the show, now rejecting half of them and worrying aloud about the remaining half.

'None of these are any damned good, let's face it!' she exclaimed, putting one small canvas after another to one side under a notice she had long since pinned to the wall that said *Rejected*. 'In fact when you take a good look, it is all just amateur rubbish.'

Waldo laughed, retrieved the rejected paintings and put them all back under the other pencilled notice that read *Selected*. From that moment neither of them took any further notice of the other. Loopy continued to move her paintings from one set to another while Waldo quietly returned them to their rightful stack.

'My dear Loopy,' he finally sighed, taking her by the hand and leading her outside into the garden and well away from her paintings. 'We have to talk. Come out onto the terrace and let's sit down, shall we?'

Outside they sat at the small iron table and Waldo helped them both to some more coffee from the Thermos flask that had been keeping it warm. Loopy lit a cigarette and sat back with her eyes closed, exhaling her first deep draw. Waldo smiled to himself, shook his head, carefully cut the end of a fresh cigar and slowly lit it, examining the end to make sure he had done a proper job before sticking it in the side of his mouth and drawing thoughtfully on it.

'I want you to know that I understand how you feel at this moment,' he said after several long, pensive puffs. 'I really do, but even so – in spite of my great and infinite compassion and understanding – *you* are going to have to take hold of yourself and not give in to your feelings, which I imagine you would describe as doubts and anxieties.'

'You can't possibly know how I feel,' Loopy replied. 'No-one but an artist can possibly understand how exposed one feels when people look at your work – or worse, don't look at it. The thought of it makes me feel as if I shall be walking around the gallery without a stitch of clothing on. No, I'm sorry, Waldo, but you really can have no idea how exposed the thought of an exhibition makes one feel.'

'I'm sure that's the very reason they call them exhibitions.'

'Can't you just be serious for one moment, please? I am having severe doubts as to whether or not I am up to facing a roomful of total strangers come to stare at my infamous *daubs* and then laughing away behind their fans.'

'Behind their *what*?' Waldo laughed.

'Their hands! I meant their hands,' Loopy

corrected herself, not finding it at all amusing. 'I really am fast coming to the conclusion that this sort of thing just – just is not me. OK?'

'No. No, it most certainly is not OK, Loopy,' Waldo replied gruffly, looking once more at the end of his cigar to make sure it was still alight. 'A lot of people are going to a lot of trouble on your behalf and they are doing so because they believe in you. In your talent. So I do not consider that it is perfectly OK for you suddenly to get cold feet. Or maybe you consider perhaps that a public exhibition of your works is not the sort of thing in which someone like you should partake?'

'I never said that! I never said such a thing!'

'I really am fast coming to the conclusion that this sort of thing just is not me?' Waldo quoted back at her.

'I meant I'm not sure I can measure up to it.'

'How do you know until you try?'

'Sure. And you know all about putting your head above the parapet, right?'

Loopy glared at him angrily and tapped the end of her cigarette so hard on the edge of the ashtray she knocked off the end. Even more angrily she ground out the now wasted smoke and got up to walk away out into the garden. Waldo let her go at first, carefully relighting his cigar, then wandered off after her, catching up with her as she reached the wall at the end of the lawns that directly overlooked the estuary.

'As a matter of academic interest you have cleared the matter with Hugh, I take it?' he asked her as she stood with her back deliberately to him. 'We don't want this coming out of the blue.'

'It doesn't really matter whether I have or not since I won't be going through with it,' Loopy answered, still well and truly on her high horse. 'So you can put that in your pipe and smoke it. Or your silly cigar rather.'

'This isn't really about whether or not this is the sort of thing in which you should partake,' Waldo said, coming to stand beside her. 'This is about something else altogether. Something that has upset you – upset you considerably, I would say.'

Loopy turned to glance at him in surprise, before turning away again. 'I want to know what Hugh was doing at your house,' she said quietly, and immediately regretted the question. 'I know – I know you said I should ask Hugh—'

'And so you should.'

'Is there something I don't know?

'Ask Hugh,' Waldo insisted. 'If you don't, your imagination will get the better of you.'

'I can't agree to this exhibition until I find out.'

'That's entirely your decision.'

Loopy remained standing with her back half turned to him.

'I saw Hugh with another woman,' she said in a low voice. 'I saw him with Meggie Gore-Stewart. The same afternoon you called on me, two weeks ago. I went for a walk, thought I saw his car, when he was meant to be in London still, and went after it. He was having some sort of tryst with Meggie. I mean I didn't hear everything – but I heard enough to make me think that – that something was going on between them.'

'As I said, Loopy,' Waldo said gently, carefully stubbing his cigar out on the wall and blowing the ash off into the wind. 'This is something you should discuss with Hugh. And now I really should go.'

Loopy said nothing to stop him, instead walking to the nearest flowerbed where she drew a light pink rose to her, inhaling its fragrance before letting the flower go to stare out across the sea.

'I was convinced Hugh was having an affair,' she said, as Waldo was on the point of leaving. 'It's a pretty dismal feeling, I assure you. To imagine the person you love is being unfaithful to you. That he's been telling you lies, carrying on behind your back.'

'I know.'

'How could you?'

'How could I what? How could I know how it feels? Because I can imagine it, Loopy. I've had my share of associations with the opposite sex, and not all of them have been sleigh rides. I know what it's like to be cheated on.'

'Not within a marriage.'

'Imagination is a powerful tool, Loopy. Besides, I have the example of my parents.'

'Your parents.'

'I think we have more pressing things to discuss than my family life.'

'I thought you were going. It looked as though you were leaving.'

'I thought I was going, too.'

'Hugh wouldn't approve of my having an exhibition,' Loopy said decisively, as if to close the matter.

'It might have been easier all round if you'd asked him first,' Waldo retorted. 'Would have saved a lot of people a lot of work.' He stared out over the stretch of water that lay between the two long fingers of land. The sea was looking particularly beautiful at that moment, with the sunlight glancing off its restless activity, neither white nor grey, just a stretch of shimmering blue and silver.

'The thing about life, Loopy, is that it's a bit like the sea. It's always changing, shifting. Life never stands still. If we understand that, then we can make of it some of each of our own lives. We mustn't stand still, just accept the way we are – or rather the way we think we are. We must rise to each and every challenge, the way the tides respond to the pull of the moon. If we don't, we drown. We drown in our own lives. We drown under waves of ennui and apathy and – worst of all – of fear. Maybe you should have an exhibition, and maybe you shouldn't. But you'll never know the answer if you don't pick up the challenge. This is an opportunity to find out something more about yourself, more about the Loopy Tate I've been hearing so much of lately – and who knows what you might find on that voyage of discovery? I'm not saying it's going to be easy – it might be sheer hell for all we know – and there again it might not. It might do what you were talking about the other day – before you let doubt creep into your mind. It might make sense of the rest of your life. And if it doesn't, what will you have lost? You'll have exposed yourself to a few derogatory comments maybe. Maybe you'll find out that you and I were wrong and that you're nothing more than a very good amateur painter – and if that's the sole sum of the bad parts, you'll soon recover. That won't kill you. And if you have to live with Hugh's disapproval – that'll only be transient. If he loves you – which I am sure he does – the ship'll soon be back on an even keel.'

'And if he doesn't?' Loopy interrupted.

'You know I can't answer that.'

'I need to walk,' Loopy said suddenly. 'I have to sort all this out.'

'Shall I leave you to it?'

'Yes,' Loopy said, striding off. Then she stopped and turned back. 'No!' she called. 'No. Come with, please? But just don't say anything. Don't say another thing. Let's just walk, OK?'

'OK.'

So they walked. They walked eastwards along the waterside path, watching the ducks and the gulls truffling for food now the tide was out, gazing at dinghies and small yachts trying to catch some sort of wind in the almost still summer afternoon, breathing in lungfuls of clean sea air and kicking pebbles along the stretch of sand where they found themselves when Loopy finally decided to break her silence.

'The trouble is, women did almost too much

during the war, you know, and now – thanks to the wise guys up there in Westminster – we're being told to go back to the way things were. And that's not making us feel so good – it's making us just a little bit fretful, making us seem a little smaller than we'd gotten used to thinking we were. And that's not good.'

'Interesting,' Waldo agreed. 'But where exactly is it taking us?'

'Try imagining what it's like, Waldo. You won't find it easy because this sort of thing doesn't happen to men – but since as you said a while back, imagination is a powerful tool, use it. Use it and try to imagine what it's like not being needed at your workplace any more. There you are – you've been beavering away, doing things you've never done before, things they said you weren't capable of doing, things *you* didn't think you were capable of doing, yet lo and behold you are. And the stuff you're doing is helping your side win the war – because believe you me, Waldo, that war wouldn't have been won if women had stayed at home. So there we all are, mighty proud of what we've done, of how we helped win the war, and what happens? They hand us back our pinnies and just expect us to tie 'em back on and go to it back at the oven and sink. I *mean*. I mean, what a waste! What a waste of ability! There we are one moment making munitions and aeroplanes, building ships and packing explosives, joining the armed services, dropping behind enemy lines as secret agents, fire fighting, delivering aeroplanes, let alone having babies without anaesthetics – and suddenly it's get back in to the kitchen time.'

'OK, OK – everything you say makes sense, but what's it to do with the matter in hand?'

'What I'm saying is it's little wonder we've lost our confidence.'

'Ah. You mean that because of being expected to be the dutiful housewife and mother once again, you've lost your nerve. Women like you have lost their self-belief and that's the reason you won't allow yourself go stick a few pictures on a wall somewhere.'

'You haven't understood a word I've said.'

Loopy began to walk more quickly.

'You're just using all this as an excuse,' said Waldo, catching up with her.

'I am not!'

'You most certainly are. You're saying that if it was still wartime it would be different – as a woman you'd not only be allowed to do such a thing, you'd be positively encouraged. But now the war is over everyone is going to stand ready to jeer, saying what in hell does this woman think she's at? Having an *art exhibition*? For God's sake, she's a woman! Doesn't she *know*? Hasn't she heard that her place is in the kitchen? Hogwash.'

'*Hogwash*?'

'Pure hogwash and utter hokum, Mrs Tate. You're trying to find some high and mighty reason for not having the nerve to go through with this. That's what you're trying to do.'

'Waldo—'

'Not that you're not damn' right what you just said about what women are expected to do now. I think that's just crazy, and is going to store up a whole lot of trouble – but like I said, it has sweet nothing to do with hanging a few daubs of paint up on a wall somewhere.'

'Waldo!' Loopy continued to protest, now looking up into his face and seeing the gleam of sheer good humour and mischief in the pair of large dark eyes looking back down at her. And finding herself being quite unable to stop herself from smiling. 'You . . .' she added weakly.

'Yes, Mrs Tate?'

'You're only too damn' right yourself, that's all.' Loopy took his arm, leading him further along the beach.

'I give in,' she said. 'I was actually coming to that – I was about to concede anyway.'

'Sure you were.'

'I just thought you ought to hear it from us ladies' point of view.'

'I was riveted. Now let's talk about this exhibition of yours, OK?'

'OK.' She stopped for a moment. 'I'll tell Hugh about it this weekend.'

'You'll tell him before,' Waldo contradicted. 'You'll telephone him and tell him. It'll be too late by the weekend. We have to start arranging things as of now.'

And so on they strolled, talking in fine detail about the exhibition that had now been agreed. It was a lovely day, still fine and unclouded, with the weather turned pleasurably cooler now as August ran into September. The breezes coming off the sea blew stronger and were more bracing, while beyond the mouth of the estuary the seas themselves could be seen to be beginning to run higher as the autumn tides began to build. With the first intimations of autumn gone was the air of oppression that had hung in the air with the all but unbearable heat wave, allowing people to move more freely and in a better mental disposition, since most were only too glad to see the end of what had been a tropical heat. Now the beaches were populated again with children playing energetic games, with barking dogs running in and out of the sea, and with lovers strolling happily hand in hand barefoot in the shallows.

Meanwhile Waldo and Loopy had reached the far end of the beach where it ended in a dramatic landscape of monumental blue-black rocks that had possibly tumbled down onto the sands centuries ago. They were about to turn for home when Loopy caught sight of a pair of lovers detached from the main body of those on the beach, lying on the sand fast in each other's arms.

'I suppose this is something else we will have to get used to in these post-war times.' Loopy raised her eyebrows.

'I guess so,' Waldo agreed. 'I have to say it's not something I can understand. I mean if you want to make love, surely the first thing you want is privacy?'

'Absolutely,' Loopy replied, before suddenly

taking Waldo's arm and swinging him sharply about.

'I take it that was something we shouldn't have seen, perhaps?'

'It's not something we shouldn't have seen,' Loopy replied, walking away with ever increasing speed. 'Rather it's *someone* we shouldn't have seen.'

'Might I enquire who?' Waldo asked, trying unsuccessfully to look behind him, while all the time being prevented from doing so.

'You can enquire as much as you like, Waldo – but I'm not telling.'

The hold on his arm tightened as Loopy increased her pace, walking as quickly as she could away from the scene of whatever it was she had just witnessed.

'Are you sure you don't want to tell me?' he pleaded as he found himself finally led off the sands and back up on to Estuary Lane. 'You seem upset.'

'I am *quite* sure I don't want to tell you,' Loopy assured him, without another backward glance. 'And you're also right about my being upset, because believe me – I am.'

Which was unsurprising really, since the young man she had seen kissing the girl at the bottom of Tumble Rocks was none other than her eldest son.

Chapter Nine

Judy Tate sat on the edge of the quays staring ahead of her, not seeing the beauty of the harbour, the sunshine and the children playing, but only grey water, grey skies, and a grey future. Walter would be home on Friday as usual, and after she had poured him his pre-dinner drink she would have, yet again, to sit at his feet and tell him as calmly as she could that there was, as yet, no good news on the baby front. As she walked home she prepared her speech, trying to invest as much optimism as she could in it and as little doom and gloom. After all, they had only been trying to conceive for – what was it – a little over twelve months now. According to what she'd heard from her friends some people took years.

She increased her speed along the pathway towards Owl Cottage, realising that when she had set out for her walk to collect some groceries from the village shop she had felt so low that she had left her beloved little Hamish behind, and he would be still sitting forlornly in the window waiting for her. Loopy had tried to comfort her with a story, only recently, of a couple she had known who had taken ten years to have their first baby and then had six, which – according to Loopy – might even have turned out to be four too many.

She took her front door key from her handbag. Soon as she could she would tell Walter that story, because it was a funny story and it might both cheer him up and encourage him. In fact they would probably end up falling about at the idea of Judy suddenly producing hordes of infants and overrunning not just their tiny cottage but possibly the whole of Bexham, and as always Walter would not be able to resist her nor she him, and the next they knew they would be upstairs in bed trying yet again to make a baby.

'No! No, we would be upstairs making love!' She suddenly corrected herself as she swung up the garden path towards the front door. 'Making love, not babies.'

As she prepared to put her key in the front door latch she heard the sound of a familiar deep voice behind her.

'The first sign of madness is talking to oneself, so they say, but who are they to say so?'

'Mr Astley!' Judy said, swinging round in complete surprise. 'What on earth are you doing here? This is hardly on your way to anywhere, is it? This being a dead end.'

'*I was following you,*' Waldo said, in a graveyard voice. '*I need the blood of a maiden every twelve hours*. I was just wandering around, wandering and wondering – wondering where this lane would lead to if I followed it – then wondering who that very pretty young woman was up ahead and then realising it was none other than young Mrs Tate. So why not say hello? And pass the time of day – after all, it is such a lovely day.'

'I'd ask you in,' Judy said. 'But Walter isn't home.'

'Isn't that some sort of contradiction? I would always hope that because her husband wasn't home, a young woman would ask me in.' As Judy turned away, looking both confused and amused, he went on, 'It's OK, Mrs Tate, I didn't mean it seriously. Please – there's really no need to look so worried.'

'My neighbour is an ardent member of the Bexham Secret Police. One look out of her window and I will be the Jezebel of the neighbourhood.'

'Then I shall leave at once, rather than risk your unblemished reputation.' Waldo half turned, imagining that he did indeed see a curtain opposite twitching.

'You don't have to go—'

'Why, but Missus *Tate*, if your husband isn't home, Ah couldn't possibly stay. What would your mammy say if I did?' Waldo teased, pushing his hat to the back of his head. 'And what would the young master have to say if he a-came a-home to find you and Ah sitting together on the stoop chatting and laughing over a mint julep? Why, missus – why, Ah would think we'd both be in for a whipping.'

As usual Judy wasn't sure which she was more

mesmerised by – the mischievous look in Waldo's eyes, or his smile.

'You're frightened to let me into your cottage, aren't you, Mrs Tate – because you think I am a dangerous influence not only on your life, but on the lives of all the women in Bexham. I am the unknown quantity, the will o' the wisp that no husband wants to meet when he comes home from work, or in your case comes home from London.'

Having opened the door, Judy entered her house, bending down to greet and pick up Hamish who was barking his usual greeting. As she did so, Waldo waltzed by them both and before she could say any more was standing in the sitting room of the little cottage, his size making it look even smaller than it was.

'I don't remember asking you in, Mr Waldo Astley,' she said primly, before going on into the kitchen to put away her shopping. Waldo watched her from the door.

'My word.' He stared at the food she was unpacking. 'I think I'd better get the American Embassy to start sending you some food parcels. That isn't really what you're living on?'

He moved behind her to the food shelf and held up a tin of stewed beef and carrots, a tin of whale meat and another of snoek.

'You can do better than this, surely. Stewed beef? Whale meat? Our army ate better than this. And as for snoek . . . until I came here I'd never even heard of the wretched *poisson*.'

'Can I offer you some tea?' Judy said, ignoring

his amazement. 'I'm just about to put the kettle on.'

'That is something the British always seem about to do. Do you think your nation was born kettle in hand? I would love a cup of tea. I really and truly have grown to like tea, believe it or not. It's also rather chic – what with it still being rationed. Gives it a somewhat risqué status. So yes – let us abandon ourselves and drink a whole pot of tea. Let us embrace life to the full. Let us live right on the edge.'

Refusing to crack even the semblance of a smile lest it should encourage her uninvited visitor to the delivery of even more absurd monologues, Judy put on the kettle, which took an age to boil as it always does when someone is watching you. She had hoped Waldo Astley might take himself off into the sitting room while she made tea, but in spite of several hints in that direction, Waldo pronounced himself quite happy where he was, and sat on the edge of the kitchen table watching her while she resolutely watched the kettle. After what seemed like the best part of half a day, the kettle finally boiled, Judy warmed the small blue and white teapot with two inches of hot water, spooned three small teaspoons of the precious leaf into the bottom of the pot, and finally filled it to the brim.

'Silly, really,' Judy said to Waldo as she took the tray through to the sitting room. 'Tea's such a precious commodity still that I get nervous making it.'

She didn't at all. She simply offered this up as an

excuse in case Waldo had noticed her hands trembling as she had spooned the tea into the pot. Why, she had no idea. She was perfectly capable of looking after herself. Having survived the Blitz and everything that Jerry had to throw at London, as they used to say, she had no fear of men such as Waldo Astley. Smiling politely at him she indicated a chair for him to take, and in return Waldo bowed in an exaggerated fashion before doing as invited.

'I see you're a gardener,' he remarked, looking out of the window.

'It's difficult to garden by the sea,' she replied, pouring tea. 'I expect you may be finding that already at your new house. It's the wind. I nearly gave up at first, but then I hit on the idea of copying the beach, and making a garden that echoed what was happening there. Like the nursery rhyme. *Mary, Mary, quite contrary, how does your garden grow? With silver bells and cockle shells.*'

'You've certainly been very successful. Even this late in the year your garden looks quite beautiful,' Waldo said, taking a cup of tea. 'May I take a closer look at it?'

He put down his tea, and then rising pushed open the French windows and stood outside surveying the garden. Judy was thankful for a moment to be alone, to compose herself, to try to cover the nerves she was feeling at being alone with Waldo in her home. She bet that her return hadn't been missed by her curtain-twitching neighbour who watched constantly from the side of her windows even when nothing was going on, and if she had noticed Judy returning she would almost certainly have noticed Waldo Astley as well, which meant that very soon the whole village would know not just that Mr Astley had arrived, but also that he had been invited in and had stayed.

The truth was that as soon as he was inside the cottage Judy simply did not know how to get rid of him. What was more, if she was going to be truthful again, quite a large part of her wanted him to stay. Suddenly it didn't seem to matter that the longer Waldo Astley stayed in Owl Cottage, the louder the rumours would become in the village. In some way his very presence filled her with confidence and liberated her from the constant feeling of failure from which she had been suffering, as if she was covered by a thin grey film which clung to her face and body wherever she turned, preventing her from seeing anything clearly.

Helped by such thoughts as well as the strength of the tea she had brewed, Judy pulled herself together while Waldo continued to gaze out at the imaginative layout of her garden, the beauty she had created out of rounded pebbles and shells, and of strong plants that could cope with seaside conditions.

'This garden says a great deal about you, did you know that?'

'In what way exactly?'

'A love of adventure. A hatred of being shut in.'

'How could you tell that just from my garden?'

'The use of shells – and pieces of mirror, for

instance. Mirror represents a sense of claustrophobia, while the sea shells return you to the sea, not only to where you came from but to where you are happiest.'

'The sea shells are taking the place of the flowers whose seeds we can't get anywhere right at the moment – and mirror has always been used in all sorts of gardens to make them look bigger. It's quite a vogue in London at the moment.'

Waldo smiled at her, but his dark eyes turned from studying her profile back to the garden. 'The choice of colour in the plants you do have is interesting,' he continued in his deep, mellifluous voice. 'Not too much blue, so that's a tendency to veer away from convention and adopt a carefree attitude to what people think, while the reds and the pinks—'

'I like hot colours in a small dark garden but they make Walter cringe. I expect you feel the same.'

'Not at all. On the contrary I love contrast. Chalk and cheese are my favourite two media.'

'My mother always says put a redhead or a blonde in pink or red and every man in the room will become fascinated.'

'I like bold, and I love unconventional. And I too love adventure.'

Waldo had now returned into the room to sit down opposite Judy and continue drinking his tea, his eyes never leaving her face.

'My life isn't always going to be here,' Judy found herself saying, as if answering some unasked question. 'This isn't going to be how I pass the rest of my life. Walter and I have great plans.'

'I am very glad to hear it, Mrs Tate – even though it is no business of mine whatsoever.'

'I don't know whether you know about what happened to my husband or not?'

'Of course, Mrs Tate. His heroism is well known. As is his miraculous return from what must have seemed to you to be the dead. How long was he gone? Was it really all the war?'

'Yes.'

'My.'

Waldo left unsaid what he was thinking and what Judy knew he was thinking: that it must have been very difficult when he did finally turn up out of the blue. Instead he just smiled sympathetically while Judy enquired whether he would like some more tea.

'Thank you,' he said, handing her back his cup. 'That was delicious.'

'It wasn't easy,' Judy said suddenly, again finding herself volunteering information she had been absolutely intent on not divulging. 'In fact it wasn't at all easy.'

'No, it can't have been,' Waldo agreed. 'In fact I cannot begin to imagine what it must have been like, suddenly for the man you thought was dead to turn up on your doorstep. Romantic yes – certainly. Sort of thing Hollywood might imagine they could handle. I say "might". The difficulties two people faced having to rebuild a relationship one of them had thought was dead and buried.'

Aware that he was staring at her, as if to elicit a

response, Judy found herself suddenly tongue-tied and unable to make a sensible reply.

'Maybe you should write it,' he suddenly suggested. 'Maybe it could make your fortune.'

'I'm not a writer,' Judy came in hastily. 'My writing never got beyond schoolgirl letters home.'

'You never know till you try.' Waldo smiled. 'Ask your mother-in-law.'

'Why? Is she thinking of writing something?'

'No. No, her thing is painting, which it seems is something none of you lot take much notice of.' As Judy coloured and lowered her eyes to her teacup, he went on. 'But to get back to this book you might write – given the huge interest in the subject of women dealing with their men when they have returned from war – either when they are demobbed or as in your case through some sort of miraculous resurrection – you could be on your way .'

Judy knew he was provoking her quite deliberately, but this time managed to be more careful, asking only as to the state of his second cup of tea.

'My tea is just fine, thank you, Mrs Tate,' he returned. 'But please – I am being serious here. Think of how your book would appeal to women – to all those who had to live without their men for five or six years. Who had to bring up their families single-handed, cope with the daily round, stay faithful – or not as the case might be – who had to wait, wait, and wait some more. Waiting to see whether the guy they loved was going to get blown to bits in the corner of some foreign field or step off the train at their local station changed into someone they didn't know any longer. You of all people could give a pretty first-hand depiction of how that must have been.'

'If you don't mind, I don't think this is the sort of thing a woman should discuss with a near perfect stranger.'

'I like the near perfect bit.' Waldo smiled. 'But I don't go for the stranger designation.'

'I hardly know you, Mr Astley.'

'Then get to know me better, Mrs Tate.'

'It wouldn't be proper for me to do so. I'm a married woman, if you remember.'

'Which is the whole point of this conversation, if you remember.'

'Are you trying to say that the whole point of following me here, of coming into my house uninvited, Mr Astley—'

'Please. You sound cross. I don't want you to be cross with me.'

'I just can't believe that the whole purpose of arriving on my doorstep unannounced and uninvited was to suggest I might write a book.'

'What do you think the idea was, Mrs Tate?'

To cover yet another attack of the *carnations*, as Judy called her blushes, she quickly picked up the tea tray, excused herself and hurried out to the kitchen. To her dismay she heard the sound of Waldo following on close behind.

'I asked you what you thought my motive might be, Mrs Tate?' he said, redefining his question. 'I do hope you're not questioning my motives.'

'You're an American,' Judy replied in sudden exasperation. 'I'm sure you see – and do – these things differently.'

'You mean There Is A Code.'

'There is absolutely no need to mock.'

'I feel I am upsetting you,' Waldo said politely. 'Forgive me. I must leave at once.'

'No!' Judy could have bitten her tongue but it was too late. 'I mean – no. No, don't go yet. Not because of a misunderstanding – because that's all it is. We just misunderstood each other, I think. You were being somewhat too forthright and I – I was being far too stuffy.'

'I understand,' Waldo replied. 'But it really was my fault. I hadn't given the matter proper thought. That's the way I am – impulsive and consequently more often than not tactless. Please forgive me if I have upset you. It really wasn't my intention.'

'Which was?'

'To talk to you. I like talking to you.'

'I don't know what to think,' Judy said, her mood suddenly dipping. 'Other than I could do with a rather stiff gin. How about you, Mr Astley?'

'Now I'm confused. First you want me to go – now you're offering me alcohol. And as we all know, that's the stuff we take to find the truth too late.'

Judy shrugged and opened a kitchen cupboard, to take out a bottle of gin and a bottle of whisky.

'I have some Scotch as well. Something tells me you're not a gin man.'

'What I am is easily persuaded.'

While Judy was making the drinks she dared to ask Waldo for an explanation about something that had long been intriguing her.

'Why did you stand outside my parents-in-law's house that Sunday last winter? Was there a reason for it? Because it was rather extraordinary. Were you trying to embarrass me, for some reason?'

'No, no,' Waldo assured her, his eyes brimful of good humour. 'I would never try to embarrass you. I only ever want to help you.'

'Help? Where was the help in that?'

'You looked so *sad*. So I wanted to make you laugh. That always helps.'

'I wasn't sad,' Judy said, defensively.

'You were. Your eyes had this deep down sadness. I saw it when I nearly knocked you down in the snow. You looked to me as if you needed to be challenged to laugh. Like when you're a child and you're told not to giggle in church, or when you're at tea with your grandmother. You needed the challenge – at least it seemed to me you did.'

'How could you know? You didn't know anything about me then, even less than you do now.'

'But I was right, wasn't I?'

'You can work that one out for yourself,' Judy told him, handing him his drink.

'I was right,' Waldo said with a big smile, before sitting down at the kitchen table.

This time as they talked Waldo hardly had to prompt Judy at all, nor did she need the gin to get her going. She simply found that she wanted to talk and so she did, unprompted. In fact she hardly touched the drink in front of her for the first half-hour other than the occasional sip. She didn't even consider why she was telling Waldo what she was telling him, let alone how she began to do so. She just quite simply found herself at this place, at this time, with this person, in the company of the truth.

'To begin with I got married,' Judy found herself saying. 'I did what my friend Meggie Gore-Stewart was advised not to do – to get married in the middle of a war. I didn't see why not. Walter and I fell in love the moment we met, so I suppose it was an inevitability. Although we both lived in Bexham, we'd never really met, not properly, and then all of a sudden there he was and there I was, and we fell in love. Then there was all that fear and all that excitement as well, the thought that we might not live to see another day – something we all felt. We'd known war was coming for some time, so perhaps we were all looking to fall in love, I don't know – anyway—' She looked across at Waldo and paused. Then took a deep breath and continued. 'Anyway, we knew we were in love, we just didn't know whether they'd let us get married – my mother put up an awful amount of flak about it. She really is the very worst sort of snob, you know.'

'Is there a really good sort of snob, I wonder?'

'I doubt it.' Judy smiled. 'One thing I hate and that's snobbery.'

'We don't suffer from it at all,' Waldo replied

wryly. 'We Americans. We just judge people on how much they're worth.'

'Anyway, as I was saying, Walter and I knew we were in love, we weren't sure we could get married, so – well, to put it bluntly I wasn't a virgin when we married.'

'Good for you. You'd have been crazy to have been so. You very well might never have seen Walter again. Go on.'

'We did manage to get married – after me having to spend a spell in Scotland cooling my heels by order of my mother. Then as soon as we were married Walter was sent to Norway, after which I hardly heard a thing until a telegram came saying that the Admiralty feared that Walter Tate RNVR was missing believed killed.' She paused. 'And so we went into mourning, all of us, and all in our completely different ways. My father-in-law went up to London and stayed there as much as he could, despite the bombing, my mother-in-law nearly killed herself with drink, and I – I, well, I joined the WVS. Which was possibly the saving of me, particularly since finally I had to give up on Walter.'

'And you never heard a word?'

'Not a thing.' Judy thought for a moment. 'Then the war came to a close, I spent VE day and night in London, got tight and tearful by turns like everyone else, and came home to Bexham.'

'And then?'

'And then.' Judy's hand went down to stroke the top of Hamish's head. 'And then Walter returned.

Literally from the dead, he came back across those fields, over there, one summer evening, just as I was laying the table. I don't know why that's important, except I was still laying for two—'

'I'd say that's important.' Waldo had become very still, his eyes never leaving Judy's face.

'I knew it was him because—' The tears suddenly came into Judy's eyes, and she felt furious with herself because she hated public displays of emotion.

'You knew it was him because?' Waldo prompted.

'I knew it was Walter because he was singing a Gilbert and Sullivan song that he had always loved as a little boy. It was a song that Loopy would never allow to be played once she thought of him as being dead. But – there it was. The song. With Walter singing it.' She wiped the back of one hand across her eyes. 'I thought I was mad. I thought because I had been living alone that I was imagining it all, but no – there he was. As large as life. Not dead at all. Walter. Standing just there.' She pointed with her hand towards the French windows. 'It was quite incredible.'

'It must have been.'

'So much so,' Judy said slowly, 'so much so that sometimes I think I mightn't ever have recovered from it. From the shock.'

'I don't suppose you have. I don't suppose anyone would. It's like they say you never get over the grief of losing someone. You go on – you get through it – but you never get over it.'

'I never thought of it that way,' Judy stared at him. 'You get through something – but you never get over it. I see.'

'How does Walter feel? Does he talk about it?'

'No, not really. But isn't that a general rule with people who've been away at war? People come back so very different, not on the outside, but *inside*. They come back different inside. They've had to do things that civilised people shouldn't have to do, young men, barely out of school, trained to kill in a matter of weeks, then sent off to do their job. It's a wonder any of them are sane at all.'

Waldo stared at the ceiling for a moment, then rubbed his chin. 'During all the time he was lost, Walter never tried to contact you at all? Is that right?'

'He did, but it was impossible. He was in Norway, you see. After he'd been rescued from his submarine—'

'Yes, I know that part of the story – his rescue, him being the only survivor, and how he worked for the Resistance for the rest of the war—'

'Actually he wasn't in Norway all the time,' Judy interrupted. 'He actually went on sorties into Holland, and Denmark, and even into Germany.'

'Yet he could never get word to you.'

'There really wasn't any way. The one chance he did have, when a colleague who had been wounded was being smuggled first into Sweden and then hopefully back to England, Walter gave him a message to deliver – a letter or note would have been too dangerous if the man had been captured. But he died on the journey to Sweden – unknown to Walter who until the moment he turned up at the very window at which you were standing just now, hoped that his message had somehow got through to me.'

'I think after everything that happened you two are not in too bad a state at all.'

'We weren't in too good a state at first. At first Walter just couldn't settle. He couldn't sit still for longer than five minutes. One of the reasons the garden is so fine is because Walter dug it up and over at least twice, before planting it out at least three times. When he wasn't trying to find paint or tiles for the cottage or digging the garden, he would disappear for hours walking along the shore somewhere, or across the Downs. He'd just disappear without saying where he was going or when he was coming back. I got used to it, and didn't question it – finally, although it frightened me.'

'But at first . . .'

'At first I thought I would go mad.' Judy smiled. 'But I didn't. I suppose I just sat it out.'

'How did you feel about him? After all, once you decide someone is dead, and you've done your grieving—'

'I hadn't really decided he was dead. I thought he must be. I thought there was no real way he couldn't be. But I hadn't quite *decided* he was dead. And since I had always loved him, and been faithful to him, I suppose I sort of stuck it out.'

'We have an expression for that. It's called hanging on in there.'

'Much better. That's exactly what I did. I hung on in there. I shouldn't really tell you this—' She stopped and stared at him.

'You can always put it in the book,' Waldo teased.

'I really shouldn't tell you this,' Judy continued slowly, not looking at Waldo. 'But for a long time after his return it wasn't as if we were even married. Then one day – one night – it was as if Walter had suddenly made a decision. He'd been out for one of his marathon walks, I had gone to bed – and then the next thing I knew he was in bed with me. Because up until then we hadn't been sharing the same bedroom. After that, we sort of managed to make all the pieces fit again. Finally everything made sense.'

'Everything?'

'Yes. Just about everything.'

'Just about. OK.' Walter drained his glass and refilled it to the quarter mark. 'OK.'

'But now it seems we can't have children.'

Waldo's glass was to his lips as she spoke, and he just held it there, without drinking, without moving. Finally he replaced it slowly on the table and looked at Judy.

'Now that's something perhaps you really shouldn't be telling me?'

Judy shook her head. 'No.'

'Then why are you? Because you have to tell somebody?'

'I shouldn't have told you.'

'So why did you?'

'I don't know. I suppose because I find – I find I *can* tell you things.'

'I'm very flattered.' Waldo smiled. 'And in return I can tell you it is no bad thing – because I just may be able to help you here.'

'I trust you're not thinking along the traditional lines of how to get a girl pregnant.'

Waldo smiled and shook his head. 'Will you trust me?'

'My father always says never trust anyone who asks you to trust them. He says that if you are trustworthy you never have to ask the question.'

'Your father is completely right. I don't know why I said that.' Waldo thought for a minute. 'So let's just return to the whys and the wherefores. My old mammy used to say the surest way to get a woman pregnant was to make her man jealous.'

'I wouldn't even begin to know how to do that. Walter has absolutely nothing to be jealous about.'

'Yet.' Waldo smiled at her and finished his drink. 'You are familiar with Shakespeare, I take it? With *Othello* in particular?'

'I'm to be Desdemona?' Judy made a strangled sound.

'And I am to be Iago.'

'You don't know Walter,' Judy argued. 'To be an Iago you would have to be very familiar with your Othello. And besides, I don't want to end up suffocated by a pillow, thanks.'

'You won't be,' Waldo assured her cheerfully, rising from the table. 'Now please don't bother to see me out. It's important that you don't.'

'In case my curtain-twitcher is watching?'

'Just don't bother to see me out, that's all.'

Wishing his hostess goodnight, Waldo collected his hat and let himself quietly out of the cottage – something which oddly enough he did backwards, leaving the front door ajar as he did so. Judy, clearing up in the kitchen, was out of sight of Waldo as indeed he was of her. With his back to the lane and his large frame excluding any glimpse of what was going on in front of him, Waldo then performed his favourite old party trick, the looking-as-though-he-was-being-kissed routine. Putting his right hand across round the back of his neck and crossing his left arm so that his left hand would be seen at the side of his waist, he then kissed thin air, while gently moving the fingers of his hands on neck and waist. Anyone watching from behind would be sure that Mr Waldo Astley was doing more than shaking hands with the young woman who had just entertained him to tea and then to drinks, and who knew what else?

Which was exactly the impression Waldo wished to give the person behind the slowly twitching curtains in the cottage opposite, as, having carefully closed the front door without moving from his position in order to make it look as though whoever it was who had been in his arms had returned within, he adjusted his straw hat at an even jauntier angle and wandered off down the twilit lane, whistling happily to himself while the net curtains fell slowly back into place.

Chapter Ten

At last Dauncy was home. Summer was nearly gone, but as far as Loopy was concerned it began all over again on the return of her youngest son.

'My,' she sighed, after she had hugged him welcome and stood back to appraise her boy. 'My oh my, but I dare swear you have *grown*.'

'I am nearly *nineteen*, Mother!' Dauncy laughed, able now to put down his hand luggage. 'I stopped growing years ago. Hey – I have missed this place.'

'You sound quite American.'

'That cannot be altogether surprising – seeing I spent most of the summer there.'

'I hope it wasn't as unbearably hot as the summer here. I thought we should all *melt*.'

Dauncy was as delighted to be reunited with his family as they were to have him back home. Being the youngest he had always had a special place in all their hearts as each of them considered he needed their protection. As a consequence, rather than being spoiled, which could so easily have been the case, despite the war and all its sorrows the youngest Tate grew up emotionally secure and confident, the most perfectly adjusted of the three boys. In fact, he was sufficiently self-assured to be immediately attractive to everyone. Whereas Walter was still the homecoming hero, and John the business success, young Dauncy now found his own fame as the most *sportif* and the most personable of the three Tate boys. So much so that he had barely been home for twenty-four hours when the invitations began arriving for him to go sailing, to play tennis, to grace cocktail parties and dances with his presence.

Naturally Dauncy allowed himself to be fêted, while privately confiding to his mother that, after his hectic time in America, he would really rather prefer just to relax with family, play a bit of tennis and golf but most of all take *Dingy*, the family's ancient but speedy little sailing boat, out whenever possible. The very first day he sailed *Dingy* out into the estuary he was immediately noticed, and then watched, by a man in a garden on the north shore, a man much taken to watching events unfold in the little fishing port opposite which he now lived. Perhaps if he had realised this Dauncy would have felt uneasy, but as it was he merely set sail with a carefree heart and a determination to enjoy his precious time at home.

The man watching him was of course Waldo, and he too was happy. He was happy with his new house, with Rusty's care of it, and in particular with the restoration work that Peter Sykes and two friends were carrying out in their spare time. Far from being irreparable, the roof, as Peter had forecast, had been easily fixed, so that all that now remained to be done was the redecoration and the furnishing. Of course, once Peter had finished the initial repairs, Waldo had further plans for the house, but being all too aware of the rumours that were now circulating around him, about how he was managing to get things done that others could not get done, he delayed doing anything more.

He was also in the Todds' bad books for being responsible for the defection of not only Peter and Rusty from their household but also their much doted over grandson Tam. Waldo expressed his concerns to Rusty, but Rusty just shrugged it all off.

'Look, Mr Astley, I been to hell and back on snow shoes, so I couldn't care any more, so don't you worry, really. We're really happy where we are now, honestly, and we can't thank you enough, so don't you worry.'

So Waldo gave up that concern and instead enjoyed the good care that Rusty lavished on him as well as the honest toil that her husband was putting into building up their joint business. But just now his interests were on something quite different as through his field glasses he watched the handsome young man skilfully handling the blue-painted yacht that was dancing across the windswept waters of the Sound running at full tide below his lawns. Much taken with the young sailor's skill and dexterity, Waldo found himself watching for far longer than he had intended, which was how he followed the little yacht home through his binoculars and saw it being dragged up on shore on the stretch of beach that ran directly below the Tate residence and was usually reserved for their craft.

'This must be the prodigal returned,' he said to himself, still watching through his glasses. 'And then there were three brothers Tate.'

Once Dauncy was out of his sight, having let himself into the family property through the heavy old iron gate in the south garden wall, Waldo dropped his glasses, allowing them to swing round his neck on their leather strap as he contemplated his next move. He could see no possible objection to the request he was planning, although he judged there would be plenty of initial opposition. Indeed, the thought of it amused him as he strolled back up the lawns towards his new marine residence. Rusty, dressed in a pretty blue cotton dress, her hair brushed on top of her head, was busy laying his lunch out on the terrace, while to one side of the house Tam played on a garden swing. It was, Waldo thought, an idyllic sight. The sun shining out of a cloudless blue sky, glinting brightly off the waves and still hot enough to allow him to take off his jacket and hang it on the back of his chair as he sat down to taste a delicious salad of freshly caught crab washed down with a bottle of Chablis he had purchased under the counter from Richards at the Three Tuns. He smiled across at Tam who was now being pushed on the swing by his mother. Some way or another they would all of them remember this moment, the sunshine, the child on the swing and Rusty in her blue dress. It was a painting of a moment.

It was in the now thriving public house that the opportunity for which Waldo had been waiting arose that very Saturday, the day of the annual Bexham rowing races, a fixture said to date back to the Middle Ages when Grisham, the nearest small fishing port to Bexham, became involved in a rivalry with the latter that had lasted through the centuries to the present day. History had it that the rivalry was nothing to do with fishing skills or the size of catches but had been based rather on prowess and myth, the prowess being the strength of the Sussex longboat men and the myth being how far out to sea they rowed during their fishing excursions. At first boat had followed boat out into the Channel to see exactly how far they did in fact row, but this type of challenge ended when a freak storm blew up during one such match, sinking both longboats and claiming the lives of two dozen fishermen, a blow it was said from which neither of the little fishing villages recovered for half a century.

Many years therefore passed before the challenge between the ports could be renewed, the rules of the contest being redrawn by the womenfolk, who, although prepared to lose their husbands and sons to the sea in the natural order of things, were determined not to increase the odds of their being prematurely widowed by the staging of an absurdly dangerous rowing competition. For the competition was infinitely more risky than any daily fishing expedition, since both crews, fuelled by alcohol and rivalry, would row out far beyond the normal limits in order to prove their point. So the match became a straightforward boat race held in the relative safety of the estuary at full tide. Before the war it had been a famous local attraction, but this was the first year it had been held since global hostilities had ceased, and not unnaturally was not nearly as well attended as in previous times.

Even so, as it turned out, it was still a busy and successful day for the village, with at least two hundred or so visitors descending on Bexham and bringing a welcome albeit brief influx of commerce.

'But as I always say,' Richards had announced authoritatively after lunch as Meggie helped him to wash up dozens of pint glasses in anticipation of even livelier trade in the evening, 'and as I always have said, if people enjoy themselves they will come back again and spend even more.'

'Of course,' Meggie had replied, poker-faced. 'You used always to say that – when? When you were serving dinner, was it? Or polishing the silver.'

'This was in one of my former lives, Miss Megs,' Richards had told her, without batting an eyelid. 'This was when I was deeply in trade, selling fish off a slab in Billingsgate Market.'

He eyed her as if in challenge, but Meggie knew better than to take Richards up on anything to do with one of his previous incarnations. All she knew was that some time in his previous life, whenever and whatever it had been, had made him an expert on everything from fish to how to lay a banquet. How this had all happened before he went to work for her grandmother after the first world war it never occurred to Meggie to ask, but happen it must have, surely, or Richards would not have ended up with such a fund of knowledge that ranged from the mind-boggling to the quite utterly trivial.

To help with local trade, not least that of the Three Tuns, the race itself was staged as late in the afternoon as possible, depending naturally on the tides, and since this particular year high tide was at 5.20 p.m. the trade in the old inn that evening was as brisk as anyone could remember since the dark days of the war. Blessed with a fine sunny evening, the drinkers spilled out on to the quays where they sat drinking and eating in the warm September sunshine, while inside the regulars stayed drinking where they always drank, as if afraid that should they forsake their regular bar stool or seat in the window they would never be able to reclaim it. Meggie, enjoying the day to the full, had stayed on to help Richards behind the bar, much to her old butler's delight since her glamour helped to pull the punters and keep them drinking.

Waldo, who for once had wandered in more or less unnoticed, was most impressed by Meggie's performance behind the polished copper bar. He was taken not only by her apparent skill at pulling pints, which by now he knew to be quite a considerable art, but by her entire manner. Since her now famous cocktail party he had really only caught the occasional glimpse of her, either walking briskly through the village with her small shopping basket on one arm and her blond hair well concealed under a patterned silk headscarf, or whizzing past, far too fast for anyone's safety, in her ruby red Austin 10. Yet few though those glimpses had been, they had been enough to intrigue him, since Miss Gore-Stewart was undoubtedly one of those women with a very well defined aura.

As far as Waldo was concerned, from a purely academic point of view, Miss Meggie Gore-Stewart had what Hollywood called *It* – that indefinable appeal of the star, that palpable sense of mystery and glamour. Tonight as he watched her at work behind the bar, he got a heightened sense of her allure, because he supposed to himself that she surely must be slumming it? She had on something in silk that obviously had seen better days, which he imagined Miss Gore-Stewart had now decided would suffice for much less elegant occasions than the ones for which it had originally been purchased. The dress was a dark red, with short puffed sleeves and a quite considerable *décolletage* in which the stream of male customers who formed an almost constant queue to be served by her were taking an inordinate and unashamed delight. With her customary applomb Meggie was ignoring the innuendoes and the open flirtations, deciding only to deliver choice put-downs to those who over-stepped the limit, several of which Waldo was privileged to overhear, and all of which did nothing to deter the male population from returning to the bar for more.

Waldo stood at one corner of the bar sipping his whisky and soda watching the unusual barmaid. He half hoped to catch her eye so that she and not Richards would come over and take his next order, and another part of him hoped that she would do nothing of the sort, so that he could simply go on observing her and appreciating her performance. After some time, Meggie, turning to get something from behind her, seemed to catch sight of him, or at any rate glance in his direction, but then the moment passed and she turned back to the next customer, and Waldo, it would seem, became as interesting to her as the pints she was pulling, or the whisky she happened to be pouring the attentive customer.

Once again the barman who stood in front of him was Richards, wearing his best and most expectant landlord's face.

'OK,' Waldo said, finishing his whisky. 'Hit me again, Mr Richards. Large Scotch, thank you.'

'I feel sure you would rather be drinking Bourbon, Mr Astley,' Richards replied, carefully measuring the whisky into the glass.

'I would if you kept some. Maybe I should bring you back a few bottles after my next trip?'

'You are returning to America, sir?'

'Not necessarily. Not necessarily at all. On the other hand, I could be – I even might be.'

With a smile, and knowing that everyone around him was not only listening but interested, Waldo paid his money over, splashed some soda into the Scotch and leaned back against the wall behind him.

Meggie was still down the other end of the bar, her back turned to him, serving some of the victorious Bexham crew. Observing this, Waldo lit his cigar and surveyed the rest of the inhabitants of the pub. At that moment the person he had been hoping to see strolled in through the pub door, dressed in his tennis whites, with sweat still on his brow. By an extension of such good chance, the newcomer happened to come and stand up at the bar, next to Waldo.

'Good evening, young sir.' Waldo smiled, his lit cigar now firmly in his mouth. 'Good game?'

Dauncy Tate smiled, but at the same time looked rueful.

'Thought it might be a bit of a walk over, but there's life in the old man yet. As a matter of fact I was playing my father.'

'Did you beat him?'

Dauncy paused, looking Waldo in the eye. 'What do you think, sir?'

'I'd say it went to a third set, which you won 7-5 after a series of deuces.'

'That's really quite incredible,' Dauncy laughed. 'Where were you hiding?'

'I used to play tennis with my uncle, who was damn good too, as it happens, but he didn't much like getting beat by a whippersnapper like me, so the better I got the closer I kept the score line.' Waldo inhaled some cigar smoke. 'Drink, young man?'

'Sure, yup, thank you. I'd like some beer, please. One thing I missed in your country – a decent glass of British beer. I'm Dauncy Tate, by the way, and I've just come back from the States. I can speak American, a little, not much, but a little.'

'That's great, you can teach me, I'm forgetting – fast. Waldo Astley.'

They shook hands, before Waldo nodded at him, and waited for Meggie who was just about to serve another young man to move up the bar towards them.

'Another pint, please, Miss Gore-Stewart.'

Mickey Todd, the young man whom Meggie was about to serve, put his glass down on the bar and smiled at Meggie, before somewhat incongruously lighting up a self-rolled cigarette with a gold lighter.

Meggie watched him as she filled his glass with what was currently passing as beer. 'Smart lighter, Mickey.'

Mickey glanced at it briefly before quickly slipping it back into his pocket again.

'Yes.' He took his glass from Meggie. 'I got it in France – on D Day. The spoils of war, you know. Gold, too. Real blooming gold it is.' He grinned. 'Cheers!'

'Could I see it for a moment?' Meggie leaned over the bar to Mickey and Mickey put his hand in his pocket to fetch the lighter back out.

'Course you can, Miss Gore-Stewart.' He grinned. 'Your word is my command. Hey!'

It was then he noticed his lighter had gone missing, picked from his pocket by one of his drinking mates to light his own smoke.

'Hey, Paul! Give that lighter back here!' he shouted, pushing a couple of his friends out of the way. But the game was on, as one by one the gang threw the lighter from one to another, keeping it out of Mickey's reach.

'Some other time, Mickey!' Meggie called. 'I've got a busy bar here!'

Happily that was as near as Meggie got to discovering the identity of the man who killed her German lover. A man who had risked his life to protect her while she posed as his mistress, sending messages out of Germany to SOE in London.

Down the other end of the bar, after yet another round, tongues were now well and truly loosened, and Dauncy and Waldo had become fast new friends. However, Dauncy was regretfully indicating that he was going to have to leave shortly, since it was high time he got home and changed for his parents' dinner party.

'Can't be late, you know how it is, since it's for me, in honour of my return. Wouldn't be taken too well. Will you excuse me, Mr Astley, sir?'

'But of course,' Waldo replied gracefully. 'I've not only kept you, I've been hogging your company. But before you sprint off, I wonder would you do me a favour? I wondered whether it might be possible for you to teach me how to sail as brilliantly as you?'

Dauncy stared at him over the top of the pint he was just finishing.

'How do you know how well I sail?'

'How did I know the result of your tennis match? Because I have second sight!' Waldo laughed. 'Hell, I spied you in the estuary this morning, and you looked pretty good to me. And what I need most of all is someone with local knowledge to help me brush up my sailing techniques.'

'I should be happy to oblige, sir.' Dauncy handed his empty glass to Meggie with hardly a look, as he was still staring intently at Waldo. As it happened Meggie was too. 'How long are you going to be here? There's not a lot of easy sailing weather ahead, I'm afraid.'

'I live here, young man. I am now a resident of Bexham – at least this is one of my residencies. And because of that I intend to be able to sail as well as I can be taught to sail.'

'Very well,' Dauncy nodded. 'When I've got a bit more organised we'll give it a go. You may not make the grade, you do realise that.'

'Of course. And if I don't you have my permission to throw me overboard. You going to the dance here later on?'

'Thought I might, once the grown-ups at home get fed up with me.'

'Very well, I'll probably see you there, or rather here, later.'

Dauncy laughed, picked up his second tennis sweater, bade Waldo farewell and wandered out of the bar in the unhurried manner of a young man who knows he is both home and at home. Waldo watched him go, puffed on his cigar and pretended not to know that someone else had been listening in on their conversation.

'Why ask poor old Dauncy to teach you?' a voice said from behind him. Waldo knew at once to whom it belonged. He also knew that Meggie must have been listening in, that was after all a barmaid's perks. 'Why ask him?' she persisted 'There are plenty of qualified instructors at the Yacht Club, you know.'

'Yes, I did know. Thank you.'

'I suppose you asked him because you thought you might get poor old Dauncy's services for free.'

'No, I didn't.' Waldo turned and looked at the young woman who was challening him so overtly. 'No, Miss Gore-Stewart, that really wasn't the case at all.'

With a polite smile Waldo placed his empty whisky glass on the bar and left the pub. Meggie stared at it before deciding to leave the glass.

Naturally Dauncy told his family over dinner of his meeting with Waldo Astley in the Three Tuns, as he was bound to do. Besides his immediate family of father, mother, two brothers and sister-in-law, there were six other guests sitting down to dinner at Shelborne that night. The Wilkinsons who sailed with Hugh, the Smith-Hughesons, who owned one of the large estates that backed from Bexham up on to the edge of Goodstock Lane, and Caroline Percy and Georgina Fairfax, whom Loopy had invited to keep John and Dauncy entertained. Both of them were the daughters of rich men and both were busy being all but ignored by the Tate brothers, who dreaded Loopy's attempts at matchmaking, until Dauncy dropped his bombshell about his meeting in the pub and the party ground to a sudden silence.

'What on earth have I said?' Dauncy laughed. 'What's the matter? Have I shaken hands with the devil?'

'No, no – no of course you haven't, darling,' Loopy quickly assured him with a smile. 'It must be twenty past and an angel's passing overhead.'

'It's ten to,' Hugh corrected her, 'and I cannot imagine for a moment why we have all lost our tongues. Mr Astley is a most interesting fellow, most interesting.'

'I thought I remember you said you found him rather attractive?' one of the guests asked Loopy.

'I don't recall saying any such thing!' Loopy gave a little laugh, hoping to turn the conversation on its head and make light of it. 'In fact I'm almost sure that was *your* first impression, Georgina. Gracious no.'

'*I* actually find him very charming,' Judy put in quickly, not wanting to see her mother-in-law embarrassed any further.

'And when have you had the chance to discover the beauty of his character, might I ask?' Walter teased, tapping the table lightly with a knife. 'Is this some handsome acquaintance you've been cultivating in my absence?'

It was Judy's turn to look embarrassed. She went to say something, but before she could Loopy came to her rescue.

'Bexham is a small place and people bump into each other. People also talk – and from what I've heard—'

'From what *I* have heard,' John interrupted, 'Waldo Astley's a bit of a show-off who can't keep his nose out of other people's business.'

'That's not like you, John.' Loopy frowned. 'And quite wrong. Why on earth should you say such a thing?'

'Because that is the impression I have gathered, Mother. He uses people apparently, just to suit himself—'

'Such as? Like who, please?'

'Well – the poor old *garagiste* on the hill, for instance. Sykes, isn't that his name? Astley moved in on his business and then not content with that he has set about getting the poor fellow to restore his house,' Jakie Smith-Hugheson chimed in.

'Yes, I gather old Mr Todd is furious with his son-in-law.'

'Mmm. How about that? And not content with buying the only garage he must buy himself a house in Bexham too. The Wiltons' house no less. He'll end up buying up everything, mark my words.'

'No, Walter,' Loopy put in. 'I think that's quite wrong. Really, I do.'

'Not only does he get Sykes to do all his labour on the cheap,' John went on, taking up the general chorus. 'But he moves Sykes's wife, Rusty, in as his housekeeper. Old Mrs Todd is stunned beyond words, they told me down at the Three Tuns. She's forever moaning about how she's not allowed to see her grandson now.'

'Hark at you. You surprise me. You sound like a bunch of schoolgirls envying someone else having a better time than them. Why, if I didn't know you better, I would almost think you were all jealous of Mr Waldo Astley.' Loopy stared round at her guests and family, feeling vaguely ashamed of them.

'Jealous?' they all chorused, looking at each other, and Walter laughed out loud.

'Why should we be jealous of Waldo Astley, Mother?'

'That is something at which I can only guess, Walter,' Loopy told him lightly. 'Doubtless you can tell yourself the real reason.'

Judy kept her napkin to her face, this time to hide not her blushes but a private smile.

'We hear all sorts of things about him,' Sheila Wilkinson continued. 'Down at the Yacht Club a lot of people are saying that he might be – well, that he might be some sort of – what do they call them over there, George?' she asked, turning to her purple-nosed husband.

'How should I know? Hoodlums, mobsters,

search me. They say all sorts of things at the club. The truth is that he could be anything, anything at all.'

'I don't think so,' Loopy insisted quietly. 'I really don't think so.'

'Could be part of organised crime, that sort of thing,' George continued blithely.

'How rather exciting,' Caroline Percy put in. 'I've always had a bit of a secret penchant for the underworld, all dead bodies and guns and things.'

'We heard he was buying up Bexham lock, stock and barrel in order to move his family in, that soon there will hardly be a decent house that isn't in his ownership,' Helena Smith-Hugheson put in, an expression of such boredom on her face that it seemed she might fall asleep before she even reached the end of her comments. 'And really, it would hardly be surprising. It's because we're so frightfully poor, don't-cher-know? Rich outsiders know they can buy up everything, and there's nothing we can do about it.'

'Well, there is something,' Loopy put in with some asperity. '*We* could start building houses again, *we* could start rewarding the returning forces, and most of all we could start being less *bureaucratic*. The end of the Roman Empire was caused by letting an indifferent class of person take over the bureaucratic running of everything, which brought about total inertia in the populace, and consequently the ruination of Rome. And that is a *fact*.'

There was a short silence as everyone stared at their hostess, and Loopy feigned sweet innocence, although hoping all the time that no-one would challenge her. Only she knew that she was actually quoting something Waldo Astley had said to her.

'Can't imagine why on earth this Astley fellow picked on Bexham, that's the real mystery,' George Wilkinson announced. 'It's not as if he's a sailor.'

'It appears he's going to be,' his wife said, nodding towards Dauncy. 'Seeing he's intent on young Dauncy here teaching him the ropes.'

'Tell you what, Dauncy.' George laughed. 'Why don't you take him out and show him a thing or two? Make sure he gets a good few clouts to the bonce with the old jib and a couple of good duckin's, and he might choose to stay at home in future and twiddle his thumbs, or preferably high-tail it out of Bexham and leave us all to get on with our lives.'

'Might go off the whole idea of Bexham altogether,' Helena Smith-Hugheson agreed with a complacent smile.

'I thought he seemed a more than half-decent sort of chap actually,' Dauncy said staunchly. 'Besides, I'd like to give him a few sailing lessons, it might make living here a bit more interesting for him— if he's taken to sailing.'

Everyone except his mother stared at Dauncy as if he'd taken leave of his senses.

'If you want a first mate, just give a shout,' Caroline Percy said to him with her sweetest smile, hoping to beguile the handsome young man with not only her good humour but also her really quite exceptional bustline.

'Very kind, Caro.' Dauncy thanked her with his bright smile. 'But you can't be too careful. After all, he might be packing a gat.'

'I trust he isn't hoping to be invited by anyone who matters,' Helena Smith-Hugheson sighed to Loopy later when the ladies had retired.

'I should imagine that's the very last thing Mr Astley wishes, Helena,' Loopy replied. 'Truly, the very last.'

There was hope for an invitation that night, but Waldo wasn't nursing it. Oddly enough the person living in hope was Meggie, who had stayed on at the Three Tuns to help Richards and other volunteers with the refreshment side of the hop that was being held in the large hall used for functions that was attached to the back of the pub. A four-piece dance band hired from Radnor especially for the occasion was playing its way through the usual repertoire of tunes for this sort of affair, the band comprising tenor saxophone, piano, bass and drums, their sound and rhythm good enough to have most people on the floor and dancing within half an hour of striking up.

By now the dance was a good two hours old, and Meggie, relieved of her duties by Richards for a well-earned break, had sat her weary self down on a hardback chair to one corner of the makeshift band from where she could observe the activities on the dance floor. There weren't a lot of people she knew except by sight a group lads from the fishing families and some of the girls she would see hanging round the shops in the High Street, or sitting swinging their long suntanned legs on the capstans outside on the quays. A number of the younger visitors to Bexham had stayed on for the dance, in the hope of picking up some of the local talent, but from the amount of giggling and grouping of the girls around the room the poor things weren't achieving much success.

Two people she did know, however, were two people whom she was surprised to see were there at all, namely young Dauncy Tate and his new friend Waldo Astley. Much to her relief she saw Waldo encouraging Dauncy to go and dance with a very pretty red-haired girl who was unknown to Meggie, but was possibly the most striking young woman present, so outstandingly pretty in fact that only one young man before Dauncy had even dared ask her to dance. She took no time at all in accepting the dashing young Tate's invitation, Meggie noted with interest, lighting a fresh cigarette.

She watched them for some time, slowly smoking her cigarette and remembering dancing with Davey. He had been a wonderful dancer, light on his feet, quick, with that ability to always make his partner feel as if she were a better dancer than she really was. Not that Meggie was a bad dancer – far from it. Davey always used to compliment her on her grace and her lightness, saying that when they danced he could barely feel her in his arms.

Smiling at the memory, Meggie turned back to the bar just as Waldo appeared to order himself a lemonade to quench his thirst. He was standing less than four feet away, but he steadfastly ignored her, which irritated Meggie since she happened to know that he'd spent a good deal of the evening watching her closely, trying to catch her eye on several occasions, something which she'd steadfastly and deliberately ignored. But now it seemed it was her turn to be ignored and it began to irritate her. Why she couldn't understand, since up to that moment she'd always found the man himself without merit, so assured was he, so confident of his charm and his persuasion. Yet now she found herself being piqued by his quite wilful lack of interest and that in turn irritated her further. After all, if anyone was to ignore anyone, it should be Miss Meggie Gore-Stewart ignoring Mr Waldo Astley – not vice-versa.

Then suddenly she saw him turn and stare right at her, catching her eyes with his before she had time to avoid them. After what can only have been a split second of time, Meggie swung her head away, blew out a plume of smoke and pretended to laugh and smile at someone across the room. The next thing she knew was that an extremely tall and more than a little drunk stranger had staggered across the room and asked her to dance. Afraid he was going to topple over right on top of her, Meggie tried to get up off her chair and escape, but she could not. The man was standing with one hand either side of her shoulders gripping the back of her chair, his head not six inches from her face as he repeated his request for a dance.

And then he was gone, as quickly as he had arrived, except he didn't depart on his feet. Instead he found himself sliding on his more than ample backside across the dance floor to roars of derisory laughter from friends and strangers alike. When Meggie looked up she saw Waldo standing in front of her, dusting his hands together before adjusting his hallmark bow tie.

'Since you won't be dancing with him, I guess, Miss Gore-Stewart,' he said, 'perhaps you will do me the honour?'

He gave a little bow and extended a hand. For a moment Meggie hesitated. Then with a small sigh, accompanied by a little raise of her eyes to heaven, she got up and allowed Waldo to lead her by her hand on to the dance floor. He put his right hand in the small of her back, so lightly that she could hardly feel the contact, took her right hand in his left, and proceeded to quickstep Meggie quite beautifully and skilfully around the floor. After only two choruses of 'Pennies From Heaven' Meggie discovered to her amusement that they seemed to have the dance floor to themselves. Everyone else had retired to the bar, or to the edges, to watch this display of what must have looked like exhibition dancing, so expert was her partner and fortunately so expert also was she, able to keep right there with him every step, reverse, twist and turn of the way, all the time keeping her gaze straight over her partner's right shoulder in the traditional manner.

She barely heard the girl vocalist sing her chorus, being only aware of the thrill of being danced with beautifully for the first time since she had danced with Davey. It was heaven to be in a man's arms like this again, not thinking of anything except dancing. As the number finished and the onlookers broke into spontaneous applause, Waldo bowed, thanked her, and led her back to her seat where he left her without saying another word. Meggie remained where she was, ignoring the stares of the curious and the admiring, taking a cigarette out of her case and lighting it while trying to compose herself. Most of all she was trying to dissuade herself of a dawning truth: that not even Davey Kinnersley had managed to have quite such an electrifying effect on her as Waldo Astley had just had, so much so that when she held her small gold lighter up to light her fresh cigarette she saw that her hand was shaking quite considerably.

Calmed and distracted by her smoke, she looked slowly about her to see where her dancing partner had gone. But he was nowhere to be seen. Meggie sat where she was for a moment thinking that he might have hidden from her but still be watching, and reluctant for him to see that she was actually looking round for him. As casually as she could, she got to her feet, wandered along the bar and round the other side of the hall. But it seemed Waldo had altogether vanished.

Daumcy was still there, dancing slowly with his delightfully pretty partner. Meggie waited until the number was finished then quietly asked Dauncy if he knew where his companion might have gone.

'Absolutely,' he replied with his brilliant smile. 'He's gone home.'

'But you can sail!' Dauncy exclaimed, laughing as Waldo swung *Dingy* to perfectly, heading her back into the wind. 'You can sail very well!'

'Not quite well enough!' Waldo called back over the wind. 'And I never said I couldn't sail, young man! I just said I wanted you to teach me to sail as well as *you*!'

'I can't do that in an afternoon, Mr Astley! That might take a good few months!'

'I don't expect to learn what you have learned over the years! I just want to learn more of the theory so that I can practise!'

'You'll need a boat!'

'Then I shall find one! Or you will find me one?'

After an entire afternoon spent sailing in waters becoming increasingly troublesome as the first of the autumn winds started to blow in off the sea, an exhausted Waldo and a still relatively fresh Dauncy repaired to the Three Tuns where the latter insisted Waldo should at least try to acquire a taste for draught English ale. Waldo tried his best with half a pint but got no further than a couple of distasteful mouthfuls.

'It is a taste you have to get used to,' Dauncy

laughed, ordering a whisky from Richards to help restore his companion's good nature.

'I think I would rather drink bathwater, Dauncy, I mean it. And please – do call me Waldo, since I have already taken the liberty of first-naming you. You shouldn't have any difficulty with that, seeing that you have just spent a considerable time in the land of apparent social intimacy.'

'I like America,' Dauncy protested. 'I won't hear a word against it.'

'Good man,' Waldo said. 'I do too. Love it. Love England too. Your good health, Dauncy.'

'Yours too, Waldo.'

'Dauncy is a none too common name, I would guess,' Waldo observed after they had finished their mutual toast.

'Not at all. We're all named after my mother's family firm, John Walter Dauncy. John, Walter and Dauncy. And you? I'd say Waldo was a none too common name either.'

'It's short for Waldophanophosteropous,' Waldo replied with a sigh. 'Which means Wisest Son Of An Extremely Stupid Tribe.'

'The Astley tribe?'

'The AS in our name should be spelled A double S,' Waldo growled, drinking some more whisky, and then selecting a cigar from his case.

'Your family is what? Your family isn't a success, you mean?'

'My family – young sir – is the greatest of successes, if you quantify success by the amount of money banked.'

'I see.'

Dauncy, a little intimidated by this information, took a sup of his ale and lapsed into silence, uncertain how to pursue this tack. Waldo looked sideways at him and grinned.

'It's OK – this sort of thing doesn't embarrass me. I guess the English don't wash their family laundry in public that often, at least not the well bred English – but Americans are different. We tell it all, much to the amazement of our European friends. My family and I don't hit it off – simple as that really. It was finally suggested by my uncle that I should take a trip to Europe ostensibly to pick up a bit more refinement, but really to get out of his hair – and so since nothing could please me more, here I am. Or rather here I still am. I began my travels before the war, and now the war is over I picked up where I left off.'

'*Bexham* was on your itinerary?' Dauncy wondered in some amusement. 'I can't imagine what attracted you here – and then to *stay* here. And to buy a house.'

'No,' Waldo said, suddenly surprisingly serious. 'No, Dauncy, I don't suppose you can imagine what attracted me here. But as to why I should choose to buy a seaside house here, I don't think that would take a lot of imagining.'

'You can't find this more charming than say Nantucket, or Martha's Vineyard, or – say – Long Island?'

'Let's say it's different,' Waldo replied. 'And then let's leave it at that. As the man says – there's no accounting for taste. Now let me get you a decent drink – or are you still too young for spirits?'

'Hardly,' Dauncy replied. 'I'm due for my call-up papers any day.'

Waldo looked round at him again, this time with surprise, before he realised what his friend was saying.

'Oh sure! I was forgetting.' He nodded. 'National Service. You're at the age, of course.'

'Can't say I'm looking forward to it.'

'You'll go in the Navy, I guess.'

'I guess.' Dauncy smiled. 'Not so bad, really.'

'Then you had better start to learn how to drink rum,' Waldo announced. 'Landlord – a whisky, please, and a good tot of your finest rum!'

Despite the growing intensity of the gossip surrounding Waldo and his ever increasing activities, Loopy watched the friendship between her youngest son and Waldo develop with only the faintest of interest and certainly no concern. Besides, she was far too busy preparing for her show during the weekdays when Hugh was absent in London to pay much attention to the backbiting. Anyway, she had her own problems. She still hadn't told Hugh about her exhibition, and as yet no good opportunity to do so had occurred, for when Hugh was not sailing, or at the Yacht Club, it seemed to Loopy he was busy trying to stick his oar in where it might not be wanted, most particularly with Dauncy.

'I take it he's paying you for all these sailing lessons,' he was now demanding of his youngest son at the family lunch on the last Sunday of September. 'He'd better be paying you, or really, I'm afraid I don't see the point of you seeing so much of the fellow. It's not as though he's a contemporary of yours. So if he's not recompensing you in some way, I can't see the point at all.'

'The point is, Pa, Waldo wants to learn how to sail really *well* which as it happens he's already doing – and I happen to enjoy teaching him.'

'I just hope he's paying you for it, that's all,' Hugh insisted, at which Loopy frowned. She really couldn't quite see what that had to do with anything, just as she couldn't for the life of her understand this growing antipathy within the bosom of her family to a man in whom she herself could only see good.

'Waldo's good company, Pa,' Dauncy was saying. 'I'm learning a lot from him. *And* he's not stuffy.'

This last remark was made not unkindly but in Dauncy's usual airy way. Loopy laughed, partly from relief, and partly because it was true. Waldo was certainly not stuffy, not like most of the other men of her acquaintance in Bexham.

'That doesn't answer my question, young man.'

'I didn't realise it *was* a question, Pa,' Dauncy stated lightly.

'He may be good company, but he's teaching you a whole lot of bad habits,' Walter put in, helping himself to more wine.

'Such as?' Dauncy gave his brother a particularly stern *thanks very much for that* look.

'Such as drinking rum chasers with your beer.'

'Who told you?'

'Bexham is a very small place, little bro.'

'If I'm old enough to be called up for National Service, I'm old enough to drink rum.'

'Mr Astley's thinking, no doubt,' John chipped in, eyeing his watch and wondering when he could safely sneak away to meet Mattie.

'Perfectly sound thinking I would say,' Dauncy replied. 'Waldo says I'd look an idiot if I get half throttled when the rum ration's passed around – and I agree with him.'

'And I agree with him too. I think Waldo has a very good point,' Loopy said, ringing her bell once more in the increasingly faint hope of summoning Gwen from the kitchen. 'We were all perfectly happy to send Dauncy to America on his own to travel about any old how – and really, compared to that what's a few tots of rum?' Loopy threw her husband a good hard look while she continued to ring her little bell.

'Depends who you're drinking them with,' John muttered.

'What *is* it with all of you about Waldo Astley?' Loopy exclaimed in sudden exasperation. 'And you in particular, John.'

John at once dropped his eyes, pretending to brush some crumbs off the table with his napkin to avoid his mother's stare. She had already accosted him about his relationship with Mattie and had only been prevented from taking the matter up with his father by John's not altogether convincing protestations that there was nothing between himself and Mattie Eastcott that was really at all serious. Naturally, having witnessed their completely serious embrace on the beach, Loopy had not been at all persuaded and had warned John about the perils of becoming too deeply involved with a young woman who had a reputation for being fast as well as a son born out of wedlock. John was her eldest and much was expected of him, so he could put from his head any idea he might have of marrying the girl. At which John had begged her to agree to a moratorium on the matter until he had sorted himself out emotionally, and above all not to say a word to his father until he had done so.

Reluctantly Loopy had agreed, her reluctance born out of her belief that the longer the matter remained undebated by his parents the more deeply John was going to become involved with someone Loopy could not help but think of as being entirely unsuitable for him. Yet such was her love for her eldest son, and such was the look in his eyes when he pleaded with her to give him some more time, that Loopy had been persuaded to give him her word.

But now, the more John made unkind remarks about someone Loopy regarded as the soul of consideration and kindness, the more Loopy wondered at the wisdom of the promise she had made him.

'Be warned, John, because I am serious. I will not have these unkind aspersions cast on someone who has done no harm to you or to anyone sitting at this table. Is that understood?'

'Yes, Mother.' John looked as unrepentant as his father looked bored, and Gwen had still not appeared with the pudding.

'I wonder why you should be so keen to leap to this chap's defence, my love,' Hugh remarked. Having given up on the pudding's ever appearing, he tapped a Senior Service cigarette on his silver case before putting it in his mouth.

'Because none of you seem able to find one good word to say about him.'

'Or could it be—' Hugh said slowly, flicking his cigarette alight with his small gold Ronson and looking down the table at his wife, 'might it be because he's got you some sort of exhibition of your paintings in London?'

Astounded into silence, Loopy stared blankly across the dining table at her husband, who in return just raised his eyebrows, blowing a line of blue smoke out of one corner of his mouth.

'As someone recently remarked, Bexham is a very small place, my dear.'

'*You* told him?' Loopy repeated disbelievingly as accompanied by Waldo she walked a distant headland. 'I just can't believe it was you who told him!'

'I told him, Loopy,' Waldo agreed, 'because I was quite certain that you were not going to. At least not until the very last moment – and then God knows what might have happened.'

'I would *not* have told him at the last minute.'

'So what do you call this? You have ten days to go till the opening – your pictures have to be in London next week to be hung – and you think Hugh isn't going to notice anything?' Waldo stopped and looked at Loopy quizically. 'What were you going to tell him? That you had sent them off to be cleaned, or revarnished?'

'You don't know Hugh well enough to tell him something like this. You don't. You don't know him well enough to discuss *my* personal business with him – to discuss something that could affect my relationship with *my* husband! I've a good mind to call this damned exhibition off.'

'Please yourself,' Waldo said calmly.

'I simply don't understand why you think you were in a position to tell my husband something as important as this.'

'That's simple. He wanted to know what was going on between us.'

Loopy put a hand to her throat and stared wide-eyed at Waldo. 'Hugh thought there was something going on between us?'

'You think that an unlikely notion?' Waldo said, raising his eyebrows as high as he could to make her laugh.

'Be serious, Waldo.'

'OK. I shall be serious. It's perfectly all right for you to suspect that your husband might be having an affair with Meggie, but not all right for your husband to think that you and I might be having an affair. Isn't that sort of against all your fair is fair all round principles?'

'You just surprised me, that's all.' Loopy looked vaguely unsettled.

'You people,' Waldo sighed. 'I don't know, really I don't.'

'Which people? Who do you mean by you people?'

'The lot of you sometimes,' Waldo replied in quiet exasperation. 'Each and every one of you.'

'Leaving aside what you might think about each and every one of us,' Loopy said tightly, 'perhaps you'd just like to explain the circumstances of your revelation to Hugh. Did you come to him – or did he seek you out? I find it hard to understand how you became this intimate when you hardly know each other.'

'We might not know each other that well,' Waldo said after a pause. 'But we see quite a lot of each other.'

'I don't see how.'

'Confidential, I'm afraid.'

'You're not a mason, surely?'

Waldo stared at her then threw back his head and laughed. 'No, Loopy – I most certainly am not a Mason.'

'Then how can it be confidential? What could you possibly have between you that should give you confidentiality – unless . . . my God, you're not?' Loopy stared at Waldo with a mixture of dismay and amazement. 'You're not one of Hugh's bogeys, are you?'

'Hugh's bogeys?'

'That's what John calls his— the people who work for him. His bogeys. My God, you're not one of them, surely?'

Waldo gave her the look that he knew always made her smile, half tilting his head at her and slightly widening his eyes.

'Wonderful view from here, don't you think?' he remarked, taking her arm and continuing to walk her along the cliff path. Loopy sighed and shook her head sadly, knowing that by the rules that bound them this conversation was at an end.

'I should hate you, really, but I don't.'

'So what do you do for me?'

'I like you, Waldo, that's what I do. You're a friend. As a matter of fact I consider you to be a really good friend.'

'That's exactly what I want to be to you.'

'Then that's good. Now let's just enjoy our walk, shall we?'

For a moment as they ambled in friendly silence along the clifftop path Loopy's thoughts turned to Meggie, and to her husband, but as those thoughts began to make her feel uncomfortable she took hold of the arm that was linked to hers, at the same time deciding to banish all further contemplation of the unknown, preferring instead to enjoy both the sea views and the present company.

All of a sudden she felt oddly independent, and

she relished the moment, embracing the new found feeling as strongly as she was embracing the arm that held her, knowing that somehow this newly discovered independence was something that was long overdue.

Chapter Eleven

The brief object of Loopy's discomfort bumped into Mattie in Dr Farnsworth's surgery the following Monday. Mattie was very poorly, with a streaming cold that had turned into something with all the hallmarks of the influenza that had broken out generally in the region, albeit somewhat earlier than was usually expected.

'You got the flu as well?' she asked Meggie. 'Because if you have, you have my sympathy.'

'No,' Meggie said, edging slightly away from Mattie and wishing she hadn't chosen to sit down next to her in the crowded surgery. 'I had some sort of bug in the summer, and it hasn't cleared up. Left me with a rather unattractive cough.'

'Cigarettes probably,' Mattie said, sounding muffled as she held a handkerchief to her face. 'I don't care what anyone says, I don't think they do us any good at all, except of course reduce our appetites.'

'I can't smoke at all at the moment,' Meggie said regretfully. 'All it does is make me cough.'

'I've cut right down,' Mattie said, stuffing her

hankie back up the sleeve of her dress. 'Down to ten a day now.'

'Bully,' Meggie said, tossing back her head. 'That's about what I'm used to getting through before breakfast – until this damn' cough.'

When Meggie finally got in to see Dr Farnsworth he himself was just stubbing out a cigarette in an ashtray, which Meggie recognised at once as having been purloined from the Three Tuns.

'Good,' the doctor said, indicating the chair opposite his desk. 'Sit. Sit you down. Good. And how are we today?'

'Absolutely top hole,' Meggie drawled. 'Hence my visit.'

Dr Farnsworth looked up, surprised. 'I was merely being conversational, Miss Gore Stewart. Obviously if you were feeling altogether well I dare say you *wouldn't* be here. So what is wrong with us today? Feeling a bit—'

'I have this cough,' Meggie interrupted. 'I've had it since the summer – since early summer in fact – and it's making me feel rather washed out.'

Dr Farnsworth duly listened to her chest, felt the glands in her throat, looked at her tonsils and took the opportunity of listening to her chest once more, a part of the examination over which he seemed to linger unduly.

'You're making a bit of a meal of this, aren't you?' Meggie said, sitting up and pulling her sweater back down over her breasts. 'It's only a throaty cough.'

'You've been feeling tired, you say?' Farnsworth

stood back, having pulled his stethoscope out of his ears. 'A bit washed out.'

'I haven't been sleeping well, not me at all, actually. I learned to sleep anywhere during the war, haystacks, trains, backs of lorries, but now with this cough I'm awake half the night and nothing brings relief.'

'You're a smoker, aren't you?'

'So are you.'

'I'm not the one being examined for a bad cough, Miss Gore-Stewart.'

'Are you saying I should stop smoking? Because if so I promise you I am taking in half my usual amount, due to this graveyard cough.'

'How many are you in the habit of smoking a day, normally, Miss Gore-Stewart?'

'Normally?' Meggie paused, thinking. 'Normally I smoke too many, Dr Farnsworth. Now I am smoking far less than too many, but still I suppose too many.'

'Then cut down. That's all you need to do – cut down. You don't have to cut it out altogether, just cut down, if you're a heavy smoker. There's nothing intrinsically wrong with tobacco – in fact there's a school of thought that holds that it clears the mind and helps concentration. I certainly find that. It's also considerably helped my daughter's asthma, so you don't have to think *oh I must stop smoking altogether*. It's the same with anything done to excess. Excess is what's harmful, not necessarily the ingredient. Same goes with alcohol, aspirin, and food of course. You're coughing because you're really not giving your lungs a chance to recover, that's all. A little respite between cigarettes and you'd be surprised. The body is a remarkable piece of machinery, Miss Gore-Stewart, with quite remarkable powers not only of recovery but of self-restoration. How many *do* you smoke a day?'

'I don't count. I told you. Sometimes more, when I'm a bit – you know. During the war I smoked two or three packets – when I could get them.'

'If I were you, I'd cut it down to one packet a day. You've been overdoing it, that's all. Simply a case of overdoing it. You won't believe the difference if you can cut back to about twenty a day. You really don't need more than that. I find I don't. Anything more than twenty a day is just – well. Overdoing it.'

Meggie returned to the outside world armed with a large bottle of cough linctus and a supply of Fisherman's Friend to keep her cough at bay. Relieved that there was nothing wrong with her other than a bad dose of excess, she was determined to take Dr Farnsworth's advice and do her best to cut back to one packet of Players a day, a target she believed was well within her capabilities, if – for instance, as she confided to Mattie as she left the surgery – she gave up smoking in bed, and particularly before she got up in the morning. She vowed to herself that those were cigarettes she would now do without.

Feeling better for her visit to the surgery, she lengthened her stride and walked with increased confidence back to Cucklington House, only to find a letter from her lawyers advising her that the matter she had tried to put out of her mind in the hope of some miracle's occurring had come to a head, and the sale of her grandmother's beloved seaside home was no longer a consideration, but an absolute necessity.

Having absorbed the contents of the letter, Meggie lit a fresh cigarette and went to the drinks tray for a gin. The unimaginable had happened. She was about to lose the last thing in her life that she truly loved.

Waldo used his trip to London bearing Loopy's precious paintings carefully wrapped up in the back of his Buick to introduce Lionel to the city's fashionably active bridge circuit. After delivering the paintings to the gallery in Cork Street and instructing one of the assistants to unwrap but not to begin hanging the pictures until he returned the following day, he drove on to an address in Mayfair where he met Lionel, and they both changed into black tie for the evening's play.

Admiring the elegant surroundings in which he found himself, Lionel could not help wondering to whom the apartment might belong, only to be told by Waldo that it didn't belong to anyone as such, at least not to anyone that he knew personally since it was a rental.

'It has quite an art collection for what you call "a rental",' Lionel observed shrewdly, sitting on one of the twin beds in the bedroom and carefully tying the shoelaces of his patent leather shoes.

'That's because it's a very expensive rental, Lionel,' Waldo replied. 'And because the guy who rents it has very good taste.'

'Might we have a bracer before we leave?' Lionel enquired, as Waldo stood checking his bow tie in the mirror above the drawing room fireplace.

'Most certainly not, Lionel,' Waldo reprimanded him. 'No alcohol either before or during the game. Afterwards you may get as smashed as you wish, your only consideration being that if we lose, you pay.'

They took a taxicab to the venue, a large private house in a very large garden somewhere in Hampstead. This was a part of London that was largely unknown to Lionel, so he had absolutely no bearing on where exactly he was, or the status of the house – at least not until he entered and saw the furnishings and the art collection. It was obviously the home of a very rich person, in the shape of a small rotund and entirely bald middle-aged man introducing himself as George Beck Hampton, their host for the evening. There were six tables in all, each one of them supervised by a white-gloved referee positioned behind the chair to be occupied by North. Lionel was duly introduced only to those people at whose table he and Waldo would first be playing, their opponents being foreign while happily speaking, to Lionel's particular relief, impeccable English. There was no real emphasis placed upon the size of the stakes other than that they were to be of the usual order and that all debts must be cleared before leaving either by cash or by guaranteed banker's cheque.

Lionel looked immediately discomfited by this, even though Waldo had put him entirely in the picture, and glanced across the table at his partner. Waldo ignored the look. Instead he started to engage in small talk with the man on his left playing East, as the pre-prepared hands in sealed envelopes were put on the table in front of each person seated North. Five minutes later play was allowed to commence.

There was no real reason for Lionel to be nervous yet he nevertheless found that the hands that held his cards were quite definitely sweating. He knew he was an excellent player and that – more importantly – Waldo had underwritten the entire evening, as a consequence of which he personally had nothing to lose. No, what he feared was making a complete ass of himself, which was why it seemed to him that he was half dead with fright.

Because of his catatonic state he opened the first hand Two No Trumps instead of One, ended up in a contract of six hearts and went four light, doubled. Waldo did not even bother to exchange a look. The next hand their opponents contracted to make a modest Two No Trumps, Lionel doubled on the strength of a long line of clubs headed by the king, led the fourth of the suit to a void in Waldo's hand and his opponents made their contract with ease, plus three overtricks. Again, Waldo did not do so much as look even vaguely in Lionel's direction, preferring instead to study at length the magnificent chandelier under which they were all seated.

Twenty minutes later the two of them left their first table the losers, scoring nothing to their opponents' two thousand eight hundred points.

'Which is?' Lionel muttered at Waldo as they headed for the next table.

'Which is what?'

'How much are we down, Waldo?'

'Two thousand eight hundred. You should know. You had the scorecard.'

'How much money is that?'

'You really wouldn't want to know, Lionel. You might play even more incompetently.'

'I did not play incompetently!' Lionel insisted, a little too vociferously. 'Nervously, perhaps – I was a little nervous, no doubt, but incompetence at the card table is not in my repertoire.'

'Your repertoire was loaded with it in that rubber, my friend. Now forget about the score, forget about the money, forget about these no-hopers, because believe me, Lionel, there isn't one guy here who can hold a candle to you let alone to us – all except that Egyptian over there who is about the best player in the world – so settle down, and enjoy yourself. Play some cards. And stop looking like a constipated crocodile.'

'That's what I look like?'

'The spit darned image, my dear fellow, the spit darned image. You should be in a Florida swamp, not on the London circuit.'

Far from upsetting him, somehow Waldo's

utterly raffish and devil-may-care attitude actually settled Lionel, so that the moment bidding started at their second table he began to play with his old flair and skill, imagining himself to be back in Gloria Bishop's modest little drawing room, playing as usual with Waldo against Gloria and the vicar. From that moment on Waldo and Lionel could not lose, or at least only when Waldo wanted them to do so in order to lure their opponents into a false sense of security. Knowing Waldo's game as well as he did now, Lionel suffered no blue fit when he heard his partner wildly overbid, or just as rashly double a contract their opponents were practically certain to make, and simply played his part to perfection. The result was that at eleven o'clock precisely, when game was called, not only were Waldo and he the evening's overall winners, but their final tally of points was five and a half thousand points clear of the next pair. For their prize they received a cash payment of two hundred and fifty pounds each. Naturally Lionel accepted the money as if it was an everyday occurrence, as he did the banker's cheque for the sum of five hundred and fifty pounds, to be split between the partners fifty-fifty.

The taxi ride home to Mayfair was a silent affair, Lionel saying not a word, and Waldo preferring to puff contentedly away on his Havana. After a while he did, however, start to shake with silent laughter, as Lionel merely stared ahead of him at the cab driver's back, dumbstruck. Following Waldo's short attack of glee, as the taxi was turning off Park Lane into Mount Street, Lionel seemed to wake from his shock, and demanded to know what Waldo had been finding so funny.

'Why, my dear chap!' Waldo exclaimed. 'Why, your face, of course! Your dear face! You should see it! Why, you look as though you are sitting on something very sharp and extremely upright! Never have I seen such a face! It is too perfect for words!'

Seeing the point, Lionel also started at last to laugh. Bexham might beckon, but just at that moment he was in heaven, and he knew it, and that was where he planned on staying.

The next morning Waldo went to the gallery to help hang Loopy's exhibition. Loopy had already arrived and with the help of two of the gallery's young assistants had already begun the task, only for Waldo to take command and order everything to be taken down and hung again. By late afternoon it was done, and even the increasingly nervous artist herself had to admit to being pleased with the arrangement of her pictures on the walls. Waldo wondered what she was going to do with herself that evening and was surprised to learn that she intended to catch the 6.10 home from Waterloo.

'Would it not be wiser for you to stay up in town now?' he asked. 'There are all sorts of incidental details still to be looked after – interviews, photographs, further preparatory work and all that stuff. You have a flat in town, don't you?

Surely it would be altogether wiser for you to stay up here with your husband?'

'That's the whole point, Waldo,' Loopy explained, checking her watch. 'Hugh isn't in town. I had a telephone call just after lunch to say he was returning home because he wasn't feeling at all well. So I really must get back to him.'

'Nothing serious, I hope? This influenza bug's running riot.'

'He said something about pains in his chest. He sounded rather worried – at least for Hugh he did. He normally stiffens that already pretty starched British upper lip at times of distress. So I really think I ought to go home.'

'Very well.' Waldo nodded. 'I'd offer to drive you home, but firstly I have an unbreakable engagement this evening and secondly I don't see as I'd be a whole lot of use at Hugh's bedside.'

'I think that's my job, Waldo.' Loopy smiled, kissing him goodbye on the cheek. 'You've done your job,' she added, indicating the hung paintings. 'And a good job, too.'

Waldo would have liked to run Loopy back down to Sussex, thereby both helping her and being in her company, but as he and Lionel changed for the evening he knew that it was quite out of the question. This was the only chance they were going to have of a match with the great Egyptian card player who also happened to be one of the game's heaviest gamblers.

For the first time in his life as far as bridge went

Waldo felt a sudden attack of nerves. Looking round at his playing partner as they both stood tying their bow ties he wondered whether they really were quite up to the challenge. Peter Bottros's regular playing partner, Estelle Van der Beek, was an extremely rich South African widow who was also considered one of the very best contract bridge players on the circuit. As a duo they were rarely beaten at the level at which they would be playing this evening, a single-table challenge of the best of seven rubbers, naturally dealt. As an added incentive the stakes were to be even higher than the preceding night's, although Waldo was wise enough not to inform Lionel of this point. Even though Lionel stood at no financial risk whatsoever, Waldo appreciated the fact that he suffered nerves on behalf of Waldo's wallet, and made absolutely no mention of the upping of the ante.

The game was held in Mr Bottros's suite of rooms at the top of the Dorchester Hotel in Park Lane. Waldo and Lionel ate a light meal of chicken and salad in the restaurant downstairs before proceeding up to the arena, where Waldo formally introduced Lionel to their opponents since they had not met or played against each other during the previous evening's entertainment. A number of spectators were present, including James Banks, the British film star, and two members of the Shadow Cabinet. Lionel, having already been lectured by Waldo about distraction, to his surprise found the strength not to be overawed by the distinguished audience nor sidelined by any small talk. Instead – again as advised – he kept himself to himself and remained very much on the sidelines, drinking fresh fruit juice and eating small pieces of dark chocolate from his pocket in order to keep up his energy while Waldo, as ever apparently at his ease, coped with the social niceties until it was time to play.

For the first two rubbers the cards simply ran against them. In fact as Lionel found himself with the third hand in succession in which he held less than six points and was thus unable to respond to Waldo's opening bid he got that feeling familiar to any bridge player that it was going to be one of those nights when he would never be dealt a decent hand.

To compound his growing anxiety Waldo began to bid against his opponents' obviously strong hands, trying to force them into a higher contract than they wanted, but Bottros and the beautiful Mrs Van der Beek were not to be bullied and twice left Waldo doubled in contracts he had no possible chance of making.

At first Lionel believed this to be part of Waldo's tactics, but when he found himself and his partner three rubbers down without a point on their score-cards, he realised it was not part of any game plan and that they were, in fact, in serious trouble. Their opponents only needed one more rubber to win the challenge and the purse, the current rubber standing at one game each with their opponents sixty points below the line and now looking the odds on favourites. Lionel tried to catch Waldo's eye just for some sign of encouragement, but Waldo refused to look up from the hand of cards that had been freshly dealt to him. Worse, for the first time since Lionel had known him he saw him scowling, his mouth turned deeply down at the corners, his forehead lined with concern and his normally big bright eyes small and darkly glittering. If the cards at which Waldo was staring were as bad as the temper shown on his face, then Lionel thought all chance was gone.

Except he had been dealt eight hearts headed by the ace and knave, the singleton ace of clubs, the queen, knave, ten and seven of spades and a void in diamonds, eighteen points if he allowed three for the void and certainly a hand both of strength and of peculiar enough distribution to more than justify an opening bid. But it wasn't him to open. It was the person on his right, East, Peter Bottros, who opened Two Diamonds, a bid given the conventions being employed that demanded a response from his partner, however weak her hand. Lionel's logical bid should have been to open Two Hearts, to show his long suit and sufficiency of points to overcall such a big opener, but, knowing that if he did so Mrs Van der Beek would be excused a response, in a moment of what was to turn out to be inspiration he passed. He passed on what was undoubtedly an extremely strong hand, one strong enough to go to game and secure the vital rubber.

'No bid,' he said.

Mrs Van der Beek playing West now had to

respond, even though she held a hand containing precisely five points, the queen of diamonds and a void in hearts, her only possible bid being the minimum raise.

'Three Diamonds,' she called, which could be taken to show minimum support in her partner's suit, or absolutely nothing. It would all depend on Waldo's bid. Should he have enough points to open then Bottros could read his partner's call as zero support and either back out, or bid on, depending entirely on the strength of his own call and the meaning of any opening bid by North.

But Waldo, sitting North, also in a moment of sheer inspiration – or perhaps simply of genius – passed.

'No bid,' he said evenly – and the trap was sprung.

Unable to resist the plunge with three rubbers in the bag and more than halfway to the winning game, Bottros reviewed his hand, a hand that contained eight diamonds to the ace, king, knave and ten, the king and queen of clubs, the queen and ten of hearts and the singleton king of spades – and gambled. After all, in a way, he had nothing to lose if they went down on this contract since they were so far ahead, and since his opponents obviously had nothing, to judge from their lack of bids, then his partner's bid was perhaps intended to show him support in his chosen suit. Ideally he knew she should have bid another suit if her hand was strong enough to encourage him to go to game, or jump to Three Diamonds, but instead of reading the bid correctly he allowed for an error, thus forcing himself into one – and a far greater one than his partner's simple minimum raise.

'Five Diamonds,' he called, reckoning on finding at least the queen of trumps in his partner's hand plus either the ace of spades, or failing that a void in the suit.

Now it was Lionel's turn, and of course everyone watching as well as his two opponents expected Lionel to pass, but he didn't. This was the moment to strike, and strike he did with a deadly precision, a move and a bid that was to remain with him for the rest of his days.

'Five Hearts,' he called, his eyes correctly fixed on his cards so that he could not catch sight of either his partner's reaction or that of his opponents, even though he knew it was a bid to drive the opposition to distraction. They must either call what they must perceive as his bluff or raise their level to a Small Slam, a contract Lionel knew to be outside their reach.

Mrs Van der Beek did not bid because she could not, but she most certainly did call and not unnaturally she doubled.

Waldo passed.

On the strength of the double and the belief that Lionel's bid was motivated by desperation, Bottros went to Six Diamonds.

Whereupon Lionel calmly proceeded to bid a Grand Slam.

'Seven Hearts,' he called, hoping against hope that his so far silent partner could fill the dangerously glaring gaps in his hand. Their opponents obviously had possibly every Diamond between them, and – Lionel imagined given the odd distribution – one of them must have a void in another suit, the odds being that the suit in which they would be critically short would be hearts. So Seven Hearts it was, and if they were to go down then it would be with all guns blazing.

'Double,' said Mrs Van der Beek, again not unnaturally.

'Redouble,' said Waldo, much to Lionel's private and utter delight, because he knew at such a crucial stage in the game Waldo would not risk the chance of such an expensive calamity unless he had realised that his own hand must contain the ingredients missing in his partner's.

Now their opponents had no place to go. Seven Spades was clearly impossible, seeing Lionel had four spades headed by the queen and the jack and a singleton ace of clubs which surely must score since the odds were one thousand to one against either of their opponents having a void in clubs, and Seven No Trumps on the strength of Lionel's ace of clubs alone was a non-starter.

So the contract was Seven Hearts doubled and redoubled by South, a contract that had been greeted with the odd not so quiet gasp from certain members of the distinguished audience. Mrs Van der Beek quite correctly led a diamond to her partner's as yet undisclosed but obviously held ace, Waldo as Dummy placed his hand down on the table, and the other three players studied it. Waldo quietly asked if he might be excused, his opponents agreed, and he left the room, leaving behind him face up on the table the king of hearts and two low ones, five low clubs to the knave, the ace of spades heading three lower spades and a singleton diamond.

As soon as dummy was disclosed Lionel knew he would need a finesse to win – he would need to bluff out the king of spades. The queen of trumps was bound to fall, even if Bottros held both the outstanding trump cards, since ace, king of trumps played would bring about her demise. But while the queen of hearts presented no problem, the king of spades did if it lay to the right of Dummy's Ace. Should it do so he would go down by one trick which while not being a disaster would not constitute a victory either – and at this point of the match a victory was the only thing of any use to them. Should they lose this hand, and the next, then the match was gone.

So Lionel had to gamble, but instead of playing for a finesse he took a major risk. From the distribution of the cards that were visible to him, Lionel knew his only chance of real salvation lay in assuming that Bottros was holding the king of spades as a singleton. So having drawn trumps he played the ace of spades from dummy and to his well concealed delight saw the singleton king fall to it. The rest of the hand was a lay-down, a concession he now politely requested and which was immediately granted.

Against all odds the crucial rubber was won and not only were Waldo and Lionel back in the game, they were back in the money, to the tune of four and a half thousand points.

'Top of the world,' he muttered to himself as he marked up the scorecard. 'Top of the world – top of the world, and if that's not, what is?'

Which indeed at that moment he truly was.

'That indeed was the turning point, my dear chap,' Waldo told Lionel as they were reviewing the evening's play on their way back to Waldo's borrowed apartment. 'A truly inspired passage of play, of which I have to say I knew you to be capable.'

'I have to confess I didn't,' Lionel replied, filling his pipe carefully, anxious not to spill any of his precious tobacco, an accident that had every likelihood of happening due to the speed at which the cabbie was driving. 'And I forgot to mention your particular notable act – your moment of true sang-froid. Getting up from the table when you had laid down Dummy and asking to be excused. That I have to say showed real aplomb.'

'Aplomb,' Waldo mused. 'I like the word aplomb. And I like to think that's what you thought I was showing. Actually I was so nervous I had to remove myself to the gentlemen's to be quietly sick.'

Lionel turned to look at his friend in amazement.

'You? Sick?' he asked, noticing of a sudden that Waldo did have dark shadows under his eyes. 'I never would have thought it of you, my dear fellow, not ever.'

'Sick with nerves. I don't think I have ever been so near the brink before. You completely wrong-footed me with your eleventh-hour bid – and then when I looked at my hand and realised we might have a perfect fit suddenly I found my stomach rushing upwards to my throat.' Waldo gave a laugh of great enjoyment then relit his cigar. 'It was a shoo-in from then, old chap, wouldn't you say?' he continued. 'Took the wind completely out of their sails.'

'I wouldn't say a four-three victory which was finally achieved after one game all in the final rubber was exactly what you call a shoo-in, Waldo.'

'We were never under pressure from the moment of that slam, dear fellow. We had them on the back foot, rocked by indecision, with their confidence completely evaporated. We could have won when we liked, as we liked.'

'You do have to have the cards, Waldo.'

'You have to have *some* cards – but more than anything, my dear fellow, you have to have great skill – in bidding, in defence, and in attack. They were all over the shop after your magnificent coup – while we were invincible in every sphere. We could have picked them off when we liked – and in fact if you remember how the play went, that is exactly what we did.'

While Waldo sat back and enjoyed the rest of his cigar, Lionel reviewed the last hands and realised his friend was absolutely right. They had been sitting in what Waldo described as the Catbird seat, a term derived it appeared from baseball, which meant that they were in total control of every aspect of the game from that historic and dramatic moment – and the more he thought about it the more Lionel glowed with pride. In all his life he had never been as excited as he was now. In his heightened state of euphoria he saw that his life had been dull and orderly not by accident but by design, and with the advent of Waldo with his insistence of dropping Lionel right in the deep end of the bridge world, he had at last come of age. He had ceased to be the little grey man that since Gloria Bishop's youthful rejection of him he felt he had become. The only thing that made him sad at this moment of triumph was that his wife Maude was not there to share his excitement and pride.

If only things had been different, he thought to himself as he puffed at his pipe, if only he had appreciated his wife more and allowed her the proper room in his life, if he had created a proper marriage for them both instead of excluding her, she might not have been compelled to take an active part in the wretched war, might not have got herself killed and might this very moment be waiting at home for his return. They would celebrate together, raiding his cellar for a bottle of the champagnes he kept but never drank, and then they would dance. They would dance just as they used to when they first met. They might even dance Maude's favourite – what was it? Yes. The

Black Bottom. Dee dum dee dee. Whatever that meant.

Waldo was talking.

'By the way, old chap, what about your new admirer? Mrs Estelle Van der Beek? My – after the game she could hardly keep her eyes off you, let alone those diamond-studded hands.'

'Nonsense!' Lionel reddened. 'She was simply being polite. Sociable. Good-looking woman, though,' he added, half to himself and half to Waldo.

Waldo laughed.

'Now, don't be shy. She has fallen for you hook, line and sinker, Lionel, believe you me. I saw it for myself. You have quite won the heart of one of South Africa's richest widows. Just you wait and see – she will be driving down to Bexham to take tea with you at any moment, I predict it.'

'I hardly think so,' Lionel retorted. 'Most particularly not when she finds out that I have a daughter and grandson living at home with me. Enough to put off any rich widow for life, I should imagine.'

Of course he had indeed found himself flattered by the close attention Mrs Van der Beek had paid him over the buffet supper after the titanic card game, but pleased as he was by the compliments she had paid him about his card play in front of the most distinguished members of their enthralled audience, Lionel considered her flirtation to be a will-o'-the-wisp. To his mind Mrs Van der Beek was simply going through the social motions, something at which she was undoubtedly expert coming from a background such as hers. And Lionel was too much of a realist not to know that by the next morning the memory of Lionel Eastcott would be consigned to oblivion as Mrs Van der Beek returned to her personal circle. Nevertheless, Lionel was flattered, and excited. He was, after all, still a man.

'Penny for them,' Waldo said, as the taxi drew up outside their destination. 'Or might I guess?'

'It really is none of your business,' Lionel replied, preparing to alight. 'You may read my thoughts at the bridge table as much as you like – but what goes on in my head at all other times is strictly out of bounds.'

Again Waldo laughed, and leaned forward to pay off the cabbie.

At Waldo's suggestion they returned home to Bexham a little later in the day than Lionel would have wished, eventually driven there at great speed by Waldo in his magnificent Jaguar.

In contrast to his high spirits of the night before, Lionel found his companion for once oddly silent, and wondered whether this might be due to the telephone call he knew Waldo had received earlier that day. He didn't wish to pry since he felt he didn't know his friend quite well enough to enquire after what Lionel always called private grief, so he puffed away at his new pipe and watched the last of the summer landscape flash by his window in a blur of soft early autumn pastels.

Finally, as they motored across the Downs just to the north of Churchester, Waldo apologised for his silence and explained to Lionel that he was a little preoccupied with personal matters, which although nothing of a serious nature had given him cause for concern. The now seemingly permanently affable Lionel assured him that, as well as understanding, after the high excitement of the previous evening he himself was only too happy to enjoy the drive in relative quiet. Waldo thanked him for his forbearance, and lapsed once more into silence, only to break it moments later with a friendly slap on Lionel's right knee.

'I nearly forgot, old chap,' he said. 'There was a call for you as well – but you were still sound out, so I took the message. Mrs Van der Beek would be very grateful if you would telephone her at the Dorchester on your arrival home the first moment you find you have free.'

He glanced round at Lionel, raised his eyebrows, and then returned his concentration to his driving, leaving Lionel to pretend to frown out of the window as if he was shocked and displeased.

Loopy paced the carpet in the drawing room, walking up and down the same line in its pattern as she waited for the doctor to finish his examination of her husband and descend with his opinion.

She had gone home the previous evening to hear that although Hugh had taken to his bed feeling unwell he hadn't called the doctor. It was typical of him and very worrying.

'No need to call the doctor. It's sure to be just indigestion,' Hugh moaned, facing the bedroom wall, and looking of a sudden, to Loopy anyway, about ten years old.

'What nonsense. If you have pains in your chest for God's sake, Hugh, it could be something serious!'

'They're not really pains as such. Not any more. Please – you know me. I'd rather not make a fuss if it weren't necessary. So why not wait until morning?'

Loopy nearly told Hugh that if there really was something wrong with him he could be dead by the morning, but the look in her husband's eyes prevented her. It wasn't a look of illness or fear, but rather one of fleeting guilt.

First thing in the morning, when she'd hardly had time to get herself properly dressed, a sudden urgent call from Hugh's bedroom summoned her back to his bedside, where she found him lying propped up on his pillows with a frown on his face and a hand on his chest. Naturally she went straight to the telephone, only to be told by Dr Farnsworth that he had many other more serious calls to make.

'But suppose my husband's suffering from a heart attack, doctor?'

'If he was, believe you me you'd soon know about it, Mrs Tate.'

Eventually, after a long morning alternating between anxiety over Hugh and anxiety over her exhibition, Loopy heard Gwen letting Dr

Farnsworth into the house. She finally stopped her measured pacing of the carpet when he had finished his examination of her husband.

'Well?' Loopy asked at once, as Dr Farnsworth ambled into the room, black Gladstone bag in one hand, his other hand searching his pocket for his packet of cigarettes.

'That coffee still hot?' he wondered, nodding at the pot on a tray by the window. Loopy shook her head in return and lit one of her own cigarettes. 'Then I wouldn't say no to a sherry. It's been one of those mornings.'

Loopy eyed the untidy bear of a man who was now lighting an untipped cigarette with a cheap nickel lighter, and with an inward sigh poured a small glass of Dry Fly from the decanter.

'So how is my husband?' she asked, handing over the drink. 'Is it his heart?'

'Hard to say really,' Dr Farnsworth replied, sinking into an armchair. 'I mean I don't think for one moment it is – but then I can't be sure without a fuller examination.'

'Then shouldn't you perhaps be arranging that?'

'If the patient shows any sign of worsening, I certainly shall, Mrs Tate. Fear not. Fear thee not.'

The doctor drank half the glass of sherry in one, and tapped his ash into the fireplace.

'Yes, it really has been one of those mornings. Two strangulated hernias – not one but two, mind you – and a prolapsed womb. Not the ideal end to a busy week. As for this flu bug—'

'What do you suggest we do about my

husband?' Loopy interrupted. 'He said he thought it was just indigestion.'

'You know, sometimes I wonder why I bothered to study medicine, Mrs Tate. I take it you know how many years it takes to become a doctor? Yet the number of patients one has who think they can diagnose what's wrong with them.' Doctor Farnsworth shook his head and finished his sherry. 'It could well be indigestion – but then I would rather be the one who decided that, not the patient. I'll look in again on Monday.'

He rose to his feet, brushed off some ash he had carelessly spilt down the front of his grubby yellow waistcoat and picked up his bag.

'In the meantime?' Loopy stopped him by the door. 'What am I supposed to do in the meantime, please?'

'What any good wife should do, I imagine, Mrs Tate,' Dr Farnsworth replied with ill concealed irritation. 'Keep a weather eye on him and see to his needs. And give me a call if your husband worsens. I'll see myself out.'

'Oh!' Loopy cried in exasperation after the doctor had departed. 'Oh! Oh! *Oh*!'

To her amazement she found herself actually stamping her foot, and her amazement was entirely genuine since Loopy Tate most certainly was not a foot-stamper. But then as far as she was concerned, the man in the room immediately above her head was most certainly not suffering from any heart problems, at least not ones that could be solved by either medicine or surgery. Out of her frustration she was just about to pour herself a glass of sherry when on the floor above her she heard the banging of the stick she had left by her husband's bed for emergency calling.

'What is it? Darling?' she enquired, after hurrying upstairs to find Hugh propped up against his pillows reading a newspaper which he at once put down with a sigh, just in time to assume his best sickly smile.

'A little broth, I think, Loopy dear,' he said weakly. 'A little thin chicken broth with some pearl barley in it, and some toast, would be very welcome. Oh – and a lightly boiled egg perhaps.'

'Did the doctor say you could eat?'

'He said I must eat to keep up my strength.'

'I'll see what Gwen can rustle up.'

'I'd rather you yourself did any rustling up that had to be done, Loopy darling. Gwen always over-boils my eggs. And burns the toast.'

'I have things to do—'

'I'm really very sorry about this,' Hugh said, his fingers playing at the edges of the newspaper's pages. 'It couldn't have happened at a worse time; and I'm really so sorry.'

'For yourself? Or what, Hugh? I don't understand what you're sorry about, really I don't. No-one can help being ill, after all. No-one designs when they are ill, do they?'

'I'm sorry about your exhibition, of course, darling.' He looked at her with clear, strong and very bright eyes. 'You having to miss the opening and all that, because of me. That was the last thing

I would have wanted, to be ill just before your opening.'

'I don't remember anyone saying I was going to miss the opening, Hugh.'

'I know,' Hugh continued, staring sadly out of the window with a faraway look in his eyes, not having heard, 'I know just how much this exhibition means to you.'

'No, you don't, Hugh. You couldn't possibly know how much this exhibition means to me. No-one could know that. Not even I know it, yet.'

'I think I do,' Hugh clasped his hands together now, like a cleric. 'And I'm just so sorry.'

'Tell you what, let's take it day by day, shall we, Hugh? See how you are tomorrow, and so on, yes? And if you're feeling better Sunday night or Monday morning – always provided you are on the mend – then I'll take myself up to town for the opening and then come right back down again. How does that sound to you?'

'Absolutely fine. Provided I'm all right, of course. But honestly, Loopy, the way I'm feeling now – the pains keep coming and going, you know – the way I'm feeling now I doubt very much if I'm going to be much better by Monday.'

'I sort of doubt that too, Hugh. But we'll see, won't we? We'll just wait and see.'

As Loopy was overseeing Hugh's precious egg and toast, Waldo arrived. Refusing Loopy's offer of some refreshment, Waldo asked her to stay out of the way while he took himself upstairs to see Hugh. Loopy protested weakly that her husband really shouldn't have visitors, but Waldo took no notice because he didn't believe it and neither did Loopy. With a small smile she took herself off back to the kitchen while Waldo vaulted up the stairs two at a time and bounded into Hugh's room, catching him by surprise in the middle of the act of lighting a cigarette.

'Very bad for your ticker, old boy,' Waldo said as he took the freshly lit Senior Service and tossed it out of the open window. 'And what's more, you're very bad for mine.'

'What the hell are you doing here, Waldo? I thought you were in Berlin.'

'I postponed Berlin till next week, *old bean*.'

'No, Waldo. You can't just postpone things like the Berlin trip to suit you.'

'I just have, old man. And I will continue to do so if and when I feel like it. I'm not working for you, you know – I'm working *with* you, remember? And there's nothing that can't wait for a day or two in Berlin.'

'As I just said, no can do.'

'Yes can do, and you're a rogue, Hugh, and a spoilsport. Besides being a spoilt brat.'

'You can't just burst into my bedroom and talk to me like that!' Hugh protested.

'Really?' Waldo smiled. 'Didn't you see me just do it? Want me to do it all over again?'

'I am not very well, Waldo. I have had these pains in my chest—'

'Sure you have – and I'm growing a tail. Now I have orders for you—'

'I do not take orders from you, Waldo. Don't be absurd.'

'In this instance you're going to. I don't expect you to get better this instant – but in about five minutes, that will be fine. OK?'

'What are you talking about?' Hugh protested. 'I can't just get better when I feel like it.'

'There's to be a distinct improvement by tonight, so much so that by tomorrow morning you're going to be amazed how well you are,' Waldo continued. 'And by evening – why, you are going to be just as right as rain.'

'You've taken leave of your senses.'

'No, no, you're the one who's done that – because if you don't do what I say, I am going to spill the famous beans.'

'I do not have the faintest idea what you're talking about.'

'I'm going to tell your wife all about you and Miss Meggie Gore-Stewart.'

Hugh stared at him intently, his hands gripping the top of his crisp linen bed sheet.

'There is nothing to tell about Meggie and me, and you damn well know it.'

'Is there something wrong with you? Are you ill, well, or faking it? While we're playing truth dare and promise—'

'There is nothing whatsoever between Meggie and me and you know it, Waldo.'

'Who's your wife going to believe, Hugh? You or me? At the moment I am considerably more in her favour than you are, *old bean*.'

'There is nothing whatsoever between Meggie—and do stop saying old bean.'

'You keep saying there's nothing between you and Meggie – and as I keep asking, who is going to believe you? *Old boy?* If you don't pull yourself together, old sport, and allow your beautiful wife to enjoy one of the most exciting things that has happened to her, not only shall I refuse to go to Germany on behalf of your government and do what only I can do there – I'll tell you what else I'm going to do.'

'I'm all ears, Astley,' Hugh said tightly. 'But I can tell you this in advance – no deal.'

'You'll change your mind when you've listened to this,' Waldo assured him. 'If you don't play ball – well, since you are too ill to move from your bed, and since you demand absolute first rate nursing care and attention during the next few days while they find out what exactly is wrong with you, at my expense I shall have you transported to the very best of nursing homes on the south coast, where not only will you receive much better care and attention than you would at home, they will also run exhaustive – and possibly some rather painful – tests to establish exactly what is causing these sudden pains in your chest.'

'You wouldn't dare.' Hugh stared up at him in undisguised horror.

Waldo smiled and picked up the telephone by Hugh's bed, dialling for the operator. Having given her the required number he held the receiver to Hugh's ear.

'The Pines Nursing Home and Clinic,' a voice said. 'Can I help you?'

'Hello,' Waldo said, taking the phone away from Hugh and placing it to his own ear. 'The Pines Nursing Home? This is Mr Waldo Astley speaking. I telephoned you earlier today about a friend of mine who needs nursing and examination – that's right – Captain Hugh Tate, Shelborne, Bexham on Sea – absolutely correct. I just want to make sure you still have a bed for him? Good. Thank you so much – I shall call you back in about an hour to confirm or cancel. Good day to you.'

Waldo smiled at Hugh who glowered back at him. 'Feeling better yet?'

'I feel worse by the minute,' Hugh growled.

'Excellent. And conscience doth make cowards of us all. Thanks to you I now have to make the return trip to London in order that the show will go on – which I assure you it most certainly will, Captain Tate. And so I bid you good day – and get well soon. Real soon.'

Hugh's recovery was purely remarkable. That evening he was well enough to take a double whisky and a good helping of fish pie followed by rhubarb and custard, and the following day he was well enough to be up and dressed and down for a roast lunch. Having left him in the tender care of Judy while she went back up to London to put the finishing touches to the hanging of her pictures and give interviews to two less than half interested art critics, Loopy returned to Bexham in time to witness her husband's return to full and glorious health.

'I wonder what it might have been,' she mused over lunch.

'What I first thought, I imagine,' Hugh replied. 'A bad attack of indigestion.'

'Oh, of course!' Loopy said. 'Acid indigestion. Of course!'

Chapter Twelve

No-one was looking at the paintings, no-one at all. It had been bad enough at first when it had seemed that no-one was going to show up at all, and after over half an hour of surveying a room empty of all but Waldo, the two gallery assistants and herself Loopy was all for calling it a day and a very bad one at that. Then suddenly as if on cue the place filled up with a crowd of chattering people, many of whom seemed to know each other, and those that didn't being soon introduced. As they helped themselves liberally to the drink on offer a cocktail party quickly developed, and within another quarter of an hour it was barely possible to see any of the hung paintings due to a fog of cigarette smoke from the gathered assembly.

'Going very well, I would say,' one of the gallery assistants remarked *en passant*. She was a pretty blonde woman of great style, typical of the kind hired by galleries for very little money, only too glad to leave their equally chic homes, and possibly their boring husbands, to go out to work for free in smart places in which they might get snapped for *The Tatler*.

Since by now even fewer people were paying any attention to the paintings Loopy was utterly amazed by the young woman's remark, so much so that she grabbed Waldo's arm as he ambled by, and dragged him to one side.

'No-one has looked at the paintings at all!' she hissed out of the side of her mouth. 'No-one – but no-one!'

'I keep telling you, Loopy – this is the way it is at openings.'

'People go to the opening of an exhibition and don't look at the work? You're kidding me!'

'We all do it.'

'Never! Never once in my life!'

'Never once? Not even when you were young?'

'Well yes – I suppose I might have done when I was young, yes – but that's different.'

'A lot of these people are young, Loopy.'

'So, there are some bright young things here. But there are also some not so young and not so bright older things – and they're all carrying on as if it's a cocktail party!'

'The way of the world – or rather the way of the art world. Now come on, try to relax. I know this is probably one of the worst moments of your life – but try to enjoy it.'

'*One* of the worst? It is *the* worst! I never for one moment imagined I would feel so – so exposed! Having a lot of total strangers arrive up here, to not stare at your work!'

'If you're that nervous, you should be happy that's what they're doing. You should be rejoicing that they all have their backs to your paintings. If you're feeling that exposed, they're doing the right thing, surely?'

'You're incorrigible, Waldo.' Loopy laughed, at last. 'You really are. I feel as if I have nothing on, actually.'

'OK, a fellow can dream.' Waldo gave a little cough, and then smiled. 'Now I am going to leave you in the very capable hands of Adam Forster here, who is already a fan and has been dying to talk to you all evening, while I go off and try to find out what the word on the street is.'

Before she could protest, Loopy found herself engaged in conversation with a tall, lanky, bespectacled young man with a shock of frizzy hair, half of which seemed to fall across his eyes so that he spent most of the time tossing his head back. In her highly nervous state the motion started to mesmerise Loopy even as she pretended to listen to his opinions on everything from politics to Art.

'Good news!' Waldo exclaimed happily on his return some half an hour later. 'You seen how many red dots there are?'

Loopy looked around, and then eased her way through the throng to the nearest wall to discover that four out of the eight paintings hanging on it had small red dots fixed to them to show they were sold. Hardly able to contain her delight, she proceeded to do a tour of the gallery as best she could, coming to the happy conclusion that over fifty per cent of the paintings on show had already been accounted for. Hardly able to believe her good fortune she threaded her way back through the buzzing guests to find Waldo.

'I have another surprise for you, Mrs Tate – turn round slowly, and try not to drop down dead from shock.'

Loopy did as asked, to find Hugh standing in front of her dressed in his best and bearing a bunch of flowers cut from their garden.

'Hugh! Oh, Hugh – what a lovely surprise!'

Loopy flung her arms round her husband. Taken quite aback, he was forced to hold his bouquet to one side, and laughed as Loopy hugged him, almost desperately.

'Oh, Hugh! Hugh darling!' Tears were welling in Loopy's eyes. 'I can't tell you what this means! I really can't!'

'Really?' Hugh smiled. 'I say.' He cleared his throat

'This is wonderful, Hugh! I can't tell you!' She stood back. 'And guess what? I even seem to have sold some paintings. There must be a lot of people here with more money than taste.'

Hugh chuckled. 'That's terrific, Loopy,' he said. 'How many do you think you might have sold?'

'Might have? Have have! I've sold nearly half!'

'I say. Nearly *half*? I *say*!'

Hugh laughed aloud, obviously delighted, beaming at Loopy as she took him by the hand to lead him past some of her red-dotted paintings.

'Well, I do say,' Hugh said, smiling with

pleasure. 'You must be quite good after all.'

'Well, I suppose I can't be all bad,' Loopy concluded dreamily, staring yet again at a picture with a red dot on it.

'Sorry – excuse me – but are you the artist?' a young man asked, having overheard. 'You're more than not bad, if I may say so – in fact you are extremely talented. And even prettier than some of your pictures.'

'But much more expensive,' Hugh said with a proprietary smile, pulling Loopy slightly to him. 'You couldn't possibly afford her.'

'Thank you,' Loopy said to the young man. 'You're most kind.'

The young man smiled as Hugh steered Loopy away to a corner of the gallery where there was a little more space.

'First of all, my apologies,' Hugh said. 'For being quite such an oaf. And a spoilt one at that.'

'I forgive you,' Loopy said, refusing to dissemble. 'Even though you were really quite awful.'

Hugh smiled, somewhat chastened, and to alleviate his discomfort Loopy leaned forward and kissed him briefly on the lips.

'Don't worry, I never stopped loving you, Hugh. That would be impossible.'

'You had every right to do so,' Hugh countered. 'Don't know what came over me.'

'Something mysterious.'

'Jealousy.' He sighed.

'Understandable. I used to be terribly jealous of the Navy,' Loopy admitted with a smile.

'Really? Even so, you didn't take to your bed when I went to sea and pretend to be dying.'

'I felt like it.'

They looked at each other, their love and faith still as firmly in place as it had ever been.

'I have another apology,' Hugh said as quietly as he could over the noise of the party. 'I was very dismissive of your paintings and I had no right to be.'

'No – no you didn't,' Loopy agreed, slightly surprising Hugh once more as he had hoped for a little mollification. 'That I do agree with wholeheartedly. You really shouldn't have been quite so dismissive because it's not as if you're a philistine. You know a lot about painting – in fact you do have quite an eye. And that's what hurt. If you'd just been a bonehead then I would have understood. At least I would have understood a little better. But you're not, so yes, you should have known better.'

'Jealousy again, I suppose,' Hugh sighed. 'I was jealous in case you would start spending more time in your studio than you did with me.'

'No chance.' Loopy smiled. 'But I've been jealous as well – and about something far more serious. I've been suffering paroxysms of jealousy about you and your young girlfriend.'

'You mean Meggie, I suppose,' Hugh replied quietly. 'And if you do, I assure you that you have absolutely no cause for any anxiety on that score.'

'I saw you in the car that afternoon. That

afternoon by the old boatyard. I heard most of what you were saying as well.'

'I thought that was you in the shadows.'

'You saw me?'

'I thought it might be you. Only thought. I only got a glimpse. Look – can we talk about this over dinner?'

'No. We don't want to spoil our appetites.'

'It won't,' Hugh assured her with a smile. 'I was just trying to persuade her to come back to work for me.'

'I know that now.'

'Did you ever doubt it?'

'No,' Loopy said quickly. 'No, not for a moment.'

She looked at him. She was lying, of course, because she had doubted him entirely, but that was her fault, not his, and so there was no point in berating someone who was in fact quite innocent. If she was angry with anyone that person would have to be herself, since her pain was all due to her own imaginings. She could have asked Hugh at any time about Meggie but she had chosen not to, just as she could have told him at any time about her exhibition but had not. And the reason she had not wanted any sort of direct confrontation with her husband was not her husband's fault. It was her own fault entirely, and the reason for her intransigence was the doubt she was nursing not about Hugh but about herself – about her talent for painting and her ongoing worth as a wife and a mother. What she had been feeling was what so many women of her age felt as they saw their children growing up and getting married and having babies, and their husbands apparently losing a certain amount of interest in them. Suddenly she had felt unwanted and unloved and rather than face up to her own misgivings and examine their validity she had taken the easier path, that of suspecting her husband of having an affair when in fact he was perfectly blameless, and of making him take the responsibility for the serious self-doubts she had concerning her art by trying to turn his indifference to her work into a reason for not seeing her exhibition through.

She looked round once more to see how many of her paintings carried the all important red dot and saw to her enormous delight that one of the gallery assistants was marking two more paintings as sold.

Imagine, she thought to herself. *Imagine if I had been weak-minded enough to give in. Just imagine – this wonderful day would never have happened. It just doesn't bear thinking about.*

Hugh took one of her hands and turned her round to him.

'I'm sorry,' he said. 'I perhaps should have waited till dinner. This wasn't really the time or the place.'

'On the contrary, Hugh,' Loopy replied, touching his cheek with one hand. 'This is absolutely the time and absolutely the place.'

Waldo accepted an invitation to join Hugh and Loopy for a celebratory dinner at the Savoy. He had tried to insist that they should go on their own, but since the show had been a runaway success the numbers at dinner were growing fast and both Hugh and Loopy pressed Waldo so ardently that naturally he agreed, safe in the knowledge that he would not be – as he put it – an all too obvious loner. Promising to join the party as quickly as he could, Waldo waited until they had left before making his way to the back of the gallery and a brass-studded leather-covered door marked *Private*.

'Hello?' he said, after knocking once. 'You there, Dick? It's Waldo.'

The announcement of his arrival gave the young woman who was standing talking to the owner of the gallery just enough time to slip quietly into the adjoining office, which she did with a finger held tightly to her lips.

'Might I come in?' Waldo asked from outside, pushing the door open. 'I know what you get up to in here. So I'm always careful.'

'I'm all alone,' the large, balding man behind the desk told him. 'And wishing I wasn't.'

'You gallery owners are worse than film producers,' Waldo told him. 'And that's saying something.'

'A great success, it would seem.' Richard Oliver got up and went to a cupboard to fetch a bottle of brandy. 'Shall we drink to it?'

'Why not? I haven't touched a drop all evening,' Waldo returned. 'Too busy propping up the genius.'

Richard Oliver poured them both a good shot of expensive French cognac and sat back down, indicating a chair opposite his desk to Waldo.

'I'm still a little too nervous to sit, if you don't mind.'

'I don't understand why you should be nervous,' Richard Oliver said. 'What was there to be nervous about?'

'How Loopy would take it, I guess. Good God, Dick – there was everything to be nervous about! Suppose nobody had showed?'

Richard Oliver shook his head. 'No chance. Not in this Gallery. When people get an invite to an opening here, they come.'

'You get my drift.'

'So how many paintings "Sold", eh?'

Waldo looked hard at his friend and suddenly smiled. 'Guess,' he said.

'Don't tell me you bought the lot. That really would be a little excessive – not to say suspicious.'

'Over sixty per cent have been sold, Dick.'

Richard Oliver whistled and raised his eyebrows. 'Going to cost you, Waldo. You know how expensive I am.'

'I only bought four.'

It was the gallery owner's turn to stare. 'You're joking.'

'I most certainly am not joking.'

'You only bought four? So who the heck bought all the others?'

Waldo shrugged. 'I did my bit. I told that pretty assistant of yours—'

'Gabriella?'

'I told her which pictures to dot and when,

which she did – and the next thing we knew, when we were about to dot some more, your other assistant—'

'Elizabeth. Lizzie Mells.'

'She was sticking up red dots all over the place. I was about to say hang on – thinking she was being just a little previous – when Gabriella and I realised they were all genuine sales. We saw the buyers' happy faces – Lizzie went and checked them. I don't think I need even have bothered to sticker my four. I think they'd have sold anyway.'

Richard now stared at Waldo in a keen, pensive way. 'I had better get her to agree to some sort of contract – verbal or otherwise.'

'Really? I thought you said she was – what was it? A moderately talented little amateur.'

'Yes, all right.' Richard smiled. 'I am never going to live it down, am I?'

'I won't say a word. I promise.'

'In return for?'

Waldo smiled. 'In return for excusing me the gallery charge.'

'On no – no, come on, Waldo!' Richard protested. 'A chap has to make a living! And the deal was you rent the gallery—'

'I know what the deal *was*, Richard. But things are a little different now. I *was* going to pay the rent for the gallery – sure – because you thought you were only going to make commission on four or five cheapish little paintings – bought by me. But now look. Look what's happened now. You've sold over half of what you have on the walls to bona fide buyers – to people who know a thing or three – and judging from what young Adam Forster was saying to me earlier there is going to be quite a piece about Mrs Tate somewhere in tomorrow's evening paper – so you have found yourself a new artist, but really.'

'*You* have found me a *hot* new artist, Waldo.' Richard smiled and then nodded. 'OK. Deal. I'll let you off the rent – provided Mrs Tate agrees to some sort of contract with me.'

'I can guarantee that.'

After he was gone, off to join the celebrations at the Savoy, the young woman who had exiled herself to the next-door room reappeared in Richard Oliver's office in a much more thoughtful mood than the one in which she had left it. Richard offered her a drink, which she accepted, lighting a Du Maurier with a small gold lighter while it was poured and sinking elegantly into the chair whose comforts Waldo had refused earlier.

'Well, well, well,' she said slowly, in a bad Cockney voice. 'Well I never did.'

'And what did you never do, Miss Gore-Stewart?' Richard asked, handing her a glass of cognac.

'He really did all that?' Meggie wondered, now in her own voice. 'Mr Waldo Astley arranged all this? He really did?'

'Why should that surprise you? That's the kind of chap he is.'

Meggie shook her head slowly from side to side. 'I really had no idea.'

'I don't suppose you did.' Richard laughed, sitting back down. 'People are always getting Waldo wrong. They think he's a black marketeer, or a playboy, or just some rich card-playing Lothario who's got nothing better to do than gamble and speculate. That's not Waldo Astley at all.'

'How come you know him? Mind you – who doesn't know Mr Waldo Astley nowadays.'

'My father and his father did a lot of business. My old man bought a lot of paintings for Astley Senior, before the war. Not a nice man.'

'But rich.'

'Could say. But you must know Waldo as well as I, since he's bought a house in good old Bexham?'

'Our paths have hardly crossed,' Meggie replied. 'I only really know him through – well, through the Tates, actually. I've hardly exchanged more than a few words with him.'

'Then you're missing out, Meggie dear. Mr Waldo Astley is really quite a fellow.'

'So it seems,' Meggie agreed, looking thoughtful. 'So it would seem.'

Before he left for Germany, Waldo made a discovery that was to have repercussions. He found a boat; or more correctly he discovered a boat. He was back in Bexham, preparing for his journey, when Rusty knocked on his study door asking him if he had a moment. Despite being behind with his travel arrangements, Waldo abandoned his affairs and followed her over to her family's boatyard on the southern shore of the estuary where she showed him a small fourteen-footer that her father and brother Mickey had been busy preparing for sale.

'It's a very pretty craft, Rusty,' Waldo agreed, trying not to look at his watch. 'But it's not really the kind of boat to which I can honestly say I am attracted. I'm an old-fashioned guy with tastes too grand for my wallet. If I'm going to buy something it will have to be an ocean-going lady with a bit of style.'

He let his gaze wander round the boatyard, penetrating the darker corners and the large greying cobwebs that hung almost like ropes at some points, taking in the half-organised chaos that surrounded him. It was then that he noticed a good-looking craft lying half on its side, in a bad state of disrepair.

'That is rather the kind of thing I want, Rusty,' he said, pointing it out. 'Except in a seaworthy condition.'

'Wouldn't everyone,' Rusty agreed, somewhat sadly. 'She was the most lovely lady, the best there was, in my opinion. Tight, fast and . . . you know – had a whole lot to her you just can't describe.'

'The way boats do.'

'You do know about boats then, Mr Astley? I thought you were a novice.'

'I know nothing about boats. As they say, I just know what I like. To whom does it belong?'

'The man who owned it's dead. Killed in the war.'

Waldo frowned, and walked towards the ruined

craft to take a better look at it. 'The *Light Heart*', he read. 'Has to be some boat with a name like that. Who was the man who died? Was he what you call a Bexhamite, Rusty?'

'I suppose so. He certainly grew up here, spent all his holidays here, and he sailed here all the time – so yes, I suppose so. His family had a house here as well. He was a terrific bloke – an absolute hero really. David Kinnersley. Everyone liked Mr Kinnersley.' She fell silent, remembering Mr Kinnersley, how dashing he had been, fair-haired, handsome, always laughing. 'He looked like something on the flicks, you know, like Errol Flynn or someone. In fact come to think of it he was just like something out of the flicks. Always setting off cross Channel in the worst weather to rescue people from the Nazis. They smuggled them through Denmark, you know, and he brought them back here to Bexham, and after that to London. Didn't matter what, he always came back with as many as he could manage. Makes your heart turn over just to think of how many times he went backwards and forwards. Then of course there was Dunkirk – and when the call went out to rescue our army off the beaches, of course he was off in the *Light Heart*, hardly before the broadcast was even ended. That was Mr Kinnersley.'

Rusty stopped, of a sudden turning away from the sight of the *Light Heart* as if it was a dead body, not a boat.

'That's OK, Rusty,' Waldo said, noting this. 'You

don't have to tell me any more – not if you don't want to.'

'Thanks,' Rusty replied. 'I know I don't. As a matter of fact, I've hardly ever spoken about this to anyone really. About the *Light Heart* and about – about Mr Kinnersley really. I had a bit of a crush on him, you see. More than a bit of a crush actually – I was daft about him. He didn't treat me like a girl, he treated me like a proper first mate. And what with being left-handed and having red hair, you can imagine I'd had a right time of it at school. But he wasn't like that, Mr Kinnersley wasn't. He was different – didn't treat you as if you should have been a boy, or shouldn't have had red hair. Or shouldn't be left-handed. Saying there had to be something wrong with your brain if you were left-handed.'

'Nothing wrong with your brain, young lad.'

'No, there isn't, is there?' Rusty grinned at him. 'Anyway – when the balloon went up about Dunkirk, off I went with him. I wasn't going to do nothing, was I? I wasn't going to sit at home knitting socks and doing what all the other girls and their mums were doing. I smuggled myself on board the *Light Heart*. It wasn't much of a risk 'cos I knew once we was out to sea, I knew Mr Kinnersley would treat me like he always treated me, because, like I said, that was the kind of man he was. Not just a hero but a gentleman.'

'And what happened?' Waldo wondered out of the silence. 'Or don't you want to talk about it?'

'I thought maybe you knew.'

'Nope.' Waldo shook his head.

'He got killed, Mr Astley,' Rusty said. 'Got drowned on the second trip – trying to save my brother. Nothing anyone could do.'

Another silence ensued, during which Rusty tidied up some loose ropes that were hanging in a jumble from various fixings on the boat, keeping her face turned away from Waldo, who watched her sympathetically.

'Fine,' he said suddenly. 'If you ask me there's only one thing for it, Rusty, and that is to get this lovely boat shipshape again and back into commission. Least we can do in honour of its dead skipper. How do we go about finding out more about her, do you think? Technically who owns her now?'

Rusty shrugged her shoulders, winding rope round a rusting old cleat.

'I don't know,' she said with a frown. 'Mr Kinnersley could have left it to Meggie Gore-Stewart. I mean they were engaged at the time. I don't know, to be quite honest.'

'I didn't know Meggie had been engaged.'

'Mr Kinnersley and she'd known each other since they were kids. Meggie was sent down here for her health, and they learned how to sail together as kids – then when they grew up . . .' Rusty turned away. 'They got engaged,' she muttered, finding yet more rope to untangle. 'Someone told me they were going to tie the knot before the war but her family said no or something. Anyway – anyway they didn't, and then Mr Kinnersley was killed at Dunkirk. If the *Light Heart* does belong to Meggie now, she might sell it because I do know she needs the money. According to Dad she's even had to put her house up for sale.'

'Cucklington?' Waldo could hardly believe his ears. 'But I understand that's the family house. That it's always been in the Gore-Stewart family—'

'That's as maybe, Mr Astley. But she's got to sell it now. Something to do with her dead parents' debts or something. I don't know. I don't understand these things.'

'I see.' Waldo examined the end of his cigar now, as if that might provide him with a solution. 'In that case we shall have to think of something else, won't we, Mrs Rusty Sykes? And as it so happens, I think I have just actually thought of it. But I'm going to need your discretion in the matter.' He gave a small cough, and stuck the unlit cigar back in his mouth.

'Discretion?' Rusty wrinkled her nose at him in bewilderment. 'How do you mean my discretion, Mr Astley?'

'What I mean is – to put it quite impolitely – I'm going to need you to keep that mouth of yours well and truly shut.'

Rusty hesitated, looking suddenly thoughtful as Waldo glanced down at his watch, mindful of the fact that he hadn't yet begun his packing.

'You can do that for me, Rusty, can't you?'

'Course I can, Mr Astley. You know I can.' She looked at Waldo directly in the eyes, her mouth set firmly. 'You know you can trust me.'

'I have no doubt about that, Rusty,' he replied. 'I never had.'

Judy received one last visit from Waldo before he left for Germany. Not that Judy was aware of his destination, only that he was going to be away on business for a few days.

But this time, instead of visiting her at Owl Cottage, he came to collect her in his Jaguar so that there was absolutely no chance at all that any of the curtain-twitchers down her lane could miss his call. Nor in fact that any Bexhamite could fail to spot them cruising round the village with the soft top down taking what looked like infinite pleasure in each other's company.

'You have yet to tell me whether or not this is having any effect,' Waldo pointed out as he drove slowly round the streets of Bexham.

'Whether what's having any effect?' Judy asked, nonplussed.

'My role as Iago, of course.'

'Oh. It's hard to tell, really.'

'I don't see why. Either your husband is behaving differently to you or he's not. Or – for instance – somebody might have said something to you?' Waldo looked round at her. 'Like that divine mother-in-law of yours. Has Loopy said anything to you about being careful whose company you keep, or anything like that?'

'Loopy's too wrapped up in her painting, particularly since the success of her exhibition. But anyway, even if anyone had said anything to Loopy, Loopy always makes a point of forgetting all about it, by-mistake-on-purpose. She's neither a gossip nor a scold. But who knows? Maybe Walter has been told by someone about my being seen around with you because he keeps telephoning me during the week. Which is something he really never does. Then last week he brought me home the biggest bunch of flowers you've ever seen. Oh yes – then this week he rang up suddenly and said he'd decided to take me to dinner at the Savoy.'

'And you say nothing's *different*?' Waldo laughed. 'And are you going to go?'

Judy turned and stared at Waldo for a brief second, and then redirected her gaze out of the car window.

'Of course.'

'Not necessarily. It's not necessarily of course. Is it?'

Judy gave a small sigh. Waldo had a way of putting his finger on everything and he was right as usual. When Walter had asked her, a part of her had wanted to say no – and she didn't know why. A part of her didn't want to go up to London on the train to meet Walter at the Savoy, and she knew now that the reason for her reluctance was sitting beside her in the driver's seat. Compared to Waldo with all his electricity, his plans and daring, Walter now seemed faintly dull.

'Yes, of course I want to go,' she repeated. 'Of course I do.'

Whereupon Waldo stopped the car without

any warning, the way a parent might when a child in its care was misbehaving and had to be reprimanded.

'Right, it's home truth time,' Waldo said, perturbing Judy who glanced at him anxiously. 'You think you've fallen in love with me when you've done nothing of the sort.'

'How dare you?' Judy gasped. 'How *dare* you?' Outraged, and without any good reason as she was well aware, she turned bright red and immediately looked away.

'Just listen, and don't get on a high horse,' Waldo said. 'You think that making yourself believe that you've fallen in love will somehow help mollify the pain you feel about Walter's apparent indifference to you, other than simply wanting to have a child by you. But if you stop to think, this might be the only way Walter has of telling you that he loves you. I don't think we can know what Walter has been through. Maybe it was so terrifying that he can't even begin to speak about it because it might start to haunt him all over again. The terrible thing is you were separated for all those years when you should have been growing together as a couple but instead you spent them growing apart from each other. Then he comes home and you both expect it to be as it was – but that's impossible. War changes people, particularly people as sensitive as Walter. What you were going to have to do when Walter suddenly reappeared back in your life was to start again, but you didn't. You both started where you thought you had left off, which was really somewhere where neither of you had ever been.'

Judy fell to a long and thoughtful silence. Two or three times she went to say something then thought better of it, remaining silent and wondering at everything Waldo had just told her. At last she took his hand and held it.

'I should be angry, I suppose,' she said.

'Why? Because you think I've been leading you on?'

'Haven't you?'

'There are all sorts of ways of arriving at the truth, Judy.'

'I see that now. And thank you. I've been an idiot – only thinking of myself and not of Walter at all. This plan of yours to make Walter come to his senses by my appearing to flirt with you – it was just a smoke screen, wasn't it? I'm the one you wanted to make see sense – yes?'

'It's a double-edged sword,' Waldo replied. 'Maybe Walter has to come to his senses, too. And maybe he will when the word gets about even more.'

'About this?'

'About you and me being seen together.'

Waldo smiled at her. Then, starting the car up again, he turned its nose up a lane to a beauty spot high on the hills that overlooked the estuary and the headland. As he drove he continued to talk.

'You haven't had it easy, you know, either of you,' he said. 'Let's face it – a husband who comes back to you after such a long absence, totally changed by experiences not of his choosing, must seem like a stranger.' Judy said nothing to contradict this, so Waldo continued. 'So to get back to your proposed dinner date – meeting him for dinner, where there are no distractions, where you have to concentrate on him and him alone, maybe it's what you need. It could be a turning point. He might start to be able to talk, to be able to tell you things that he hasn't been able to tell you before. He might – although I pray to God he doesn't – he might even want to confess something to you, something shocking or terrifying, but something that might help you to understand you *both* better. Tell me – how many times have you and Walter been out to dinner alone since he came back? I don't mean dinner parties – I mean *out* to dinner.'

Judy thought for a moment. 'Not once.'

'I rest my case.'

Waldo pulled the Jaguar off the lane and on to a track that led towards the clifftops.

'Why are you doing this, Waldo?' Judy suddenly asked as he was parking the car. 'Why are you taking such a proprietary interest in Walter and me?'

'Because I like you very much – both of you. Because maybe I wish I was Walter. Maybe John even, or Peter Sykes or your father-in-law – I don't know. I wouldn't mind being any of you.'

'Don't you like being you?'

'I don't think I know who I am. That's the whole problem. Just don't know.'

Having reached the end of the track, Waldo pulled the car into the small clearing that served as a parking place. Swinging the low door open, he got quickly out of the Jaguar and stood at the top of the hill looking out over the view, with the stiff sea breeze ruffling his thick dark hair. After a moment, Judy opened the passenger door and went to stand beside him.

'Come on,' he said. 'Let's walk.'

They walked along the clifftop path, the wind in their faces, and below them boats sailing on the white-capped blue sea.

'Why did you come here, Waldo? Why did you come to Bexham?' Judy asked after they had walked a good half-mile, and as she did so she wondered that she'd never thought to ask him before, so involved in her own muddled life had he become.

'I had to, Judy,' Waldo replied, still looking out to sea. 'My father died last year when I was in Europe and I sailed back for his funeral. We were never close – in fact we didn't get on at all, even though I was his only child, and that's kind of odd, but there you are. He was a most unpleasant man by the time I got to know him, and by the time I'd got some polish and therefore could have been maybe a little more interesting to him, he went and died. It was very sudden. He was out riding his favourite horse, and he never came back. His horse did, but Pa didn't. They found him up in the hills, dead from either a heart attack or a massive stroke.'

'You've never mentioned your family before.' Judy took a scarf out from her coat pocket and tied it in the wartime manner, knotting it on top of her head to keep out the wind.

'For several reasons – the main one being I don't really have a family. I had a father, but I never knew my mother. She gave birth to me, then left two days later.' Waldo shrugged, sinking his hands deep in his pockets. 'Possibly the problem was my father. He was a very hard and a somewhat bitter man – although why, God alone knows. He was absurdly rich and had everything most people want. Except the affection of others. He was, as I say, very rich and therefore very influential, but deeply, deeply unhappy. I don't know what happened between him and my mother but all the time I was growing up she was never referred to, not once, by my father – and apart from me there was no visible trace of her ever having been in his life. He'd forbidden everyone in the household, everyone in his family, ever to mention her name, and my father being my father no-one questioned him. No-one disobeyed. It was the law.'

'How on earth did you survive? More than that, how did you turn out so well?'

'I don't know about well – but thank you. As for how I survived, put that down to Bags. Bags – the greatest mammy in the world. Everything I am I owe to Bags. Bags was big – no, Bags was huge – she still is, God bless her. Bigger than ever. Bags is enormous, very black and very wonderful. She arrived the day my mother left because my father sacked everyone in the house who had worked for my mother, and he drove into town and came back with Bags, whose husband had worked for my father on his estate until he'd died in a lumber accident. Bags brought me up, loved me, took care of me, nursed me when I was sick, put up with me. Bags was my mother – and it was Bags who found out about my mother.'

Judy took Waldo's arm, holding onto him tightly as they negotiated the now narrowing coastal path cut into the side of the hill before turning and retracing their tracks.

'Did Bags know your mother?'

Waldo shook his head. 'Like I said, by the time I was a teenager it was as if my mother had never existed. We lived a pretty peripatetic life – Carolina, New York, Monterey, Long Island, New England – and the more we moved about from one house to another the less connection there was with the past. The only link was Bags, and no – she'd never known my mother. She said that once in town, when she was young, she thought she'd caught sight of my mother in my father's car – she had this vague picture of a beautiful blonde woman passing her by, waving at her and smiling, and that was that. Bags was only a kid then herself, you see. So my father and my mother must have been married for quite a few years before I was born, because Bags says she started work for my father, coincidentally, on the morning of her twentieth birthday and she thinks she was about fifteen when she saw my mother that once.'

'So how did she find out about her? If she never knew her?'

Waldo stopped for a while to take in the view

of the blue sea that ran out it seemed to endless horizons.

'My father kept her on after he'd sent me to Europe, which was odd since he hardly visited Carolina once I was gone, and once war had broken out. When I went back to America for his funeral – we buried him down South – Bags grabbed hold of me – literally, before we'd even buried Pa – and gave me an envelope containing a couple of photographs of someone Bags thought could be my mother. They were scorched, as if they'd been pulled from a fire.'

'Where on earth did Bags find them?'

'In a bedroom – or to be rather more precise in a bed. She had been told by my father's land agent to get rid of any old bedding and mattresses and replace them because he was going to do some pretty elaborate entertaining back home due to the fact he was planning on running for Governor, so he was intending to refurbish the family home which had fallen into disrepair. When Bags was turning over an old mattress on the bed in one of the dressing rooms off the main bedroom—'

'I like *one* of the dressing rooms.' Judy laughed. 'Must be some house.'

'It's a typical South Carolina mansion. Anyway, out of the mattress, through a hole someone had made in the side of it obviously to hide things – out fell this little package. Soon as Bags saw the contents she hid them away until she could get them to me, most of all because of what was written on the back.'

'And what *was* written on the back?'

'Well might you ask, Mrs Tate,' Waldo replied, looking down at the little fishing port that lay far below them. 'On the back of one of them – a photograph of a handsome young man and a stunningly beautiful young woman – was written in pencil – as clear as the day they were written – the words *Bexham 1917*'.

Judy stared up at Waldo, but then something else caught her eye.

'Heavens above!' she exclaimed, looking over Waldo's shoulder. 'Here's Walter.'

'So what happened to you, Mr Know It All?' Hugh wondered when he met Waldo at Northolt Aerodrome prior to Waldo's departure for Germany.

'Your son-in-law got hold of the wrong end of a stick.' Waldo sighed, doing his best to keep his blackened eye wide open.

'Knowing you I suspect that was rather what you wanted him to do.'

'I could have just done with suspicions being raised, Captain Tate, not fists. Still, amazing what a good piece of black market beef will do.'

'These should help you even more on your way,' Hugh said, nodding to his aide who handed over to Waldo several large parcels wrapped in brown paper and tied up with string. 'One thousand Lucky Strike, twenty-four pounds of coffee, twenty-four dozen eggs – so don't go getting careless – and one thousand boxes of matches.'

'Matches are in short supply now?' Waldo exclaimed in surprise.

'Sixty Deutschmarks a box. You should be able to buy a lot of information with that cargo – and here are the letters you have to post.'

Hugh gave him a large white envelope that Waldo immediately slipped into his official-looking despatch case.

'Bon voyage,' Hugh said, shaking him by the hand. 'Come to dinner when you get back.'

'You bet,' Waldo said. Then he took his leave and climbed up the steps at the side of the waiting Dakota to get on board.

Hugh watched the plane taking off, and sighed.

'Let's hope all goes well,' his companion volunteered brightly.

Hugh shook his head. 'Yes.' He turned to the young officer still standing at his side watching the now airborne aeroplane. 'Yes, let's hope,' he agreed. 'Since Berlin is his destination, that's all we can do.'

Chapter Thirteen

Judy's parents, Sir Arthur and Lady Melton, were away, and since Gardiner their old maid was too Judy had to check up on the house for them. She called up to Walter to tell him where she was going and that she wouldn't be long.

'Wait for me!' came the anxious reply. 'Wait, Jude! I want to come with you!'

Their evening out at the Savoy had been just the success Waldo had forecast. They had indeed discovered each other all over again. From the moment Judy stepped out of her taxi in evening dress to be met by Walter beautifully turned out in his white tie and tails, it was as if this was their first date. There had been no war, there was no hardship to endure and no personal misery or anxiety. They drank cocktails at the bar and dined at a table in a window overlooking the Thames, intoxicated by the magic of the moment. Judy had never seen Walter in such lighthearted spirits, not even when she had met him in those now distant days before the war. Somehow the times then had been so full of foreboding and the future so fraught with danger that it seemed as if they did not have time to laugh as they were laughing now, or to dance like they were dancing now, or even to flirt with each other the way they were flirting now.

As they danced after dinner to the music of Porter and Gershwin Walter felt as if he was seeing the beautiful girl in his arms for the very first time, and it seemed as though all memories of the sinking of his submarine and the terrible subsequent days in Norway that turned into years of fighting for his life as well as the lives of his new comrades were expunged from his mind. It was as if a door down a long dark corridor in his mind suddenly banged shut, and when it did so Walter felt as though his whole heart had lightened and his eyes had grown suddenly bright.

'I love you, do you know that?' he whispered, kissing the soft curl of her hair just above her forehead. 'I know I don't tell you enough, but I love you just the same. You're a wonderful, wonderful girl and I'm a lucky man.'

'I love you too, Walter,' Judy replied as he danced her slowly round the floor, which at that moment seemed to hang suspended somewhere in space. 'I've loved you from the moment we met and I shall go on loving you for the rest of my life.'

'I'm sorry about how I've been, Judy. I didn't mean to be like that.'

'I know, Walter. It's all right.'

'I couldn't help myself. It was as if – it was as if the sky kept falling down on me, as if there was hardly ever any daylight.'

'It's all right, Walter – you have nothing to apologise about. If anyone should apologise—'

'It certainly isn't you, my darling. You have done nothing wrong whatsoever.'

'I think I have, Walter. But nothing deliberately wrong. I should have been more understanding. I should have been more – more loving.'

Walter eased her a little away from him so that he could look down into her eyes. He smiled at her, then kissed her once more on the forehead.

'Nobody could have been more loving than you,' he assured her. 'Whenever I had one of my really black moods on – and I'd look up and see you sitting there, reading your book or doing your sewing, and you'd look back at me with those big anxious eyes, I could just feel your love. I couldn't do much about it, I couldn't say anything at the time – and God knows I wanted to, but I just couldn't – but it was just the fact that – well. That you were still there. That you were sitting it out, sitting out what must have been a terrible time for you, that was what counted. Because you were still there I knew you had to still love me.'

'Which I did, Walter. And which I do now more than ever.'

And now Walter was hurtling down the stairs of the cottage after her, still calling for her to wait, leaping off the staircase and grabbing Judy by the hands as she was getting Hamish's lead and a coat for herself.

'I really do want to come with you!' he laughed. 'So don't you dare go without me!'

Grinning up at her he sat on the bottom step and started to pull on his outdoor shoes. Judy smiled back at him, clipping the tartan lead onto her little dog's collar. Hamish barked joyously, knowing a walk was in the offing.

'I'm only going to check up on the house, Walter. I'm not going to be long.'

'I don't care, Mrs Tate. I do not want to miss a moment of your company.'

'OK – if you get bored that's your hard cheese.'

'Jolly hockey sticks!' Walter laughed teasingly. 'Up school and at 'em.'

'Don't start,' Judy warned. 'Or I'll set Hamish on to you. I thought you wanted to begin clearing up the leaves?'

'I did – but now I have other things in mind.' Walter stood up, shoelaces tied, and kissed her full on the mouth. 'Come along, Mrs Tate,' he ordered. 'At the double.'

He took Hamish's lead from her and jogged out of the cottage in front of her. Judy laughed and ran on up the lane behind him.

'That was a wonderful night last night,' Judy said, when they'd slowed down to a walk to continue hand in hand. 'Thank you so much.'

'You don't have to thank me!' Walter laughed. 'I just wish we could have afforded to stay the night.'

'I don't. There's nothing quite like one's own bed.'

'No.' Walter turned and smiled at her. 'No, there isn't, is there?'

They walked along for a while in silence,

swinging arms the way young lovers sometimes do, caught up in their memories of the night before and thinking hopefully of the happiness that could lie ahead for them now.

'One thing I meant to ask you – that I have to ask you,' Walter said, breaking it. 'Did you flirt with Waldo on purpose, Judy? To make me jealous?'

'I never flirted with him once,' Judy replied with perfect truth.

'Very well.' Walter mock sighed. 'Did he flirt with *you* on purpose?'

'Well of course!' Judy laughed. 'What else did you think that was all about?'

'I was *meant* to get jealous?'

'It was Waldo's own rendition – is that the word? Waldo's *interpretation* of Othello. Better. Waldo's *rendition* of Iago.'

Walter frowned as he thought about this, then raised his eyebrows. 'Likes to sail close to the wind, doesn't he?'

'He has been taking sailing lessons from Dauncy,' Judy teased.

'He didn't learn that sort of jiggery pokery from young bro.'

'He got a black eye for his trouble.'

'Lucky I didn't knock him over the cliff.' Walter snorted.

'You couldn't have done that. Waldo was too strong for you.'

'No he wasn't!'

'He was, too. He managed to make sure you didn't hit him again.'

'I thought once was quite enough!' Walter protested, shadow boxing as he walked.

'Walter – Waldo's twice your weight!' Judy laughed. 'And probably twice as strong!'

'I hope he's not twice as attractive,' Walter said suddenly, stopping his boxing and dropping back to a walk. 'Is he?'

'Of course he isn't. He's not one quarter as attractive as you.'

'I don't know. He seems to have the whole of Bexham womanhood at his feet.'

'He is not nearly as attractive as you, silly,' Judy assured him. 'And even if he was, so what? You're the one I *lerve*.'

'Promise?'

'Cross my heart and hope to.' Judy crossed her heart in an elaborate schoolgirl way which always made Walter laugh.

'I believe you, Mrs Tate,' he said. 'But there's thousands that wouldn't.'

Judy smiled and slipped her arm through his, walking as close to him as she could.

'I wouldn't blame you – or rather I wouldn't *have* blamed you,' Walter said thoughtfully. 'If you had found him attractive and – well. And had a bit of a fling, say. Because let's face it, I was being a pain.'

'No you weren't.'

'Of course I was. But it was difficult – coming home. Coming home after all that time.'

'Of course it was.'

'Particularly when I found out that you hadn't got any messages. That you thought – that you didn't know I was still alive and kicking. I think walking through that gate back there – into the garden – I think now that was the hardest thing I ever had to do. Harder than anything I had to face during the war. I had no idea what you'd think of me. Whether you still – you still felt anything. Three years is one hell of a long time. I quite expected you to have forgotten all about me – even if you had known I was still alive. I mean *three years*, Judy? And then suddenly there I am again, except I'm not, because I'm not the same me, and you – you hardly even knew the old me, so what were you to make of it? I'll tell you what it was like, shall I? For me anyway. It was as if I'd taken off all my clothes in 1942 to go for a swim in the sea, left them there on the beach, only I didn't come back again. Not for three years. Then when I did I picked up my clothes where I'd left them and expected them still to fit me – which of course they didn't. They couldn't. They were bound either to hang off me, or be too tight, or just look all wrong – they were never going to fit me after all that time. Poor you.' He stopped and turned to Judy, standing in front of her in the path that led up to the front door of her parents' house. 'You were meant to just take it or leave it. You were meant to welcome back with open arms this stranger in ill fitting clothes who hardly knew himself let alone his wife.' He shook his head and looked sadly at her. 'Poor darling Judy – how I missed you. God how I missed you – not just when I was away from you but even when I was back home and couldn't reach you. I've missed you so much.'

Judy took both his hands in hers and kissed him. 'It's all right, darling,' she said quietly. 'It's all over now. Everything's going to be all right.'

'Yes,' Walter said decisively, all doubts at last banished. 'Yes it is, isn't it?'

'Of course it is.'

'And I suppose we've got old Iago to thank for it, have we?'

'I think he played a part.' Judy smiled. 'But most of all I say, thank God.'

She opened the front door of her old family home with a large iron latchkey and they stepped into the cool darkness of the hall. Judy went to turn the lights on but Walter stopped her, drawing her back to him.

'No, I like it like this, There's something about old houses when they're empty. Something exciting.'

Judy knew what he meant. Whenever she had been left alone in the house when she was a girl, she often felt a peculiar thrill from it, as if there was danger in being solitary. She seemed to be getting that same thrill, but it wasn't a sense of danger that was exciting her. It was something else.

'Do you remember?' she asked, taking Walter's hand and leading him through the hall.

'Of course I remember. What sort of person do you think I am?' He laughed

'Do you think it was wrong?'

'Not a bit. We thought we might not ever see

each other again. Which as it turned out, wasn't far from the truth.'

'I used to worry so much about it. I really thought I'd go straight to hell.'

Walter smiled and held her hand even more tightly as he leaned over and opened a door.

'What are you doing, Walter?'

'What do you think?' He smiled mischievously. 'Putting Hamish in the kitchen.'

He pushed the little dog gently into the kitchen and shut the door behind him.

'Do you think he'll be all right in there, Walter?'

'I think he'll be perfectly all right in there. Come on.'

'Do you think we should?' Judy asked fearfully as they tiptoed in semi-darkness down the rest of the corridor towards the conservatory that lay at the back of the house.

'Your parents are hardly going to burst through the door, are they?'

'I thought they were before. I was convinced they were before.'

Walter laughed and opened the heavy double doors of the conservatory. At once they were both hit by the tropical warmth of the huge glassed room as well as overcome with the heady intoxicating smell of the jasmine.

'That smell. My God, the jasmine was out then, too.'

'Afterwards I carried the scent of these flowers wherever I was.'

Judy sighed, standing quite still, looking around,

remembering. 'It was romantic.' She turned to him and Walter kissed her, before slowly and carefully beginning to undo the pearl buttons on her blouse.

'But there's a big difference this time, Mrs Tate. This time I'm not going away from you. I'm never going to go away again – not ever, I hope.'

After which he kissed her again.

And again.

And again.

'You've been asked to dinner, Mattie!' John called upstairs in excitement after Lionel had let him in and retired to the quiet of the drawing room to study his latest book on bridge technique. 'Mattie?'

Mattie hurried out of her bedroom and appeared on the landing.

'I've been what?' she echoed. 'Asked to *dinner*? When?'

John held out his hand to beckon her down to him, and Mattie hopped down the stairs two at a time, missing out the last four to jump straight into John's arms.

'They haven't actually given a date yet, set a day – you know – they have a somewhat full social calendar,' John said, slightly evasively. 'But when I brought the subject up about you and me, instead of the usual objections et cetera, my mother smiled and said that it would be very nice if one day I brought you home to meet them properly. And have dinner.'

'That's wonderful,' Mattie said cautiously. 'But you really have no idea when?'

'Just that obviously it will be very soon, or they wouldn't have bothered to mention it,' John said happily, before kissing her on the cheek. 'I think they're sort of finally coming to their senses. Trying to be reasonable – just in case I rush off with you to Gretna Green.'

'I wonder why they've suddenly started coming to their senses, as you call it,' Mattie said. 'As far as your father was concerned I thought we didn't have a chance.'

'Search me,' John shrugged. 'It can't just be the success of Mamma's exhibition. That sort of thing wouldn't affect the dear parents' attitude to you and me.'

'So what could it be?'

'Maybe what they've come to realise is how mad I am about you and that there's no point in any further resistance.' John grinned and then kissed Mattie gently on the mouth. He had discovered recently that he could resist most things, but not Mattie's luscious, full lips.

'Will you two lovebirds stop billing and cooing and come in here for a drink?' Lionel called. 'A man could die of thirst!'

'And talking of sea changes—' John nodded towards the sitting room. Mattie widened her eyes and shrugged her shoulders.

'Don't ask me. Must be something in the air.' She laughed. 'Or maybe in the gin!'

In his armchair by the fireside, Lionel smiled to himself as he began a new chapter on Slam Bidding. He knew exactly what the young people were talking about without even having to hear, just as well as he knew the explanation for his own change. It was nothing to do with Waldo's and his triumph at the card table, nor indeed with the delectable as well as extremely rich Mrs Van der Beek's growing interest in him – although he would be a fool not to admit that carried quite a considerable sway – but all to do with Waldo's apparently idle conversation one evening subsequent to their famous victory when they were discussing how they had actually pulled it off.

'By taking a risk, of course, my dear fellow!' Waldo had laughed. 'Drinking from the far side of the cup no less.'

'That is not a characteristic of mine, Waldo,' Lionel had replied, surprised. 'That is not the sort of person I am.'

'You were that night, and you don't regret it, do you?'

'No, but I do wonder at it.'

'You took a risk, but what were you risking? Reputation only. What other people might or might not think of you, and what you might or might not think of yourself. You weren't risking your money – it doesn't matter about mine because that's academic at this point – and so you weren't risking your livelihood, simply your reputation, and what is that anyway? Reputation is nothing without achievement and achievement is never arrived at without risk. So let's admire risk, shall we? Let's raise our glasses and drink to risk –

because without the taking of it, we are all absolute dullards.'

The more he'd thought about Waldo's words, the more Lionel had considered them to contain the right kind of truth. Applying them to himself, and to the way he looked at life, of a sudden changed him, in every way. To start with, he decided not to employ Ellen any more. Since he had learned to cook in the war, he would now learn to keep house and thereby ensure himself a great deal more privacy – important if Mrs Van der Beek came to visit, say, which Lionel very well thought she might.

'It's not doing you any good coming here, and, frankly, it's getting me down,' he told Ellen, making sure to take a kindly tone. 'There's a much better position for you at Sir Arthur and Lady Melton's at the top of the village. I met old Gardiner in the street and she's all for giving up now, so why not go up to the Manor—'

'I know where Lady Melton lives, thank you, Mr Eastcott.'

Ellen had sniffed, removed her pinny, gone to see Lady Melton, and been taken on for twice the money.

For a few days Mattie had kept wondering aloud who would do the housework, to which Lionel kept replying that he would, and that it would be good for him, until Mattie had to admit that the house was a great deal cleaner now that Ellen had gone and the atmosphere a great deal more cheerful.

Lionel's next concern had been with his daughter. If he continued to oppose Mattie's romance, it would surely be what Waldo would call playing safe, and really what mattered now was that John Tate obviously adored Mathilda. So it might be a terrible thing to spoil their chance of happiness together. Besides, Lionel further considered, if anyone was taking risks, it was surely John and Mattie, and since they were more than prepared to do so, why not let them? Having come to his conclusions Lionel decided he would sit down and put such thoughts as he had on the matter in a letter to John's parents, in an attempt to bring some common sense to bear on the situation. This he had finally done, which was why he was now sitting so contentedly by his fireside with a freshly poured gin and tonic and a newly opened book without a single proper care in the world.

Meggie, on the other hand, found herself suddenly full of cares. Through her agents she seemed quite unable to raise any interest in Cucklington House, at least not at the price she was asking, a price which both she and they considered eminently reasonable for such a beautiful and historic house. It seemed no-one in these days had much interest in buying a place of such architectural merit, particularly in Sussex, but more especially since poor old Cucklington House required a considerable amount of repair at a time when, due to building restrictions, repairs of such magnitude were all but forbidden. Yet Meggie *had* to sell. She had taxes to pay and debts to meet and no income other than the few shillings her former butler insisted she take for helping out behind the bar. Her grandmother had left her a certain amount of money for sure, but she had also very generously left her the great, grand old house without for a moment thinking how much it would cost to repair.

Then too there were the problems she had inherited from her parents. She had lost them both out of the blue when their car veered off the highway one night when they were returning home from an all night party at Cape Cod, crashing in flames at the bottom of a steep wooded valley. Typically they had made absolutely no provision for their only child, assuming in their usual feckless way that since Meggie was the apple of her grandmother's eye their daughter had already inherited a small fortune when Madame Gran had died in 1940. Such had not, alas, been the case, and finally Meggie found herself far from rich, having inherited only a crumbling house as well as a great many effects for which little money could be raised from anywhere, shortages having extended themselves not just to food and petrol, but to people's disposable incomes as well.

Meggie thought more about her parents now that they were gone than she did when they had been alive. During their lifetime she had thought of them hardly at all because she hardly saw them. Her father had been posted to the US at the start of the war, and what with his being in the diplomatic service, and extremely handsome with a beautiful wife, doors were opened to them everywhere, and the doors that opened in New York led to a far more enjoyable social life than the one they had abandoned in war-torn London. Within six months of settling in New York her father had resigned his diplomatic post and accepted an extremely lucrative position on the board of a highly successful firm of investment bankers. Nevertheless, the Gore-Stewarts went through their money as if they owned a private mint, Sir Anthony adding to their growing financial difficulties by his unsuccessful but compulsive gambling. By the time their car had swerved fatally off the highway, the Gore-Stewarts were not just heavily in debt, they were all but penniless.

The consequences of her parents' irresponsibility meant that Meggie, being the honourable soul that she was, had to sell off what little there was left of the Gore-Stewart goods and chattels in order to try to pay off some of her parents' creditors, as well as some hefty back taxes. Paintings went to auction at the very worst time, although thanks to her many good and decent connections some of the finest of the family collection went straight to private buyers for proper sums of money. Silver was sold and jewellery too, items left to her by Madame Gran and the few bits and pieces her mother had somehow managed to keep out of hock. When all duties and liabilities had been met, all poor Meggie had left was the beautiful but crumbling Cucklington House, a place that was fast becoming a white elephant as the agents kept endlessly hinting.

'There really are no other assets you can realise?' her lawyers kept asking her, unaware of the two paintings she had kept for herself, one being hers by right anyway, and the King Charles I drinking cup she just could not bear to be quite parted from since it had been her grandmother's prize possession.

'Unless you find some form of employment and find it soon, Miss Gore-Stewart,' they kept warning her, 'you could well be facing bankruptcy. Could you not perhaps go back to work for your former employers? After all, you had a very distinguished career during the war.'

Meggie found this last remark hilarious, since bound by the Official Secrets Act she was quite unable to discuss the matter of further employment with His Majesty's Secret Service. Once she had fully realised the depths of her financial difficulties, she had indeed contemplated a return to the Service, and for that reason had allowed Hugh Tate to make professional advances to her, but had soon thought better of it. For a start the pay was atrocious, and secondly, although she had actually been briefed as to the political expectations of the next few years, her heart really was *not* in peacetime espionage the way it had been in wartime. To her it was a totally different game. And while realising that it was just as important if not more so – with the birth of nuclear weapons and the mounting tensions between Russia and the West –

she was too realistic not to know that her personality was not cut out for that kind of cloak and dagger stuff, which explained her complete rejection of Hugh's professional advances that afternoon in his car on Bexham Quay.

'We do have to repeat our warnings, Miss Gore-Stewart,' her lawyers had persisted both verbally and by letter. 'If you do not find some way to achieve solvency then you face the very real prospect of bankruptcy.'

'Bankruptcy be damned,' Meggie would toast, whenever she had finished her work at the Three Tuns. 'Let them throw me into a debtors' prison – see if I care!'

Once the pub was closed she and Richards would sit in the half darkened lounge and reminisce, Richards sticking valiantly to his brew of big strong cups of tea, Meggie drinking cognac from a crate smuggled in from an old Breton comrade in the French Resistance.

But memories are heady things, and inevitably, as the hours grew shorter and dawn more imminent, Richards and Meggie would either be in tears at the recollection of some tragedy, or in paroxysms of helpless laughter. As the light came creeping under the old shuttered windows, and the first rays of the autumn sun began to warm the still waters in the harbour, Meggie would light her last cigarette for what was no longer the night but was now a new day, and wander slowly home smoking and watching the gulls wheel above the little fishing boats returning, listening to the gentle awakening of her favourite place in the whole world.

'And you're not going to be enjoying life as much as you'd like to enjoy it unless you get a grip on your smoking,' Dr Farnsworth warned her when Meggie visited him the day after Waldo had flown off to Berlin. 'That cough of yours is if anything worse, and I don't like what I'm hearing in your chest at all.'

'Very well.' Meggie sighed over-dramatically, narrowing her eyes at the medic. 'Have it your own way. I'll give up the weed altogether. Will that make you happy?'

'I think it would be a wise move, Miss Gore-Stewart. Since you don't seem to be able to cut down. I do think the only thing would be for you to give it up altogether.'

'Just like that.'

'I'm very much afraid so.'

'And of course, we all know how easy it is, to give up smoking.'

'If you don't give up, you could be storing all sorts of trouble up for yourself in the future, and the not so distant one at that. Suck sweets – see if you can't find someone to get you some American chewing gum, on the quiet. But take more care – because your system is running down, Miss Gore-Stewart.'

The doctor watched her leave the surgery, and once she was gone and the door was closed he thankfully lit up a Capstan Full Strength.

As Meggie left the surgery she knew the

wretched doctor was talking sense. She had tried cutting down, but within less than a week she found she was back to her full complement without even realising it. The trouble was not only her weak will as far as smoking went, but the fact that she had no difficulty whatsoever in getting hold of cigarettes due to the constant flow of contraband that streamed into the cellars of the Three Tuns. She was making herself ill, and she knew it without the doctor's having to tell her. She felt desperately tired all the time, so much so that unless she was either smoking or drinking she only wanted to sleep, and not just a nap. She wanted to sleep for ever. The dry cough that had plagued her all summer was becoming habitual as autumn wore on.

Richards kept nagging her to eat more, but due perhaps to always being on the run in Europe during the war Meggie now had little appetite. Besides, she hated eating alone and always had done. She would start out with every intention of being sensible but generally after the first couple of drinks she always seemed to forget to eat. It was the same when she was in company. Rather than hold up the party while she finished what was in front of her, she left it. The result was she was growing thin, painfully thin she considered as she looked at herself in the glass that night, too thin to attract any man and that was for certain. Not that there was any man who in her consideration was worth attracting, she thought as she sat down on the edge of her bed, lighting up what she promised would be her last cigarette ever – well, if not ever, at least for a very long time indeed. No, there wasn't any man even remotely interested in her, and she wasn't remotely interested in any man either.

Except now there was a man, but he was a most unlikely man, and quite possibly a highly unsuitable man as well. Yet ever since that day – the day of the Regatta, the night of the dance – hardly a quiet moment had gone by when Meggie hadn't thought about him.

'I mean, Waldo Astley for God's sake!' she said to herself, tossing and turning on her bed. 'Of all the idiot men to get a crush on! I must have taken leave of my senses!'

And now I probably won't ever see him again, Meggie thought in misery, as she fell back on her bed, lying there and staring up at the ceiling. *I won't see him again because he's only going to go and get himself killed on one of Hugh's derring-do missions, dropping off secret documents in Berlin and trying to buy information from double agents in return for black market goods. God in heaven, I thought all this nonsense was over anyway – but apparently it's not, because apparently according to Hugh the Russkis are going to try to kick us out of Berlin anyway. Just as well I'm sleeping alone at the moment.* Meggie sighed as she slipped under her bedclothes in her underwear, too tired to change into a nightgown. *I'd probably talk in my sleep, blow the gaff and get sent to the bloody Tower.* She fell asleep early, far too early to be tired, but still she dreamed.

She dreamed that she was wandering in a garden, and she met her beloved, long dead Davey, and he led her through sweet scented places, talking to her, making her laugh and cry at the same time, while she kept saying to him over and over again *I knew I'd find you again, I knew I would*. But Davey kept shaking his head and pointing ahead of her to someone in the distance. As she drew nearer and nearer, Davey seemed to drop further and further back, until he was no longer by her side, and she stood by the side of someone else.

Of a sudden Meggie woke up, her face still wet with tears, and remembering her dream she turned her face into her pillow, longing all at once for the person by whose side she knew she most wanted to be.

The cards, however, promised a dramatic turn in her fortunes, both financially and romantically. Meggie was a great reader of cards as well as other popular runes such as the position of tea leaves in an empty cup, and above all the positions of the stars and planets. She had even been known to consult visiting fortune-tellers who travelled through Bexham in the summer months, setting up their tents and attracting a brisk trade from the young, the superstitious, and the curious.

Meggie's grandmother, Madame Gran, had never approved of fortune-telling, Ouija boards, table rolling with glasses, or any other kind of occult occupation, maintaining as she did that if there was indeed another world, then it was a world best left to itself. *Put a foot in the door,* she used to say, *and the door will fly open and unleash something over which you would have no control.*

It wasn't until her grandmother was long gone to the next world that Meggie found out from Richards why Madame Gran had been so strict on this score. It seemed that one midsummer night at Cucklington she and a party of her friends had relaxed the rules, lowered the lights, and with the aid of a glass and a set of cut-out letters had tried to call up spirits from the other world. Unfortunately they had succeeded all too well, conjuring up it seemed the ghost of a footman who had strangled his girlfriend, and himself been killed by the other servants. Having been invited back to the house where he had been murdered, he persisted in making his presence felt in many unpleasant and evil ways, and it took several visits from the vicar to get rid of his malignant spirit. Richards maintained that after that Madame Gran had needed no convincing about the existence of ghosts, but was assured that the correct and only place for them was in the *next* world.

Meggie appreciated her grandmother's caution, and yet now could not resist consulting her pack of cards night after night, obsessed by the idea that they might either confirm or deny this sudden and unexpected change in her emotions. At first it seemed she was to be disappointed, and that the indications of any change in her fortunes were just yet more marsh lights. For a start Waldo failed to return from his trip when he had been expected to do so, at least according to Hugh from whom Meggie learned unofficially that the trip had not been expected to take more than a week. Yet it was now well over ten days since Waldo had left Bexham and there was still no sign of his return. Unable to tell her more, Hugh tried to reassure her by saying that there was nothing at all to worry about, although of course privately Hugh knew very well that anyone pursuing the sort of business Waldo Astley was pursuing in Berlin ran the very real risk of being killed by either side, which was precisely what Meggie imagined.

On top of which she had developed an acute and rather severe chest infection as well as her ongoing cough, a contagion that raised her temperature alarmingly and made her take to her bed, a place Meggie only ever used for either sleep or pleasure. Finally, bored to distraction by her confinement, Meggie dosed herself up with aspirin and returned to work at the Three Tuns where she promptly passed out the same evening trying to help shift beer barrels in the cellars.

In answer to a call Dr Farnsworth reluctantly paid a visit to Cucklington House the following morning, where he found her being nursed with devotion and solicitude by Richards who had left the Three Tuns in the charge of Neil, a new young barman he had just taken on to help him cope with the increase in business.

'She's been quite delirious during the night, doctor,' Richards said. 'Her temperature went up to over 103 at one point and I've had to change not only her night things but her bed sheets, twice.'

'It's this wretched influenza bug,' Dr Farnsworth said, with a shake of his head. 'It's knocking everyone over like ninepins, and quite rushing me off my feet. I'm going to put her on a course of M&B. She'll also need two aspirin every four hours and plenty of liquid to replace all this lost fluid. If she worsens, call me at once – otherwise I'll be in again tomorrow morning. She should respond to the M&B pretty quickly. I'm finding most of my patients are up and about within the week provided we hit this wretched bug early enough. So long as she doesn't miss a dose and you keep her well topped up with aspirin, we should see this temperature down within a day or so.'

Worryingly enough, far from beginning to fall as predicted Meggie's temperature shot up to 104 the following night. She became more and more delirious before falling into what Richards feared might be some sort of coma, and he was forced to call Dr Farnsworth out once more, this time in the small hours of the morning.

After much grumbling on the other end of the telephone the doctor turned up on the doorstep of Cucklington House with his flannel pyjama trousers showing underneath his tweed suit and distinctly reeking of whisky.

'Think I'm going down with the damn' thing myself now,' he grumbled as Richards let him in. 'All these blasted house visits, of course. Still – that's how it goes. Occupational hazard.'

'Miss Gore-Stewart is critically ill, doctor,' Richards announced in his gravest tones, slipping back to his former role. 'Otherwise I would not of course have bothered you.'

'You're a doctor now, are you, Richards?' Farnsworth muttered as he followed Richards up the stairs. 'Not content with being a pot man you're a doctor now, are you?'

'I am merely reporting on the state of the patient, doctor.' Richards stood aside and admitted the doctor into the sickroom where Meggie lay on her pillows, her beautiful face ashen, her hair matted from sweat.

Dr Farnsworth put down his Gladstone bag, sneezed, and wiped his nose on a large red spotted handkerchief, before feeling his patient's forehead.

'I'd say the fever has abated,' he said, straightening up and pulling a thermometer from his jacket pocket. 'If I'm not very much mistaken.'

Placing the thermometer carefully under one arm of the still comatose Meggie, Dr Farnsworth then helped himself to a good swig of some sort of syrup he took from his bag and blew his nose loudly.

'Bit of a scourge this, Richards,' he said. 'Hope you don't get it or we sufferers won't even be able to drown our sorrows at your noted hostelry, will we? Not what we want at all. If the pub closes, Bexham closes. Not even Hitler managed to close the Three Tuns. Not even the Little Corporal managed that.' He sneezed again.

'If you come to my hostelry and do that, Dr Farnsworth, then there's every chance I shall contract the bug, and then the Three Tuns will be forced to close, believe me.' Richards sniffed.

'Hmmmm,' Dr Farnsworth said with a sideways look at the upright figure beside him. 'I should imagine all your organs are far too well pickled by now to succumb to any infection.'

'You may well be right, Dr Farnsworth,' Richards replied, permitting himself a small smile. 'Alcohol is indeed a very fine preservative, which is obviously why you have stayed healthy for so long. Why we enjoy your custom at the Three Tuns so regularly.'

'I was right,' Dr Farnsworth said, ignoring him, having retrieved and examined his thermometer. 'Ninety-nine point two. I would say we are well and truly out of the woods.'

'Thank God for that.' Richards turned away, about to go in search of fresh bedlinen. 'She's been that delirious, telling me to move the rats off her bed and the spiders off the walls, I really thought I'd lost her.'

And from that moment Meggie's luck changed, just as the cards had predicted, for the very next day Richards took a telephone call from her lawyers on her behalf, explaining that his patient was still far too weak to take the call in person. As soon as he had heard the good news, Richards replaced the telephone and sighed with relief. Then he proceeded upstairs at his usual dignified pace even though the news he was about to break was exceptional.

Meggie was propped up on a pile of freshly slipped pillows, her hair brushed, a little lipstick applied to her mouth and a tiny bit of colour to her cheeks. Snatched it would seem from the jaws of death she looked prettier than Richards could ever remember seeing her, her frailty and helplessness adding to her innate and captivating beauty.

'Now, Miss Megs,' he began, coming to the side of her bed with his hands held folded in front of him. 'I forbid you to get out of bed and jump with joy when I impart my glad tidings. You may be allowed one small shout of pleasure if you wish, although even that may bring on a coughing fit so I'm not really sure, not at all.'

'What is it, Richards?' Meggie asked anxiously. 'I heard the telephone ringing.'

'Indeed. And for once it has rung with glad tidings. As we know, this dear place has been up for sale for some time now—'

'We have a *buyer*?' Meggie's eyes widened in astonishment. 'Well?'

'Cucklington has been on the market alas without success for some time now and your agents decided, as you know—'

'Stale bread, Richards,' Meggie interrupted. 'We all know the state of play, their latest ruse being to invite sealed bids, and the highest wins. Desperation point, I should have thought.'

'And the closing date was yesterday, which of

course neither of us was in any fit state to remember, *was* we, dear?'

Meggie kicked the bedclothes feebly and groaned at Richards, wishing he would get on with it, something of which he never seemed capable.

'No we *wasn't,*' she retorted. 'Now get on with it, you daft old bat.'

'Three bids, Miss Megs. Two absurdly low, at least a thousand pounds under the last asking price – and one . . .' Richards deliberately let his voice peter out, raising his eyebrows ever higher and making his mouth ever smaller.

'One *what*, Richards? One what *for God's sake*?'

'One – preposterously and absurdly high.'

'High?' Meggie bit her lip and her long-fingered, pale-skinned hands moved restlessly across the top of the sheet. 'Absurdly high?'

'Preposterously so. Unbelievably so. Laughably so.'

'So it's not genuine then? Someone larking about, do you mean?'

'Most certainly not, Miss Megs. The bid enclosed a banker's cheque as a deposit should the bid be successful, and your man is conferring with his man *e'en the noo* to confirm the details.'

Meggie frowned again and then puffed out her cheeks.

'So go on – tell me. How preposterously, absurdly, ridiculously high was the winning bid?'

'Hold on to your wig, milady.' Richards sighed dramatically. 'It was five thousand more than was originally asked.'

'Five *thousand*?' Meggie gasped. '*Five thousand pounds*, Richards?'

'No, five thousand brass farthings, you silly scarecrow. Of course it's five thousand pounds.'

'Good grief,' Meggie said, all but inaudibly. 'But if this is true—'

'It's true, it's true. You're not delirious, you're not dead and gone to heaven. You're better, your temperature is down, and to cap it all some lunatic is going to pay you five thousand pounds too much for this dear old wreck of a mansion.'

'But who?' Meggie wondered, eyes popping. 'Who would be potty, crazy, or even stupid enough to do that?'

'Search me, your high and mightiness. Some madcap by the name of Pat – Pat for Patrick I imagine – Mr Patrick O'Henry, apparently, an eccentric Irish inventor, so they tell me.'

'Mr O'Henry has to be quite some inventor to be willing to pay that sort of money for dear old Cucklington, Richards.' Meggie sighed. 'And you do realise what this means. Don't you?'

'I do indeed, Miss Megs.' Richards sighed in return. 'It means at last I might be able to claim all the back pay I'm owed.'

The only setback to the change in Meggie's fortunes was the continued non-appearance of Waldo Astley whose absence became more noticeable with each passing day, not only to Meggie but to everyone who had become involved with him in the deceptively short space of time he had been in Bexham.

Peter and Rusty Sykes awaited his return without knowing anything about the sorts of risks he was running yet with a feeling of mounting concern, as if instinctively they realised that whatever it was their employer was doing it was certainly not in the normal run of things. Rusty was also anxious because her father and her brother Mickey had been hard at work on the *Light Heart* to meet the deadline set down by Mr Astley yet now he was nowhere to be seen, nor was there any word from him, and what was worse the money he had deposited against the repairs was fast running out. Judy Tate awaited his return because she was dying to tell him how well things were going between her and Walter, just as Loopy was hardly able to contain her eagerness to see him again. She thought even Waldo, with his seemingly unstoppable enthusiasm and optimism, would not be able to believe that before Loopy's exhibition had finally closed she'd managed to sell another eight paintings. Even the Reverend Anderson prayed for a quick return. He and Waldo had become good friends over the months, their opening dialogue about the poverty of the vicar's sermons having been a turning point in the clergyman's life, since shortly after that he had discarded his books of pre-prepared sermons and begun thinking for himself. The fine and unexpected result of this was that his preaching had improved immeasurably and with it had grown a true affection for his maverick parishioner. Naturally Hugh Tate found himself praying for the safe return of his intrepid young agent, a man whose audacity and courage he had admired from the time he first met him in the bar of the Paris Ritz in 1945, only hours after the liberation of the city.

But most of all Waldo's safe return was prayed for by Meggie Gore-Stewart, who'd at last realised that she had finally and much against her better judgement of course, fallen in love with the engaging American of the dark eyes and the mysterious ways. The Highwayman, as she liked to think of him, seemed to have kidnapped her off her chair that evening at the dance, and galloped recklessly off with her emotions.

But still there was no word.

In desperation Meggie sought out Hugh, only to be answered with a sad shake of the head and a shrug of the shoulders. Waldo Astley had gone to Berlin, had arrived safely, had posted his continued presence and then, once again, disappeared.

The days became weeks, and while Meggie gradually seemed to recover from her fever, and dutifully joined in the celebrations at the Three Tuns that accompanied the wedding of Princess Elizabeth to her dashing naval prince, it seemed to her that instead of the future Queen of England walking down the aisle it was her and Waldo, while the bells of the Abbey became those of the ancient Saxon church of Bexham, pealing out merrily across the estuary in celebration of one of the most unexpected marriages in their recent history.

But now it was December, and the days were growing colder and shorter as everyone prepared for Christmas, hoping against hope that this winter was not going to be as severe as the last, as well as that the absence of their American friend had not become a permanency. But as the children opened fresh doors on their home-made Advent calendars and hung them back on their bedroom doors, there was still no news from Berlin.

Then, just as dramatically as he had disappeared, Waldo Astley returned.

He was first seen walking down Bexham High Street with what seemed to the people who knew him an even larger cigar than ever clamped between his perfect white teeth, his arms full of parcels wrapped in shining red paper.

What the people who saw him did not know, but Rusty and Peter Sykes knew, was that this was not his first day back. They had been surprised by him a good ten days before, but had been sworn to secrecy when he arrived at the dead of one night with his left arm in a sling and a deep scar running down his forehead through his left eyebrow to finish on the top of his cheek. Naturally Rusty was the first to wonder why the secrecy was necessary when everyone had been waiting for so long to welcome him home. Equally naturally, Waldo told her to mind her own business.

'Your wife's bossier than my old mammy,' he grumbled good-humouredly to Peter. 'I don't wish to see anyone, and I don't wish anyone to know that I'm here, and that's all there is to it.'

Rusty suspected that there was actually a good deal more to it than that, because she had gone through an experience that had left her scarred and wounded as well. She knew how memories could haunt a person and said so, which made Waldo growl at her; but instead of asking her to leave for stepping so far out of line, which she was quite sure he would, after a long while and several deep sighs he told her to sit down by his bedside while he took her into his confidence.

'It's not these silly injuries that are plaguing me, Rusty. Sure, they hurt at the time and they still hurt me now – but it isn't them that's the bother. It's what I saw. That's what gets to you, as you know. It's the real life dilemmas that stay with you – people's pain and misery and despair. You know what I'm talking about so I can say it to you, Rusty. The things I saw in Berlin – they'll stay with me for the rest of my days. And there was damn all I could do about it. There's damn all any of us can do about it. We complain about what it's like in this country – how things should be better having won the war – but we're OK. I mean we are really OK compared with what those folks in Berlin are going through right now. Believe you me, they're going to take a long time to shift, the memories I have of those people. Oh boy.'

Rusty said nothing because there was nothing

she could say. She just stayed with him as he lay there in silence, and watched an almost shocking tear rolling unashamedly down one of his cheeks before he turned his face from her and fell into a deep and troubled sleep.

Five days before Christmas, everything changed when Rusty heard the sound of whistling coming from inside his bedroom and moments later saw her employer emerge dressed in his best dark suit and crisply laundered white shirt and best red silk bow tie. He smiled at her, donned his famous black slouch hat and left the house with his arms full of presents for his friends, all of whom he called on in turn, leaving their houses only when he extracted from them a promise that they would tell no-one else of his return.

He called on Lionel, whom he found in company with his daughter Mattie and her friend John Tate. He dropped into the vicarage and enjoyed a tot of hot whisky and lemon with the Reverend and Mrs Anderson; he paid his respects to Richards and his loyal band of locals in the Three Tuns. He called in on the Tates and found them all busy decorating their tree, Loopy, Hugh, Walter, Judy and Dauncy. It was hard to know who was the most astonished or pleased to see him out of them all, and finally he knocked on the door of Cucklington House, with only one red-wrapped present left.

Meggie opened the door. When she saw who it was she laughed, burst into tears, laughed again and finally and thankfully threw her arms around his neck.

'Remind me to go away a lot more often, Miss Gore-Stewart,' he said, smiling broadly, the expression in his eyes unseen over Meggie's shoulder. 'Or is this the sort of greeting you always extend to Santa Claus?'

'You're such a bloody fool,' Meggie said, wiping away her tears quickly. 'And a bloody awful sort of man to boot.'

'In that case don't boot me out,' Waldo replied. 'At least not until you see what I've bought you.'

'I haven't bought you anything,' Meggie lied. 'But only because I didn't think I'd ever see you again. I thought you'd just taken off – in the same way as you arrived here. Out of the blue. In a puff of smoke. And I'm not opening this now – it's unlucky.'

She took the carefully wrapped present and put it under her Christmas tree, which was decorated with pre-war lanterns lit from inside by tiny bulbs, large real glass baubles, and strange-looking pieces that her grandmother had collected down the years and had always put away on Twelfth Night until the following December when once again it was time to deck the halls and house with holly.

'Why should you worry about ever seeing me again?' Waldo asked, his face all innocence. 'Why, the last time we saw each other—'

'No.' Meggie held up a hand, at the same time crossing to the drinks tray. 'Don't talk like that – don't let's talk about it at all. You disappeared and I think you did it just to frighten me. I do not like people disappearing. A lot of people have disappeared from my life, there one minute and gone the next, and I don't want it to happen any more.'

Seeing her expression Waldo pulled her back towards him and took her hands in his.

'If you're thinking how I'm thinking,' he said. 'Of what I'm thinking—'

'Anyway, I'm glad you're all dressed up,' Meggie said, interrupting him. 'Now you sit there and enjoy your drink while I go and change.'

'You don't have to change. You look great; so glam.'

'I want to look even more glam, as you call it, thank you.' Meggie tossed back her blond hair and smiled at him, putting one hand to his cheek. 'So just preserve that soul of yours in patience, as Richards used to say when we were growing up, and wait for a transformation.'

'You're the boss.' Waldo smiled, took the hand that was held to his face and kissed the palm. 'Just don't be long. And by the way – what's the occasion?'

'It's Christmas, fathead. And we're going to a party.'

They didn't have to go far – in fact they didn't have to go anywhere, because the party was being thrown by Meggie right there in Cucklington House. Having changed into a stunning albeit pre-war cocktail ensemble of matte crêpe tunic jacket with a velvet front matching the underlying dress, and found a precious pair of silk stockings and her favourite evening shoes, Meggie brushed her hair until it shone – adding the final embellishment of jewelled combs either side of her face – then hurried down the back stairs straight to the kitchen and her emergency larder. As she prepared a tray of cold chicken, fresh ham and cheeses and took out a bottle of chilled Bollinger from her ancient pre-war Frigidaire – the food and drink having been of course provided by Richards and his team of trusty smugglers from the Three Tuns – from upstairs she heard the sound of Waldo playing carols on her Blüthner.

As she came closer to him, walking quietly down the service corridor and out across the hall, she could now hear him singing as well. He was singing 'In the Deep Midwinter', which just happened to be her favourite carol, and he was singing it in a beautiful round baritone, filling the house with Christmas and her heart with unaccustomed joy.

She stopped outside the drawing room and waited until he had finished.

'Don't you know anything a little more – well, you know – festive? Something we can all sing?' she remarked casually, putting the tray down. 'Something those of us without wonderful deep brown velvet voices can sing? Instead of all this recherché stuff?'

At once a poker-faced Waldo began to play a terrible pub-like version of 'While Shepherds Watched', the words of which Meggie immediately amended to the schoolgirl version.

While Shepherds washed their socks by night
All seated round the tub
A bar of Sunlight soap came down
And they began to scrub!

Waldo shook his head tragic-sad at her, as if she was a hopeless cause, and transposed the carol at once into a minor key, which made it impossible for Meggie to continue singing her mock version.

'Clever clogs,' she said, opening the champagne. 'Spoilsport.'

'I'm a musical *puriste*, Miss Gore-Stewart,' Waldo said in his best Grand American, very Harvard, very Long Island. 'I simply cannot sta-and the classics being *traduced*.'

'All right, Schubert.' Meggie sighed, sitting beside him on the piano stool, their champagne on the piano before them. 'Play me "White Christmas" then. I just love "White Christmas". Gives me goose bumps.'

'I'll sing it only if you let me kiss your goose bumps better.'

'That's a deal.'

And it was. They were both as good as their word.

'Isn't this a bit sudden?' Waldo wondered as he sat with Meggie in his arms on the sofa before a roaring log fire. 'And before you laugh, I'm serious.'

'No, on the contrary, Mr Astley,' Meggie replied. 'I think it's a little late. I hate wasting time – and when I think of the time we've wasted. All that lovely, long hot summer. All those swims, those walks, that lazing on the beach. It's purely criminal the time we've wasted not being together.'

'You hadn't got a good word to say for me,' Waldo observed. 'I know. You hadn't got a good word to say for me, about me or to me—'

'And didn't you know? That is always a sure sign.' Meggie laughed, with another toss of her hair. 'Besides, you wouldn't even look my way, so you are certainly not one to talk, Mr Waldo Astley.'

'I was dazzled. Blinded. Terrified by your charms.'

'*Et ta soeur*, as they say in *la belle France*.'

'It's true. No it isn't – because I did look at you. I looked at you a great deal and it was you who wouldn't look at me. The day of the famous Regatta. When you were helping in the Three Tuns – in that low cut red dress of yours, and your hair all awry. You looked so different from your usual cool, poised self. I couldn't stop looking at you.'

'I know.' Meggie smiled. 'I know.'

'You do? Well now, I sure would like to know how – you never looked at me once.'

'Women can feel these things. I'm not sure about men, but women certainly can. Anyway, there's a mirror behind the bar.'

Waldo laughed and lit his cigar. 'You still wouldn't look, though.'

'I danced with you at the hop afterwards, didn't I?'

'Sure you did. No, as a matter of fact, you didn't.

You let me dance with you. You looked past me the whole time. In fact you spent the whole time looking over my shoulder. I got the distinct impression you thought I'd been rolling in a cow barn and wouldn't touch me with a haymaking fork.'

'Shows what you know. I didn't dare look at you. I didn't dare dance with you – because I didn't know what would have happened. I felt out of control.'

'I wonder why?' Waldo mused. 'I felt just the same.'

'So, as the saying goes – we were meant for each other. Big sigh.'

'You're making fun.'

'Only because it's *so serious.*'

'I have a favourite cliché, too. *Then they woke up and found it was all a dream.*'

'Could be, could be.' Meggie looked at him and then kissed him tenderly. 'Somehow I don't think so – except—' She stopped, remembering a specific dream, and frowned. 'Except, sometimes one does dream, and the dream does change one's mind.'

'Let's dance,' Waldo suggested, of a sudden, getting to his feet. 'I want to dance with you again.'

'I'm out of needles,' she replied. 'Rather, I mean the gramophone is. I forgot to get some new needles.'

'We don't need the gramophone. I just want to dance with you.'

'Very well,' Meggie agreed. 'What do you intend

to do? Play the piano one-handed while we dance round the stool?'

'No. I shall be both the band and the singer, and we shall smooch. OK?'

'Suits me.'

Waldo opened his arms to her and took her in them. She felt as if she had always danced with him, it was that good a fit. He sang 'The Nearness of You' as they danced, and after that he hummed it. She held him and he held her and the room went round, and the world too.

Later, as they undressed each other, she saw the wound in his shoulder. 'How did it happen?' she whispered, shocked.

'Someone shot me. And missed,' Waldo whispered back.

'They didn't miss. They hit you.'

'They missed killing me. Sucks boo to them.'

'Who wanted to kill you?'

'One or the other. I don't know. I was where I shouldn't have been – which was where I should have been because I had to – and someone let someone else know, someone who shouldn't have known – and the consequence was someone took a shot at me.'

'Six inches lower. God, Waldo, another few inches.' Meggie stared at the scar.

'It didn't happen, Meggie.'

'And what about your face?' She gently kissed the scar that ran down as it were through his eye. 'What happened to this dear, beautiful face of yours? Was that a bullet, too? Looks more like a duelling scar. Have you been duelling in Germany?'

Waldo laughed and kissed her right back. 'No duel,' he told her. 'I was drunk – and walked into a glass door. In the hotel.'

'You fool.'

'I didn't mean to.'

'What did you mean to do?'

'I didn't mean to do this, Meggie. But, boy, am I glad I am.'

'Why didn't you mean to do this, Waldo? You against this sort of thing?'

'Not on political or religious grounds. No. Not on moral grounds either. When I say I didn't mean it to happen – I didn't mean that.'

'He thought he saw an elephant, sitting on the stair.'

'Would you be shocked to know that this is the first time?'

'The first time what? That you've made love? Don't tell me that!'

'That I've been *in* love. I never thought I would fall *in* love. Now – come here, Miss Gore-Stewart, before I pass out from desire.'

'Do you have the photographs with you?' Meggie asked as they sat downstairs by the fire, much later, having a midnight feast from the tray Meggie had prepared for their dinner.

'They're at my house.' Waldo drained the last of his champagne and stared at his glass with something close to regret.

Having finished her food, Meggie suddenly longed for a cigarette, but resisted, in spite of knowing there was an emergency pack locked away in the desk. To distract herself she poured them both another half-glass of wine then turned the empty bottle on its head in the ice bucket. 'So. There are just two. And that's all you have to go on. Two snapshots and the words *Bexham 1917* written on the back of one of them.'

'Not a lot, is it?' Waldo agreed, taking a cigar from his coat pocket.

'And nobody has been able to help.'

'It's a long time ago now. Who's alive who's going to remember? I don't even know what month the photographs were taken or where. I know that my father must have been here, because it's his writing on the back. That's all I do know.'

'Maybe he had a relative here. He'd have to have some reason – because I'm absolutely sure there were very few Americans in 1917 who were choosing Bexham in little old West Sussex for their vacations. He must have known somebody here.' Meggie wrinkled her nose and looked at him. 'They must have had a love affair or he wouldn't have tried to burn the photographs, or rather someone wouldn't have tried to burn them.'

'Then maybe it went wrong and left him the bitter man I came to know all too well? I always had the feeling that he had been happy once, but that it had ended suddenly. That happiness had been snatched away from him. That's why I came here, just to see . . .'

'Just to see?' Meggie turned to look at him as he fell silent.

'Just to see,' he said again, and then finally smiling at her, 'what would happen. And look what has happened. Like him, perhaps, I have fallen in love for the first time – in Bexham.'

Chapter Fourteen

The van drove round to the tradesmen's entrance at the back of the house, the delivery driver being familiar with the layout of Cucklington. He had brought the other consignments down from London when they were ready to be returned to their owner, a journey he enjoyed making not only because he himself had been brought up only ten miles from Bexham, but also because he had fallen in love with the owner of the house when he had made the first delivery. Indeed, as he opened the back of his smartly painted black and green van, he hoped and prayed it would be his heroine, Miss Gore-Stewart, who opened the door to him.

And of course, since Richards had long since left to take up his duties as the landlord of the local public house, the delivery boy's prayers were answered and Meggie opened the back door to him in person, dressed in a bright red wool dressing gown piped in white and red kid slippers, with her blond hair pulled tightly back and tied with black ribbon. Despite her early morning attire, to her little admirer she was still the most beautiful creature on whom he had ever set eyes.

'Delivery from Barnstaple and Brown, miss,' he stammered. 'I understand you're expecting it.'

'As a matter of fact, in the excitement I had completely forgotten all about it,' Meggie replied, examining the delivery chitty before staring back at him with clear blue eyes. 'The excitement of Christmas, that is.'

'Only three days to go now, miss. And, you know, I still get all excited like. Even though I know it's daft.'

'I don't think it's daft at all. I think it would be much more daft not to get excited about Christmas. Now, if you wouldn't mind carrying that through to the hall for me and unpacking it, I'll get you some refreshments.'

The delivery boy took the wooden crate through as directed, easing off the nailed planks of soft-wood with a screwdriver he kept in his pocket and carefully removing the newspaper that his employers had rolled into balls as a means of insulation and protection for the cargo. Finally and with even greater care he removed the painting from the case, picked off a couple of flakes of news-paper from the frame, and stood it up against the side of a large armchair that stood by the fireplace in the hall to await its owner's return.

Meggie was back moments later with a tray bearing a mug of hot tea and a plate of hot buttered toast in a muffin dish that she set down on the hall table before standing back to appraise her restored painting.

'Yes, that is brilliant,' she said finally. 'I'm always a little frightened about having paintings repaired when they've been damaged, but they really have done a brilliant job. And now – thanks to the sale of the house – I don't have to get rid of it. It can come with me wherever I go.'

'Mr Barnstaple said he thinks it's one of the best Herbert Wilkinsons he's seen for a long time,' the delivery boy offered.

'He didn't paint a lot of portraits, apparently,' Meggie said, staring at the painting with her head on one side. 'Wilkinson was mostly known for his landscapes, so they tell me. Now. Now all we have to do is find a new home for it.'

Had the painting been hanging where it had hung before, Waldo would have seen it the moment he walked in the front door. As it was, Meggie had decided to hang it in the library above her writing desk, and because of this Waldo didn't see it until he had poured them both a drink in the drawing room. He was about to produce the photographs that he had gone home to collect, when Meggie took him by the hand and led him towards the library.

'I want you to see something first,' she said. 'One of my favourite paintings has come home. It got damaged about nine months ago – fell off the wall – and I got it back this morning.' She threw open the library door. 'I bet like me you'll find it rather special.'

Meggie preceded him into the room, but as she turned to see his reaction she saw Waldo was already transfixed.

'Good heavens above, Waldo,' she said, hurrying back to him. 'Waldo, whatever is the matter with you?'

'You won't believe this, Meggie, but the woman in this painting is the woman in my photographs.'

'I'm very sorry to disappoint you, Mr Astley, but my mother could not possibly have been your mother,' Meggie teased him after they had sat trying to puzzle it all out.

'I don't see why,' Waldo said, still worried, and not entirely convinced. 'She could have got pregnant, returned to America, had me—'

'Waldo?' Meggie smiled at him, shutting him up as she did so. 'Pipe down, and listen. My mother and father got married in 1918, after the war was over. The women in the photograph and in this portrait do look a little alike, I agree, but only because they are costumed in dresses and hats of the period.'

'No, no, I won't have it, he cried! I insist my father came here, fell in love with your mother, and we're really brother and sister. Our romance is doomed, and we will have to go to the vicar to be shriven.'

They both laughed.

'Now there's a notion.' Meggie handed Waldo a cup of coffee, and some buttered toast on a plate.

'A Greek tragedy in Bexham. That would be more than the poor vicar could take.'

'It would give him a good theme for a sermon. Something along the lines of *do not do unto your brother, or sister, what you would do unto another.*'

'Why Waldo Astley!' Meggie said, in her best mock-shocked Southern American.

'He'd have a full house all right.'

'Leaving that aside, are you really telling me you came all the way from America simply because of two old snaps. Is that really true?' Meggie bit into her toast, relishing food for the first time for months.

'I suppose in a way, yes, and in another way, no.' Waldo leaned back in the old red velvet chair and of a sudden stared past Meggie. 'I came to Bexham because of the snaps, as you call them – and also because of Hugh Tate whom I met, if you remember, in Paris in '45. But it wasn't *just* because of either of those things I came here. I think I came because something had happened here, to my father, and I felt that. According to my uncle it was not just my mother running off that closed his heart for ever. It was closed already, which was why she ran off. He suffered some huge disappointment, some heartbreak perhaps. I know it sounds a bit melodramatic, but the mystery of why my father had always been so full of rancour and hatred was beginning to worry me. I wanted to try to find out what it was – because it had to be *something*. Instead of which, it seems that instead of something I've found someone. And now I have, it kind of solves it all. If something happened to my father here, something that changed his life utterly – and not for the good – then what's happened to me must surely balance the books.'

Meggie smiled at him a smile as warm as spring sunshine, then leaned over and kissed him. 'That's just the nicest thing, Waldo. What a lovely thing to say.'

'I say it because I can because it's true, Meggie,' Waldo replied. 'Finding someone is more important than finding out some vague half-truth to do with someone else. Funny thing is – I don't care any longer what that thing might have been. That's history. My father's history. I have to live mine now, and that's what matters. And my history is here – with you.'

'I think it's time to pull a cracker,' Meggie said gently. 'I think we should let Christmas commence. Because I'd say we most surely have more to celebrate than we can possibly imagine.'

Everyone gave parties over the next week. Even though they were still a long way from the land of plenty, the people of Bexham had saved what they could and bought what they could, and what they couldn't buy they made, and what they couldn't make they imagined.

Christmas Day dawned cold, but with a fine frost high on the Downs that made the faded grasses sparkle and the hedgerows glint. As usual Bexham Church was fuller than it ever was during the rest of the year, but Stephen Anderson no longer minded this since he had come to appreciate that sometimes a congregation of two dozen people who were there to worship in earnest could be even more fulfilling for a priest than a church full of people whose minds were more on the roast turkey than the mysteries of the Trinity.

After Matins Waldo and Meggie were invited to the Tates' for drinks, where, with an air of caution in her voice, Judy, in what she thought was a low voice, whispered to Waldo that she might be pregnant.

'I take it the Savoy dinner went OK, then?' Waldo asked straightfaced, once Walter was well out of earshot.

'You were absolutely right – it worked like a dream,' Judy replied. 'But if you really want to know, I'd say that my rumoured flirtation with a certain person – no names no pack drill – did even more than a lovely dinner at the Savoy for two. It acted like a fifty megawatt charge to our relationship.'

'Tell that to my left eye.' Waldo sighed.

Judy laughed and looked across the room. 'Now, only John and Mattie to go, really,' she said. 'Poor John's on tenterhooks. His parents have indicated that they wish to ask Mattie to dinner, but they haven't announced the date for it yet. John keeps wondering if they didn't really mean it, if it will never really happen.'

'It will happen. If it's meant to happen, it does. It's just difficult waiting for the moment, that's all.'

Loopy and Hugh tried once more to persuade

Waldo and Meggie to stay for Christmas lunch but they refused, having made a private arrangement to dine at Cucklington House for what Meggie knew was to be her last Christmas there.

Waldo and Meggie had prepared the lunch together and together they cooked it, Waldo surprising Meggie by how good he was in the kitchen and Meggie surprising Walter by how good she was, both having assumed that having been brought up in rich households neither of them would be really that good at preparing a full scale meal, even though it was only for two. They cooked side by side in perfect harmony, preparing a traditionally delicious Christmas dinner, albeit with a fresh farm chicken in place of the turkey they had not managed to secure in time.

Yet although there were only the two of them sitting in the large dining room at Cucklington, a dark-panelled room which Meggie had decorated with an abundance of candles arrayed all around the room in old jam jars and beautiful traditional arrangements of dark green shiny red-berried holly intertwined with mistletoe and ivy, it seemed that there were six if not a dozen times as many people at the table, so hilarious was the conversation as the two of them ate their way through their mouth-watering dinner. Happily there were still good wines to be plundered from the cellars, although it took some looking, a task that Meggie conferred upon Waldo since she was spooked by the spirits she was convinced remained in some sort of limbo in the subterranean rooms of the large house.

The fearless Waldo, innocent of any such ghostly accounts and stoutly maintaining that no good American should be put off by medieval spirits, returned with two bottles of ancient Vosné-Romanée, a Château Lafitte, and some extremely ancient crusted port. By the time it was the hour to listen to the King's speech, the two of them were – as Meggie put it – well and truly toasted.

After King George had finished addressing the nation, they exchanged presents, Meggie having at the eleventh hour decided to give Waldo a pair of antique gold cufflinks that had belonged to her grandfather as well as a leatherbound edition of *Great Expectations* which she had learned by chance from Judy was one of Waldo's favourite books. Waldo presented her once again with his box beautifully wrapped in the shiniest of red papers. She opened it to find a door key.

'Fine,' she said, her blue eyes narrowing. 'You have me here, sir. Is this one of your quaint jests, perhaps? Or something symbolic?'

'Why, it is neither, madam,' Waldo replied, entering into the spirit of things. 'It is but a plain unvarnished front door key.'

'To the house in which I already live, sir. To a house indeed already sold, sir, moreover.'

'Sold to someone who now has found someone to whom to give it.'

'Oh, no. Not the mysterious inventor Mr O'Whatsit?' Meggie said slowly, as she realised. 'No, Waldo Astley – now you go *too* far.'

'I do so hate to see houses go out of the family.'

'But your bid was *ridiculous*!'

'What I love most of all about you is your unfailing gratitude,' Waldo scolded. 'I had no idea of what anyone else would bid. And when I asked privately—'

'They said to themselves rich Yank, let's push him up.'

'Well, of course. But I knew it was all in a very good *cause*.'

'Ever since you arrived here because of two burned up photographs, all Bexham seems to have done is scrounge from you. It doesn't seem right.'

'What you really mean is, ever since I arrived here I keep throwing my money about, isn't that it?'

'Well, if you insist on being vulgar . . .' Meggie shrugged her shoulders, but remembering all the backbiting and criticism with which Waldo's generosity had been greeted she sighed. 'Most people suspect good motives. It always follows that if you're generous, you must be self-serving. It's true, isn't it? What they say – that no good deed goes unpunished.'

'Oh sure, but don't worry.' Waldo laughed. 'I'm used to people disliking my generosity, and believe me I do nothing I don't want to. They say money doesn't buy happiness, but I don't go along with that. It might not buy *you*, the guy with all the money, happiness – but it certainly can buy happiness for other people. I got that out of this cracker.' Meggie groaned and Waldo continued. 'As you might have guessed, I'm pretty rich, Meggie.

Actually pretty absurdly so – and through none of my own brilliance, I assure you. My father made several fortunes, and let me tell you no-one comes by all that money purely legitimately. I have this sense that a lot of his money came from places where it shouldn't have – and if that was the case, I reckoned that if it came from bad use, why not put it to some good use.'

'You are really quite a remarkable person, Mr Astley,' Meggie said, taking his hand. 'And now – you know what I am going to do with this key you have just given me?'

'I do not have even the vaguest of ideas, madam.'

'I am going to get up,' Meggie said, after which she did just that. 'And I am going to go to the front door, and I am going to lock the door from the inside and hide the key so you will not be able to leave until I say so.'

'And now I shall tell you something, Miss Gore-Stewart,' Waldo replied. 'That little idea of yours just suits me fine.'

But as far as parties proper rather than improper went the party voted best of all by all and sundry was the all day open house Waldo and Meggie threw the following day at Cucklington House. It seemed that at one point or other of the day every person who lived in Bexham arrived for a drink and a good wish. Some stayed for hours, others just dropped in with a small present, or a card, or just to present the compliments of the season. The drink flowed, tray after tray of Rusty's homemade mince pies were consumed, and Waldo sang at the piano while people danced in the drawing room until the bell atop the old Saxon church chimed midnight and the revellers finally staggered home, all except Rusty and Richards who stayed at their own insistence to help clear up the house.

When the Sykeses had finally retired and Richards had ambled back to the Three Tuns, Meggie damped down the fire and locked up the rest of the house while Waldo, now recovered from what he called post-host exhaustion, sat at his piano playing a favourite piece of Schumann.

'I haven't really thanked you for your present, Waldo,' Meggie called to him, over the closing bars of *Träumerei*. 'But I think that's because I didn't know how to.'

'I know how you can thank me,' Waldo said. 'By staying just as you are . . .'

At which he at once began to play 'Stay As Sweet As You Are', his rich sonorous baritone filling the lovely drawing room and floating up to the ceiling where, it seemed to Meggie, it stayed, floating around the room like the cloud of happiness on which she found she was now sitting.

Mattie gazed at herself in the mirror in her newly made home sewn winter dress. It was a three-quarter length shirtwaist style frock, remodelled from one of Lady Melton's pre-war winter gowns, and as she turned herself every which way to examine it Mattie saw it to be very flattering and that it showed her off to her best. But pretty though she undoubtedly looked she felt the very opposite. She had never felt less self-assured in all her life, just at the moment when she needed all her poise and self-belief most. For at long last the formal invitation to dine with the Tates had arrived and tonight was the appointed night.

And now it was here, now the time she had longed so much for had finally come, she felt gauche, unattractive and timid, as if the occasion was going to prove to be far beyond her social capabilities, as if in fact she was making the most terrible mistake in thinking that John's parents were going to ratify their association. What could she have been thinking? she wondered miserably as she sank onto her dressing table stool to stare glumly at herself in her looking glass, with her chin propped up on her fists. She should have known that the Tates could never accept her. Enough people had told her so, heavens above. Accept somebody not only with her past but with an illegitimate child? It really was completely absurd to think that they might. It was worse than absurd, it was extremely embarrassing.

At that moment Mattie felt like chucking the whole thing in – like tearing her newly fashioned dress off, throwing it in the waste basket and climbing into her bed where she would remain until all this stupidity had blown over and calamity had been avoided. Because sure as eggs, she thought, that is what it is going to be – calamitous. It didn't matter any more how much John loved her and she him, nor the way he had accepted so completely what had happened to her in the war without question or criticism, just as she had understood and accepted what had happened to John, when believing his brother to be dead he had found himself falling in love with the woman he thought was now Walter's widow. It mattered not that both she and John were perfectly content to accept each other for what they were because if John's parents were not, then they had no future as a couple, at least not as a respectable couple. They could perhaps run away somewhere and either live together or get married in some register office or other, but in her heart of hearts Mattie knew that this was not what John would want. John Tate came from a very close and loving family, and what he would want was for the parents who loved him to love the woman that he now loved.

So, much as Mattie wanted to see the evening through, even if it ended in defeat, and not to let John down, suddenly it seemed that all her courage had evaporated. Indeed, the normally optimistic and resolute Mattie now felt so utterly without hope that instead of getting on with preparing herself for what she had so foolishly hoped would be her big night, all she felt like was taking her clothes back off and clambering into her bed.

If it had not been for the sudden knock on her door, Mattie might well have done just that, but hearing her father's cheerful voice outside asking if he could come in there was little she could do but go to the door and speak to him.

'Yes?' she asked, allowing just her face to appear in the narrow opening. 'Is something the matter?'

'On the contrary, I thought something must be the matter with you,' Lionel reported. 'I know you women take the best part of a year and a day to get ready, but you can't afford to be late. The Tates are not people to be kept waiting.'

'I'm not going,' Mattie said feebly, doing her best to close the door.

'Of course you are – don't be so damn' stupid.' Lionel pushed the door open and gained an easy admittance, so surprised was his daughter by his resolution, let alone his language. 'I thought you might be fuffing about,' her father continued. 'But believe you me, there's no need to. You can save all this sort of behaviour for your wedding day.'

'Who said anything about wedding days?' Mattie asked, nervously fiddling with her hair, which was already done beautifully.

'Oh, for goodness' sake,' Lionel groaned. 'What on earth do you think this is all about, Mattie? They're not asking you to dinner with their eldest boy just to talk about the weather.'

'They could be asking me up to tell me I'm not suitable, Daddy.'

'Not suitable? Not suitable? You?' Lionel threw back his head and roared with laughter in a most un-Lionel Eastcott-like way. 'Why' – he beamed, putting both his hands on her shoulders – 'I've never seen anything more suitable! Let alone anything quite as lovely. So come along now, Mathilda. I've got the car out for you. I'd drive you myself, but then there'd be no-one here to look after young Max. Off you go, now. And don't you dare come back here without a ring on your finger.'

Kissing her a fond farewell, Lionel watched Mattie walk off down the garden path before closing the front door and leaning his back against it.

'Fingers crossed,' he said out loud. 'Fingers crossed the old letter's done the trick.'

Twice on the short drive from her home to the Tates' Mattie stopped the car and thought about turning back for home, the second time seriously considering the option. She could easily plead illness, have her father telephone the house and say she had suddenly been laid low with some bug or other, and then – and then what? For a start her father would never agree to making any such excuse for her, and even if he did, she would only be delaying the inevitable. Sooner or later she would have to face the Tates and come to terms with the objections she just knew they were going to put in her and John's way – her past – her child – her social *unsuitability* – so really she might just as well bite on the famous bullet and have done with it now. Putting the car back into gear she drove on through the village and headed up the lane to Shelborne. As she proceeded to her delight and surprise she found her confidence flooding back. She had realised that even to think of ducking out on this evening would mean that she was ashamed of herself and, more important, ashamed of her beloved little boy, Max.

So in spite of having to ring the bell three times to gain admittance, by the time Gwen finally opened the front door Mattie was her old self.

'Sorry, miss.' The maid sighed. 'It's the captain. He's banging away at the old joanna, as you can hear – and when he's banging away that loud it's as much as I can do to hear me own thoughts.'

To the sound of her host singing and playing loudly at his grand piano, Gwen took Mattie's coat, put it over her arm and pushed the door to the drawing room open with her free hand.

'Miss Eastcott,' she announced. The group around the piano took no notice whatsoever. 'I said! Miss Eastcott!' Gwen bellowed.

At last Loopy heard. She had her back to the door, and was busy mixing cocktails at the same time as joining in the general sing-song, but somehow over the general noise and cacophony she managed to hear Gwen's announcement and turned to see Mattie standing in the doorway. At once she waved to her newly arrived guest as if greeting someone who had just boarded a yacht from ashore, beckoning her to come over at once, which Mattie did, noting and envying her hostess's elegance, dressed as she was in a silk patterned evening skirt and white silk shirt over which she had thrown a silk cardigan. Hugh Tate also looked relaxed and elegant in his plum velvet smoking jacket and white silk cravat. Seeing the new arrival, he at once stopped playing and rose to his feet.

'Most dreadfully sorry, Miss Eastcott,' he said,

coming round from the piano. 'We'll really have to get Gwen a loudhailer, I'd say.'

Mattie shook hands with the Tates, who both seemed genuinely pleased to see her, while John hovered, smiling too much.

'Bang on time, too,' he said too loudly. 'I said you were an ace timekeeper.'

'My military training, I'm afraid,' Mattie explained. 'Left its indelible mark.'

'Army, John tells me,' Hugh said. 'Staff driver, weren't you?'

'Absolutely. Staff driver, that was me.'

'Drive anyone interesting?'

Mattie felt John's glance but didn't return it. 'Some five star generals,' she said evenly. 'In fact I was attached to one in particular.'

'One of ours or one of theirs?'

'An American.'

'Anyone we'd know?'

'General Michael Rafferty.'

'Rafferty? Oh, quite a fellow, Rafferty. One of the D-Day boys. You had a big cheese in the back of your car. Quite the war hero.'

'He was a very nice man. He was a pleasure to drive. Very nice manners,' she added inconsequentially.

'Guests, Hugh?' said Loopy, prompted by Gwen struggling with an armful of fresh coats while kicking the drawing room door open backwards with one foot.

A very jolly older couple were introduced to Mattie, Major John and Caroline Haskett-Smith, friends apparently of the Tates' from Bexham Yacht Club and the sort of people Mattie's father always described as the *backbone* of England. In spite of a bad war wound that necessitated the use of a heavy walking stick, Major Haskett-Smith was as spry as could be, while his tall and slender wife, her handsome face weather-beaten from her sailing days, was as wry as her husband was nimble. Having survived the worst of wars, it seemed they were determined to enjoy the rest of their lives to the full.

Soon the room was full of laughter as everyone regaled everyone else with the latest in local gossip, their tongues quickly loosened by Loopy's absolutely perfectly made dry Martinis. Far from feeling estranged, Mattie felt oddly at ease, as if the moment she had walked into the drawing room she had been accepted. From the continued riotous behaviour at dinner in the yellow painted dining room there was no reason to suppose that the mood might suddenly alter, and that Hugh Tate would bring an end to the happy proceedings by banging on the table for silence before announcing that in both his and his wife's opinion it would be by far the best thing if Miss Mathilda Eastcott removed herself from their eldest son's affections and returned to her modest little home immediately. Mattie smiled inwardly when she thought of this, amused, because such a ludicrous scene was exactly the sort of fancy that had run through her mind as she was getting ready for the evening.

But now instead she found herself laughing and

talking freely to the people who she had been convinced were about to shun her. Here she sat at ease in elegant surroundings, eating dinner off fine china and drinking wine from cut glass without one disparaging remark being passed about her. She would give anything to be accepted by this elegant and sophisticated family. Now it would seem that she was about to be just that, and yet Mattie's inner fears were not quite allayed. Having lived through the war she knew all too well about false dawns, about the weeks of quiet when one hoped the bombing was at an end, only to have such hopes dashed by the arrival of the Doodlebug or the V2, or some other dreadful weapon of mass destruction. So she knew better than to count her chickens, even though so far all the portents had been more than favourable.

In fact it was almost too idyllic to be true. It was too much to hope for, too much to want, and the seed of doubt had been sown when Hugh Tate had asked her whom she had driven? Remembering certain rumours about John's father and his possible involvement with government intelligence, all at once Mattie got the feeling that perhaps Hugh Tate *knew* – and that was the reason not only for the brief but what had now become in Mattie's mind *pointed* conversation before dinner but for her very invitation here. Perhaps any moment now, when everyone had finished their dinner, John's father was indeed going to bang the table for silence, but instead of merely sending her home and banishing her from his son's life, first he was going to reveal not just her secret, but the identity of the father of her child.

For the rest of the meal Mattie found she could hardly eat a thing.

'Let's go for a walk, shall we?' John said to her, more as an order than an idea, after dinner had been finished without any terrible revelations on the part of Mattie's host. Everyone had gathered again around the piano to be entertained by Hugh and Loopy, who was singing some Noel Coward song in a light but sweet soprano, so it was an ideal opportunity for the young couple to take themselves off into the garden.

Which was where Mattie very soon found herself, before she had time to utter a word.

'What on earth got into you over dinner?' John asked with a laugh that did not altogether conceal his concern. 'One minute you're the life and soul, and the next you look as though you'd just received a tragic telegram.'

'No I didn't,' Mattie protested. 'It was just that everyone else was being so awfully entertaining. Major Haskett-Smith's story about escaping from prison camp and meeting up with those American airmen, Hank and Buddy, dressed as women, was hilarious.'

'Made all the funnier by the fact that they were in such danger.'

'I couldn't possibly compete with that.'

'It wasn't your sudden silence,' John said. 'It was the look you got on your face. Come on.'

'I don't know,' Mattie protested. 'I just suddenly – I don't know. I got tongue-tied.'

'You?' John laughed again. 'Dearest darling Mattie, the day you get tongue-tied is the day I start painting my nails.'

'I think it's because – it's because it was such a wonderful evening,' Mattie blurted out as John, with her hand in his, led her down the lawns.

'And that turned you into Ophelia?'

'I didn't want it ever to end.'

'And it won't,' John said quietly, turning her to him. 'Why should it?'

'Why shouldn't it? It's just an evening.'

'It won't end because there'll be lots more evenings like this,' John said. 'Hundreds of them.'

'And?' Mattie shrugged, feeling certain that she would never be a part of them.

'And you're going to be enjoying them—'

'I am?'

'Because we're going to get married.'

'We are?' Mattie said, now totally wrong-footed. 'I mean are we?'

'Sorry,' John said, pulling a mock sorry face. 'I didn't phrase that very well. Let's try again, shall we?' He dropped to one knee and took her hand. 'Mattie – my darling –'

'Don't fool about, John,' Mattie warned. 'I mean it.'

'I am not fooling about, Mattie.'

'Have you asked your parents?'

'Of course I have asked my parents! Not that I have to ask my parents, being over twenty-one—'

'You know what I mean, John. What I meant was have you *told* your parents?'

'I have told them, Mattie, I have asked them, Mattie, I have declared it to them, stated it to them, I have consulted them, debated it with them—'

'John – be serious.'

'I am being serious, Mattie! I am being *serious*!'

'And?' Mattie asked cautiously, expecting the spell to break at any moment – suspecting that this must be the most dreadful tease, and that as soon as she said yes, everyone would pour out of the drawing room into the garden, holding their sides with laughter.

'And we have their blessing!'

'We what?' Mattie asked, quite sure her ears had deceived her.

'We have their blessing.'

'And . . . and Max?'

'And and and Max too!' John laughed. 'Why shouldn't Max have their blessing as well? My parents can't wait for him to join the family. They said so, only last night. Dad – having brought up three sons – he can't wait to help bring up another. Teach Max sailing, and cricket, and golf – he'll be playing trains and table tennis, and charades at Christmas. He can't wait! Between his two grandfathers poor young Max won't be given a moment's peace, at least that's what Mother says.'

'Are you sure, John?' was all Mattie could ask. 'I mean it's an awful lot to ask.'

'Why?' John grinned. 'I love you, Mattie Eastcott – I love you and because I love you I love your son, and because they love me my parents love you – and your son – and even if they weren't my parents they would still love you. I know that for a fact. Because that's the sort of people they are – and more importantly because that's the sort of person you are. Someone everyone loves.'

John kissed her slowly and sweetly and Mattie kept her eyes open right through the kiss, staring at the bright stars above her to make sure she was awake and not dreaming. After which John took a small red leather box out of his pocket and opened it, revealing a beautiful single diamond ring whose very brilliance seemed to capture the whole of the night in its irridescence.

'You only have to agree to one thing,' John whispered. 'Besides agreeing to marry me.'

'Oh, I've agreed to that, John Tate,' Mattie whispered. 'I agreed to that the moment you asked me.'

'Then the only other thing you have to agree to is to marry me as soon as you can. I don't want to waste any more of my life *not* being married to you, if you don't mind.'

'Oh, very well,' Mattie said with a teasing sigh. 'If you insist.'

'I do. I insist with all my heart.'

Despite the fact that John was looking and sounding more intense than she had ever heard him, Mattie was only half listening to him. The rest of her was thinking about how her life was changing for ever and ever, and in only a few minutes. She was going to be part of Shelborne. She was really going to be able to sit down for dinner with John and his parents and their friends – she was going to be related by marriage to Walter and Judy and Dauncy, and be a proper part of that close and happy family. No longer would she be *that Mattie Eastcott who had the illegitimate baby.* That part of her life was over now and for ever. Now she was to be Mathilda Tate.

But while they embraced and kissed and celebrated their bliss, what neither of them would ever know was that it was Lionel Eastcott's letter to Hugh that had finally swept away the Tates' objections to John and Mattie's relationship. Indeed, what Lionel had written to Hugh on behalf of the two young lovers had made not just Hugh but also his more broadminded wife feel ashamed of the stand they had taken against John's romance, albeit that it had been a more or less unspoken one.

Lionel had written, in his precise but surprisingly sensitive hand –

> *There has been a terrible war. Young people make mistakes in war, but they only make mistakes because the older generation have made an even greater one in failing to stand up to a great and terrible enemy. In failing to mend errors of diplomacy, in indulging in fear and indecision, our generation brought war upon themselves. In my view those mistakes are far greater than the mistake of one young girl who succumbed to a love affair which resulted in a baby being born. To stand in the way of the next generation's*

happiness, at whatever cost to one's family pride, is surely to add to the misery of man, and woman, kind. Millions upon millions have been killed so that the few who are left behind can be free and happy. I know that, and I think you know that. You must accept that John loves Mattie, as I have had to accept that Mattie loves John, and much as I will miss my daughter I know that to do otherwise than to wish her well would be to bring yet more shame on our generation.

Hugh had shown Loopy the letter, the expression on his face that of a man who has just fallen over a trip wire.

'He's absolutely right of course, Loopy,' he said. 'We may not approve of what happened to Mattie, but it is something we should accept, like the all-important fact that John loves her. We must withdraw any objections that we might have and ask Mathilda up here to meet us properly, as soon as possible. I know it takes a bit of getting used to because whatever Lionel Eastcott says and however right he might be, one's eldest son marrying a girl with what our old gardener used to call "a foal at foot" does need a little bit of time to get used to. But used to it we shall be and *I* have to say, having read what her *father* had to say, I feel more than a bit ashamed of myself. I shall look forward to welcoming Mathilda – and that little boy of hers – into our family. And making them both feel a part of it.'

Loopy had already come to this conclusion before Lionel Eastcott's letter had arrived but knew it was only proper that she should wait for Hugh to come to his own conclusion, even though she felt that in good time he would most probably come round to her way of thinking.

But then Lionel's letter had brought matters to a head much sooner than she had imagined. Of course she'd always liked Mathilda, and even admired her for her honesty and resolution, and although it had been a shock at first when she'd seen them kissing on the beach that day, Loopy now accepted that they loved each other, in the only way possible; with good grace.

Chapter Fifteen

As it happened that winter was not nearly as severe as the one that had preceded it, yet the weather was still cold and damp enough to bring with it the usual seasonal afflictions. Once again Meggie was among those struck down with the flu, but happily this particular attack was not apparently as bad as the previous one. Even so she had, albeit reluctantly, been forced to take to her bed with a raised temperature. Dr Farnsworth attended her as usual, and Waldo only left her bedside every now and then in order to prepare his patient a light repast.

'This is not much of a way to start the New Year,' Meggie grumbled as she lay in her bed staring out at the grey wintry skies. 'And now you say you've got to go away.'

'I'm not going anywhere until you're better, Meggie,' Waldo reassured her. 'That's a promise.'

'I hope to God it isn't more bogey business,' Meggie said with an exaggerated sigh. 'Now I've found you I don't want to go and damn' well lose you.'

'Stop worrying.' Waldo put his hand on hers but did not – so Meggie noticed – contradict her.

'So where are you going?'

'I'm going to London to see the King.'

'Waldo—'

'I am going to America, on business,' he replied.

'America? That's miles away!'

'Anywhere is miles away from you, sweetheart. The end of the bed here is miles away from you. Now stop fretting. I have to go – it's family business to do with my father's estate, and since there's only me I have to attend to the winding up of all his affairs.'

'You'll be away for ages.'

'I'll be away for two or three weeks tops. OK?'

'No it is not OK,' Meggie said, with a sudden frown. 'I bet that blighter Hugh's sending you back to Germany or somewhere nasty. You said yourself the other day that the Berlin thing's getting worse by the moment.'

'I am going to America, Meggie – you can count on it. And you're wrong about Berlin. Berlin's cooled down at the moment. No-one reckons anybody's going to do anything for a month or two – and some believe that the whole thing is just one big Russian bluff. Things are a lot worse back home as it happens – although our trouble's coming from the coal miners, not the Reds. So I might get back to find no home fires burning and no trains running. Who knows, you could have picked the best place to be.' He kissed her on the forehead, at the same time checking her pulse.

'Nice and steady,' he said. 'I reckon you'll be up and about in no time.'

'I don't,' Meggie said gloomily. 'I had – what do you call them?'

'Depends what They are.'

'When your heart beats very fast – and sort of flutters.'

'Palpitations. You had palpitations?'

'Sort of. Last night – and I felt terribly feverish as well.'

'I don't remember you saying anything about that.'

'It's obviously just part and parcel of the flu,' Meggie decided. 'I had the same sort of thing last time.'

'Did you mention this to Doc Farnsbarn?'

'Farns*worth*. I didn't bother because I'm sure that's all it is. I remember my grandmother saying people get palpitations when they run these up and down fevers – and taking all these aspirin doesn't much help either.'

'You're telling me because you're worried, that's is, isn't it?'

'No.' Meggie looked at him directly. 'No, I'm telling you to stop you going away.'

'OK,' Waldo agreed. 'Then I'll postpone my trip. I won't set a foot outside Bexham until you are pronounced one hundred and fifty-three per cent fit. How's that?'

'I just hate being in bed, that's all. Except when you're in it, of course.'

Waldo kissed her cheek, but changed his date of

sailing remaining behind in Bexham until Meggie was allowed up, which in fact she was after a further three days' bed rest. Doctor's orders were to take things quietly and easily at first, but Meggie – never one to be restrained – was out and about walking the lanes round her beloved house within twenty-four hours and hiking round the headlands after a further forty-eight. Waldo, delighted with the rapid and obviously complete restoration of her good health, immediately set about replanning his departure, much to the dismay of Meggie, who at once threatened a relapse if he insisted on going.

'I only wish I didn't have to, sweetheart,' Waldo assured her. 'But if I'm to keep up this profligate lifestyle – buying houses for my beloved and the like – then I am going to have to assure the security of my future income.'

It was the day before he departed and he was taking Meggie for a drive in his Jaguar, their first call being her favourite walk on the Downs.

It was one of those rare late February days when the skies suddenly clear and you can almost feel the world beginning to turn on its axis and the ground beginning to warm under your feet. High up on the Downs a light breeze seemed to carry the first hint of spring on its air as they walked on the old, wonderfully springy turf. When they had reached the highest point of their ramble they stopped to rest on a knoll and watch two hares boxing not fifty yards from where they stood.

'This is more like it,' Meggie sighed, holding one

of his arms tightly in both of hers. 'This is exactly how everything should be. God's in his heaven – all's right with the world.'

'So right – because to me this place *is* heaven,' Waldo replied. 'Most of all because it's here that I found *you*.'

'When you think how much we hated each other when we met.'

'I never hated you.'

'You thought I was stuck up and arrogant.'

'I thought you were wholly delightful.'

'And weren't you right?'

'No, not for a moment,' Waldo teased. 'I certainly never thought I could be this happy.'

'You never thought you could fall in love, according to you,' Meggie reminded him.

'No, I never did. I didn't think I could fall in love, but now that I have I can't believe my good fortune. I can't believe not only that you love me but that you love me as much as you say you do, and I can't believe quite how much I love you.'

'Me too,' Meggie agreed. 'Ditto.'

'Now come along, young lady,' Waldo said, quickly consulting his watch. 'I don't have all day – and there's something I have to show you.'

'Not another of your surprises?' Meggie said mock wearily, thinking that it couldn't possibly be so.

'Could be. Could be,' Waldo replied, leading her back down the hill. 'And I can't wait to see the look in those beautiful blue eyes of yours.'

* * *

By now she was lying a mile and a half down the coast from Mr Todd's yard, moored near a dry dock Mr Todd used when building or restoring boats. The covers were off her, the paint and the varnishes were bone dry, the sails were mended and furled, every leak had been stopped and sealed and the engine had been stripped and re-built. The *Light Heart* was seaworthy once again.

Both Meggie and Waldo stood staring at her, Waldo not having seen sight of her since he'd commissioned her repairs, and Meggie not having seen her since the day she'd last sailed on her with Davey, what now seemed like a century ago.

'I don't believe this,' Meggie said, gripping Waldo's arm. 'How did you manage it, Waldo? And why did you do it? Did you have to buy her? Surely she still belongs to the Kinnersley family?'

'One thing at a time, sweetheart,' Waldo replied. 'I didn't manage it, Mr Todd here did – he and Mickey. Yes I did have to buy her and yes the Kinnersley clan had forgotten all about her. I had my lawyers look into it, and since the owners weren't remotely interested in getting her shipshape I paid them a more than fair price and then commissioned Mr Todd and his son to refit her and make her one hundred per cent seaworthy. And haven't they done a first rate job? She's like new.'

Mickey, who was standing nearby, grinned, as pleased as Punch, while old Mr Todd just sort of twitched and touched his old blue yachting cap in recognition of the compliment before returning to the task of getting his pipe lit in the sea breeze.

'But why, Waldo? Is she another part of your Grand Plan? Are you going to sail her round the world singlehanded or something?'

'I'd have to ask your permission first – because you're her new owner.'

Meggie turned and stared, first at him, then at the *Light Heart*, then back at Waldo.

'You are completely and entirely nuts,' she said. 'And I love you even more. You shouldn't have. You really shouldn't – but I'm so very, very glad you did. I can't tell you what this means to me. You'll have to wait till we get home.'

At that she suddenly walked away from him down the beach, sank her hands deeply into her coat pockets and pretended very hard to examine every inch of the beautiful boat bobbing out on the estuary. Waldo watched her happily, puffing away at a freshly lit cigar.

'Is she ready to sail now?' Meggie called up to him. 'I mean everything's been done to her that needs to be done?'

'I guess so!' Waldo called back. 'I guess as ready as she'll ever be! But we'd freeze to death out there!'

'We could go home and put on our warmest clothes, Waldo,' Meggie said as she came back to join him. 'We could wrap up really well and take her out just for a potter round the estuary after lunch. We needn't go out to sea, even. We could just go upriver a bit and then back again. Please,

Waldo? Please? Just to get the feel of her on water again? Just a weeny teeny little trip? Please? The prettiest of pretty pleases?'

Waldo grinned, sighed and went to consult Mr Todd and Mickey about the sea-readiness of the *Light Heart* while Meggie, pulling her fur coat tightly round her and double-wrapping her neck in her wool scarf, hurried back down the beach to stare out at the moored yacht resplendent in her bright new blue paintwork. Yet she didn't look like new. The Todds had skilfully managed the restoration so that they had kept the character of the beautiful old craft, so much so that she looked as if she had never left the water other than to be keel-cleaned, repainted and varnished. She looked just like she had looked when David Kinnersley had owned her, a perfectly and meticulously owned craft that inspired everyone who stopped to look at her. She looked as she had always looked – she looked to be part of the beauty of the sea.

They hurried back to their respective homes to change into their warmest clothes, Waldo returning in his car to collect Meggie after half an hour's absence. She met him at her front door, pretending to be unable to move, walk or speak, so muffled up was she.

'You are looking at eight layers of wool,' she growled from behind her thick red scarf. 'You are about to go sailing with a very large sheep.'

'Speak for yourself,' Waldo laughed. 'I'm toast!'

But they were glad of all their insulation because

even though there wasn't a great deal of wind that afternoon, out on the water it was a good ten degrees colder than it had been on dry land. Since there wasn't enough of a breeze to merit unfurling any canvas, they pottered quite happily about the estuary and a couple of miles up the River Bex using only the engine to power them, but even so it did enable them to get the feel of the wonderful old boat on the water.

'She's as yar as ever!' Meggie called with delight as she took the helm. 'She just seems to float over the sea! Rather than in it!'

Waldo sat with his back against the cabin hatch and his cigar alight, beaming with pleasure at the sight of Meggie dressed in her bright yellow oilskins and matching sou'wester pulled on over all her warm clothes. He was utterly captivated by her, and as she steered the *Light Heart* back towards the quayside, their joint inaugural jaunt nearly done, he couldn't help being filled with wonder all over again at the turn his life had taken.

When they reached the harbour he nimbly jumped ashore with painter in hand and tied the boat up to a mooring ring, before holding a hand out to help Meggie from the boat. As she came ashore, Waldo smiled at her then lifted her up in his arms and began to carry her up the quay as a bridegroom carries his bride over the threshold.

'Any particular significance to this?' Meggie asked him wryly.

'I don't know,' Waldo replied happily. 'I just felt this is a very special kind of moment.'

'Me too,' Meggie agreed, settling down in his arms. 'My thoughts entirely, actually.'

They sat in a window seat of the *Three Tuns* drinking whisky and looking out over the estuary where the tide was now on the turn. The sky was still a clear light winter blue, dotted with flocks of sea birds searching for food. A small brightly painted red and yellow fishing boat had just left the harbour, headed eastward for the open sea, while a handful of resolute yachtsmen were swinging their craft on towards their deep water moorings, their day's sailing done.

'You're to look after yourself when I'm gone, Meggie,' Waldo said.

'When you're away, Waldo,' she corrected him. 'Not when you're gone.'

'You know what I mean, sweetheart. You've had a nasty case of the flu and it can sometimes leave you feeling a bit run down.'

'I promise I shall look both ways crossing the road.' Meggie sighed, leaning over the table and holding up a lighted match for Waldo's sputtering cigar. 'I shan't play with scissors, or matches, or fall asleep with a lighted cigarette in my hand – particularly since I don't smoke no more, boss.'

'I know I fuss, but it's not always a bad thing,' Waldo replied, taking a small notebook and pencil from his pocket. 'Which is why I want to give you a name and number – just in case. I notice you still have that nasty cough, and just in case it turns into anything – or simply won't go away – just in case

– here's the name and number of a top guy. Dr Farnsbarn's OK for a village medicine man, but Albert Schweitzer he ain't, and I want to make sure that while I'm away this time, if you do need anything you're going to get it from the best. He's a general specialist, and he's a buddy of mine – we play a lot of cards together – and he's also the guy who took the bullet from my chest. I only saw him last week, as it happens, for a check-up before I go away, and I told him about you. So he'll know what to expect. He's already fitting steel bars to his windows.'

'Very funny I do not think, Mr Astley,' Meggie said, taking the slip of paper from his hand and looking at the name, trying to maintain her air of devil may care but secretly happy that she now had someone who wanted to look after her because he loved her. 'Very well,' she sighed, folding and pocketing the paper. 'If my hair catches fire I'll give him a ring.'

'You do that. Now come on – I have to leave in just over an hour.'

'If you have that much time we could have another drink.'

Waldo looked at her and shook his head very sadly. 'It isn't the drink I'd be wanting, Miss Meggie,' he said in his stage Irish. 'Sure it isn't the drink at all, at all.'

He thought she was still fast asleep as he slipped out of her bed and back into his clothes. But he was barely into his underthings before a warm arm snaked out from under the blanket and wrapped itself around his waist.

'How can I possibly let you go after that,' she whispered. 'If I had a gun I'd hold it to your head and keep you as my prisoner.'

'All I can say is it's a pity you don't have that gun,' Waldo answered back. 'But since you don't, I shall have to overpower you with one more kiss and make my escape.'

He kissed her for the last time and held her warm, soft and fragrant self to him, burying his face in her hair and holding her as tight as he could.

'I love you, Meggie,' he said. 'Not just now, but always.'

'You always pinch my lines,' Meggie grumbled. 'Now I don't know what to say. Except that I love you too, and for ever more as well.'

'That'll do me just fine,' Waldo said, gently letting her go. 'Bye, sweetheart – you just take good care of yourself.'

'God, how I hate life.' Meggie sighed dramatically, falling back onto her pillow, one arm folded over her eyes not against the light but to blind her against what was happening. 'Why can't it all be just a little more straightforward?'

'Because it wouldn't be any fun, that's why,' Waldo replied, pulling his polo neck sweater over his head. 'Now go back to sleep – and when you wake up—'

'You'll be gone.'

'When you wake up I'll be back.'

Bending down, he kissed her once more on the

lips. This time two long and slender arms wrapped themselves around the back of his neck and tried to pull him back down on to the bed.

'No.' Waldo resisted. 'Don't make this any harder than it already is.'

'I hate you,' Meggie said, her eyes locked on his. 'I hate you for making me feel like this. I really, really hate you.'

'Ditto.' Waldo grinned. 'Now go to sleep. That's an order.'

Meggie didn't obey, as he knew she wouldn't. She just lay there while Waldo finished dressing, watching him silently, committing every last thing to her memory. Before he went he pulled the soft wool blankets up under her chin, tucking her into her bed. Not daring to kiss her again, he kissed the tip of one finger instead and planted it on the centre of her mouth.

She promptly seized the tip of the finger in her perfect white teeth and held it there.

'Ow,' Waldo said gently.

'That's to teach you for going,' Meggie growled, then rolled on to her side away from him.

'Love you the most,' he said from the doorway.

But the figure now huddled under the bedclothes said nothing. The figure under the bedclothes was not the sort of person to be heard to be crying.

There was not a lot to occupy Meggie's mind over the next few days as she tried to get used to life without Waldo, thinking as she did how ridiculous it was to find herself feeling as she did when only a matter of weeks before she had been an utterly independent person, able to cope with everything life had to throw at her without relying on anybody in particular. Yet now here she was, all because of this thing called Love, wondering how she was going to cope with even the most mundane tasks and routines without Waldo. She thought of him all the time, from the moment she woke up in the morning, usually after a night spent dreaming about him, right through the day up to going to bed at night, possibly to spend yet another fitful night dreaming about him again.

So when she found herself getting involved in the preparations for Mattie and John's marriage it came as a relief. For a few hours of the day she could stop herself mooching and involve herself instead in the utterly enjoyable business of helping Mattie Eastcott prepare for her wedding.

The main problem was, as always with the shortages, the wedding gown. By the time Meggie had become reinvolved with her circle of friends it seemed that the situation was so grim that Mattie was trying to get herself used to the notion of walking up the aisle in her tennis dress.

'If only I'd worn my mother's wedding dress, you could have borrowed that,' Judy sighed. 'We're both exactly the same size so it would have fitted you perfectly – but she gave it to some museum or other. The beading alone apparently makes it invaluable.'

'Beading.' Meggie frowned, and then smiled. 'I

remember . . . an old white dress with gorgeous beading on it in the attic at home. I remember seeing it when we were going through the things up there when I'd put the house up for sale.'

'Then what are we waiting for, girls?' Judy smiled excitedly. 'Let's go play in the attic.'

They hurried over to Cucklington House and up to the dusty and dark old attics, lit only by one dim and cloudy light bulb that swung in the draught generated by a missing pane in the grubby window. Meggie soon found what she was looking for, an old sea trunk, the label on its handle clearly marked OLD CLOTHES in Richards's best copper-plate writing.

From within Meggie took a beautiful gown and held it up.

'Gracious heavens, that is so beautiful,' Mattie almost whispered, carefully feeling the material with one hand as Meggie stood up, holding it against her. 'How old is it? It must be *quite* old.'

'Turn of the century I'd say,' Judy guessed, appraising the exquisite garment, her head on one side.

'Not bad,' Meggie said. 'About 1910-ish I think. If you look at the slender cut, and the slightly raised waist line.'

'I love that beaded lace bodice,' Mattie said. 'And this pleated silk top—'

'And look at the sleeves,' Judy remarked. 'Look at the way they're almost sort of sculpted – and look? They've got matching pearl decorations here at four points.'

'The skirt's quite a lot heavier,' Meggie said, holding the bottom of the gown out before her. 'And it has a little train. See? Must be wonderful on.'

'Put it on, then,' Judy urged. 'Go on, Megs – try it on.'

Meggie hesitated, holding the dress once more up against her before deciding.

'There's no point,' she said. 'Anyway I'm far too tall for it. Who we want to see it on is *Mattie*. Come on, Mattie. It should be perfect for you, darling – and being a light cream we should be able to find an old piece of lace for your head somewhere . . .'

'I can't possibly wear this,' Mattie said. 'It wouldn't be fair.'

'Like I just said, cloth ears.' Meggie clicked her tongue. 'I'm far too much of a beanpole for this. I towered above my grandmother, so come on – let's go downstairs and try it on you.'

'Are you sure, Meggie?' Mattie asked.

'Don't start getting wet,' Meggie warned her. 'You're getting an awfully wet look about the old eyes. Come on.'

Once down the rickety attic steps the three of them made their way along the corridor to one of the main bedrooms, which Meggie unlocked. It had not been occupied since Madame Gran's day and as Meggie went in ahead to draw back the curtains Judy and Mattie could see that it was as if time had not dared to move even its second hand on within its pale cerise portals. The dressing table, large and lace-flounced, the glass drops on all the light fittings cascading down the faded silk walls, the curtains, exquisitely pleated and carefully draped, caught up at points by silk rosettes, the large Aubusson rug with just a hint of Versailles, the palely painted lithographs of ancestors set about with cherubs, the gold-painted putti holding up the bedhead, the bed itself silk covered, the trimmings so tightly pleated that, it seemed to Judy and Mattie, they must be a work of art in themselves, so intricate were their workings, so precise the stitches that held them. The whole room transported them all back into an age of leisured elegance, something they would never now know.

'Heavens.' Judy stared about her. 'It's a bit like being in a shrine.'

'It is a shrine.' Meggie laughed. 'It's dear old Richards's shrine to Madame Gran, the only woman ever in his life.' She fell silent for a moment, fondly remembering the wonderful woman who had brought her up, who had steered her through all the difficult times of her young life and had set her on the road to self-determination. She knew she owed Madame Gran everything and as always when put in mind of her resolved to make sure to try to continue honouring her memory. 'Of course, now Waldo has bought Cuckers, I might have to work on him to keep it like this,' she said idly.

'Waldo has what?' Judy asked, even more astonished than Mattie.

'Sorry,' Meggie said, pulling a face as she laid the gown on the bed. 'I thought you knew. I thought I told you. Waldo bought the house. And gave it back to me.'

She smiled, remembering the moment she had unwrapped the key to the house and saw Waldo's delighted face watching her – and how they had joked and laughed and then how they had embraced; and as she did she felt a strange, sad and quite inexplicable ache in her heart, so powerful that she suddenly had to sit down.

'Are you all right?' Judy asked, hurrying over to her.

'Waldo bought you Cucklington?' Mattie echoed, her back to the other two as she stood examining the lovely silver set on the dressing table. 'We have to face it, Waldo really is the most amazing man.'

'I'm fine, Judy,' Meggie said quietly, taking Judy's hand and getting back up, throwing Mattie an anxious look, determined not to let anything spoil this moment. 'I just got this sudden – I don't know. It wasn't déjà vu, exactly – but it felt as if it was something – something prescient. Do you ever get that feeling? Probably not,' she concluded quickly, seeing the concern on her friend's face. 'I think I probably had a little too much gin last night. Come on, Mattie – time to get you undressed and dressed.'

'Did Waldo really give you this place, Meggie? You're not making it up? Because that has to be the most romantic thing I have ever heard,' Mattie said as Judy and Meggie began to undress her. Meggie related the whole tale of how a certain eccentric

Irish inventor had sent in the highest bid, a buyer who in fact turned out to be Waldo, who had bought it for Meggie as her Christmas present.

'He's obviously going to propose then, isn't he?' Mattie said, standing before them in her petticoat.

'There's nothing obvious in this life, darling,' Meggie replied. 'And you're going to have to take your slip off.'

'I'm *freezing*.'

'And the bride wore goosebumps,' Meggie observed. '*Off*'.

'Of course he'll propose,' Judy smiled. 'The point is, will you accept?'

'I accepted the house, didn't I?'

'That would be bribing you. And knowing you, you don't bribe easily.'

'Even if he hadn't given me the house, and the *Light Heart*—'

'He gave you the *Light Heart* as well?' Mattie gasped.

'Just put the dress on, Mattie – here.'

Meggie, being the tallest, lifted the dress up above Mattie's head. Mattie put both her arms up straight and Meggie eased and dropped the exquisite garment on to Mattie's lithe, trim figure. 'As if it had been made for you.'

'Really?'

'Go and take a look.'

'I suppose I will – you know.'

For some reason it only now came to Meggie that she and Waldo really were going to marry.

'So,' Judy said as they gathered round the floor

standing dressing glass. 'So there could be a summer wedding at Cucklington House, could there?'

'Do you think it's all right? Me getting married in white, I mean?' Mattie asked anxiously as the thought occurred to her, but not for the first time.

'Perfectly,' Meggie assured her, carefully pulling the dress down at the back so that all the creases disappeared. 'Particularly since the dress isn't white – it's cream.'

'You know what I mean, Megs.'

'Who cares?' Meggie laughed. 'It's what you want that matters. And you look wonderful.'

Meggie began to cough as they all stood admiring the beautiful sight. Unfortunately, rather than just being a bout it turned into a fit, so in order to avoid any more anxious looks from her two friends Meggie hurried off into the large bathroom off the bedroom and quickly drank some water. She stood for a moment, clutching the sides of the hand basin and taking deep breaths to stop herself from coughing any more, and much to her relief after a few more well stifled splutters the fit was over. Wiping from her eyes the tears the coughing had caused, she adjusted her hair and returned to the bedroom, where it seemed Judy and Mattie were so involved in admiring the beautiful gown in which Mattie was to be married that they had quite forgotten Meggie's sudden disorder.

But Meggie hadn't. Nor had she forgotten the strange turn that had caused her to sit down so suddenly on the bed, with her breath seemingly stuck in her throat and her heart pounding like a hammer in her chest.

'Coffee,' she remembered later, when she was alone and sitting by the fire she had laid for herself in the library. 'It happens every time I drink too much coffee.'

The more she thought about it the more she saw it was true. Richards had sourced a supply of fine French coffee from his contacts, and Meggie had fallen happily back into her pre-war addictive days. Normally she had restricted the amount she drank, knowing that there had been other occasions when she had been left in a highly agitated state after taking in too much caffeine. But now, since giving up smoking, she had begun to drink too much coffee. Only that morning, having woken after a good night's sleep to find herself feeling oddly exhausted, Meggie had staggered down to the kitchen and made herself a large and extremely strong pot to get her motoring, as she called it.

Even so, the combination of such a bad coughing fit and the reaction to an overdose of caffeine had left her quietly shaken. Retrieving the piece of paper from her overcoat pocket, a name and number she thought she would have no need of, Meggie put in a call to Waldo's friend in Harley Street, who agreed to see her as soon as she could get herself up to London.

'I could come up tomorrow,' Meggie said, 'if you could see me then.'

'I owe our mutual friend Waldo so much money

at cards,' a cheerful voice informed her on the other end of the line, 'that if you insisted, I'd see you the day before yesterday.'

Again after a good night's sleep, helped by a large draught of cognac before retiring, Meggie awoke feeling utterly exhausted and wondered at first if she was going to be able to make it out of bed. For a while she lay staring out of her window at the daybreak, wondering what sort of legacy the wretched influenza might have left her with. From her brief and cryptic conversations with Dr Farnsworth she knew that that winter's bug had been a particularly virulent one, so she wouldn't be at all surprised to find that it had left her with some chronic infection, just as it had done apparently in the cases of several of Farnsworth's patients. But rather than return to the local surgery for yet another superficial examination followed by yet another dose of Farnsworth's bromides, Meggie thought she owed it not only to herself but to Waldo as well to have herself properly examined by the man Waldo said was the best in his class.

'I'd like you to stay in the clinic overnight,' the good-humoured Dr Wright told Meggie after he had listened to her case history and completed his initial examination. 'There's absolutely nothing for you to get concerned about, but in order to run a full and exhaustive series of tests – which I do for all my patients who come to me with the post-effects of influenza, I assure you – I really need you to stay in my care for twenty-four hours. It involves no unpleasant procedures, I promise. Some further X-rays certainly, but I want to do a full chest X-ray and I want to run some blood tests, too, and some other niggling little examinations which take time and a bit of patience on your part – but that's all. By lunchtime tomorrow we shall have all the results and I'll be in the best position possible to tell you what ails you, as they say, if anything.'

'Other than an addiction to French coffee,' Meggie said, doing her blouse back up. 'And a long but now a no-more habit of smoking.'

'The moment you give up smoking is the moment you start to recover,' Dr Wright assured her.

'You think smoking's that terrible?'

'No, I don't think smoking's terrible, because I smoke, Miss Gore-Stewart. But I'm absolutely convinced it's not good for us, whatever the Government says.'

Judy was waiting in Lionel's sitting room for Mattie to come back from picking Max up from school and start cutting out the bridesmaids' dresses. She stared down at the material, remembering her own less than glamorous appearance at her wartime wedding and how she had insisted on wearing her WVS uniform and not her mother's wedding dress. How upset her mother had been! Judy clicked her tongue in irritation as she realised what a stubborn little fool *she* had been, more intent on impressing the village with her patriotism than pleasing her mother to whom she owed so much.

She would do anything to be able to redress that moment. As she started to open out the swathe of material on the table in front of her she imagined herself walking back through the narrow streets of the village until she reached the beautiful old house that was her family home. The housekeeper would, as ever, open the door and announce her to her mother, who would be seated in front of a small fire in the morning room reading the *Daily Telegraph*. She would look up in surprise, the way she always did when Judy visited her, even when she was expected, before slowly lowering her newspaper, taking off her glasses and gazing curiously at her daughter.

Mamma, Judy heard herself saying, *I've come to say sorry to you, about not wearing your dress on my wedding day. I've come to say sorry for being selfish and not thinking of you.*

As always when she had this fantasy, her mother said nothing. All she did was give a small sniff, raise her eyebrows as if to say *it's a little late now* and return to her reading. Now, hearing the front door of Mattie's house close and the sound of Max's piping voice, Judy quickly returned to reality, vowing never to visit that particular land of make-believe again, knowing that there was no point – that even if it wasn't make-believe but reality, the fact was that however sincere her apology it would do no good whatsoever. Her getting married in uniform had for some reason hurt her mother beyond measure, and there was nothing Judy could do about it now.

It had been bad enough telling her mother recently that she was expecting a child. Lady Melton had greeted the news with the kind of look on her face she usually wore when having spotted greenfly on her precious roses. To her it was bad enough one's daughter getting pregnant – but to talk about it was compounding the felony, as she indicated to said daughter in no uncertain terms. Having hoped her good news might bring her mother some happiness, Judy left the house feeling as though she and Walter had managed to do something utterly shaming.

So it was with no little relief that she greeted her returning friend Mattie, who had now appeared in the living room having handed her son over to his grandfather to have his tea.

'I still can't believe Waldo Astley actually bought Cucklington House for Meggie,' Mattie exclaimed as she sat down opposite Judy to help cut out. 'How lucky can one person get? And when you think what they thought of each other when they first met. According to you, anyway.' Mattie shook her head, an amazed expression on her face as she readied the pinking scissors.

'I think Meggie was *badly* in need of some good luck,' Judy replied. 'Davey, the war, all her work under cover in France and Germany, having had to sell everything when her parents died. We're all inclined to think life's been a bit of a cakewalk for Meggie, when in fact it's been far from it.'

Mattie looked up momentarily, caught by Judy's reprimand, before beginning to cut. 'We all need a bit of luck, Judy,' she replied as her scissors click-clacked into life. 'I didn't mean it that way. John and I are certainly going to need it – otherwise we're not going to be able to get married in Bexham church. John's father is doing his best, but you know a lot of vicars won't marry a couple if the bride has a child.'

'Reverend Anderson will marry you,' Judy said quickly, looking up. 'He's a friend of the family.'

Mattie pursed her lips and frowned. 'Crossed fingers department, Judy,' she replied. 'If it was just up to the Reverend Anderson there'd be no problem – but Daddy says otherwise. At least so he's heard.'

Midway through the following morning Dr Wright, considered by most to be the top general specialist in the country, stood in front of the row of illuminated X-rays that hung on the wall in front of him. He stood with his hands behind his back and his chin punched slightly forward, as if examining a set of rather fine prints or other works of art, hardly moving except to shift his weight occasionally from one foot to the other or to tilt his handsome, craggy head to right or left.

'Hmmmm,' he said to himself thoughtfully, 'Mmmmm'.

Then he took himself slowly through to his office.

'Helen?' he called through the door that led to his secretary's room. 'Is Miss Gore-Stewart up and about yet? I told Nurse Bradshaw to make sure she was ready for me at eleven.'

Meggie in fact had been up and ready for over an hour, sitting in Dr Wright's outside office idly flicking through copy after copy of *The Tatler* and *Bystander* without seeing one photograph or reading one word. So when Dr Wright's secretary popped her head round the door to tell her she was needed, Meggie was practically up and out of the waiting area before she had finished speaking.

'I hope it's good news, Dr Wright,' she said after she had sat down nonchalantly stretching out her silk-stockinged legs in front of her. 'One thing I cannot abide hearing from doctors is any sort of truth.'

Dr Wright looked at the beautiful woman opposite him, who was so stunning and arresting that for once he was able to see a patient as the extraordinarily attractive and vibrant creature she was rather than a collection of organs inside a skeleton and epidermis.

'Then I shall, I am glad to say, be very much in your good books,' he replied with a smile, closing the confidential file in front of him. 'There is a certain amount of gloom, alas, but very little doom, you'll be happy to hear.'

'I could have done with an utterly clean bill of H, Dr Wright,' she replied. 'I'm the sort of person who likes things to be either one thing or t'other.'

'With a bit of care, and good management we shall very soon have you entirely one thing and not the other, I hope,' he replied. 'But there is absolutely no doubt at all you have had a very bad infection.'

'Have had? Well, that sounds a bit more cheerful.'

'I apologise. I phrased that wrongly. You have had and still do have a bad infection in your lungs and in your chest.'

'So it's not coffee.'

'No.'

'And it's not just the smokes.'

'The smokes as you call them haven't helped – but no, it's not just the smokes, and it's not just the coffee. I'll try to keep it as simple as I can – not because I don't believe you'd be able to understand the medical ins and outs, but because I think really they're irrelevant, and they might even alarm you. So this is it in a nutshell. You have contracted some particularly nasty infection that has attacked the chest and respiratory system. It's more than likely this is part and parcel of the influenza epidemic, but it could also be something quite separate from it. But no matter – whatever caused it, the treatment remains the same.'

'Not more bedrest,' Meggie groaned. 'I'll shoot myself if you send me back to me bed.'

'I agree,' the specialist smiled. 'I cannot stand being sent to my bed. In fact sometimes I think it makes patients sicker to be sent to bed than to be allowed downstairs to sit and read or listen to the radio. Resting in bed doesn't always help. But then it depends on the patient.'

'I'm a lot better sitting up than lying down,' Meggie assured him. 'At least when I'm ill, that is.'

'You're going to have to take things a bit easy for a while, Miss Gore-Stewart. A lot of your trouble possibly stems from the fact that you haven't given your body a chance to recover properly from this infection. What would have been ideal would have been for you to take two or three months off somewhere – even at home actually, it doesn't matter where. Just doing nothing. But according to you – at least what I learned from our talk yesterday you find doing nothing all but impossible.'

''Fraid so,' Meggie said, a little alarmed at the prospect that by her wilfulness she might have damaged her health. 'But obviously from your tone this is what I'm now going to have to do for a while. Not very much.'

'Even less if possible, if we're to get you one hundred per cent yourself again. So here's the regime. It's going to sound mighty boring, but believe you me this is really what you have to do to get better. I'm going to put you on an extensive menu of drugs in order to try to hit this infection on the head, and while you're on these I want you to stay indoors for the next two weeks doing as little as possible – and in this case what I mean is nothing at all. You're to treat yourself as if you were an invalid, which means no excitement and no leaving the house. Every afternoon you are to go to your bed for a two-hour rest, and then when you get up you are to do nothing more energetic than read or listen to the radio.' Dr

Wright raised a warning finger when he saw his patient about to protest. 'If you don't – because that's the question everyone asks at this point – if you don't do as I advise you won't get better, it's as simple as that.'

'You mean it's as bad as that.'

'I mean it's as simple as that. After a fortnight, provided the medication's doing its stuff, you'll be able to start getting out and about a little, and after another couple of weeks there's no reason to suppose you can't slowly get back to rebuilding a normal existence – provided the drugs are doing their stuff. Do you have staff?'

'Yes,' Meggie lied initially, before changing her mind. 'No. I live alone.'

'You'll need a nurse, and a housekeeper. I can organise the nurse if you could perhaps organise the latter?'

Meggie nodded. 'How shall I know if the pills are doing the trick?' she asked, doing her best not to sound anxious.

'I shall be in touch with your GP who will keep a weather eye on you, as will I – and before you ask how that will be possible, as I said, our friend Waldo holds an awful lot of my IOUs. Besides, my family lives in Sussex, not a million miles from Bexham, so it's not exactly off my beat.'

'I see.'

While Dr Wright, having smiled briefly but comfortingly at her, proceeded to write out several prescriptions, Meggie took stock and considered her position.

In her heart of hearts she had known there was something wrong with her, and from the way she had been feeling of late she had feared the worst, so at least this diagnosis had relieved the very blackest of her fears. She also believed the man sitting on the other side of the desk implicitly. Not only had she liked him at first sight, but she was aware the reason why she had liked him was because she felt she could trust him, so she knew she must do as he said. Waldo was going to be away for at least two weeks if not longer, so if all went well she could be up and about by the time he got home, if not well on the way to a full recovery. So for once in a life full previously of stubbornness, Meggie decided to do exactly as told, take her medicine, obey her advisers, and give herself the best possible chance of being in the best possible shape for the moment for which she was living: Waldo's return.

'Good,' Henry Wright said as he handed her a sheaf of prescriptions. 'Before you go I'll give you a parcel of the medicines you're going to have to take straight away, and I'm also going to give you a shot of something that's going to make you feel considerably more at ease. It's all right' – he smiled in answer to Meggie's anxious look – 'it's only an injection of iron and vitamins. You came up by train, did you not?' Meggie nodded. 'At this time of year, with the weather being so entirely unreliable, I'd much rather not have you exposed to any such vagaries, so forgive the presumption but I have made arrangements to have you driven home. Don't worry about the expense. Likewise about the nursing care. Waldo told me that he'll cover all the costs incurred.'

'You've spoken to Waldo?'

'No, no. No, this was something we agreed in advance. Should it be necessary. Don't look so surprised, Miss Gore-Stewart. You must surely know Waldo well enough by now to realise he is not a man to leave any stone unturned.'

'He can't have known I was ill.'

'No. But he certainly suspected you might not be exactly well.'

Having personally seen Meggie off from his clinic, safely tucked up in the back of the car hired to drive her back to Sussex, Henry Wright returned to his consulting room and sat down behind his desk. As he did so, Helen his secretary came in and handed him another medical file in a brown folder.

'You asked to see this, Dr Wright,' she said. 'As soon as the results were through. I've just this minute finished typing it up.'

'Thank you, Helen,' Henry Wright said, taking the file from her and putting it down in front of him. 'I'll read it immediately.'

But he didn't. After Helen had left the room, Henry lit one of the four cigarettes he permitted himself a day and turned his chair round so that he could look at the painting hanging on his wall. Waldo had told him about the artist, and being a bit of a collector he had hurried along to the Oliver Gallery and been unable to resist buying one of the few of the exquisite paintings that had remained unsold.

He stared at it long and hard, allowing himself to be taken into the picture, to be transported to a spot on a beach somewhere where the sun always shone hot and strong, and the sea ran deep blue and cool. He could feel the light sand between his toes and the wind rustling his hair while the sounds of children playing and dogs barking came faintly into earshot.

Then he turned his chair back and his attention to the folder on his desk which was marked *Mr Waldo Astley. Confidential.*

Once he had read it, he read it again, then replacing the copies of the X-rays inside the folder he looked at his watch and buzzed through to Helen.

'What time is it over there now, Helen? Do you know?' he enquired.

'Still the wee small hours, Dr Wright,' came the reply. 'At least they're certainly not up and about yet. It's only about six a.m.'

'Then I think a cable is in order,' he said. 'In fact it might be the better way to go. Can you come in here in a couple of shakes? After I've composed what I must say? And take it down? Thank you.'

As the cable was being wired across the Atlantic Waldo was on his way to a meeting with the other side at the Plaza Hotel. He had refused yet another office meeting because meetings in offices were inclined to get overheated, particularly when they involved subjects as touchy as this, and had insisted on the impartiality of the lounge in a big hotel. Besides, he was very fond of the Plaza and provided he got a move on he'd have time for some of their delicious *Oeufs Benedict* and a pot of coffee before battle commenced. His hopes were dashed, however, for on his arrival in spite of his promptness he spied the other side already in place and waiting.

'I don't know why we're bothering,' the tall, extremely handsome and expensively groomed woman he had come to meet said at his approach, not bothering either to stand or extend a hand in greeting. 'I haven't changed my mind.'

'Then I have to wonder at the purpose of this meeting.'

'Why – to see you of course, Waldo. What else? To see my lovely, rich husband.'

At exactly the moment Waldo was signalling for someone to fetch them some fresh coffee, a fellow American was also on the look-out for refreshment, some four thousand miles away in Bexham. Having admired the pretty little town from the wheel of his rented car, he was searching for somewhere he could get a drink and maybe a sandwich. His eye fell on a black and white painted sign advertising the local inn. Following the arrow he soon found himself at the side of the large public house that dominated the quays and turned his car into the car park at the rear of the building.

Still unfamiliar with the English licensing laws he found to his disappointment that the doors to the bars were all locked, and was about to leave when a young man who was just depositing a crate of empty beer bottles outside a side door asked if he could be of assistance.

'I was looking for some refreshment,' the stranger said. 'But I guess you're all shut up.'

'The bars are, sir, to non-residents,' the young man replied. 'But the inn itself is open and we could certainly manage you some tea and toast, or a soft drink if that's your preference.'

'That would be dandy,' the American said. 'That would be most kind.'

He followed the young man back into the inn through the side door, which he realised was possibly the main entrance to judge from the small table inside lit by a standard lamp and bearing a large register for the signing-in of guests. His guide led him on to a small lounge overlooking the harbour and leading into the lounge bar which as the American visitor could see was firmly under wraps, judging from the tea towels draped over the beer pumps and the lack of any lighting. But the view from the lounge was first class and the furniture comfortable, and within no time at all the stranger was happily tucking into a plate of delicious cucumber sandwiches washed down with a pot of first class Darjeeling tea.

'I trust everything is to your satisfaction?' a tall, lugubrious man enquired, appearing out of the shadows of the bar as the American was finishing his first cup of tea.

'Quite excellent, thank you,' his visitor replied,

carefully wiping his mouth on a linen napkin. 'The sandwiches are everything cucumber sandwiches should be and the tea – for which I have acquired quite a taste over the years – is most refreshing.'

'Then I take it you have visited our shores before,' Richards said. 'Since coffee is your national drink, rather than tea, obviously.'

The American laughed and extended a hand.

'Rafferty,' he said. 'Michael Rafferty. How do you do?'

'How do you do, sir. Richards, the landlord.'

'Mr Richards.'

'Mr Rafferty.'

'Are you over here on what I understand you call your vacation?'

'Well yes in one way, Mr Richards, and no in another. Initially it was business. I'm with the military and had to attend some meetings in Paris and Munich about this Berlin business.'

'Which seems to be worsening by the hour,' Richards said, beginning to turn on some lights in the lounge bar. 'It looks like the Russkis mean business.'

'Let's hope not, but I must admit it isn't getting any better. Anyway, having concluded my business I thought I'd allow myself a few days' vacation here in England on my way home. Visit some old stamping grounds.'

'You were stationed here, sir?'

'No, no – just a place I visited once. And rather fell in love with.'

'Our little Bexham?'

'No, Bexham I have not visited previously. No, I stayed at a lovely old inn quite near here, I believe. The Golden Eagle, I think it was called.'

'Of course. In Middlehurst. A very fine establishment. And are you travelling by yourself, sir? Or accompanied by your family?'

'My family are all back in the States,' Michael Rafferty replied. 'My children, that is. I lost my wife nearly two years ago now.'

'I'm sorry to hear that, sir,' Richards said, removing the tea towels off the beer pumps and raising the flap in the bar. 'How very sad.'

'It was a great blow,' Michael Rafferty agreed. 'We'd been childhood sweethearts. It didn't seem at all fair, I must say. I'd survived four years of hell and high water, and my poor wife who had been without a day's illness in her life dropped dead suddenly of a brain haemorrhage. Here—' Michael Rafferty had got to his feet and followed Richards over to the bar, taking his wallet out of his pocket. 'These are my children,' he said, producing several photographs. 'And this was Carena. This was my wife Carena.'

Richards found himself looking at the picture of a very pretty woman, open-faced, smiling easily but with very resolute eyes. It was a look that reminded Richards so much of someone that for a moment he felt as though he knew the dead woman, as if he had seen her almost every day of his life.

'Charming,' he heard himself murmuring as

Michael Rafferty put away his snapshots. 'What a charming young family. And what a terrible tragedy.'

'Yes,' Michael agreed. 'Yes, it was. It was so utterly unexpected. And I guess that's what made it so unbearable. The very – the terrible sudden shock.'

Both men fell to silence, Michael left with a memory and Richards with a sense of puzzled bewilderment.

'Still, life has to go on,' he heard his visitor saying, as he turned to regard the wonderful view out along the quays and over the estuary which was now running up to high tide. 'There's no point in standing still. None at all.'

Richards nodded but said nothing, now going about the business of opening the bar officially, unbolting the two front doors that stood either side of the big bay window. At the end of the jetty he could see a group of figures, young women, some with their children and some alone, standing there gossiping, just too far away to be recognisable.

'So what do I owe you, Mr Richards?' Michael enquired. 'For that excellent tea.'

'Half a crown should cover it, sir,' Richards replied. 'One shilling and ninepence for the sandwiches and—'

'No need to break it down, I assure you.' Michael laughed. 'Cheap at the price for such a delicious confection. There we are, and thank you.'

Michael handed Richards half a crown, and returned to his table to slip sixpence under the cup for the service. Then he hesitated, knowing that he simply had to ask the question before he left, because asking the question had been the whole point of his visit. And if anyone knew the answer it must surely be the landlord of a hostelry that quite obviously dominated the life of the village. Either he or the vicar, and Michael knew that as far as his question was concerned he might be better off asking the landlord.

'I wonder if you happen to know a young woman by the name of Mathilda Eastcott?' he asked, as lightly as he could. 'At least I think that was her name. Mathilda Eastcott – yes, I'm sure it was. I only really knew her as *Mattie*.'

'Indeed, sir?' Richards regarded him from under his carefully combed and tufted thick black eyebrows. 'You must have known this young lady quite well to address her thus.'

Michael managed to conceal his smile of delight at the positively Shakespearean quality of the landlord's reply and just nodded instead.

'She was my driver,' he replied. 'When I was in London during the war I was allotted a driver and this charming young woman – Miss Mathilda Eastcott – drove me everywhere, all the time I was stationed here. And I remember when we – I remember when we were talking about our homes and where we came from and all that stuff, she told me all about Bexham. Made it sound like a fairy tale – which indeed I have to say it is. I think this little harbour is one of the most enchanting places I've seen in England. Anywhere, in fact.'

'Hence your visit, sir,' Richards concluded, setting out fresh ash trays on the tables and stopping to stare out of the bow window when he came to that particular table. The group of young women had broken up now, and dispersed. Two of them were walking up towards the pub, with a handsome little boy between them, hand in hand with both the young women who swung him happily off the ground whenever they could. 'Hence your visit.'

'I thought I had to see it for myself,' Michael replied. 'And while I was here—'

'While you were here, you thought you'd get back in touch with your pretty young driver.'

'Why not? Life's too short,' Michael said, suddenly embarrassed enough to find himself colouring, which he saw Richards noting as he turned slowly to look at him. 'Is something the matter?'

'Not at all, sir, forgive me,' Richards replied, returning to his ash-tray duty. 'It's just that I thought – no, it was nothing at all, sir. Please forgive me.'

Even so, Richards stole another glance at the trio that now stood almost at the foot of the pub steps. Judy Tate, Mattie Eastcott and who he now realised with shock was a miniature version of the man standing in the shadows behind him. In truth, if the child had been put to stand beside the tall American behind him, Richards knew that nine out of ten people would inevitably have come to the same conclusion. He sated briefly at his duster, wondering.

'So?' Michael Rafferty was asking him again. 'This is a very small place, a close community I would imagine, so if young Miss Eastcott still lived here I would think you might well know of her and her whereabouts.'

Richards straightened himself up slowly and nodded, one eye still on the action without.

'You're absolutely correct, sir. Miss Eastcott did come from these parts and did in fact dwell in Bexham right up until last year.'

'Until last *year*?' Michael asked impatiently. 'Why – where is she now? What happened last year?'

'Last year, sir, young Miss Eastcott fell in love with a childhood friend and got married. She then left our little village and has settled down very happily somewhere near Oxford.'

'I see,' Michael said, which he did indeed, although somewhat absurdly he still found himself wanting to ask if Richards was sure. He prevented himself from doing so, sensing how ludicrous such a question might seem. 'I see,' he repeated. 'I'm very glad to hear it, Mr Richards. Very glad indeed. She was a very nice young woman, full of character and extremely courageous. So I'm very glad she's found happiness, married and settled down. Very glad indeed.'

'We all are, sir,' Richards replied. 'She was a most popular young woman and everyone was very fond of her. We all wanted nothing but the best for Miss Eastcott.'

'Good,' Michael concluded. 'Now I must be on

my way. Thank you again for your kind hospitality, and for the pleasure of having tea here at your lovely old inn.'

'Any time you're passing, sir,' Richards said, still with an eye on the two women and the little boy, all three of whom now looked as if they were intent on climbing the steps up into the lounge bar. 'May I show you out?'

'I rather think I shall go out the front way if I may,' Michael said, throwing a spanner slap in the works. 'I fancy a stroll to the end of the jetty and a good dose of fresh sea air.'

'These steps are somewhat steep, sir – and a little treacherous for those who don't know them.'

'Don't you worry about me, Richards. I've scaled the cliffs of Brittany.' With a smile Michael Rafferty made for the right hand door, giving Richards the break he so desperately needed, seeing that Judy, Mattie and young Max were about to enter the left hand one.

'Allow me, sir,' Richards said, putting his not inconsiderable bulk between his departing visitor and the incoming party. 'And pray do take care on the steps.'

His professed concern was enough to make Michael look down at the steps he was about to descend, and so pay not the slightest attention to the two pretty young women and the handsome little boy who entered the bar behind him at the exact moment of his departure.

As he left, Richards shut the door, flooded with an enormous sense of relief. At once he turned to the new arrivals and swept them up to the bar well out of sight of the window.

'Is something the matter, Mr Richards?' Mattie asked.

'I do hope not,' Richards said. 'Although your father did sound a little agitated.'

'Daddy? What are you talking about? Daddy can't have been in already – you've only just opened.'

'He telephoned me – said if I saw you I was to ask you to return home immediately. And no, he didn't say why – so if I were you, Miss Eastcott—'

'It's all right, Richards!' Mattie called back over her shoulder as she hurried out of the bar and down the side corridor, with Max firmly attached to one hand. 'I'm on my way!'

Judy stared after her, then back at Richards. 'Think I should go with her?'

'I wouldn't bother, Mrs Tate,' Richards replied suavely, lying through his teeth. 'As far as I could gather Mr Eastcott had simply misplaced the can opener.'

Having served Judy with her usual gin and tonic, and made sure his American was still way down the far end of the jetty, Richards slipped off to his office to quietly telephone Lionel Eastcott. Without putting him fully in the picture, he told him just enough for Mattie's father to appreciate that there was danger lurking down in the harbour, so he should keep his daughter at home until well after dark.

'Thank you, Richards,' Lionel said gruffly. 'I shall owe you several large Angostura and tonics for this.'

'And don't worry, Mr Eastcott.' Richards sighed. 'I shall claim each and every one of them.

There was continuing drama the other side of the Atlantic, too, Waldo at the moment managing considerably less well than Richards had in solving his own dilemma.

'If you won't give me a divorce—' he said yet again.

'Which I will not—' his wife repeated yet again.

'Then what do you want, Dolores?'

'More money?'

'If you agree to a divorce, Dolores, I shall make sure you're a very rich woman. Your lawyers have the proposed settlement. You've seen the figures.'

'This isn't just about money, Waldo.'

'It isn't? You surprise me. I'm not the guilty party, remember? You were the one who was unfaithful. On our honeymoon, too. You could at least have waited till we'd got home.'

'You're going to have to prove I was unfaithful, Waldo dear,' Dolores said, tightening her smile.

'You mean I'm going to have to prove you have been consistently unfaithful, Dolores.'

'You said it, Waldo.'

'Why won't you give me a divorce? You know our marriage was a disaster. You know it never even existed. So come on – be reasonable.'

'Why do you want a divorce?'

'Why do you think?'

'You want to get married again?'

'That really is none of your affair, Dolores.'

'I do hope you haven't been unfaithful, Waldo. It could cost you.'

Waldo said nothing for a moment, suddenly mindful of the fact that had Dolores been smart enough she could have kept him under surveillance. She could certainly afford to have done so, yet even though the thought had startled Waldo he knew at once it couldn't be the case. Had it been so Dolores would not have hesitated to file against him immediately, such was her truly appalling lust for money.

'OK, here's how,' he said. 'Suppose we look again at this proposed settlement.'

'Waldo sweetie,' Dolores interrupted, lighting up a fresh king size smoke. 'As far as your proposed settlement goes, you know what you can do with it.'

'Cable for Mr Waldo Astley! Cable for Mr Waldo Astley!' a bellhop announced, accompanied by the ringing of his bell and a show of Waldo's name chalked on his call board. 'Cable for Mr Waldo Astley!'

Waldo excused himself and made for the desk, tipping the bellhop a buck on his way through and being rewarded with a delighted smile from the boy and a touch to his pill box hat. Collecting the cable, which had been sent over from his hotel, he tore it open, knowing that if it was from England it was bound to be bad news. When he saw from whom the cable came, he became certain of the sort of tidings it bore.

'Oh, my God,' he whispered after he had read the contents twice. 'Oh, dear God,' he said even more quietly, and crumpled the telegram in one hand.

When she finally arrived back at Cucklington House early that evening, Meggie found Rusty waiting for her, with fires lit in all the rooms Meggie normally used.

'Waldo?' she asked, as she draped her coat over a chair in the hall. 'I take it this is more of Waldo's crystal ball stuff.'

'Dr Wright rang Mr Richards, which apparently Mr Astley had instructed him to do should there be any need while he was away, and Mr Richards rang me,' Rusty replied, stoking up the fire in the drawing room while Meggie poured herself a large gin and tonic. 'With Mr Astley being away, I can do your housekeeping, if that's all right, Meggie?'

'What about Tam? What about Peter?'

'Peter's fine with the idea, and believe it or not Mum and Dad agreed to look after Tam – but not at their house. Mum's coming to stay with us.'

'Good Lord.' Meggie grinned with open surprise. 'Don't tell me you've got the tiger by the tail.'

'Seems that way.' Rusty shrugged.

'What brought about the change?'

'I'm pregnant again,' Rusty said shyly.

'But I thought—'

'Me too,' Rusty interrupted. 'But it seems I was wrong. Seems I was wrong before too – I wasn't the only one that went a bit off the rails. Seems that Mum couldn't handle it either. Which was why she acted so funny. She and Dad. That and what everyone was saying to them – that it was all my fault.' Rusty shrugged happily. 'Says she's tickled pink. And when I said *suppose it's a little girl?* she said *it's what you want, isn't it.*'

'Good,' Meggie said. 'Well done you.'

'Right.' Rusty grinned. 'So is that all right then? Me helping you out?'

'Can't think of anything more all righter,' Meggie replied. 'Just tell me when and if I'm being an even bigger bore than ever.'

Sensing that she needed some time to herself, Rusty tactfully withdrew and went to prepare a light supper along the lines of Richards's suggestions, some fresh Dover sole and homemade treacle tart, the sort of meal that could easily be eaten off a tray by the fireside. While she was gone, Meggie sat in her favourite high-backed chair by the fire, nursing her drink and surveying the small table by her side that was now covered with her pills and medicine bottles. Looking at the French carriage clock above the fireplace she saw it was time for her next *fizzy*, as Henry Wright had christened them. She rather liked these *fizzies* as they induced a slow feeling in her of happy euphoria. And after a couple of days such as Meggie had just experienced she most certainly felt like a bit of euphoria.

* * *

'Is this expected to make a drastic difference?' Dolores wondered, having undone Waldo's cable, read it and tossed it back at him.

'I wonder what keeps you alive, Dolores,' Waldo said carefully. 'It certainly isn't a heart.'

Dolores stared. She hated Waldo. Most of all she hated him for being such a goody-goody.

Dolores smiled. She smiled directly at Waldo and kept on smiling. 'What if I still say no to a divorce?'

'I will make sure I become a widower.'

'You don't meant that,' she murmured.

'You don't know that I don't mean it, do you, Dolores?'

There was a long pause.

'Double the settlement,' she said suddenly, and picked up the pen.

They both knew what would happen next. Waldo's lawyer would book them on a plane to Rio where the divorce would be put through quicker than the flight. After which Waldo would take the next plane to England. Meanwhile, he took a cab to his favourite bar and drank himself into a state of semi-oblivion.

As he stood in the Reverend Anderson's untidy study, covered in books and old pieces of paper with scribbled ideas for sermons written in an indecipherable hand, Hugh Tate could not help feeling like a small boy up before his headmaster. This feeling was brought home to him even more forcibly by the way that Stephen was staring at him over the top of his spectacles, a deeply worried frown furrowing his brow, making poor Hugh feel all the more as though he had been caught breaking bounds.

'I'm all for it, of course, all for it,' he said. 'These are my parishioners and I feel like you that they are entitled as much as anyone to a church wedding. But.'

'But what?' Hugh stared at Stephen, who averted his gaze to look down at the carpet.

'The bishop, you know,' Stephen said, and since he groaned after he had said it Hugh took it that his friend the vicar did not altogether agree with what he was going to have to say. 'He's a bit of an awful stickler, Hugh. An out and out traditionalist, and the long and the short of it is—'

'He won't allow you to marry John and Mattie in Bexham Church.'

'In a nutshell, Hugh. In a nutshell.'

'Because of the little boy.'

'Of course. *Of course*. In line with much of current Church thinking he considers the moral fibre of this country has been damaged and that steps must be taken to repair the fabric.'

'Which means not allowing two young people who are very much in love the pleasure and the blessing of a church wedding.'

'In a nutshell, Hugh – in a nutshell.'

'Are these your feelings, too? Do you go along with that sort of reactionary claptrap?'

'Me? Me?' Stephen squeaked. 'Good Lord no – you know me, Hugh. You know me.'

'I thought I did,' Hugh replied. 'But if you're telling me you have to stand in line with this ruling, then I don't know you at all.'

'It isn't *me*, Hugh,' Stephen protested. 'It's the way these things are.'

'I honestly thought our friend Waldo had stopped you running along mental tram lines.'

Stephen looked duly ashamed, blushed and stared even harder at the carpet. 'I don't think we have much choice really.'

'Oh, I think we do. What would happen if you just went ahead and married John and Mattie?'

'What would *happen*?'

'Yes, Stephen. What would happen? God wouldn't descend from heaven in a fiery chariot, surely. Would He? And smite you dead? Smite the lot of us dead in fact for having the nerve to marry two people who are very much in love in a church when one of them has a child already? Didn't Jesus say suffer the little children? Isn't the Bible full of warnings about those who do harm to the most innocent? You tell me, Stephen, because you're the expert on these matters. I'm just an old sailor who believes that God is good and merciful and that sometimes the Church is full of a lot of old hooey.'

'I see,' Stephen said, swallowing and now staring up at the ceiling. 'I *see*.'

'So what are you going to do?'

'What am I going to do?'

'Yes. You. Because if you don't do something, you're going to be looking at a half-empty church in future.'

'I'm generally looking at a half-empty church, Hugh.'

'You're going to be looking at half of that half-empty church!'

'This is a sort of blackmail, isn't it?'

'While what the Church is saying isn't?'

'Ah.' Stephen nodded. '*Ah.*'

'Ah ha,' Hugh agreed. '*Ah ha.*'

'Then married they shall be,' Stephen decided. 'In Bexham Church. By me.'

'And God will not descend in a fiery chariot.'

'I very much doubt it. And if He does, it'll make a nice story for the *Bexham Echo*.'

'And what do you think will happen to you?'

'I shall get hauled over the coals. And I shall get reprimanded by the new bishop.'

'Is that all?'

'It had better be. Because if they try anything else I shall hand in my collar.'

'Good man,' Hugh said. 'That's the spirit. Why?'

'Because you're right, Hugh, that's why,' Stephen replied earnestly. 'Because otherwise there was no point in us fighting the war.'

Chapter Sixteen

For once in her life Meggie did as she was told. She obeyed Dr Wright's orders to the letter and the consequence was that after her first week of enforced rest and all the medicines she felt considerably improved. Her cough had all but gone, her appetite was returning, albeit in a diminished form, the pains in her chest had disappeared and she was sleeping better. Even the deep exhaustion from which she had been suffering seemed to be on the wane, prompting Rusty to remark that she was really beginning to look herself again.

Meggie thought it wasn't only the medication that was helping her recovery, but also the couple of transatlantic telephone calls she had received from Waldo, however indistinct they might have been. Besides the fact that he loved her, which he shouted down the line at every possible opportunity, she also gathered that if all continued to go as well as it was he would be home earlier than intended, particularly since he intended to fly home by stratocruiser. Meggie, who hated the thought of him flying the Atlantic, for once didn't press him to come home by boat, so anxious was she to be reunited with him.

'I love you, Meggie!' he shouted for the last time. 'Next time you hear me I'll be calling up the stairs!'

Six days later Meggie was awoken from her afternoon sleep by someone kissing her tenderly on the lips.

'Hiya, honey,' whispered an all too familiar voice. 'Bad luck! I'm home.'

Meggie stared at him, blinking her eyes, trying to make sure this wasn't a dream, that the dark eyed man sitting beside her on the bed really was Waldo.

'You might have waited to come home until I was up,' she said, staring at him. 'You're not seeing me at my best.'

'This is the best as far as I'm concerned, darling.' He smiled. 'I wouldn't care if I found you down the coal hole covered in soot. You look beautiful.'

'I look as if I've just woken up,' Meggie complained, looking past him at her reflection in the distant mirror. 'And look at my hair.'

'I could do with a bath and a shave myself,' Waldo said. 'As well as a change of clothes. Why don't I pop back home and freshen up – and meet you back here for cocktails? I'm sure you've got a lot to tell me.'

'I have? About what?'

'About how much you missed me. And about how much you love me.'

'And what have you got in your beak for me, mister?'

'Just you wait and see.'

* * *

After she had bathed, Meggie stood in her best silk underwear in front of her wardrobe wondering what to wear for the evening. She had just decided to take down one of the simple black taffeta short evening dresses that she knew Waldo loved and that she knew set off her colouring to the best advantage when her eye fell on another of Waldo's favourites, the dress he claimed she was wearing the moment he knew he was in love with her, the night of the Regatta when she had been serving behind the packed bar, her old red silk dress with the puffed sleeves.

She took it down and held it up to herself in the mirror. She'd had it cleaned since that night and even though it was old, and perhaps even a little old-fashioned, the colour still did wonders for her, as did the cut, once she had slipped into it. She had lost a little weight, but Meggie thought that was all to the good since the dress now fitted her to perfection. This time at her neck she added one of her grandmother's beautiful necklaces, tiny diamonds shaped like a small pendant which showed off the elegance of her slender neck and somehow seemed to bring even more colour to the dress.

'I am at a loss for words,' Waldo said when he saw her. 'And before you say anything about pigs flying I mean it. You look just out of the world.'

'You look pretty handsome too,' Meggie said, taking him by the hand and leading him over to the drinks. 'I like you best in everything you wear.'

'That's clever – I must remember that.'

'No point – wouldn't be true about everybody. But it's true about you. You look wonderful in everything.' She kissed him, touched his cheek with one of her long-fingered, elegant hands, which he grabbed at once to kiss in the palm, and then asked him to make the drinks.

'Is it OK you drinking?' he asked. 'Aren't you taking medication?'

'Henry didn't say anything about not drinking.'

'It's Henry now, is it? I think I'll put a ban on any further housecalls.'

'You don't have to worry. He's only called here twenty-three times. Or is it twenty-four?'

'And how does he think his patient is?'

'He thinks his patient is gorgeous.'

'How does he think her general health is?'

'As gorgeous as she is. Now make me the perfect dry Martini. I always put too much vermouth in mine. How's your health, by the way?'

'Mine?' Waldo picked up the gin bottle. 'Couldn't be better. Why should you enquire about my health? There's not been anything wrong with me.'

'That's what you think,' Meggie teased, poker-faced.

'Did Henry say anything to you?' Waldo asked with a frown, pouring a tiny measure of vermouth into the shaker.

'Why should Henry say anything to me about you?' Meggie laughed. 'Unless there *is* something wrong—'

'I told you,' Waldo interrupted. 'Henry looked after me after I'd been shot. When I got back. I had a check up with him before I went away.'

'I know you did. No need to be ratty.'

'I wasn't being ratty.' Waldo grinned, shaking the cocktails. 'I just didn't want you worrying, that's all.'

'I'm not worried.'

'Good. And neither am I.' Waldo leaned over and kissed her, then poured them both the perfect cocktail.

'To you,' Waldo said, holding up his glass. 'To the most intoxicating thing I know. Martinis included.'

'To you,' Meggie returned. 'May your shadow never grow less.'

'I like that. Where did you get that?'

'I have an Irish uncle.'

They sipped their delicious drinks then moved over to sit opposite each other by the fireside.

'You really do look amazing,' Waldo said. 'I don't think I've ever seen a vision quite so lovely.'

'Thank you. But keep your looks strictly above knee level.'

'Knee level? And miss out on those glorious legs?'

'My legs are not always what they should be!'

'They look pretty wonderful to me.'

'How. I. Have. Missed. You.'

Meggie smiled and raised her glass. 'Let me count the ways. In the morning—'

'In the evening,' Waldo put in.

'All the time,' Meggie finished, simply. Waldo kissed her. Meggie smiled. 'So tell me all about your trip. Did you bring me home anything nice? I do hope you brought me something indescribably unrepeatably gorgeous?'

'Pretty much so,' Waldo agreed. 'I brought you back an unencumbered me.'

'Unencumbered?' Meggie frowned at him. 'Don't get. What do you mean?'

'I have come back . . .' Waldo said, 'a free man.'

'So why didn't you tell me?' Meggie demanded later over dinner.

'Why on earth do you imagine? I'd fallen in love with you. I didn't want to lose you.'

'But supposing she hadn't suddenly granted you a divorce for whatever the reason was—'

'She had good reason.'

'No, but what would you have done, Waldo? If someone just refuses—'

'I'd have asked you to live in sin with me instead.'

'Instead of what?'

'Marrying me.'

'You haven't asked me to marry you.'

'Yet. Would now be a good time?'

'She sounds absolutely frightful, your thankfully ex-wife. How on earth did you come to marry her in the first place?'

'Will you marry *me*?'

'I can't understand how you could have been so duped.'

'*Will* you marry me?'

'I mean you of all people—'

'I didn't know anything about women. I was a lamb to the slaughter. The moment we married she changed – seriously. One minute she was all sweetness and innocence and the next minute – oh boy. She was out there – on the prowl. I imagine the condition has a medical name. Now for the last time, will you marry me?'

'Well of course I will,' Meggie replied, almost grumpily. 'Now tell me all over again how you two met.'

He had brought her back a ring, a single diamond like Mattie's, but considerably larger. He had also brought her a diamond brooch to match, and a diamond necklace just in case she said yes. He made her put the necklace on then he led her upstairs, took off her clothes and made love to her in only the necklace.

'When would you like to get married, Meggie?' he wondered as they lay together in the darkness.

'Would yesterday be too soon?'

'Not soon enough. I shall start putting all the arrangements in hand immediately.'

'I have an idea,' Meggie said the next morning as they ate breakfast.

'You look tired,' Waldo said. 'I kept you up too late.'

'You look tired as well. I kept you up too late.'

'By the way, what did the good doctor Henry say about making love?'

'Making love isn't something Englishmen recognise.'

'I'm sure he must have said something about too much excitement.'

'Excitement isn't something Englishmen recognise.'

With his bare foot Waldo found her bare leg under the table and gently booted it.

'You know what I mean.'

'Now what was your big idea, darling?'

'Mattie and John are getting married soon. Why don't we get married on the same day?'

'And have a double wedding? Isn't that the sort of idea people like you go *ooer* at? I know I do. Anyway, it wouldn't be fair to crowd their act.'

It was Meggie's turn to kick him under the table.

'Ow,' Waldo said. 'That was my war wound.'

'Very funny. I didn't mean a double wedding. I can't think of anything more *ooer*. Anyway, they wouldn't let the likes of you get married in a church. You're divorced, spit, spit. We could do a Register office job then share a huge great splendiferous, fantasmaganic, and absolutely magnifichentous knees-up. We do have all the same friends – know all the same people. At least I do. You don't have any friends at all and don't know anybody.'

'Could be, could be,' Waldo said, thinking about it. 'Have to ask John and Mattie though.'

'Well of course we're going to ask John and Mattie!' Meggie exclaimed. 'You don't think we're just going to turn up at their reception and help ourselves.'

'I think we might be getting an invitation to the wedding anyway,' Waldo said poker-faced. 'And that means the reception as well – where all our friends will be – so why bother telling them? They'll only make us pay half.'

Meggie couldn't hold a straight face any longer and burst into laughter, followed by Waldo. Unfortunately the laughing caused a coughing fit and Waldo was quickly despatched up to Meggie's bedroom to fetch a foul-tasting linctus and a phial of bright red pills, which he did, trying not to look worried.

'Ta muchly,' Meggie gasped, after she had dosed herself. 'I haven't had a coughing fit since God knows when. All your fault, making me laugh.'

'Then that's a good sign,' Waldo said, lifting her gently up from her chair. 'But even so, I think after that we'd better go back to the book and have you put your feet up.'

'Henry said I'd have to get worse before I got better, so here I am – being worse.'

'Don't you dare get any worse.'

'Any worse? Look at me! Look, I'm fine, really, Waldo, I'm fine!' Meggie protested. 'I'm as right as rain, though why rain's right *searchez moi*. I really am all right. In fact I feel so good I feel like dancing. So come on, let's dance.'

'OK – we'll dance.'

Waldo took her in his arms and smooched her slowly round the kitchen once and then out into the hall and then, lifting her up in his arms, carried her all the way upstairs.

'But this time no excitement,' he whispered as he laid her down on her bed. 'Just one kiss, that's all.'

There were six kisses, but no matter because that really was all. Two minutes after he had kissed her for the last time, Meggie fell into a deep and happy, if exhausted, sleep.

All the Tates, young and older, were delighted when Waldo called and proposed the notion. Waldo went by himself because Meggie and he were agreed that if she was to be restored to her bonny self by the date set for their wedding then she must abide strictly by Henry Wright's orders, and they included no further excitement, at least not until they were married. Promising to return the next day to discuss the plans and the guest list, Waldo ambled off.

'I hope Waldo's all right,' Loopy said to Hugh after she had watched him drive away from the house. 'He doesn't look quite well.'

'He's just flown all the way back from America, Loopy,' Hugh said. 'And what with the time difference and the length of the flight a chap's bound to look a bit washed out.'

'He doesn't look washed out, Hugh,' Loopy said. 'It's his eyes. He looks simply dreadful. Next time you see him, take a good look at the dark shadows under his eyes. As well as the look in them.'

* * *

Hugh did, and of course being Hugh saw nothing to trouble him. He had often seen Waldo coming off duty, as it were, and on those occasions according to Hugh he looked a whole lot worse, so a few shadows under a chap's eyes weren't going to concern the Spymaster whatsoever. In fact the more he saw Waldo the better he thought he looked and said as much to Loopy, who was forced to agree that perhaps she had been fussing too much.

'Even so, Hugh, believe me, I know,' she said in conclusion. 'Something's troubling him.'

'Wedding bell jitters, I'll be bound.' Hugh grunted. 'Remember me? Couldn't even eat my soup without spilling it. All Waldo's suffering from is the well known Wedding Bell Jits.'

By the time the month of May rolled in after a sodden April, the weather had suddenly turned to full spring. The plan was for the two couples to get married on the same day, Waldo and Meggie going first to be wed at the register office in Churchester at midday, accompanied only by a small party of friends which included the Sykeses and Walter and Judy Tate. Lionel to act as Waldo's best man. They didn't invite anyone else because they knew that everyone else would be too busy getting ready for the big church wedding to be held at three o'clock, so in spite of some hearty and heavy protestations from the Tate clan Meggie and Waldo insisted it was all for the best and stuck to their plan.

Waldo paid a visit to London to collect the suit he had ordered from his tailors in Savile Row. He also took time to keep an appointment with Henry Wright.

'You sure this is OK, Henry?' he said, doing up his shirt after his examination. 'It's all right going through with this?'

'Of course,' Henry said. 'It's not going to change anything, and if you've been following my instructions—'

'To the letter.'

'Then why not? Personally I think it's wonderful.'

'And you are coming?'

'Try and stop me.'

In spite of her recovery, which seemed to be gaining a new momentum, Meggie was banned from accompanying Waldo to London to do her wedding shopping. Naturally she protested, arguing that she couldn't possibly find anything suitable for her wedding and for the Tates' celebrations locally, to which Waldo replied that if Muhammad couldn't get to the mountain, the mountain would come to Muhammad. Sure enough, two days later a dark green Harrods van arrived outside Cucklington House, followed by a small dark red Austin 10 from which two impeccably attired middle-aged ladies disembarked to supervise the delivery of two dozen ensembles from which Miss Gore-Stewart would be required to choose her wedding outfit.

Surprised and thrilled, Meggie carefully sifted

through the choices before her, listening to the advice of the two good ladies and trying on several of their recommendations before deciding on a two piece New Look suit in dark blue, with white piqué sleeves and collar, topped off with a small veiled hat in the two matching colours. Everyone agreed it was the perfect choice, all except Waldo who was banished to the gardens to smoke a cigar while the final selection of gloves and shoes was being made.

When he saw her come into the Register office on the morning of their wedding, however, he was happily nearly speechless.

'Meggie Gore-Stewart.'

'Very soon you'll have to call me *Mrs* Astley,' she replied smartly.

'You're perfection. You're Mickey Mouse – you're cellophane.'

'And you – are a large Napoleon brandy.'

'I'm so nervous I could do with one.'

They took each other as man and wife and the bridegroom kissed the bride, for a little too long according to the registrar who cleared his throat but with a beaming smile reminded them that he had several other couples to marry that day. As she walked out of the office on Waldo's arm, with Waldo unable to take his eyes off her, Meggie thought she would burst with the sheer happiness of the moment. Afraid that it all might suddenly end, she held Waldo's arm with all her strength, so forcefully in fact that Waldo had to remind her he wasn't going anywhere – for once.

'You'd better not,' Meggie warned him as they

stood on the steps outside having their photographs taken. 'One wrong move, buster, and you are a dead man.'

'Having felt what your naked foot can do at the breakfast table, Mrs Astley,' Waldo returned, 'I heed your warning.'

After a celebratory bottle of French champagne back at the Three Tuns, enjoyed of course as it should be in the *cocktail* lounge, it was on up the High Street and into the church, where in the most traditional of English ceremonies, and therefore the most deeply moving, Lionel Eastcott gave his daughter Mathilda away to John Sebastian Tate, eldest son of Captain and Mrs Hugh Tate of Shelborne, Bexham. The bride looked so beautiful in the antique Gore-Stewart gown that the stalwart John Tate all but piped his bright blue eyes when he saw her walking up the aisle to him. Walter was his best man, and Dauncy, on leave from National Service, was his chief usher. The church was packed with friends and well-wishers, so crowded in fact that as Mr George from the post office remarked – he thought it was only the whole of Bexham what had been invited, not all the neighbouring villages too.

Eschewing tradition, the couple came down the aisle not to Mendelssohn but to Mozart, to the joyous wedding march from *The Marriage of Figaro*, and even further from tradition – or at least her own custom – Mrs Waldo Astley found it difficult to stop herself from crying through almost all the ceremony.

'Remind me not to take you to too many weddings,' Waldo muttered, lending his new bride his only handkerchief.

'It's these stupid pills,' Meggie whispered, attempting to smile. 'They make one so awfully waterlogged.'

The reception was an entire success, blessed by warm spring sunshine and catered for by the ever redoubtable Richards, whose team of smugglers must have been working nocturnal overtime to be able to bring ashore all the wonderful foods and wines that the guests enjoyed.

'Actually,' Meggie said, as she and Waldo sat on the wall at the end of the garden drinking champagne, 'actually this has been such fun I vote we all get married more often.'

'Do you mean *all* of us?' Waldo enquired. 'Or all of *us*?'

'I don't mind if you get married six times, Waldo,' Meggie replied with an even smile. 'Long as every wedding day is like this, and as long as it's always *me* you're marrying.'

'On my heart of hearts, my darling, when I feel like marrying again, you will be the very top of my list, as well as number two, three, four, five and six.'

'And who shall be number seven and eight?' Meggie wondered, looking at him imperiously.

'Loopy,' Waldo said. 'Then you again.'

'I heard my name,' Loopy said, stopping to sit beside them. 'Hope you're not taking it in vain.'

'Nope,' Meggie assured her. 'Waldo was just

saying he'd marry you after he's married me six more times.'

'Sounds a good arrangement.' Loopy laughed. 'Except I might *not* accept.'

'If you didn't, Loopy,' Waldo said, 'then I'd have to return to Miss Gore-Stewart here again.'

'Mrs Waldo Astley if you don't mind.'

'So – are you going anywhere nice on honeymoon?'

'We haven't planned a thing, Loopy – my belief being that, to paraphrase Mark Twain, wherever Meggie is – is heaven.'

Meggie turned round and murmured, 'You say the nicest things.'

'I say the nicest things other people have said first.'

'That simply is not true. Some of the nicest, nicest things I have ever heard anyone say have to have been said by you. And that's an order.'

'We thought we might take the *Light Heart* out for a few trips, if the weather stays like this. Sail down the coast – stay the night at a few seaside inns,' Waldo said, taking Meggie's hand. 'It was Meggie's idea. Said that's what she'd like to do, very best of all.'

'Say, that does sound romantic,' Loopy replied. 'Hugh and I used to sail all the way down to Land's End some summers. Sleep in those lovely deserted Cornish coves at night, at anchor. I can't think of anything more romantic.'

'Cornwall here we come,' Meggie said happily. 'All aboard.'

* * *

They missed out on the next two days, delaying their departure until they were both fully recovered from both weddings. Waldo seemed to be even more exhausted than his wife, who in fact was up and about packing for their trip the following afternoon while he lay flat out and fast asleep on the bed.

'You OK?' Meggie asked him when he finally woke up properly late in the afternoon. 'You do know what time it is?'

'I think it's all just hit me, sweetheart,' Waldo said with the deepest of yawns, rubbing his bleary dark eyes with his closed fists. 'I think it's all just caught up with me – America, the trip there and back, all that divorce nonsense – and now all this marriage wonder. Hey, come here – come on—' He took hold of her by the hands and sat her on the bed. 'I haven't seen you all day.'

'Do you think I've changed much?'

'Almost entirely. You look even more lovely.'

Meggie kissed him and ruffled his dark hair. 'Hello, Pirate Captain.' She smiled. 'You're my very own Pirate Captain and you're just about to kidnap me, smuggle me aboard your leaky craft and carry me off to Penzance.'

'Yo ho ho,' Waldo growled. 'But first I have another little surprise for you in my locker.'

They set sail on the Tuesday following, leaving on the midday tide accompanied by an enormous tail of tin cans Dauncy and Walter had tied on to the back of the *Light Heart*. They had also writ large and clear on the back of the lovely craft JUST MARRIED in very obvious whitewashed letters. Waldo and Meggie didn't mind. They were well beyond the gates of their seventh heaven.

The weather was as fine as it had been at the weekend, sunny but with a good stiff breeze at sea enabling them to indulge in some proper sailing.

'I'm impressed,' Waldo said as Meggie took the wheel and found the line. 'You're a good sailor.'

'You're not so dusty yourself.'

'Thanks to young Dauncy. I wanted to be able to handle a boat this size and young Dauncy showed me how.'

'Not in *Dingy*, surely?' Meggie laughed.

'We hired a craft from someone at the club.'

'I don't know. You had all this planned?'

'I thought it might come to this, some time, and I didn't want to be found lacking.'

'That is you all over, Waldo darling. You're always so prepared you could have invented the Boy Scouts. Perhaps you did.'

'I'm not always that prepared, Meggie mine,' he said, more to himself than to her. 'You can't prepare for everything in this life.'

They moored off a tiny cove in Dorset on the first night, eating the first of the picnics Rusty had helped prepare for them and then sleeping well wrapped up on deck under a blanket of stars. On the second night they stayed in a small inn overlooking a sandy bay on the Devon coastline, and on the third night, after three beautiful days of perfect sailing weather, found a tiny beach in a Cornish cove which they reached by means of the small dinghy Mr Todd had thoughtfully suggested bringing for exactly this purpose. On the beach they built a bonfire of driftwood and cooked fresh mackerel they had caught earlier that day and ate with potatoes baked in their jackets in the embers of the fire.

'Why does food – food like this – just fish and spuds – why does it taste so different like this?' Meggie wondered. 'Because it always does.'

'Because it *is* different. It's in a different place, cooked on a different fire, enjoyed for different reasons.'

'I wish we could always live like this,' Meggie sighed. 'I could take the life of a native. Long as you were around, Captain.'

'I shall always be around, Meggie darling, don't you worry about that,' Waldo assured her. 'Now we have a choice of bedrooms. It's warm enough to sleep out, but where? Here? Or back on board? Or do you want to go on and find an inn?'

'Bit late for that, Captain,' Meggie said, looking at the clear skies above them. 'I vote for a night on the beach.'

'In that case I'll need to row back to the *Light Heart* to get our sleeping bags and blankets – and anything else we might need.'

'My hand luggage has my—'

'I hadn't forgotten. Will you be OK? Won't take me longer than twenty minutes.'

'Can't I come with you?'

'Of course you can.'

'But on the other hand . . .' Meggie said, looking about her, 'Maybe I'll stay and tidy up this beautiful bedroom.'

'I'll hardly be more than a minute.'

'You'd better not be,' she warned. 'I might not be here when you get back, Captain!'

Waldo rowed hard and fast back to the boat. It was easy getting out to the yacht because the tide was only just on the ebb, but after he had collected everything they might need, and more, he found the return leg tough going with the tide now fully on the turn and hurrying it seemed out to sea as fast as the moon would pull it.

Pulling the dinghy up onto the sand he suddenly staggered and fell over, stubbing his toe on a buried rock.

'Damn,' he said, getting up and hopping. 'Damn and blast, because that hurt.'

Once he had pulled himself together and got his bearings he looked round the tiny beach but of a sudden he could see no sign of Meggie. The fire was still well alight and burning with a comforting red glow against the darkening evening sky, but the place where he had left Meggie was deserted, her former presence marked only by the indentation in the sand.

'Meggie?' he called. 'Hey – Meggie sweetheart! Come out wherever you are! I give up? Come on, Meggie! I give up!'

By now he was wandering round the beach,

turning in circles as he eye-searched the tiny cove. There was no access other than from the sea, and there was nowhere really for anyone to hide – no caves, no huge rocks, just a few jagged ones too sharp to climb and hide behind, and otherwise just a sheer cliff running a hundred or so feet up above him.

'Meggie? Meggie, this isn't funny!' he cried, his heart pounding in his chest, the breath catching in this throat. 'Meggie darling – where are you! Where are you!'

Then he saw her. What he had taken in the lengthening shadows to be a rock at the edge of the sea he now saw was nothing of the sort. It was Meggie.

He hadn't far to run – twenty yards, no more – yet it felt like a marathon. Every step he took seemed to get him no nearer her. He just seemed to be running on the spot, and then it seemed as if she was moving away from him, being carried out to sea, which with sudden horror he realised she was.

Doubling his speed and hardly able to catch his breath thanks to the bullet still lodged in his lung he leaped into the sea and caught hold of the saturated shape that was Meggie – the slender, wet, bedraggled shape that was Meggie, that was still Meggie, but that was only just still Meggie.

Her eyes looked up at him faintly, as if they were unable to see him, as if they had no idea who or what he was.

'Meggie,' he whispered. 'Meggie darling – Meggie, my darling, it's me. It's Waldo. Meggie, my darling, please. Please say you can hear me. Meggie, please.'

But the eyes still just looked at him. They looked at him hopelessly and helplessly, staring at him as if he were the last thing they would see on earth.

He was carrying her back to the fire, where there was a rug, the rug they had just been sitting on, the rug where they had just been talking, and laughing, where she had wondered why everything was always so very different with him, while he had wondered why he was so happy, and now there was just the rug and the shape where they had been sitting and Meggie was dying in his arms.

'Meggie,' he whispered as he knelt down by the fire. 'Oh, please, my darling – please say something. Please.'

Gently as he could he laid her down on the rug, and wrapped the whole around her. Tearing off his sweater and shirt, he rolled the shirt into a pillow, and placed the sweater over her. Then he took one hand from under the rug and held it in both of his, and as he did so, his own heart stopped. It was ice cold. He leaned forward, noting that her eyes too had lost all life. They were dying eyes. Yet he had to keep looking into them, because if she could not hear him any more she had to know from his look how much he loved her.

For a second as he stared into her eyes it seemed to him that there was just a tiny speck of light, so he put his mouth to her ear and whispered over and over, 'Love you, Meggie, always.'

'Love you too,' her voice seemed to whisper. 'Always.'

* * *

He brought her body home covered with the blankets in which they had slept, sailing non-stop while the winds were strong, and when the wind failed he sailed by the engine. He sailed until late in the evening he saw the mouth of the Bex and the landfalls that marked the entrance to the estuary. He had made sure the tide would be running in because he didn't want to lie off waiting for the tide.

Later he remembered nothing about their arrival, about landing, about the faces when they learned what had happened, about the fishermen who raised her body off the deck and carried it in their arms on to the jetty and into the *Three Tuns* where they laid Meggie out carefully in the back room. He couldn't remember Richards coming back in with the undertakers and taking her from him for the last time. All he could remember was the pain.

'She didn't want to be buried in a graveyard, actually,' Judy said, when Waldo and she finally met to discuss the funeral. 'I don't know whether she talked to *you* about – well. About such things.'

'No. Never.'

'We did. We always talked about it when we were growing up. And of course we often talked about it during the war. Meggie didn't like graveyards. She always said the only thing anyone ever looked at in graveyards were the dates to see how old people were when they died.'

'Did she ever say what she wanted?'

'Yes. She always said she wanted a Viking's funeral.'

Waldo stared at Judy and smiled for the first time since his return.

'Yes, of course. That would be Meggie.'

'Mind you, I'm not sure whether it's allowed?'

'You can be buried at sea. No-one can stop that.'

'A Viking funeral is slightly different, Waldo. Vikings died in their boats. They were laid out in beautiful clothes, and then their boats were pushed out to sea and set on fire.'

And so when the time came Waldo and Judy laid Meggie out in a gold robe and cloak that had belonged to her grandmother, and after the funeral service in the church Waldo, Mickey Todd, Walter and John carried her coffin on their shoulders the length of the High Street and down the lane that led to the quays – and the jetty from where, with the help of a band of six strong fishermen, they placed the coffin on board the *Light Heart* on a dais covered in flowers.

They left Waldo to pay his last respects, watching as he kneeled down beside her to pray, and then barely able to watch as he kissed the pale pink rose he had plucked from her favourite rose bush and laid it carefully down on the coffin about the place where he thought her heart would be. Coming ashore, he climbed into Mr Todd's little tug and stood facing the *Light Heart* as she made her final journey, towed slowly down the estuary and out into the open seas, with the village following in a flotilla of boats, throwing wreaths of flowers after it, until finally they reached Meggie's last resting place. As Mr Todd brought his tug to a stop and came to the stern to undo the tow rope, Waldo lit the torch and with one last look, threw it aft onto a pile of oil-soaked rags.

Mr Todd took his craft to a point where they could turn about and watch.

The fire caught slowly at first, seeming at times reluctant to do its job, until at last a tongue of flame found the trail of petrol that had been laid along the deck, and seconds later the *Light Heart* was ablaze on the roughening sea.

As she watched from the safety of the tug, it seemed to Judy that she could hear Meggie's exultant voice from all those years before – 'That's what I want – a Viking's funeral' – and she could hear her laugh, that wonderful laugh. 'See to it, won't you?' How had Meggie known that Judy would?

In this way, Judy missed hearing the first few notes as Waldo began to sing the *Ave Maria* and the little flotilla retreated back to Bexham leaving behind one of its heroines.

Epilogue

Loopy laid out two Martini glasses and the cocktail jug then stood back from the table to make sure she had everything set, after which she looked at the clock and saw that not only was he late, which was so unlike him, but he was later than ever.

It was now five months since Meggie had died and Waldo had disappeared from all their lives to try to find somewhere to begin to recover from his grief. Now he was back in Bexham, and as soon as she had heard the good news Loopy had sent a note round to Cucklington House to invite him for cocktails.

'Loopy.' He arrived at the French windows, unannounced. 'I hope I have not startled you. I rang the doorbell for hours but it appears Gwen must have gone deafer than ever.'

'Waldo,' Loopy said, with unconcealed delight. 'I can't tell you how good it is to see you. Come in. Come in at once.'

He came into her drawing room trying his best, she felt sure, to look like the Waldo Astley of old, but unsurprisingly what he had been through had left its mark – not visibly so much as internally, so that he now wore the look of a man who has been through so much grieving he had little emotion left to spend. Of course he was as handsome as ever, sun-tanned, leaner than before and immaculately dressed as always, yet to Loopy he seemed to be someone to whom every new port had only spelt distraction, and every departure relief.

He had left them without notice but not without thought. Like everyone else Loopy knew of his continued generosity, of how he had given over his share of the garage business to Peter and Rusty and their family, how he had bought the freehold of the Three Tuns and gifted it to Richards in Meggie's memory, how Mickey Todd had been commissioned to build a new yacht for Waldo, inevitably named the *Light Heart II*, and how the people at the post office had been anonymously bought an allotment.

She had also heard the rumours that as soon as the housing shortage was over there were plans for the almshouses to be rebuilt for the old and the infirm, that someone had sent an anonymous donation to the cottage hospital which would keep it running for many years to come, and that the village hall was to be rebuilt and renamed the Gore-Stewart Memorial Hall. She was also well aware of the sarcasm that this generosity had bred in certain quarters, and of the fact that Waldo's nickname in the village was Mr Bountiful, or at other times The Great Provider, which Waldo, also knowing, joked about sometimes in his letters to her. What Loopy did not know, however, was why Waldo had felt compelled to do as he had done.

'That's easy,' he said. 'At least it is now that I've had time to think about it. You know I had this kind of pilgrimage I felt I had to make, to try to sort out the mystery of my father's famous photographs, but what happened instead was that I fell in love, something I thought I wasn't capable of doing. First I fell in love with Bexham, and then with Meggie – and that was what counted.'

'But before that – before you fell in love with Meggie – you started helping people long before that.'

'As I said, I was in love with Bexham. I also reckoned you all needed a bit of cheering up – everyone was so got down, so depressed. In fact you all appeared to be feeling exactly like I'd felt when I left America, and so I thought this won't do. And when I started doing this and that, here and there – you know, for the first time in my life I felt I had a purpose. Instead of being some little rich kid, I felt needed.'

'Of course you are,' Loopy assured him. 'Believe you me, Bexham's not been the same without you. How long will you be here for?'

'I've come back to stay – to live, I'm not sure for how long till I see what the natives make of me. I'm not sure I'm going to go on working for Hugh. I think maybe I've had enough of secret agents – and people taking pot shots at me.'

'There was a rumour that you weren't well.'

'I wasn't. I had a bullet in my lung after that

fracas in Berlin, and they couldn't take it out until the infection had completely died down. Took a while. But Henry – Henry Wright who looked after Meggie? He managed to extract it three weeks ago, and I'm right as rain now.'

'So if you don't do any more work for Hugh—?'

'I shall probably just retire and – as Pascal said – cultivate my garden.'

'Which garden?'

'Cucklington.'

'Meggie'd like that.'

'That's why I want to do it, Loopy.'

'What was it actually, Waldo? If you don't mind me asking? Everyone *said* it was her heart—'

'Everyone is right then.' Waldo finished his Martini and placed the cocktail glass on the table next to him. 'Henry couldn't say what caused it or when – whether it was as a result of two bad doses of influenza, or whether it was the strain of the war, or just a separate infection altogether. It was degenerative, that was all. After Henry had x-rayed her he knew at once. He cabled me in New York, telling me it was only a matter of time. There was nothing anyone could do. Except make it as painless as possible. He couldn't say for sure when it would happen. Just that it would. And that it might happen soon.'

'We all miss her so dreadfully.'

'I shall never stop missing her.' Waldo paused. 'The good thing is that because of her, because of you all really, whenever I drive into Bexham I get this coming home feeling. When I walk through the front door at Cucklington – I can feel her there. I can feel her waiting for me. I can feel her knowing that I've come home.'

'She'll always be with you at Cucklington, Waldo,' Loopy said, picking up Beanie as Waldo got to his feet. 'And so too – please God – will you.'

Loopy walked with him to her front door, where with Beanie still under her arm she kissed him on the cheek.

'I'm so glad to see you're back, Waldo.'

'So am I.'

'We're always here,' she called after him, stroking her little dog's head as she watched Waldo ambling down the drive, past the neat flowers in the borders and the small square of green lawn until he reached the road that led back to the village. A tall, elegant, lonely figure, walking back to embrace his memories.

THE END

To be continued in *The Moon at Midnight*

Charlotte Bingham would like to invite you to visit her website at www.charlottebingham.com